A Life Beyond

M.L CHURCH

Dedication

This book is dedicated to my wonderful family who believed in me enough to make me start and finish this first book, so to my wonderful wife Steph who I love more than anything and to the true inspiration for this book Lillie and Daniel I love you to the moon and back and always will

Table of Contents

Preface

The characters in this story are based on my children in name only, none of the events actually happened, most of the characters are fictional apart from a few who are school friends of my children. I chose to write this book so my children would have something to remember me by when I am no longer around to offer them guidance. It took me around a year and a half to write my story from memory and it has snowballed from there with me writing the follow up book, I suppose my biggest challenge was the story itself which came with its own challenges as some chapters took a long time for me to think of plots and twists but I got there in the end so I am excited to have finished it now, so I hope you enjoy reading this book as much as I have enjoyed writing it.

Mark Church

Introduction

The purpose of this book is to pass on my story to everyone and watch as you all enjoy it so I hope you have fun connecting with the characters.

Chapter One
The Beginning

STOP THE BELLS FROM FALLING, COMPLETE THE CIRCLE, COME
HOME come home!!!!.
 The husky voice carried across the empty plains, winding and twisting
across the land like a leaf caught on the tail of the wind, its path leading up
to the sight of a lonely figure standing on top of a hill looking out into the
distance, seemingly searching for something, lost in his own thoughts,
despair etched across his face, sadness filling his soul.

 The figure was of a tall man, a soldier of some kind, long dark hair tied up
at the back, a long flowing cape flapping in the wind behind him, his face
was a blur of dark colours with pain showing through, his hunched stance
seemed to tell a story of how this person seemed to be struggling to find
what he was searching for.
'My boy.....Come ho....' his sentenced ended before it began as he
vanished into the darkness.
With a start Daniel woke up and sat bolt upright, stretching his arms wide
and yawned the biggest yawn ever. Daniel was a twelve year old boy,
striking blond hair and the most beautiful blues eyes you had ever seen
with a face that had that look which you knew could get you into trouble
without even trying. He was born with a birthmark on his left forearm too
which was shaped like a shield with some sort of winged bird behind it, it
was a birthmark that Daniel covered up sometimes as he felt it was
embarrassing.
 'Yawn.....' Daniel felt his body loosen up,

'Woah, it's that dream again' He said to himself as he tried to process what had gone on. 'That's the same dream I've been having for the past week now, I wonder if it means anything'.

So Daniel took out his 'Dream Journal' as he called it and started writing down all the details of what had been inside his head, his journal was an old and tatty looking diary given to him on his tenth birthday by his mum, it was leather bound and smelt like a pair of old shoes and he kept it locked with the smallest padlock and key ever seen which Daniel was forever misplacing.

The diary also had a symbol on the front which largely looked like the morning sun rising behind the flat of the land, his poor diary was getting a bit ragged around the edges as he was forever dropping it and kicking it across the floor like a football, it was also full of colourful drawings and a lot of nonsense too but it did contain the dreams he was having especially in the last year or so.

So Daniel sat down on the edge of the bed half ready for school with his trousers dangling off one leg as he noted down in his diary the latest dream he'd had, about how he'd heard the same words said in the same way over and over again and how he had seen this tall lonely figure standing alone on the hill,

Daniel's mind was racing with all sorts of explanations for it, and why it was the same one he was having night after night.

'Maybe it's just nothing' Daniel sighed and closed his battered diary up.

Then all of a sudden the bedroom door burst open, which nearly took it clean off its hinges, and before Daniel had a chance to see who or what it was his face was met by what can only be described as a 'giant furball', the smell of damp dog filled Daniel's nose, his face was being licked so clean that you could eat your dinner off it.

'Bucksy!!' groaned Daniel as he managed to push the giant furball off him so he could see his face.

Bucksy was Daniel's most loyal companion, a Labrador with a coat as black as space and with eyes that weren't like any other dogs eyes, one of them a dark blue like the deepest part of the ocean and the other as green as the grass in a field, but he was just as mad as any Labrador, in fact any dog breed could be, he got up to the usual dog stuff like chasing his tail, barking at the postman when he whistled his way up the path in the morning, lying upside down on the sofa dreaming of whatever it is dogs dream about, normally chasing other dogs and the usual sniffing of every tree or lamp post.

Bucksy was the kind of companion who was never more than a few feet away from Daniel whenever he was around, he would follow him everywhere and would only settle when he knew he was safe from 'harm', it was like a King having a guard by his side 24 hours a day, that's how much Bucksy thought of his master, they were inseparable and were often getting into mischief, whether it was play fighting in the house and knocking things over or Daniel hiding in the neighbours garden and Bucksy sniffing him out and causing the local cat population to scarper and cause the kind of commotion that normally ended with Daniel's mum finding out and waiting for them to come back ready to lecture Daniel on keeping out of the neighbours gardens and hedges as they were getting damaged by the constant games of hide and sniff!!.

So that morning had seemed as normal as any other really, Bucksy was his usual clumsy self and doing his best to annoy Daniel, which he kind of enjoyed apart from when he was in the shower and an inquisitive wet and cold nose would find its way into the shower and press itself against Daniel's leg causing him to recoil in terror.

Daniel was starting his usual daily routine of getting ready for school which he really didn't like but Bucksy wouldn't leave him alone as usual.

'Bucksy!!!, get off me please' pleaded Daniel as he struggled to put on his trousers which were stuck under Bucksy's bottom.

'I need to get ready for school you big lump, and you are so not helping!!, seriously move please' said Daniel as he finally pushed his dog off of his trousers, Bucksy moved to another part of the bed and sat in front of Daniel pawing at his arm as Daniel finally relented and grabbed Bucksy by the head and started to tickle him behind his ears, then something strange happened as Daniel felt himself falling under some kind of hypnotic gaze, Bucksy's eyes seemed to turn a deathly black and there seemed to be some kind of weird connection between the two which had never been there before.

Daniel started seeing blurry images deep inside his dog's eyes and through his own thoughts also but he couldn't make them out, a voice called out to him through the haze,

'Follow....' then all of a sudden Daniel lurched back onto the bed.

'Woah, what the blooming heck was all that about?' Daniel said as he sat back on his bed, not knowing what to make of what had just happened between him and his dog.

'That was really strange, I've never felt anything like that before, Whose voice was that?, The dog's eyes.... it's as if he's trying to tell me som......',

His sentence was cut off as he could hear strange noises coming from down the hall which took his attention away from what had just happened, So he got dressed and sat there just looking at his dog who was now lying upside down on the floor with one of Daniel's socks hanging out of his mouth which he quickly dropped so he could go investigate the next bit of clothing which happened to be a pair of pyjama bottoms left on the floor.

'I mean surely it was just nothing, just look at him now' laughed Daniel as Bucksy now had his head stuck at the end of Daniel's pyjama bottoms with only this big black wet nose poking its way out of the end of the leg hole, still sniffing for the next thing to investigate.

So Daniel made his way across his bedroom seemingly forgetting about the strange event that had just happened as if his memory had been wiped, he had to jump over his sea of toys and clothes scattered around his room, past Bucksy who was frantically trying to paw the bottoms off his face without any luck,

Daniel looked back and laughed as he watched his dog run head first into the leg of the bed and letting out a yelp as the bottoms were proving to be a worthy opponent.

11

Over the sound of the growling and yelping from Daniel's room came the still muffled noise that had distracted Daniel earlier, as he moved further down the landing he realised that it was the sound of someone 'singing' quite loudly and badly along to music in their bedroom.

'LILLIE, PLEASE STOP THAT SCREECHING!! I CAN'T STAND IT ANY MORE' shouted Daniel as the music and singing got louder and more screechier the closer he got to the door,
'WHY DO YOU HAVE TO DO THIS EVERY MORNING, YOU'RE SO ANNOYING'.

Daniel was still moaning as he made his way to the bathroom to finish getting ready for school, the only place he didn't really like going, only for him to stop off at his sister's bedroom door where he then barged in to be met by his sister, Lillie, singing into a can of hairspray like it was a microphone.

Lillie was Daniel's older sister; she was thirteen years old, tall for her age and the kind of child who excelled at most things she put her mind to, she had beautiful long dark brown hair and stunning green eyes which gave off a sort of sparkle every time the sunlight caught them, she was a very sociable girl unlike Daniel who was content with having few real friends, she was always seen as the centre of attention and everyone wanted to be her friend.

Her relationship with Daniel was your typical love/hate relationship, (she loved winding him up and Daniel hated it) but she would always fiercely defend her little brother if any trouble came his way as she felt a sense of duty to look out for him, even if they didn't get on that well, she felt it was her sense of duty to keep him safe just as Bucksy seemed to do whenever Daniel was around.

So Daniel went on to tell Lillie about what had happened between him and Bucksy in the bedroom and how it was the weirdest thing he had ever felt.
'Wow Daniel....' remarked Lillie 'Just when I thought you couldn't get any weirder, then you come out with some stupid story like that!!, do you think

12

that's funny wasting my time like this??, now please get out of my room so I can get ready too!!' she barked as Daniel, looking slightly upset, replied 'I knew you wouldn't believe me, you are so annoying, I can't wait until I can move out of here!!, I've had enough, I'm going downstairs'.

 And with that Daniel went to storm out of his sister's room but instead he ended up in a heap on the floor as he tripped over a big pile of clothes that Lillie had left on the floor,

Lillie fell about laughing as she watched Daniel struggling to get up and leave her room, he managed to get to his feet looking rather embarrassed, Lillie still laughing at Daniel as he went to leave said

'Shut the door carefully on the way out and DON'T slam the do........'

She hadn't even finished the sentence when Daniel slammed her bedroom door so hard that her shelves fell off the wall covering the floor in all her perfume bottles and her big collection of books that were carefully placed in alphabetical order.

 'Oh that's just great!!, well done you idiot, don't think I'm going to pick all these up, Get back here now and clean this up', Lillie shouted in a fit of rage as she raced out of her room in hot pursuit of her brother who was already halfway down the stairs.

As Daniel ran into the kitchen to hide away from the whirlwind of rage heading his way he was greeted by the sweet soft female voice of his mother who called out to him. 'Good morning my baby boy, how are you doing today?.' Daniel stopped dead in his tracks and answered back to the woman who was standing in the way and hurriedly wiping her face as she looked like she had been crying.

 'Mum, I.....', he stopped what he was going to say and looked at his mum and knew something was troubling her, 'What's the matter?, mum I can tell you've been crying again, it's not the first time I've

seen you crying, I hear you in your room sometimes and I can hear you crying and I want to come in but I daren't, if we can help then please tell us what we can do, we don't want to see you upset anymore' Daniel's

13

mum's eyes looked heavy and swollen slightly as she answered back in the soft way in which she spoke,

'I'm fine my beautiful son, I'm just having one of those mornings, I'll be fine I promise you. So...',

Daniel's mum's face broke into a smile as she gazed upon Daniel standing in front of her, looking like a face she knew from her past, hiding whatever pain she was feeling behind her smile,

'What's going on with you two then?, it sounded like a herd of elephants up there a minute ago and then you fly down the stairs, what have you and your sister been fighting about now?'.

Lillie stormed down the stairs and into the kitchen like a tornado on its path of destruction and started moaning about what Daniel had done to her room and how it wasn't fair that she had to tidy it up when it was her brother who had wrecked all her things.

'Well..' said Stephanie, the children's mum, ' Don't worry about that now, I will have to sort it out later when you two get your bums off to school but first you need breakfast...so sit down at the table and I'll get your breakfast ready'.

So they sat down together at the table and were chatting about what was going on at school when all of a sudden Bucksy appeared at the doorway, his head still stuck in Daniel's pyjama bottoms, he managed to clatter into the chair that Daniel was sitting on and let out a yelp as his nose connected with the chair leg.

'Bucksy!!...' scowled Daniel as he looked down to be greeted by the ever inquisitive nose of his dog poking up in the air, sniffing at the smell of breakfast.

'What are you doing now? There's no food for you so go and lie down please'.

And with that Bucksy made his way round the kitchen still bumping into everything in sight and yelping every time he hit a new piece of furniture.

Lillie answered back to Daniel with a scathing tone,

'Sometimes I wonder about that dog of yours, you two seem to have the same amount of brain cells between you'

'Shut up Lillie..' said Daniel as he scowled at his sister who was poking her tongue out at him, trying to goad Daniel into a reaction which he responded as she expected.

'You're just jealous that he actually likes me and doesn't pretend to be my friend like the stupid friends you have at school'.

Stephanie threw them both a look that would stop a rampaging bull dead in its tracks and warned them both.

'If you both don't stop arguing I'll bang your heads together and you will both be grounded for a VERY long time, do you hear me?'

The children both looked at each other surprised at their mum's reaction, she never said anything like that before as she continued,

'Now please just eat up and finish getting ready for school, this sort of behaviour isn't what I need at the min.....',

Stephanie stopped halfway through what she was going to say so she didn't go too far but Daniel had already picked up on what his mum was trying to say.

'I knew something was up mum, so why are you so upset lately ' he asked in a quizzical way,

Stephanie looked up at Daniel, smiled then carefully thinking about what to say, replied to her increasingly anxious son who seemed to be just as upset that his mum was feeling this way, 'I wish I could tell you my boy but it's nothing you can help with, it's something I need to sort out on my own, even I don't know what it is at the minute, I just need some time to think that's all',

And with that she got up from the table and walked out of the kitchen leaving Lillie and Daniel each with a puzzled look on their faces as they both tried to make sense of what their mum had just said.

Daniel decided to break the eerie silence that had descended on the kitchen, he turned to his sister and muttered,

'See I told you something was up the other day and now look what you've done, you had to come downstairs and be a tell-tale didn't you, it's all YOUR fault she's upset now'.

'MY FAULT??...' Lillie replied angrily ' YOU were the one who started all this, you just kept going on at her with all your questions didn't you, no wonder she's stormed off you blooming idiot!!, I'm going to finish getting ready for school so hurry up or we'll both be late, and get that stupid mutt of yours out of the kitchen before he hurts someone'.

 Daniel bent down to help Bucksy remove the pyjama bottoms from his nose and head and muttered to himself,

'I'll give her 'stupid mutt'....' as he led Bucksy out of the kitchen and let him out into the garden.

 Daniel stood by the back door thinking about his mum and what she had said to him, all the while watching as Bucksy chased a lone crisp packet round the garden which was causing him to bark in excitement.

Daniel then decided he would get to the bottom of why his mum was so upset lately but first he would have to make the long boring walk to the place he hated most, Longmeads High School, the walk was made more enjoyable as Bucksy always joined him on his way to school, (Bucksy always seemed to know how to get back home and always greeted Daniel at the same place every day without fail... strange how he always knew where to be!!!!).

Chapter Two
School Days

   The walk to Longmeads High School was one that Daniel enjoyed as he normally got to meet his best friend along the way, Harvey Jones, the only friend that Daniel really got on with at school, they had both started school at the same time so Daniel knew he could rely on his friend to have fun with when they were at school and as they both lived in the same street, were always at each other's houses and generally spent most days in each other's company.

   The walk to school took them through the woods close to Daniel's house which was at the end of Mumbles Drive, which was situated in the sleepy town of Lullington Mulch, it was a beautiful part of the country and was a quiet but generally sunny place to live, full of endless green fields and the most stunning wooded areas this side of the country which were filled with the sound of all sorts of animals who were existing in this strangely special place. So Daniel was finally ready and as it was as hot a day as normal he left his school blazer at home and made his way out of the front door to start the walk into school as he done every week day but not before shouting out to his sister,

'Lillie, I'm leaving for school now, hurry up or you'll be late'.
Lillie stopped drying her hair to answer back to Daniel who was waiting for a reply,

'Ok, I'm just finishing up here, you go on ahead and I'll meet you on the way...oh and please don't bunk off again, you're lucky I haven't told mum about the last three times you've been caught......'.
Daniel quietly shut the front door with his sister still nattering on in the background and snuck off out of the front door and as usual he was joined

by Bucksy who was wagging his tail so fast he could almost take off. Bucksy loved the walk in with Daniel and Harvey as it meant them taking a path through the woods next to the house where they lived which was filled with all sorts of smells that caused Bucksy to run on ahead and bark at whatever had caught his attention this time.

They boys were always out together getting up to mischief and generally being kids but today there was no sign of Harvey as Daniel made his way along the road alone wondering where his friend had got to,

'Hey Bucks…' said Daniel 'wonder where Harv has got to, haven't heard his whiney voice yet!!', Bucksy barked in a way as if he was answering Daniel's question until he noticed a stick on the floor in front of him which took away his attention.

Daniel picked up the stick he saw sitting on the ground in front of his dog and got ready to throw it for Bucksy to chase as he usually done, barking away at the top of his voice so Daniel would know he was ready to fetch it for him.

'Go on Bucks….fetch it, good boy', and off his dog would run sniffing out the stick that Daniel had just thrown which he duly brought back and dropped it at his master's feet ready for him to throw out into the distance again, this time Daniel didn't hold back and launched the stick as far as he could which landed right into a clump of bushes ahead of them, then followed a strange whining noise that started coming from deep within the bush which then started to shake as if something was behind them.

Bucksy stopped dead in his tracks and waited for Daniel to catch up and he turned his head as if to say 'Wait here'.

Daniel said to Bucksy 'what is that sound? Go on boy have a look but be careful', and with that his dog set off ever so carefully like a lioness stalking its prey until he came to the shaking bush and slowly stooped down as if ready to pounce. Then, like an Olympic athlete, Bucksy launched himself into the bush, 'Grrrrr...' Bucksy growled as he had grabbed hold of something in his mouth.

18

'AAhhhh get this blooming dog off me!!!' the reply came as Bucksy slowly pulled out a leg from the bushes, followed by the second leg and eventually the rest of what looked like a scared young boy who was now covered in dirt and yelping in pain as he was pulled further out into the open, Bucksy finally let go and started barking at the muddied face looking up at him from the floor, it was Harvey looking rather angry at his friend who was doubled over laughing at him as he started pulling bits of twig out of his hair,
'Stop laughing Daniel!!, it's not funny is it?? Just look at the state of me' Harvey cried out as he surveyed the state of his coat and trousers which were muddied up from his trip through the bushes.
Daniel, still sniggering at the sight of his best friend being dragged through the bushes, had to ask the question about what was going on,
'So Harvey, please tell me why you were hiding in the bushes, you weren't trying to jump out on me again were you?, you know what happened last time you tried that don't you!!'.
Harvey gradually got to his feet, brushing his trousers and coat down and replied,
'Well, I was thinking of jumping out on you two but not from where you found me, so I sneaked ahead of you towards the woods on the path we always use then in the distance I saw something, I don't know what it was but it looked like some sort of weird shaped animal, it turned and looked at me before scurrying off into the bush which Bucksy dragged me from, so I went after it to see what it was, I managed to crawl through the gap at the bottom and saw whatever it was running off into the distance, it was so fast that I didn't get to see it properly'.
Daniel looking on with a puzzled look on his face replied to Harvey who was catching his breath back after his long winded explanation,
'Right, so you saw some sort of rabbit then??', Daniel carried on,
'But why didn't you come out after that?
Harvey carried on with his 'story' much to Daniel's amusement,
'Well I would of got out sooner but I realised I was stuck in the bush and couldn't actually move, I did hear voices coming but it didn't' sound like you

two so I stayed very still for ages, until I felt something heavy land on my head, it must of crashed through the bushes, then the next thing I know is I'm being dragged out by my trouser leg by some horrible hairy beast, I thought I was a goner but then I turn round and see it's your dog. Talk about needing new underwear!!!'.

Daniel was now laughing uncontrollably as he walked over to Harvey, put an arm around his shoulder and said,

'Come on mate, let's go, but don't worry I'll protect you 'King' Daniel is here!!.

And with that the boys walked through the woods, Daniel jumping in front of Harvey every time he heard a noise ahead and laughing as he done it and Bucksy barking at the pair of them, eventually they came to the end of the woods and to the pathway that led them to the back gates of Longmeads High School, the boys both groaned as they saw the familiar figure of the caretaker Mr Twitcher standing with the gate open muttering to himself.

'Who will it be today??, Who is the lucky one?'.

The boys filed past him and ambled off up the field and into the school grounds not looking forward to another boring day of 'learning rubbish' as Daniel so nicely put it.

As they made their way to the classroom Daniel turned to Harvey and with a miserable look on his face huffed and said,

'I can't wait until we leave this place mate, I hate it here, I want something exciting to happen for us, that way we can just stay at home', Harvey looking straight ahead as he replied,

'It would be nice for something to happen mate, like the school being taken over by aliens or coming in to find all the teachers hadn't bothered to show up for class....',

But before he could finish what he was saying a shadow was cast over the boys which made them look up and were greeted by the familiar booming figure of Daniel's form teacher, Mr Whitworthy, who was dressed in his usual clothes of the most awful dark blue suit ever seen and horrible brown shoes which were always polished to perfection, Mr Whitworthy, standing tall at the door to the classroom boomed at the two boys who were standing there waiting for some kind of punishment, replied to Harvey's fictional thought,

'Well Jones my boy, there is no chance that I won't ever turn up to school, I practically live here so don't even think about messing me around... Do you hear me?? Now Jones, run along to your form room please. And do try to stay out of trouble'.

'Y.y..yes sir!' Harvey stuttered with a reply as they both walked past the teacher and Harvey scuttled off into the next corridor where his Form Room was with Miss Jacobs and Daniel slowly made his way into the classroom and sat at his usual desk at the back of the class, he threw his school bag down and yawned as he rested his head in his hands prompting Mr Whitworthy to look up from the desk he was sitting at and noticing Daniel was completely not with it he snorted out the sort of cutting remark that made everyone else in the class turn round and look in Daniel's direction,

'Well Mr Carter, it seems like someone didn't get much sleep last night judging from your demeanour, I'm sorry if my wanting to teach you something which may serve you well in the future gets in the way of your daily rest but unfortunately I do have to do my job which DOES involve you listening, so sit up straight and pay attention!!'

Daniel fixed his gaze on his teacher and huffed as he sat back in his chair as if someone important had entered the room then replied in his sarcastic way that he had adopted since he started school,

'Well I best sit up then sir, don't want you to have to stop your ever so interesting lesson just to have to deal with me again!!'.

Mr Whitworthy grew slightly more annoyed then decided to change tact and replied in a calm voice,

'That's your last warning Carter, then it's off to the Headmaster's office if you carry on disrupting my lesson',

Daniel slumped back in his chair again and prepared for another day of boring lessons while Mr Whitworthy started his usual classroom chat.

So today was pretty much like any other day really, the sun was beating down, the birds began their morning chorus and now Daniel was looking out of the classroom window thinking about how nice it would be to go out and be in the sunshine, daydreaming about all the things he could be getting up to instead of being stuck in this boring lesson all morning listening to the droning voice of Mr Whitworthy who was pacing up and down at the front of the classroom waffling on about how 'The might of the Roman Empire shaped the world in which we live in today' , all Daniel heard was 'BLAH BLAH BLAH BLAH' as his attention was now taken up by something moving out in the school fields, Daniel craned his neck closer to the window as in the distance, right by the path that leads to the back gate he thought he saw some kind of shadow darting in and out of the bushes which then seemed to stop moving as it neared the end of the row of trees and shrubs which surrounded the school.

It was a shadow that looked like the figure of a person which Daniel soon realised that it was looking right at him now,

He craned his neck and body forward so much that he fell off his chair with a 'CRASH' which alerted Mr Whitworthy, causing him to whip his head round in Daniels direction.

'Owww, that blooming hurt!!' remarked Daniel as he slowly lifted himself off of the floor and back into his seat, dusting himself down as Mr Whitworthy strode down the classroom and stood directly in front of Daniel's desk, his oversized glasses perching on the end of his nose, Daniel hadn't noticed his teacher standing there as he turned round.

'Woah' Daniel remarked as he clapped eyes on his teacher who was standing there arms crossed, ready to dish out a punishment to him,

'Sir you scared me!!!!' He continued as he smirked at the sight of his teachers rather large glasses close to falling off his nose, they always made him laugh too as he had seen them fly off many a time during his time at school, Mr Whitworthy leant forward even closer towards Daniel's face, ready to speak but all Daniel could think of was the rather odd coffee like smell coming from his teacher's mouth, then his teacher opened his

22

mouth to reveal his yellow stained teeth which made Daniel feel queasy, then his teacher, thinking long and hard about what should be said to him spoke,

'Well Mr Carter it seems like once again you have decided that my class is too distracting for whatever it is you feel you should be doing…', all the while Daniel was watching his glasses slip further down his nose,

He continued with his usual waffling which was nearly always aimed at Daniel,

'Well I'm sure that as of this minute I know that you would of been listening extremely closely to what I have just been talking about and will easily be able to tell me about the great things that the Roman Army gave to the world…'.

Daniel decided that his reply should be one to get him sent out of the class for the day, so he looked his teacher straight in the eyes and without a single shred of guilt on his face said,

'Well I guess the Roman Army didn't give us toothpaste sir otherwise you would have used it this morning…',

The class erupted with laughter as Mr Whitworthy stood bolt upright, pushed his glasses back onto his nose and scowled at Daniel as he angrily replied,

'Right Mr Carter that's the last time….. I've never been so insulted in all my life, you are truly a despicable young man'.

The whole class fell silent as Mr Whitworthy carried on his rant at Daniel, who was now looking round the classroom at his classmates who were all whispering to each other, Mr Whitworthy continued,

'I think that you best leave this classroom right this minute as there seems to be no hope for you, Go on off to the Headmaster's office right this minute and I'll let him deal with you.

So Daniel sighed as he put his school books back in his school bag and rose out of his seat, the walk to the door looked a long way away with thirty pairs of eyes trained on him as he marched towards the front of the classroom like an inmate on his final walk, and reaching the handle ready to turn it when Mr Whitworthy turned, looked in Daniels direction and left him with something to think about, said,

'You will amount to nothing Daniel Carter, you mark my words, you are truly the worst pupil I've ever had the misfortune to teach since I started teaching and you will get no respect from anyone, That's the truth of the matter, Just remember this quote from Julius Caesar,

'Experience is a teacher of all things',' Mr Whitworthy said as he stood up straight,

'Julian who?' replied Daniel with a cheeky smirk on his face,

'JULIUS CAESAR' Mr Whitworthy shouted back angrily 'Do you not listen to anything I've taught you boy?, and seeing as I HAVE been doing this for a very long time then you will do well to remember that quote in the future, Now please leave my classroom and don't bother returning'. And Mr Whitworthy turned his attention back to his pupils and carried on as if nothing had happened, Daniel opened the door and left the classroom wondering if he had gone too far this time, looking back through the glass panel in the door as he stood there for a moment reflecting on what he had said. His gaze was met by the hand of Mr Whitworthy ushering him to move away from the door,

So Daniel picked up his bag off the floor, turned and started the walk down the corridor with the words of his teacher still ringing in his ears,

'I'll prove him wrong someday, then we will see who's right' said Daniel as he angrily pounded the wall on the way down the school corridor.

Chapter Three
Leaving It All Behind

The halls of Longmead High School were as ancient as some of the teachers who worked there with many locked doors leading off into the unknown, rumour has it (from many former pupils!!!) that they all lead to the same spot deep under the school where all the teachers would meet after the school day was done and carry out rituals cleansing their souls of evil after having to deal with the unruliness of the 'unlearned' as they were called.

Rumour also has it that a brother of one of the pupils had managed to get into the tunnels under the school but was never seen again, just the odd scream heard from deep in the belly of the school basement was heard for a few weeks it's said, but then….silence.

 But Daniel was totally uninterested by these rumours as he walked the long stone clad corridor of the school on his way once again to the Headmaster's office, looking at the pictures of the former Head teachers hanging on the walls, each one as scary as the next one,

 ' I'm sure they are all staring at me' thought Daniel as he continued his walk down the eerily silent corridor, the occasional banging door heard in the distance until he was distracted by a faint mumbling noise coming from around the next corner.

 As he rounded the corner he was confronted by the sight of Harvey sitting at a desk which had been placed outside, normally that meant that he had been in trouble too, he was humming and mumbling to himself unaware that Daniel was sneaking up behind him like a Lion hunting its prey, 'BOO' screeched Daniel as he grabbed hold of Harvey by the waist and scared him so much that Harvey shrieked like a small child does, 'YEEEEAAAAH' he went causing him to almost lift off the seat he was sitting on, Daniel on the other hand had collapsed against the wall laughing so hard as Harvey and his class work went everywhere, all over the floor and down the corridor too.

'What the blooming heck are you doing to me Daniel???, you scared the life out of me', Whimpered Harvey as he tried to recover from what had happened, Daniel had managed to bring the laughter down to a snigger as he thought about how funny it was,

'Sorry mate, I so couldn't resist it, I've never seen you jump so high!!' he replied 'Looks like you've turned even more pastey than you already are'. Harvey snorted at Daniel in a way that suggested he wasn't very happy with him,

'Not funny mate!!, it's not my fault I can't tan!! You look like you don't wash!!', he bent down from his seat to pick up all the paperwork that was lying around on the floor, muttering under his breath as Daniel just stood there watching him.

'Aren't you going to help me pick all this up, seeing as you caused this', Harvey grumpily asked Daniel.

'Nah, not my work to pick up, anyway what are you doing outside class?, what have you done this time?'

Harvey smirked as he told Daniel what had happened,

'Well you know Miss Jacobs....'

'Yes...' Daniel replied in an inquisitive way hoping that this was going to be a good story to hear, not like the ones Harvey normally tells.

'Well you know how much she goes on about all these old writers and stuff and how she tells us she's spent her life learning about each one and boring us about 'what they were trying to achieve' or something like that...',

'Right, but what happened?' Daniel looking totally confused now as Harvey carried on,

26

'She was blabbing on as usual about this writer bloke from the past and all I said was that anyone could write stuff like that and how none of it made any sense and how it was totally boring, she totally flipped at me which kind of scared me, haha'

'And she threw you out for that mate?' Daniel questioned,

'Oh no mate, I'll carry on, so I told her that I wasn't really bothered about learning about this stuff anymore as I wouldn't need it in the future seeing as I was going to be big sports star, so she screeched at me, ranting that this was the only thing she had ever cared about and her whole life was about understanding writer's….blah blah blah blah', Harvey continued his story in epic detail as Daniel looked even more confused now,

'So then I said to her 'maybe you should get out more and go and get some real friends seeing as you only care about old dead blokes', then she completely lost it and screeched at me to leave her class which caused that massive vein on her head to pop out, So here I am mate, think she may have overreacted a bit, haha'.

Daniel stood there chuckling to himself as he pictured Miss Jacobs and her massive vein making an appearance, but all of a sudden a huge gust of wind appeared as the door to Harvey's class swung open wildly almost taking Daniel's head clean off it's shoulders.

'Woah!!!' Daniel leapt back in defence as he was greeted by the sight of Miss Jacobs standing there, face looking full of anger as she caught him chatting to Harvey who was supposed to be sitting in silence,

'Right Mr Jones, first of all I sent you out of the class as once again you were being disruptive and you have completely upset me!!, second I catch you talking to Mr Carter here who, as I'm presuming, has been sent from the class too for some kind of disruption'.

Daniel decided that it was his turn to answer in his unique way,

'Ding Ding, I think we have a winner here Harvey, let's see what prize she has won!!!'.

Harvey snorted with laughter as Miss Jacobs grew angrier and by now was close to exploding,

'Right that's it, be off with you two, get down to the Heads office and don't you dare stop or I'll have you expelled, DO YOU HEAR ME!!!!'.

And with that Daniel piped up, 'Alright alright we're going, jeez I was already on my way there anyway so there's no need to shout, don't let the vein on your head pop out anymore or we will all be in trouble!!!'.

Miss Jacobs screamed at the boys like a howling banshee,

'How dare you talk to me like that, I'm in my right mind to write a letter to your parents about your disgraceful behaviour, NOW GO!!!'.

And with that Miss Jacobs turned on her heels and slammed the door shut sending a cold breeze straight through Harvey's clothes leaving the two boys sniggering to each other.

Daniel peered into the class window to see what the teacher was doing until she turned to catch him laughing and gesturing about the vein that they saw throbbing on her head earlier, to which Miss Jacobs stormed over to the class door and stood there just staring at him with her piercing evil looking eyes until Daniel finally piped up

'I think we better go mate, reckon she's going to turn into a dragon or something!!, Don't fancy being eaten today, haha'.

Harvey stood up from his desk still clutching all his paperwork and decide not to make eye contact with his teacher as he scuttled past the door and along the corridor with Daniel,

'Think I went too far this time, don't you mate?' Harvey asked inquisitively as he feared what was going to happen in the Headmaster's office, Daniel on the other hand was less than fazed by the events and tried to reassure his scared looking friend,

'Nah, I reckon it will be fine, she's only upset because you literally destroyed everything she has worked towards all her life!!, Haha'.

Harvey whacked his less than caring friend on the arm with his books as they made their way along the breezy cold corridors towards the Headmaster's office which was at the far end of the school, totally hidden out of the way from the pupils to hang about near.

The closer the boys got to the office the more Daniel started thinking about school, and what he was actually learning there which brought him to a halt, he turned to Harvey and said,

'Do you think that I really want to be here anymore mate?, I mean I'm so fed up of this place and all the teachers make me miserable, don't you think there's something out there for us to do instead of being at school?'.

Harvey looking deep in thought for a moment casually replied,

'Well, to be honest my mum will kill me if I don't do well at school, she's already threatened me with going to stay with Aunt Hilda over the summer holidays!!, so I think I'll take my chances here thanks!!',

'But surely your mum knows the amount of trouble you get into here, I know mine does' Daniel said, 'And anyway it's nearly the end of term so I'm sure we won't be missed',

Harvey, trying to take Daniel's thoughts off school had an idea, 'I tell you what mate when schools over today let's go to the Hideout and hang out then we can talk about what we are going to do'.

'Mmm, good idea mate, the Hideout does sound like a great plan and we can carry on our 'War' too' Daniel replied with a big smile on his face,

'Think we should take Bucksy too, he loves a good run around and he makes a great horse!!, I'm sure he will happily come with us mate, He always acts odd in the woods anyway' Harvey replied as their excitement level grew higher and louder.

Harvey's eyes then bulged out as he thought of an idea,

'Seeing as we are going to the hideout why not take the 'weapons' we have made, I'm sure the swords and shields are still at mine and this time Bucksy is going to be on MY side for a change, I'm looking forward to being 'The King of The Woods' this time!!'.

Daniel stopped dead in his tracks, his mind seemingly running overtime as they were edging ever closer towards the Headmaster's office when he seemed to have an idea, grabbing at Harvey's arm he told him his plan,

'Tell you what mate I've had a great idea…'said Daniel, Harvey rolled his eyes back and muttered, 'Here it comes..'. Daniel hit Harvey on his arm and continued to tell him what was going to happen,

'Why don't we go now??, Look I'm sure the teachers aren't going to miss us, I mean there's only a bit of the day left, we may as well make the most of the sunshine, all we have to do is go down this corridor, sneak past the classroom doors and get out past the front desk, then we are out of here!!'.

Harvey didn't really react with the excitement shown by Daniel apart from saying,

'You've forgotten about one thing though haven't you..'

'What are you talking about Harvey?' a confused Daniel replied.,

'Even if we get out of here, past the classrooms, past the front desk and out towards the back gate then there's still the small matter of Mr Twitcher and Rollo'. Harvey seemingly pouring water on the plan as Daniel thought for a minute or two,

'We will be fine mate, trust me, I've sneaked past him a thousand times in the past, that's the easy bit, come on mate live a little…'

Harvey stood there for a moment and processed everything that Daniel had said a worried look spread across his face but Daniel was always too persuasive for him to turn down,

'I shouldn't do Dan but…..Ok mate lets go, but if we get caught I'm blaming you for the whole thing' Harvey said as they slowly made their way down the corridor and edged closer to the front desk,

'Also I can't be bothered to sit in the Heads office while he lectures us about 'the values of a good education', blah blah blah, plus I can never stop looking at that massive mole on his cheek'

Daniel sniggered as he recalled the last time he was in the office being lectured by Mr Pole, the Headmaster, and all Daniel was looking at was the dancing mole on the side of his cheek,

'Moley Poley...haha' they said at the same time, this was their nickname for the Headmaster, they both used to believe it grew bigger the angrier he got.

Their attention turned back to the task in hand as Harvey reminded him of what they needed to do, so Daniel, whose mind was forever on the go, was assessing the situation they were both in,

'So here's what we will do...' He started to relay the plan to Harvey, ' I'll cause a distraction somehow and when it's safe you then make a run for the door, make sure you hold it open so I can get through it too otherwise I'll get seen then you'll be for it!!!.

Harvey replied to Daniel's order in his best army voice,

'Yes sir, Captain!!...Right then, are we going to do this?, I'm starting to feel like I need to get back to class and learn something the more we stand here, haha'.

So Daniel crouched down near to the open door of the office and he could hear the familiar sound of Mrs Catchpole, the school secretary, tapping away at her computer while singing gently under her breath so she couldn't be heard by anyone passing, the door to her office faced the exit of the school hence why she would need to be distracted by something to get her to face the other way so the boys could escape,

Daniel looked at Harvey and put his finger up to his lips,

'Shhhh' Letting Harvey know to be quiet so he could get to work, he took a small pebble out of his pocket, which he often collected them to keep, and slowly and quietly moved into position, pebble in hand, he was scouring the room to look for something that he could hit to cause a big enough distraction so they could run.

In the far corner of the room stood a huge metal filing cabinet which Daniel had seen and decided to use that to distract Mrs Catchpole, so he gestured to Harvey to get ready to run as he pulled his arm back and with a harder throw than was actually needed he released the pebble from his sweaty grasp and watched it fly across the room like it was in slow motion past the Secretary and straight towards the cabinet which it hit directly on the drawers with an almighty 'DONNNGGGG', Mrs Catchpole screeched in terror as the noise the cabinet made caused her to launch all the

31

paperwork she had in her hand right up in the air which in turn made her lean back on her chair too far and over she went with a 'CRASHHH'.

Daniel looked straight at Harvey who was totally oblivious to the carnage around him by now so he gave him a slap on the leg and mouthed, 'Now!!...Go!!', and with that Harvey leapt into action like a sprinter and ran at the front door which for normal people would be an easy task but this was Harvey who was rather a clumsy child, he tripped over his own feet as he neared the door and instead of opening it silently he went crashing through it like a bull in a china shop head first which caused him to squeal,

'ARRGH' he cried as he felt the full force of the heavy door against his face as his momentum took him through to the outside and he collapsed in a heap of arms and legs with only his head holding the door open.

Mrs Catchpole was totally oblivious to the commotion that was happening outside of her office as she was in a state of confusion as to why she was lying on the office floor looking up at the ceiling with handfuls of paperwork all around her, she muttered angrily,

'Whatever is going on here?, I don't remember a thing, look at all this mess!!!...' she slowly got to her feet and surveyed the mess across the whole office as Daniel waited for the right time to make a break for it, so as Mrs Catchpole was busy facing the other way slowly picking up all the paperwork she had dropped then Daniel decided that was the right time to make his escape, and with that he turned on his heels and sprinted towards the door which Harvey was still holding open with his head and looking very dazed and confused as he felt a rush of wind coming past him and the next thing he knew he was being dragged away from off of the floor and around the corner of the building out of sight.

'AAAHHH...OWWW, Stop dragging me you blooming maniac!!' Harvey moaned as Daniel kept pulling him round to the side of the building until he thought they were safe hiding in a small recess in the school building 'Think you've broke my bum!!!..' He carried on moaning with tears in his eyes as he stood up to survey the damage to his school clothes, his

32

trousers had been ripped at the knees and round the back, his shirt was stained by the gravely floor, so he stood up and whacked Daniel hard on the arm and angrily said,

'You've ripped my clothes, why were you so rough?, These were my only pair of trousers, Mums gonna go mad now, she warned me not to damage these ones or I'll have to wear my shorts instead!!'.

Daniel looked Harvey up and down and replied,

'Stop moaning mate, we're out aren't we!!', and just as he said that he heard voices coming straight towards them, Daniel gestured to Harvey to be quiet as he was still ranting about the state of his clothes,

'Shhhh...there's someone coming' Daniel whispered as he slowly peered around the corner of the wall to see Mr Proctor the Deputy Headmaster and Mr Lint the Geography teacher walking towards where they were hiding, he was sure they would be found out as the recess wasn't very big and there was just enough room for the two boys to stand, so Daniel held Harvey back right up against the wall as they approached the opening,

Daniel was wishing so hard that they wouldn't be spotted, then Harvey noticed that Daniel was kind of chanting to himself, something he had never heard before, but Harvey was frozen solid to the spot unable to move or speak,

'Eramosa...Vin Sarmo Eramosa...' was the chant Harvey heard over and over again, he closed his eyes tight and looked away in the hope the boys wouldn't be seen, totally ignoring Daniel's chanting which he was now muttering under his breath, he was completely still by now almost as if they were part of the wall somehow as the two teachers stood directly in front of the boys still talking amongst themselves, then Mr Proctor turned round to face the boys where they were standing, but nothing.

There was no booming voice demanding they come out of the hiding place, no hint of any kind that they had been seen even though the teachers were staring right at them, then Mr Proctor and Mr Lint carried on towards the front of the school and Daniel seemed to unfreeze and peered out.

'What the heck was that all about mate??' Harvey quizzically asked.

33

'What do you mean?' Daniel replied as he looked at his friend who was staring at him in a way that he had never seen before, so Harvey carried on,

'Well, first of all why the heck didn't the teachers spot us!!, I was sure we were going to be seen. The next thing was you were chanting something over and over, it was like you weren't there at all!!'

Daniel looked totally puzzled as he tried to search his memory for anything that had just happened.

'I haven't got a clue what you're on about mate, seriously I don't, I just remember holding you back then the teachers moving on, that's it!!'

'Well whatever it was I've never felt anything like it before, it was like we were….invisible or something' said Harvey as he and Daniel just stared at each other both as confused as each other.

Daniel then turned away from his friend to look out again to see if they could make a move,

'The coast is clear mate, let's go' he excitedly said as Daniel pulled at Harvey again and they made their way along the school building and off towards the path which led to the back gates of the school but as always someone was patrolling the one place that could mean huge trouble for the boys and their attempt to escape the school grounds for their weekly get together.

Chapter Four
Freedom...sort of

The school gates were the only way out of the back of the school as any other entrance had been blocked off, They were surrounded by thorny shrubs and a collection of hedgerows quite different to normal hedges and the gates themselves were arch like and very regal looking and were always well maintained, suggesting that someone spent a lot of time down this way, with today being no exception.

So as the boys made their way towards the back gates of the school Harvey was still complaining about the state of his clothes and how his mum was going to 'brain him' then Daniel suddenly stopped dead in his tracks causing Harvey to walk straight into the back of him almost tripping them both over. Harvey piped up, now rubbing his nose which had slammed into the shoulder of Daniel.

'Owww, what did you stop like that for?, it's bad enough that you've destroyed my only pair of trousers, now I think I need to go to hosp....', his angry response was cut short by Daniel putting his hand over Harvey's mouth which was still going even though Daniel was covering it,

'Shhhh Harv...I can hear something round the corner'

So Daniel poked his head as close to the corner of the hedge they were standing by to see if he could spot where the noise was coming from,

'Oh great....' Daniel sighed as he turned to Harvey to tell him what he was seeing,

'Why did he have to be here at this time!!'

Harvey pulled Daniels hand away from his mouth and looking puzzled replied,

'Who's there?? I hope it's a doctor, think you've broke my nose as well as my bum!!', so Harvey slowly leant in front of Daniel to see who was blocking the boys exit out of the school grounds and looking dejected as he muttered,

'Fantastic...it's old man Twitcher, what's he doing here at this time??'
Daniel was just as bemused to see Mr Twitcher searching the bushes that run alongside the school gates.

  Mr Twitcher was Longmeads live in caretaker, he was rather a tall man with an extremely weathered looking face and he was always carrying his favourite poking stick which he used when searching the bushes for and children who had decided to try and leave before the end of the school day, alongside him as always was his faithful but rather oversized four legged companion Rollo who loved nothing more than sniffing out any children hiding from sight.

  The caretaker loved nothing more than acting like the big hero whenever he managed to catch any children trying to escape so he could take complete credit, claiming that it was his 'extensive army training' that made him who he was (truth is he was never in the army, the story goes that he was thrown out of the army cadets on the first day because he was shouted at a lot and it upset him so he kept on crying until he got his mummy to pick him up).

  He always muttered the same thing to himself whenever he was on 'patrol' as he put it, kind of stuck on a loop in his head,

'Today's the day, today's the day when Herman catches kids who stray...'
he would mutter as Rollo let out a cross between a bark and a howl, which was his way of approval.

'Let's see who we can catch today, eh boy, my hut needs new badges!!' Mr Twitcher said excitedly as he started his usual sneaky pacing up and down along the thick hedgerows, trying to peek inside to see any sign of children in them desperate to get past him and out of the school gates. Between

36

them they had been very successful over the years, catching numerous children wanting to sneak past him but he always seemed to be one step ahead of them, whenever he caught anyone he would make up a new 'Badge of Capture' with the child's name on it and proudly display it on the wall of his tin pot shed which he called his 'Base of Operations', so over the years the walls had become almost completely covered by the names of all the children desperate to make a run for it but weren't quite clever enough to get past him and Rollo, The badges dated back well into the 1960's which shows just how long he had been working at Longmeads.

So this time Daniel and Harvey knew they needed to be extra cunning to try their luck at getting past them,

Daniel was surveying the bushes to see if there was any way of sneaking far enough through and he turned and spotted a gap right where they were standing,

'Ah Ha..' he muttered silently as he slowly slipped out of sight, Harvey was still peering ever so carefully round the end of the bush to keep an eye on Mr Twitcher and Rollo to see how far away they were from them,

'So what's the pla….Daniel???, where are you?' Harvey whispered as noticed Mr Twitcher and Rollo heading their way,

'Daniel?, Daniel!!', Harvey sounding more desperate as he searched for his friend who was nowhere to be seen and now the caretaker was yards from where he was crouching.

The next thing Harvey knew he was being lifted off his feet and was being dragged through the gap in the bushes just as Mr Twitcher and Rollo reached the spot where he had just been cowering.

Mr Twitcher looked puzzled, he took off his rather tatty old hat, scratched his head and muttered to Rollo,

'I'm sure I just heard voices boy…',

Rollo Barked fairly tamely as if to agree with him, he then turned his head towards the spot where the boys were hiding and started his usual sniffing of the bushes, hoping to seek out anyone hiding inside. Daniel lay his hand across Harvey's mouth so he couldn't screech like he normally does when

37

he gets scared by something which was just as well as all of a sudden Rollo's big wet nose started poking in through the gap at the edge of the bush and he started sniffing furiously like he had picked up a scent.

Harvey's eyes widened and he began to panic as the dog's nose got ever closer to Harvey's trainers and trouser legs, next followed the dogs big brown head into the bushes, Rollo had discovered the boys hiding place but as the space was small he was unable to bark for Mr Twitcher to look inside so instead Rollo reached out to Harvey and managed to grab onto his trouser leg and began trying to tug him out of the bushes but he was stuck up to his neck by the sheer thickness of the bush, all the while he was growling as if to say 'I've found something' but Mr Twitcher seemed to be preoccupied by something else and didn't notice his dog neck deep in the bushes struggling to free himself.

Harvey was getting more and more agitated as Rollo tugged harder at his trousers slowly pulling him backwards away from Daniel's grip, he still had his hand across Harvey's mouth trying to stop him from making too much noise that the caretaker would eventually discover them, Harvey on the other hand was trying to shout out in terror but instead was making strange noises on Daniel's hand which causes Daniel to hold it firmer each time, then he whacked Harvey on the arm and mouthed at him,

'Shhh Harv...I've got an idea!!', so he dove deep into his trouser pocket and after a bit of rummaging around exclaimed,

'Ah-ha, here it is' and he pulled small packet out and held it in front of Harvey's face,

'Look....' He quietly whispered and made sure Harvey could see what it was,

'Pepper....' He told Harvey who was more interested in getting loose from the jaws of Rollo who was still struggling to free himself plus pulling Harvey out through the bush.

So Daniel ripped the top off of the small pepper packet, carefully opened up the packet and began to sprinkle it all over Rollo's big wet nose, waiting as the pepper stuck to the poor dog.

Rollo suddenly let go of Harvey's trouser leg and instead began licking at the pepper which had now spread nicely all over his nose and tongue. 'Snort...sneeze..' went Rollo as he suddenly realised that whatever it was on his nose wasn't good for him, he managed to sneeze himself free from the bush and continued to sneeze all over the place as the boys were sniggering quietly to themselves.

Rollo was now rolling about all over the grass trying to rid himself of the pepper which by now was all licked off his nose and getting deep into his throat causing him to moan,

'Awwrrrrrr' Rollo whimpered as he pawed at his snout, trying to get his owners attention but Mr Twitcher was still oblivious to Rollo's situation because he could hear what sounded like children coming towards the back gates,

'Sounds like we've got ourselves a couple of early leavers Rollo!!!' Mr Twitcher said excitedly as he hurriedly got ready to pounce on whoever it was that was trying to leave,

'Come here boy, we don't want to be seen yet do we' He said to Rollo who was now staggering towards his owner, his eyes streaming with tears and him still sneezing every so often,

'What happened to you Rollo??, Did you get stuck in the bush again' Mr Twitcher said as he caught sight of Rollo looking worse for wear covered in branches and leaves from the bush he had just been stuck in.

All the while the boys were still hiding in the same spot too scared to move as the voice of the caretaker got slightly louder and closer to the spot where they were hiding.

They didn't dare make a sound as a sneezing Rollo plodded past the spot where they were hiding but didn't bother with the boys as he knew what had just happened and didn't fancy a repeat of it.

The next thing the boys knew was that the hole in the side of the hedge where they got in was slowly going dark as all of a sudden the backside of Mr Twitcher started to push through into the gap slowly and quietly which now seemed to scare both boys at the thought of them both being dragged

39

back into school and straight into detention, but all of a sudden Mr Twitcher stopped moving backwards, his bottom must've been about a foot away from the arm of Harvey, the boys were now completely petrified as they thought the game was up so they sat completely still, not daring to move a muscle.

Out of the corner of Harvey's eye he caught sight of something small, stripy and buzzing which was flying towards his hand, to Harvey it was the biggest bee ever!!, he was frozen to the spot as he watched it land close to his hand, Daniel had spotted it too and immediately put his hand back over Harvey's mouth as he knew he would squeal like a pig if it got any closer, all the while Mr Twitcher was completely still in the gap of the bush.

Then it happened, the insect made its way onto Harvey's hand, who was now frozen with terror, then his eyes widened and he began to breath heavily as he knew what was coming next, He was stung on the hand and started to fidget uncontrollably as the pain took over but Daniel still had his hand over Harvey's mouth which was proving harder to keep there as he jerked around.

Mr Twitcher on the other hand wasn't paying any attention to the commotion behind him as he was concentrating on his next capture, mumbling softly to himself as he sat there waiting,

'Oh goodie, another couple of pupils to add to my list!!, That's it boys come closer!!'. He muttered, all the while licking his lips in anticipation,

In the distance and getting ever closer to the spot where they were all gathered were two more Longmead pupils heading towards Mr Twitcher and Rollo,

From their voices Daniel could just about make out who it was, It sounded like Archie Jenkins and Henry Thompson coming towards them, Daniel didn't really get on with them so he was willing them to be caught so it would take the attention away from the two boys who were stuck between Mr Twitcher's looming bottom and the huge trunk in the bush which was stopping them from moving away, Harvey was still frantically swatting his arms trying to hit the bee and also trying to get Daniel to move his hand as he was struggling to catch his breath now and turning a darker shade of red than he was used to but Daniel held on because he knew if he let go then Harvey would give the game away and they along with the other two boys would be hauled in front of the Headmaster again,

'Mmpphh' Harvey tried to alert Daniel to his predicament and eventually Daniel looked at him and seeing that he was turning redder by the second released his grip ever so slightly but still wary of any noise that Harvey may make,

'Shhh…' Daniel gently whispered in his friend's ear,

'I can hear Archie and Henry coming...this is our chance to get away, just got to wait for Twitcher to catch them...so keep still and don't make a sound!!'.

And with that Daniel turned towards where Mr Twitcher was, hoping and praying he wouldn't turn round and see them.

Then all of a sudden Mr Twitcher leapt out of his hiding place like a coiled spring shouting,

'Ah-ha, I've got you!!!, looks like we are going on a nice little trip to the Heads office doesn't it,', all the while smiling like the cat that got the cream with Rollo barking with excitement alongside him as the startled boys looked at each other with total fear in their eyes, Archie then stuttered as he tried to reply to Mr Twitcher,

'B..B.but sir….I have permission to I..leave, I'm going to the dentist',

'A likely story if ever I've heard one' laughed the caretaker as Rollo started circling the two scared boys making sure they didn't make a run for it,

'Looks like we got a couple of new badges to add to the wall boy, now let's get moving' said Mr Twitcher as he spread out his arms as if to herd the boys back towards school like a couple of sheep with them still pleading their innocence,

'But sir….we need to go, my mum is waiting…..' Henry replied as they started to make their way back to the school with Mr Twitcher rubbing his hands with glee at the thought of being seen as the school 'hero' again.

41

Mr Twitcher just muttered at the boys to get a move on as there were more to catch, all the while the two boys pleading to be let go,

'Come on sir....please let us go, I have a letter.....' Archie begged and thrust a piece of paper into the caretaker's bony hand but he just smirked and screwed it up, tossing it into the nearest dustbin as they neared the school.

Now out of sight Daniel breathed a huge sigh of relief as Mr Twitcher and the boys disappeared out of sight and into the school,

'Blimey...that was close mate..' Daniel said as he craned his neck slightly to look out of the hole in the bush to see if the coast was clear, but he had totally forgotten that he was still holding his hand over Harvey's mouth as his friend punched Daniel in the leg reminding him to let go.

'Owww...Sorry mate..I totally forgot about you' Daniel said as he took his hand away from his friends mouth.

'AAAHHH, OWWWWW, jeez that hurt!!!, look at the state of my hand, that blooming bee thingy has made it look fat where it stung me, it's all your fault, if anything happens to me because of this I'll brain you' an irritated and angry Harvey scolded his friend who was now laughing at Harvey and his 'fat hand' and pushed Harvey off his legs and said,

'Hahaha, look at it, it looks like a row of sausages now!!, any way stop whining,we haven't been caught have we??, it looks like we're in the clear, see nothing to worry about, no harm done'.

'NO HARM DONE!!!!' shouted Harvey as he looked at himself and how bedraggled he looked and continued his rant at Daniel,

'I've had my head bashed in by the door, ripped my only pair of trousers and new school shirt, broke my nose on your bony back, I've been dragged through a hedge backwards, literally and for real, almost mauled to death by the biggest most ferocious dog on earth and to top it all off I've been attacked by the scariest looking bee on the planet and now I have a hand like a pack of sausages.....and you say no harm done!!!!!.'

Daniel stifling his laughter now looked Harvey up and down and said

'Stop being a big baby and let's move, I'll lend you some of my clothes when we get home, no biggie mate, now come on let's go'.

And with that the boys made their way through the rest of the network of bushes so they didn't get spotted by anyone else, Harvey was still scolding Daniel because of the state of his clothes, was following Daniel as close as he could as Daniel kept pinging the branches of the bushes back so he hit Harvey in the face,

'OWW will you stop that, just you wait until we get out of here, your so for it!!'.

Daniel eventually stopped when they reached the end of the bushes and squeezed through the hole right near the gates and they popped out onto the school field,

'Right mate, we're free now, just got to climb the gates and off into the woods we can go, totally had enough of that place'.

So Daniel starts to climb the gates, normally they are open but with Mr Twitcher not around to patrol them they have been locked,

Daniel makes easy work of the gates, scurrying up them like a professional mountain climber and pops over the top of the gates and makes his way down the other side and onto firm ground, Harvey on the other hand isn't as agile as Daniel and has a phobia of heights when it comes to climbing,

'Oh great!!!...' he mutters as he stares at the sheer size of the task in hand, the gates looming over him like a giant tree seemingly never ending in their pursuit of reaching up to the sky. Then as he gets his first foothold on the gate he feels the gate pushed backwards with force followed by a familiar noise,

'WOOF WOOF WOOF' barked an excited Bucksy as he jumped up at the gate causing Harvey to slip off and fall onto his backside on the grass.

Daniel was laughing so hard that he couldn't stand now and collapsed on the floor holding his stomach with laughter.

'Oh that's it laugh why don't you, I suppose you think that's funny..' Harvey growled in anger as Bucksy stood up on his hind legs at the gate wagging his tail at Harvey,

'Get away from me you blooming mutt, as if I'm not dirty enough as it is!!',
Daniel piped up as Harvey went to start climbing the gates again,
'Come here boy, let Harvey make a fool of himself again, hahaha',
Bucksy ambled over to his owner and sat beside him watching, his head
tilted to the side as Harvey made his way slowly up the gates, not sure
what to make of his attempt at climbing, all the way up the gates Harvey
was breathing fast and mumbling to himself,
'Don't look down, don't look down, don't look down!!'
Daniel on the other hand was now yawning away in sheer boredom, waiting
for his friend to make it over the gates,
'Come on Harv…' Daniel said as he watched the slowest ascent ever
seen, 'Get over while we still have daylight, I'm bored of waiting',
'I'll be over when I'm over' Harvey shouted,
'You know I can't stand heights, it's ok for you Mr 'not scared of anything',
I'm scared of falling flat on my face and ending up in plaster, so shut up
while I do this!!'
And finally Harvey made his way over the top of the gates and down the
other side much to the delight of Daniel who was clapping and cheering
him as he set his feet down on the pavement outside the gates.
'Finally!!!' Daniel said as Harvey dusted himself down and scowled in his
direction, Bucksy ran at Harvey barking away in delight too,
'Get away from me Bucks, You didn't help much either' said Harvey as he
pushed the dog away from him.
Bucksy always waited patiently for Daniel to come out of school and he
always seemed to know where to wait for him but today he seemed a lot
more pleased than normal to see the boys, he was constantly nudging
Daniel as he stood there talking to Harvey.
'What is it Bucks??' Daniel said looking down at his pet who was gently
pushing his nose into Daniel's hand as if to say 'Come on let's go'.
'Well I suppose seeing as we're now going to be in heaps of trouble we
may as well go', A resigned look fell across Harvey's face as he realised

they would both be in a lot of trouble if and when their parents found out about them skipping school.

So as the boys made their way along the back fence of the school and towards the woods which loomed large in the distance and was the boy's passage home Daniel turned towards the school for what seemed like a last look at school life then turned to Harvey with a determined look on his face and said,

'I can't wait to leave this place behind mate, I feel there's something else out there for me...sorry, us to look forward to but I can't quite put my finger on it at the minute'

'Yeah yeah mate, I understand, you're just not a clever as me so you'll be flipping burgers in no time, haha' laughed Harvey as they walked further down the grassy path and into the entrance to the woods surrounding the school.

'Shut up Harv..' laughed Daniel as he put his arm around his best friend's shoulder and sighed as they carried on walking away from Longmeads.

'Can't wait to leave this place for good mate, come on we've got some serious playing to do!!!'.

And with that Daniel screamed 'HAHA' as he chased after Harvey down the winding grassy paths which led into the deepest part of the woods, Harvey seemingly running for his life and laughing loudly as Bucksy barked enthusiastically and wagged his tail as he bounded after both boys who were pretending to fight one another as they all disappeared into the distance and out of sight with only the odd muffled bark heard in the distance as the boy's disappeared from sight.

Chapter Five
The Calm Before the Storm

So the boy's finally came to the edge of the woods at the end of Mumbles Drive and reflected on the events of the day so far,

'Glad you talked me into going now Dan' said Harvey as he stopped and leant against a tree to have a rest, blowing out his rosy red cheeks as he spoke,

'Don't think I could have coped with another minute in there, it's too nice out to be stuck in a classroom'.

'That's why I suggested going mate, have I ever been wrong before??' Daniel said as he raised his eyebrow in a kind of 'if you tell me I'm wrong I'll bash you' kind of way,

'Well there was that time when you got us thrown out of that shop near the school, pretending we were homeless just so you could get free food and drink!!!' Harvey reminded Daniel of how that had gone horribly wrong,

'I wasn't to know mum was going to walk in at the same time did I!!' Daniel replied,

'Any way you didn't warn me she was standing right behind me so that was your fault, I ended up grounded for two weeks thanks to you'

'Whatever...' Harvey said as the boys made their way along the road and close to Harvey's house which was surrounded by the largest hedgerow on the block with god knows what living in there,

Daniel then remembered that his mum was probably going to be in at home now,

'Cripes mate I totally forgot, mum will be in so I can't go home yet, she was supposed to be doing a half day at work, remember seeing it on the calendar before I left this morning', Harvey smugly replied to Daniel's plight,
'So you want to come in to my house until it's time for us to be home from school eh??.Hmm what should I do?.
'Come on mate, don't be a div!!...you know I'll get grounded again if mum finds out', replied Daniel as he seemingly became more desperate in his plea.
'Look it's only for a few hours, me and Bucks need to keep our heads down for a bit, can't risk being spotted by the neighbours!!'
'I'm only joking mate, of course it's ok, Mum isn't back until late tonight and she's left money for me to get a pizza' Harvey smiled as he opened the gate to let Daniel in closely followed by Bucksy who was covered in twigs and leaves as he ran past them and into the safety of the front porch and flopped down panting away with his tongue hanging out of the side of his mouth,
'What's wrong with him??' Harvey asked quizzically
'Who knows, he disappeared for a bit when we were messing around in the woods, probably chasing his shadow again'.
The boy's entered the house to be greeted by the smell of mums nasty smelling air freshener which she seemed to like but Harvey thought the smelt like old wet dog and sweaty feet,
'She's put them air freshener thingys out again!!!!' Harvey moaned as he walked in holding his nose,
'Quick get the windows open Dan…', and with that Harvey launched the air fresheners into the front garden through the open front door, even Bucksy didn't dare enter the house as they were so strong, he went and hid at the end of the porch until the smell had gone.
Eventually Bucksy sneaked into the house and plonked himself down on the cold floor behind the boys who were thinking of what to do with the rest of the day.
'So what are we going to do then Dan?? Said Harvey,
47

'Well I think first get some food as I'm starving here, feel like I'm wasting away!!' laughed Daniel as he grabbed at his stomach in a way to suggest he was in pain, 'Come on Harv let's go see what's in your cupboar.........',
But before he could finish his sentence Daniel started sniffing the air and then a look of sheer horror spread across his face,
'Oh my god, what's that smell??, It smells like nasty old shoes mixed with rotten eggs and cabbage!!!',
Harvey then started to screw his face up as the awful smell slipped deep into the back of his nostrils'
'Urrgh, that's awful!!!. Was that you?' Harvey quizzically asked Daniel
'No it blooming well wasn't!!....' He replied as they both turned to where the smell seemed to be coming from, it seems all that running and chasing in the woods had caused Bucksy to get a little over excited, he was sitting upon his front paws wagging his tail which caused the smell to waft from his direction.
'It's your dog!!!...He's let rip!!!', shouted Harvey as he grabbed a clothes peg from the shelf beside him and put it on his nose hoping to block out the smell,
'That's so nasty, what did he eat earlier??, I think I'm going to pass out!',
Daniel was holding his nose with his fingers as there was nothing to use to block out the foul smell,
'I think my eyes are melting..' Daniel moaned as Bucksy just sat and kept wagging his tail as if to say 'I can't smell anything, but here have some more'.
'Quick we need to get the windows open!!, I'm struggling to breathe here', The boy's scrambled around with the locks on the windows until they all creaked open,
'That's better...' Daniel said as they had opened all the windows downstairs and left the front door open to get rid of the smell,
Daniel looked at Harvey who was looking a little off colour now and had started to gag at the stench the dog had left behind as the peg he was using had broken in half,

'Seriously get that dog out of my house!!,' Harvey cried as Bucksy just tilted his head to the side and looked at him as if to say 'just try and move me',

'Alright, I'll take him outside, the smell has gone now though' Daniel replied as he put his hand behind Bucksy's head and gently pushed it forwards as if to move him from his sitting position,

'Come on boy, let's put you out in the garden before you do it again then we will really be in trouble'.

Harvey had walked through the kitchen and pushed the back door open wide so Daniel could let his dog out in the fresh air, as Bucksy walked past Harvey threw the dog a look that showed complete disgust for what he had done and said,

'Yeah that's it, get outside you rotten dog!!, Next time you do that you'll be left out on the porch, you're evil!!'.

'Daniel ushered the dog out and as he shut the door behind them he shouted, 'Stay, Bucks. There's a good boy. That was a good one though, hahaha'

'Right mate , now that Sir Trump-a-lot is outside let's eat!!', A hungry sounding Harvey said as he whipped open the cupboard doors to reveal a shelf full of biscuits, sandwich spreads, tins containing all sorts of food and fruits,

'Right Daniel, let's prepare a feast fit for a King, what shall we have??' as they both surveyed the contents of the fridge too where they spotted a box full with cut up chicken,

'Mmm, I'm having that!!' said Harvey as he pulled out the box and placed it on the kitchen side then dove back into the fridge to see what other delights were hidden inside,

'Harv....look!!!!!' exclaimed Daniel as he pulled out the biggest chocolate cake they had ever seen and seemed to both be drooling at the sight of it,

'I'm having a bit of that I think!!', Daniel declared as Harvey's eyes widened at the thought of cutting off a big slice of it and stuffing his face full of chocolate,

49

'It looks amazing, Let's eat!!' he said as the boy's made the kitchen look like a site of devastation as there was bread and crisp crumbs everywhere over the sides followed by chunks of chocolate cake that had fallen off and been squished into the kitchen side,

'Let's eat outside in the treehouse mate, just don't drop any in there' Harvey warned his friend as they both struggled under the weight of their oversized portions on such small plates and made their way across the grass, followed by a hungry looking Labrador, to the treehouse which was sitting proudly in the corner of the garden overlooking the most beautiful fields filled with dazzling coloured flowers and hedgerows which stretched as far as the eye could see which was in stark contrast to Daniel's house which sat on the edge of the overbearing forest filled with the tallest trees and constant noisy chatter of the animals that dwelled within it, maybe that's why Daniel liked it so much as it gave him the freedom to be with his thoughts, it was somewhere Harvey spent a lot of time as he liked to just stare out across the open fields and dream about his fantasies.

So the boy's sat down in the treehouse and began tucking into the 'feast' they had prepared when Daniel asked Harvey a kind of deep question which was not normal for him to ask,

'So now we are out mate, what should we do, I don't really want to go back to that place anymore, I feel there's something else we should be doing'

'Like what?' Harvey said as he stuffed piece of chicken into his mouth and chewed it like it was the only bit of food he'd eaten all week

'I don't know mate, I just wish something exciting would happen, like us having some sort of adventure or something, see all these things that have been going on lately with my dreams and stuff I've seen have really made me think about stuff and what I want to do and I can't have school getting in the way!!'

'Like what stuff' Harvey bluntly replied again as he shoved a bit of cake into his mouth, So Daniel went on to explain about the recurring dreams he had been having and what he had seen and heard in them and how he was struggling to understand what they meant when Harvey piped up rather excitedly,

'OH MY GOSH…. That's the weirdest thing ever!!!!, I've been having the weirdest dream too, kind of like that but all I keep seeing is a castle sitting above a town and then a load of bells hanging in this big cave type place then this odd looking guy dressed in what looks like big pyjamas keeps reaching out to me telling me to 'protect the bells, Protect what is needing protection', Or something like that, I thought I was having a nightmare, woke up sweating buckets and everything", Harvey grew more excited with every passing second.

'What do you think it means??...' he continued as his excitement level grew with every passing second,

'I dunno mate, sounds weird though doesn't it' Daniel replied in a calm manner as if he was trying to make sense of what his friend was telling him, Harvey was practically bouncing on the spot hoping that Daniel might have the answer

'I reckon it means something good is going to happen!!!, Bet it involves wizards, knights and castles!!!, oo-oo maybe we are going to be the heroes and save the land or even become great warriors!!!'

'Or it might be nothing Harv, stop getting over excited and sit still, I'm sure it's just a coincidence that we had the same kind of dream' said Daniel as he tried to make sense of it all.

'Sounds cool though mate doesn't it!!!!' Harvey said clapping his hands together and smiling the biggest smile from ear to ear at the prospect of this being real, he continued

'I mean imagine if it was real, how cool would it be, us being brave warriors and stuff, bet I get the best animal to ride on and I have the biggest sword ever!!'

'Whatever Harv..' Laughed Daniel as his mind was now going into overdrive at the thought of what might be, he sat, legs dangling over the edge of the treehouse, looking out towards the fields and wondering if it could be a sign something was going to happen or if it was just their overactive imaginations looking for a bit of fun, Harvey was still rattling on behind Daniel about slaying dragons and witches, slicing through the air with his pretend sword when something caught Daniel's eye out by the woods. It looked like the shadowy figure he had seen at school that day, it seemed to be standing still and looking towards where the boys were sitting.

'Harv.....look!!' said Daniel as he grabbed his dragon slaying friend and pulled him towards the edge of the treehouse,

'There's that shadow thing I saw earlier!!!, It's just out there by the edge of the woods, I think it's looking at us'.

Harvey dragged his arm away from Daniel who had a good grip on it and strained his eyes trying to see what Daniel was talking about,

'I can't see anything Dan...Where am I looking again??'.

But Daniel was preoccupied by the woods and what happened earlier, he seemed to be staring deep into the woods, almost hypnotised by the windy rush swirling round between the trees like a dancing ballerina, the leaves twisting and turning almost rhythmic in their flow, Daniel had blocked out all around him as he could see something in the far end of the woods which had caught his eye, then he seemed to break the trance like state he was in so Daniel this time grabbed Harvey by the head and held him in the direction he could see the mysterious shadowy figure and sharply said,

'Look again!!!!...it's right there by the edge of the trees it's just standing there'.

Harvey squinted his eyes and leant further forward to get a better look then all of a sudden he lost his balance and fell forwards.

'WOAHH' Harvey screamed as he fell forwards and went straight over the edge of the treehouse edge and landed with a thud on the floor below,

Daniel had taken his eyes off the shadow in the distance and couldn't help but laugh as he saw Harvey sitting up against the tree rubbing his bruised backside moaning away,

'That blooming hurt!!!, That's your fault again Dan...why is it whenever we're together I always get hurt or injured or stung or attacked!!!'

Harvey stood up and moaning loudly about how much pain he was in decided that he was going to stay down on the ground so he didn't get injured again,

'So can you still see whatever it is you're seeing or has it gone now?' said Harvey as he climbed up the fence slightly so he could see into the woods, Daniel looked back and as he did he saw it moving off again deeper into the woods this time,

'It's moving mate!!!, going into the woods now, can you see it??',

Harvey strained every bit of his neck to try and focus on whatever it was his friend was seeing but he couldn't see anything.

'Nope can't see a thing mate, are you sure there's something there??.....No wait I think I see something…' Harvey said as he saw something approaching the edge of the woods, he could just make out what looked like figures approaching,

'That's not what I saw' Daniel replied as all of a sudden a small group of people started walking along the path towards the back of Harvey's house, turns out they were a group of 'ramblers' who were always out walking the woods and around the countryside,

As they walked past they clocked the boy's on the other side of the fence and all said 'Hello' as they made their way past the fence where the boys were hanging over, Daniel piped up as they walked by,

'Excuse me sir..' He started, 'You haven't seen anyone else out by the woods just then have you??',

'Hello young man, no we've been walking round for hours, haven't come across a soul since we've been out, are you looking for someone?', The rather oddly dressed man replied.

'Kind of...Thought I saw something there a minute ago and then it just vanished. Not sure what it was, just curious to find out what it was I guess', Daniel replied as he huffed and his shoulders dropped.

'I reckon it was something to do with wizards and witches!!!' Harvey piped up with a large smile across his face as the odd looking man stopped in his tracks and smiled at Harvey as he took a deep breath before replying,

'Well young man, you never know do you, these woods have always been a source of wonder to many, some believe they hold magical qualities, some say they house the gateway to another world, people have gone searching in these woods and are yet to return....well that's the stories I have been told since I was a young boy growing up round here'

'Oh ok...' Harvey was taken aback by what the man claimed and for the first time in years was speechless, he muttered to himself and slowly slide down the fence out of sight, hiding from the man on the other side, Daniel was sitting there feeling rather relaxed as he didn't believe anything the man had said, he was looking down at Harvey who was cowering behind the fence now,

Daniel being Daniel laughed at his friend for slinking off out of sight then as he turned back said,

'Sounds like you're trying to scare u....' but there was no one there to be seen as Daniel stood up to see if he could spot the walkers.

'How weird is that mate!!!' Daniel beckoned Harvey up to the top of the fence,

'They've gone, there's no sign of them!'

Harvey climbed the fence post and peered over the top very slowly,

'Where have they gone?, they were just here, See I told you those woods were magical!!!, Maybe something ate them!!, OH no it's going to be us next....' Harvey panicked as he hid behind the tree shouting

'I'm too young to die!!!, Mum save me!!'

Daniel jumped down from the treehouse straight in front of his friend and picked him up and laughed at the way he was panicking,

'Haha, stop being a baby Harv...do you really believe there's some magical place hidden out there, don't forget how many times we have walked those woods, we would of seen something by now!!! You big baby, we know every part of those woods and there's nothing but trees out there, I'm pretty sure we would've seen something by now!!.

'But you never know!!...' replied Harvey

'Well I'm telling you its fine out there, any way don't forget we are going to the hideout later anyway!!' said Daniel

'Mmm, might give it a miss today mate' Harvey scaredily replied,

Daniel got his friend in a headlock and laughed as he held him tight,

'Stop being a wimp mate, as if I'd let anyone hurt my little Harvey warvey..' Harvey struggled to get free as he started hitting his friend shouting,

'Oh you're so for it now Dan, just you wait!!!' and he broke free from Daniel's grip and they started fighting just as boys did,

'Haha, I'm coming to get you!!!' Harvey shouted as he charged towards Daniel ready to pounce at him like a cat, But Daniel had other ideas and as Harvey leapt through the air as Daniel managed to step to the side and watch as his friend went flying past him with a look of terror on his face as he realised he was going to crash onto the floor,

THUMP, he went as he hit the ground hard, laying face first on the grass,

'OWWWW, that hurt!!', Harvey grimaced as he turned over just as he caught the sight of a lesser spotted Daniel flying through the air, ready to pounce on his 'prey' who was whining about his face and elbows hurting.

'Yaaahhhhh' Daniel screamed as he landed full force on top of Harvey, 'Ha-ha you're mine now!!' As he pretended to slay his prey 'dead' with a swift swoosh of his hands as if holding a sword.

Harvey went along with it, twitching his body as if in his last throes of life, body bucking like a bull, then he fell silent apart from the odd twitch, Daniel stood victorious over his slain friend, raising his arms aloft shouting,

'Ah-Ha!!! I have defeated Harvey 'The Strong', this epic battle is over, I am the win…..' He was stopped in his tracks by someone clearing their throat behind him, Daniel turned his head sheepishly, It was Harvey's mum standing there, arms crossed furiously tapping her foot on the floor as she saw that the boy's had skipped school.

'Well Well Well, what do we have here?, I'm guessing there's a good explanation for you two being at home!!' An angry Mrs Jones stormed over to Harvey who was picking himself up off the floor,

'Mum...I….' Harvey stuttered for an answer, trying to think fast,

'Harvey Maximus Jones....Don't you dare try and lie to me!!! I want an explanation right now!!!'

Daniel burst into fits of laughter as he had never heard his friend's middle name before,

'Maximus???.Hahahaha, oh my gosh that's the funniest name ever!!!, hahaha, I thought your middle name was Andrew....Maximus!!!,hahahaha'.

'Daniel Carter I suggest you be quiet!!, you're both in trouble unless someone explains to me why you are both standing in the back garden while you're supposed to be at school' Mrs Jones sternly replied.

The boy's looked at each other and at the same time said

'Boiler broke, toilets flooded' but Harvey's mum was wise to the usual type of school boy lies and demanded they tell the truth but they both fell silent,

'Well if that's the way it's going to be then Daniel I suggest you go home, I'll be calling your mum in a while just as soon as I've had a nice quiet word with Harvey here...' she replied in a calm manner,

'Don't you mean Maximus!!!...hahaha', Daniel spluttered loudly as his stomach was hurting from laughing so much,

'Right Daniel, time you went I think and take that overgrown carpet with you, he's smelling out my house!!', Mrs Jones pointing towards the back gate demanding he go,

'Alright I'm going!!! Jeez no need to be so angry!!, come on Bucks let's move' Bucksy came bounding over to Daniel and they both headed towards the back gate,

'See you later mate' Said Daniel as he turned to Harvey, but he was preoccupied by his mother chasing him across the garden towards the house ready to deliver a sweet backhander across the back of his legs for lying to her, Daniel opened the gate and huffed as he walked out of the gate with his faithful friend, he stood there long enough to hear Harvey shouting,

'I'm sorry...I'm sorryyyyyyyy!!!....', He smiled to himself as he thought about what had gone on,

'Maximus!!!!!, oh that's bad!!' he said as he shut the garden gate behind him and made his way along Mumbles Drive and back to his house at the end of the road still chuckling to himself as Bucksy walked beside him wagging his tail.

Chapter Six

And So It Begins

Daniel reached his house and quietly peered through the letterbox to hear if anyone was in,

Good, no one is in!!', he smiled as he swung the front door open and Bucksy bounded in past Daniel and off into the front room for another lay down,

Then it hit him like a sledgehammer to a wall...He could hear a voice coming from the kitchen, sounded like someone was talking on the phone,

'Yes Mr Whitworthy...I'm sure there's an explanation for this…Yes, I'll get onto it as soon as I see him',

It was his mum Stephanie, and by the sounds of it she was talking to his teacher,

'She wasn't supposed to be home for hours!!..Now I'm for it!!...' Daniel went to sneak back out of the door just as the phone slammed down and a voice shouted from the kitchen,

'Daniel Carter I know it's you, don't you dare try to sneak off!!!, I think we need to have words, come here RIGHT NOW!!',

Daniel sheepishly shut the front door and made his way towards the kitchen, passing the front room on the way where even Bucksy knew he was in trouble as he buried his nose under a pillow and whimpered.

Daniel was trying to think of a good excuse to tell his mum as to why he was home early from school but he realised it was pointless as his mum seemed to always find out the truth. And as he entered the kitchen his mum was sitting on a kitchen stool with a look that could stop a herd of buffalo in its tracks.

'Well then Daniel care to explain to me why I was just on the phone to Mr Whitworthy?? And don't even think about lying!!' Stephanie said sternly as Daniel looked at the floor hoping he could talk his way out of it.

'Well..uh..I...You see, the thing is...Look mum I really hate that school I'm at, everyone is awful to me and I'm sure the teachers don't like me!'. He tried to justify his skipping of school as his mum listened on,

'Well, I don't really feel like I belong there at all and the stuff I'm learning is pointless, I've only left class a few times'.

'A FEW TIMES!!!!...' His mum's voice getting louder and louder as she grew even angrier at what her son was saying

'Well according to your teacher, this is about the twentieth time you have sneaked out of school this term!!, How do you expect people to get on with you if you keep giving them a reason to not like you!!, You need your education now more than ever as it's not long until you take your final exams..'

'But mum....' Daniel tried to interrupt his mum but she carried on,

'Don't you 'But Mum' me!!, I am struggling to keep everything together at the moment and you aren't helping in any way, I am trying to run this house on my own, make sure you two are kept safe, if only I could get some help from your fath....'

'My what???...'Daniel questioned his mum further,

'Were you going to say father??, do you know where he is??, I think I have a right to know if there's something you need to tell me'

'I've said too much as it is Daniel, I just need you to trust me at the minute and I promise in time I will be able to tell you everything, I'm struggling with a lot of things at the minute and I need you to stop this silly behaviour as it isn't helping matters' His mum tried her best to sort of explain what the matter was,

'And what do you mean 'keep us safe?', Are we in trouble or something??', Daniel got more inquisitive as he pushed his mum for more answers which seemed to agitate her further.

'Look Daniel...I...I can't say any more but please just stop all this, I need space to try and sort all this mess out so just for now please just help me out ok?' Stephanie was becoming visibly more upset with every passing comment,

'But mum please, if this is to do with my father then I need to know!!, I want to help you as I hate seeing you this upset but I need you to tell me what's going on, Please...These dreams I've been having are really making me worried..'

Stephanie turned quick as a flash to face her son and replied,

'What dreams?? Tell me!!'

So Daniel went on to tell his mum about all the strange dreams he'd been having lately and how they were always of the same thing and of the warrior type man at the front of it all. And how Harvey had been getting the same kind of visions too, also about the incident at school with Harvey telling him he spoke weird when the teachers were near.

Stephanie's face suddenly drained of colour as she tried to process what her son was saying to her, it looked as if she knew what he was talking about, the she suddenly blurted out,

'It's too soon!!! It's too soon, I need to sort this now...'

Daniel looked puzzled as he replied,

'What are you talking about mum??, You're scaring me now'

Stephanie stood up quickly and threw her jacket on before saying to Daniel,

'Stay here Daniel, I..I need to go out for a while, please stay inside and stay out of trouble, I'll be back later I promise', and with that she shot off out of the front door slamming it behind her as she went.

'Wha...who...what the heck is going on here?' said Daniel as he stood there in a state of shock at what had just gone on.

Bucksy appeared in the kitchen doorway and walked over to Daniel as if he was comforting him,

'I'm so confused Bucks..' He said as his dog nuzzled his nose into his owner's hand.

'Come on boy, I'm going up to bed to lie down, you coming??' Daniel said as he led his dog upstairs to his bedroom and shut the door behind him, still trying to figure out what his mum was talking about.

He lay down on the bed and Bucksy jumped up and curled up at the bottom as he usually did and the pair both drifted off to sleep.

Later on as the day was passing by, Daniel was still sleeping with Bucksy lying upside down again, snoring his head off, when all of a sudden he was awoken by someone speaking to him in his dream, the figure was hazy at best but it felt so real that he was there, It seemed they were telling him something but he couldn't make out what it was,

'It's time.....'.

Daniel sat bolt upright in bed, his mind working overtime trying to figure out what had just happened when his attention was taken away from that to Bucksy, who was still sleeping a little too close to the edge of the bed, stretched and slid straight off the bed and hit the floor with a 'THUMP'.

He looked up at Daniel who was just staring at him and yawned, stretched then jumped back onto the bed again straight up to Daniel as if to say 'What's the matter?',

'That's new!!!...'Said Daniel as he tried to recall the conversation he was having,

'I swear it was the same guy I saw before, this is getting weird',

He looked at the clock and saw that it was close to tea and as he went to get up his door opened and as his eyes accustomed to the light he saw someone standing there,

'Mum??' Daniel asked,

'Not even close freak show...' It was Lillie standing there,

'So tell me why you are home early again for the hundredth time this week' She asked as Daniel just looked blankly at her,

'So what's this I hear about you skipping school then?? It's the talk of the English block as you were seen making a run for it followed by that half-witted friend of yours struggling to keep up, It's not like we didn't see you and that oddball friend of yours running out of the front door, It's not like

61

you were quiet or anything, everyone heard Harvey squealing when the door hit his head' laughed Lillie,

'Oohh right' replied Daniel as he wasn't really paying attention to his sister,

'Plus we all saw you run off towards the gates and saw Twitcher near where you were, then we watched as he took those two other boy's back to the school, I was hoping it was you two but no such luck!' Lillie carried on as her brother just sat staring into space.

'So where's mum?, Is she back yet?' asked Daniel inquisitively,

'No she's not and I don't really blame her for not being here after what you got up to today!!',

'What do you mean??' he replied to Lillie,

'Don't act all innocent with me, don't you realise what she is going through at the minute??, and with what you have been doing lately sure as hell isn't helping her, you're probably the last person she wants to speak to anyway!!' She angrily replied as her brother hung his head down,

'I want to say sorry to her, that's all!!' He muttered to Lillie as he got off the bed and got some clothes out of his cupboard,

'Well I'm sure she will love you're pointless apology, until the next time you mess up' Lillie shouted at her brother from the safety of the door so she could step back if he threw anything at her,

'Get lost Lillie, I can't be bothered to speak to you now!!, just let me know when mum's back' said Daniel as he walked towards his door, pushed his sister out and shut it behind him so he could get changed.

Daniel eventually came out of his room about an hour later after being too engrossed in his latest comic book, he wandered across the landing, Lillie was screeching away to a song in her room made by the latest boy band she was into, he covered his ears and made his way down the stairs half expecting his mum to be sitting at the table in the kitchen waiting for him but there was no sign of her,

'Mum??, mum are you here??' Daniel called out but didn't get a reply, he searched the rest of the downstairs rooms but still no sign of his mum,

'That's odd..' He remarked,

'It's almost six o'clock and she's still not home, Bit odd for her not to be here'.

All of a sudden he was greeted by his sister who had rushed down as she was now getting hungry seeing as it was tea time,

'Where's mum?' Lillie asked,

'Don't know...haven't seen her since I got back earlier' Daniel replied still searching the room for any sign of their mum, like maybe she might jump out of a cupboard to surprise them.

'It's not like her not to be here..I bet this has something to do with you and your issues at school' Lillie's response grew angrier the more she replied,

'What do you mean by that!!, You can't blame me for her not being here, maybe she's at a friend's or something' Daniel started to worry slightly at what his sister was saying to him,

'Well you're the one who has skipped most of the school year so far, it's always you getting in trouble and it's always mum having to deal with it, just look at that time you broke that massive window in the school hall with that baseball ball, who had to pay for it??..Mum did that's who, and did she tell you she had sorted it?' said an even angrier sounding Lillie as Daniel just stood there looking straight through his sister,

'Well...no...but it wasn't my fault as I told mum at the time!!' Daniel replied trying to plead his case,

'What do you mean not your fault!!, you were the only one there, you were the one holding the bat, who else is to blame if it wasn't you!!,' Lillie continued,

'Well I hope you're happy with what you are doing to mum, can't you see she's struggling lately and this isn't what she needs right now, no wonder she's not home, I can't really blame her can you!!'

Daniel looked sheepishly at his sister who was telling him off just like an adult would,

'I promise I'll sort this with mum when I see her, I'll do my best to do things differently',

63

'I really hope you do Daniel as mum needs us by the sounds of it, she doesn't need more stress put on her so sort yourself out rather quickly or else you will have me to deal with first!!' Lillie said pointing her finger in her brother's direction,

'Whatever…' Daniel replied as he walked off into the kitchen now on the hunt for food as his stomach was talking to him rather loudly,

'Shhhh you'll wake the dog up!!' Daniel jokingly said to his stomach as he searched the cupboards for something easy to make for tea, then he spotted something,

'Ah-ha!!...' He said as he reached into the back of the cupboard to pull out a tin of hot dogs, they were rather dusty but still in date.

'These will do, now where's the pans??' and with that he opened the small cupboard next to the sink and grabbed the pan out, Daniel did enjoy making food at home as his mum had taught him to cook certain easy foods so he never went hungry, it was kind of like survival training for him he thought, He left the hot dog sausages to cook and got the buns ready for himself and his sister,

'Right...buns. Check, sauce...check, hotdogs...hot...check' Daniel went through his checklist of things to do, he went to the bottom of the stairs and shouted for his sister,

'LILLIE….I've done food for us, it's ready to eat…'

The bedroom door swung open and Lillie sprang down the stairs like a deer sneering at her brother as she reached the bottom,

'I've eaten already, don't want you to poison me with whatever it is you're burning, I'm off out to Sammy's house for a bit, I told mum this morning so she's cool with it, See you later short stuff!!'.

'Oh right!!! Cheers for telling me' Daniel looked annoyed with his sister as she floated past him and swung the door open,

'Bye...don't wait up!!' she laughed as the door shut behind her and off she skipped up the path.

'Oh more for me then!!' Daniel smiled as he realised he could tuck in to all the food, then all of a sudden Bucksy appeared as if he heard something just as Daniel was making his was towards the kitchen to start on his 'feast'.

Bucksy started barking and wagging his tail in anticipation as the noise grew closer and closer,

'THUMP THUMP THUMP', went the noise at the door which sent the dog into a barking frenzy, Daniel turned round and went to answer the door, having to drag his dog out of the was first,

'Get out of the way dog!!, if you let me answer it I'll be able to see who it is, It's probably Lillie anyway!!'

He opened the door still trying to push Bucksy back,

'Forget something did w…..' Daniel said as he turned towards the open door,

'Hello mate….' Harvey mumbled,

Daniel was greeted by the chocolate covered face of his best friend who seemed to have been let out after the events of earlier,

'Oh it's you…' he muttered

'Thought it was Lillie coming back'

'Nope I've just seen her skip off down the road, she didn't even say 'Hi' when she went past, totally ignorant your sister!!' Harvey said as he barged his way past his friend only to be pounced on by Bucksy,

'AAAhhh get off me!!!...' He screamed as the dog leapt onto Harvey and started licking at his face hoping to taste the chocolate that had covered his face,

'Bucks...DOWN!!' Daniel ordered as his dog relented and sulked off back into the front room and into his bed,

'Thanks mate, not ready for 'Death By Licking' yet!!' Laughed Harvey as the boys made their way into the kitchen,

'OOOH what's cooking??, something smells gooood' sniffed Harvey as he felt his stomach talking to him again,

'Just doing a bit of food for tea as I'm starving, well it was for Lillie too but she's gone out' Daniel said as he turned off the stove and put the hot dogs in the buns ready to eat,

'I guess you want some?' Daniel said as Harvey, plate in hand already, was helping himself to three hot dogs and buns,

'No please help yourself' Laughed Daniel as he managed to pull the plate away from Harvey before they all disappeared,

'So where is your mum?? Isn't she normally here at this time?' Asked Harvey as he stuffed a hotdog bun into his gaping mouth,

'Don't know Harv….But Lillie thinks it's to do with today and stuff, saying it's my fault she isn't here as she's been upset lately,' Daniel replied as he looked at his basic tea portion and huffed,

'Oooh I see..' Harvey wasn't really paying any attention as he filled his mouth with another bun like he hadn't eaten for a week,

'So where is your mum?' Harvey asked again,

'Weren't you listening to me???...I just told you what happened!!, typical of you, always thinking with your stomach, stop shoving those hot dogs in you plank!!' Daniel growled as Harvey wasn't really paying attention to what he was telling him,

'Sorry mate I'm just peckish that's all, Not eaten for ages' Harvey replied as he eyed up more of the hot dogs that Daniel had moved away from him,

'I only left you a couple of hours ago!!..You can't be that hungry still??, Daniel replied as he pulled the plate closer to him as Harvey leant across the counter trying to steal a hot dog.

'Mum said I'm not allowed anything else to eat until later on because we stuffed our faces at mine and there's not much left in the cupboards now' Harvey looked unhappy as he remembered why he wasn't allowed to eat at home so he had come down to his friend's to feast on his food instead,

'WE stuffed our faces?? That's funny!, if I remember it was you doing all the stuffing!!' Daniel laughed as Harvey's face broke out in the cheekiest of smirks,

'Yeah alright!!!, I admit it!!!.haha' He laughed as Daniel scooped up the last hot dog and chomped it in front of Harvey's face as if to tease him.

'Mmm, best hot dog ever!!!', Daniel said as he devoured the hot dog so fast that he got hiccups,

'Haha that'll teach you for messing around!!' Laughed Harvey as Daniel's hiccups got worse,

'Any way Dan, what are you going to do then?, wait for your mum to come home so you ask if you can go out?' Harvey enquired as he was desperate to go out and play as it was still a warm sunny evening,

'Well, hic, since she's not here and Lillie's out too, hic, I don't fancy staying in while it's still, hic, nice out' Daniel said between hiccups as Harvey was laughing at the hiccups but was also copying him,

'Well that's sorted then mate, let's go out before I get even more bored, don't forget the swords and shields we made last time!!' Harvey said as he jumped off of the seat he was on and made his was swiftly towards the door just as Bucksy was coming out, Harvey had no time to avoid the dog and tripped over him in the hallway and landed head first on the floor with a 'DONK'.

Daniel let out the biggest belly laugh as he saw his friend spread eagled on the floor with Bucksy looking rather sheepish as he knew it was his fault,

'That blooming stinky mutt!!!...' Harvey bellowed,

'Why is it always me who gets hurt??..Ow now I've hurt my blooming knee!! Thanks Bucks you idiot!!', he said as he got up gingerly from the floor.

'Oh yeah, I forgot to tell you, Bucksy is coming with us, he needs a walk' Daniel replied, as soon as Bucksy heard the word 'walk' he always got excited and bounded round the hallway barking with delight as he knew they were going off into the woods which he loved as it meant he could go off exploring for whatever scent caught his nose.

'Well can you tell your dog to stop whacking me in the face with his tale, I keep getting a waft of his stinky bum!!' Harvey groaned as he pushed Bucksy away from him and said,

'Get away dog, and let me get up',

Daniel called to Bucksy who was still bounding round the hallway all the more ready to go,

'Come on boy let Mr Happy get up then we can go for a walk',
So with that Daniel went and grabbed the makeshift swords and shields
they had made days earlier and walked out the front door of the house,
Harvey shut the door just as Daniel said,
'Don't shut the doo….brilliant!!, I've left my key inside the house'
'I'm sure your mum will let you in later when we come back mate so don't
worry' Harvey tried to reassure his friend,
'Or maybe Lillie will be back, Depends if her mate gets fed up with her and
kicks her out, I know I would!!.Hahaha' Harvey laughed as he didn't really
like Daniel's sister that much.
'Yeah I suppose you're right Harv, come on let's just go before it gets too
late, I'm sure mum will figure out where I've gone if she sees the dog has
gone too.
And with that the boy's made their way towards the edge of the woods
where they stopped just before they headed towards their hideout, when all
of a sudden a wind ripped through the trees, a wind that on a day like this
shouldn't even be there, it was almost as if the woods were warning the
boy's about entering.
The bushes were being practically pushed to the floor, the trees were
swirling and creaking, branches falling all around them, then just as quick
as it started the winds stopped, when Daniel swore he heard something on
the tail of the wind as it whizzed past the boy's as they stood there.
'Did you hear that Harv??' Daniel enquired as he turned to Harvey,
'Hear what?, all I'm thinking is how windy it's just got!!, I didn't even bring a
jacket!!' Harvey moaned as he pulled his arms across his chest to help
keep himself as warm as he could,
'I swear I just heard that voice again!!!, the same one I've been hearing in
my dreams' Daniel racked his brains to try and recognise the voice again,
'What did it say this time then?, I know..' Harvey piped up
'I bet it said 'Your best friend is freezing cold, go get him a jacket so he
doesn't freeze!!', that sounds about right!' Mocked Harvey as Daniel
slapped his friend on the arm and said,

'Shut up you div!!, I'm sure I heard something like 'Nearly heeeere', It was definitely the same voice again' Daniel recalled that the voices sounded so alike and he was starting to get slightly scared this time,

'I've never been scared by these woods Harv but I'm thinking we shouldn't go in today!!, I have a bad feeling about this'

'Oh now who's the scaredy cat!!' Laughed Harvey as he mocked his friend's voice,

'OOOH the big bad woods are gonna get me!!, I'm so scared, hahaha'

Shut up Harv!!!, I'm serious what if something bad is going to happen, not sure mum will cope with any more stress' Daniel said as he had second thoughts about taking the dog in but Bucksy was strangely desperate to go into the woods today, so Bucksy walked off and made his way up alongside Harvey who was trudging up the downtrodden path as they usually done and off into the woods they walked,

'Come on Dan let's go, we've got a den to protect!' Laughed Harvey as Bucksy barked at his owner as if to say 'Come on'.

'I've got a bad feeling about this' murmured Daniel as he gingerly walked off after Harvey and Bucksy who were ahead of him.

Daniel was feeling so paranoid that he felt his every step was being watched by someone or something and it made him feel so uneasy especially as Bucksy had ran off ahead of him so he had nothing to hold onto, the further he walked into the woods the faster his footsteps became until he finally caught up with Harvey who was waiting by the slightly covered twiggy path which led to their hideout,

'What's the matter now Dan?, are you still feeling a bit off...Look let's go to the den for a bit and if you still feel uneasy then we will go back, I've been itching to get out of the house since earlier on and I don't fancy going back now, c'mon let's go', Harvey gestured to his friend as he made his way through the collection of bare branches and long grass covering the start of the path towards where they had built their den some months earlier,

Bucksy sat waiting for his owner to move, wagging his tail as he sniffed the air, Daniel was looking around nervously then he let out a big 'SIGH' and trudged through the undergrowth as Bucksy followed him through, sniffing the ground as he went along behind Daniel.

They reached the den finally which was a crudely made log and stick den, it seemed to be very sturdy from a distance but on closer inspection it looked like it might collapse at and second, the entrance was just big enough for the boy's to fit through and was big enough inside for them plus Bucksy to sit in and relax as they usually did.

As Daniel got closer to the entrance he called out,

'Harv...Harvey??,' He was nowhere to be seen,

'Where is that stupid boy Bucks??..Go find him!'. He gestured to his dog to go search around the den,

So Bucksy let out a yap as he bounded off into the undergrowth looking for Harvey sniffing at every tree and bit of bush until he got his scent, then he must of picked it up as he shot through a hole in the trees and barked as he did so,

'Bucks….Did you find him??' Daniel called out as he sat nervously by the entrance,

'Come on boy, I'm getting worried now…' The air was filled with an empty silence as Daniel sat as still as he could, listening for any sort of noise of maybe his dog or Harvey might be making when all of a sudden Bucksy appeared in front of Daniel who stood up to greet him,

'Did you find him boy?. Where could he be?'

'Bucksy sat there wagging his tail as Daniel looked around at the trees and bushes, looking for a sign of his friend hiding, Bucksy then sat up as rigid as he could, tail wagging faster as Daniel wondered what he was seeing.

'What is it boy?. Have you seen something??' Daniel said to his dog as Bucksy tilted his head to the side as if looking at something behind Daniel, Then all of a sudden Daniel felt something grab him from behind, arms wrapped around his body

'Wha…..' He shouted as he managed to spin round and just as he did that he swung a punch in the direction of whatever it was holding him back, connecting with its face,

70

'OWWWWWW my nose!!!' It was Harvey shouting in pain as he pulled his hands up to cover his face,

'You punched me!!!, Why did you do that?' He screeched as Daniel tried to focus on his friend's face,

'You sneaked up on me you idiot!, why would you do that to me!!, It's lucky I didn't hit you harder', Daniel's heart was beating fast as he tried to calm himself down, Harvey on the other hand had pulled out tissue from his trousers and was holding it over his bloodied nose,

'That really hurts!!, if you've broken it I'll never forgive you!!' Harvey wailed as he sat down against the tree holding his back, tissue still attached to his face,

'Oh shut up Harv, Just don't do that ever again alright!!!!' Daniel angrily replied as he took deep breaths trying to calm himself down.

'Alright, alright mate, I'm sorry, but I didn't deserve this!!! Owwww, it hurts so much, you've ruined my beautiful face!!' Harvey replied as he pulled the tissue away from his nose.

'Well at least it's stopped bleeding now!!' Daniel said looking at his friend's bloodied face,

'My good looks are ruined now' whined Harvey as he sniffed constantly,

'I've improved them I'd say Harv' laughed Daniel as he helped his friend up onto his feet,

'I'm sorry Harv, but you know how I'm feeling at the minute' he replied in a sad tone,

'Yeah I won't be trying to scare you anytime soon, not after what you have just done!!', Harvey said as he sniffed a few more times before the boys made their way into the den and sat around just talking about everything that had happened earlier,

'Tell you what mate I'm so tired today, think I'm gonna chill here for a bit before heading back' Harvey yawned and stretched as he lay down on the blanket and pillows that he had managed to take from home when they first built the den,

'Good idea mate let's just chill for a bit, just hope mum's home when I get back!!' Daniel sighed as he remembered how much he had hurt his mum earlier.

So the boy's lay down with Bucksy curled up close to Daniel for warmth, they were both feeling so relaxed that it wasn't long before Harvey started snoring out loud,

'Oh I guess he's asleep then' Laughed Daniel as Bucksy yawned and lay his head down on Daniel's lap, licking his lips as he got comfortable, Daniel slowly drifted into a semi deep sleep also as his worries seemed to drift away as he felt his eyes close completely.

It didn't seem that Daniel and Harvey were asleep that long before they were awoken by the sound of crunching twigs and the rustling of leaves coming from the area where the boys were gathered, Bucksy's head shot up, he sniffed the air as he raised himself up off the floor and moved silently towards the front of the den so he could see who it was approaching their location, Bucksy let out a giant 'WOOF' which should've scared just about anything off as he leapt out of the den and shot off into the bushes barking as loud as he could as he chased whatever it was through the woods.

Daniel leapt up shouting for his dog, 'Bucks...Bucks!!! What is it boy??', in the distance he could still hear his dog barking away,

Harvey sat bolt upright from his slumber and whacked his head in a low lying trunk that was sticking into the den,

'OWW, what is it with everything today!!!, I'm sure someone is trying to bump me off!!', He whined as he rubbed his sore head,

'What's wrong with you Dan?, what's that noise?' He asked as he stood up and pushed Daniel to the side to see what all the commotion was,

'Bucksy has heard something out there, sounded like it was coming this way, but he's chased it off, I hope!!', Daniel said as he scoured the bushes for any sign of his dog, when all of a sudden a figure crashed through the branches and landed in a heap on the floor swiftly followed by Bucksy who was wagging his tail with delight. It was Daniel's sister Lillie, she had been sent off to find him as his mum was now home and she wanted them home for tea,

'There you are!!!..I've been looking for you everywhere, did you not hear me shouting?' she ranted as the boy's just looked at her and laughed as she was covered in all sorts of things from the trees and bushes outside,

'What are you laughing at?, it's that dog of yours fault I look like this!!, I thought I heard noises from where you are now so I crept through the bushes only to be chased by a big black furry thing...' Lillie was pointing at Bucksy who was still wagging his tail and barking in a way that suggested he had done a 'good deed',

'So I ran straight through the bushes, trying to get away when HE jumped on me and pushed me through here, I thought I was going to be eaten!!'

'Good boy Bucks..' Daniel smiled as he patted his faithful companion on the head,

'But next time can you try and eat her!!' Harvey piped up and laughed as he threw Bucksy a sweet.

'Not funny you silly little boy!!' replied an angry Lillie as she went to walk towards the boy's, grabbing Daniel by the jumper as she told them they needed to go,

'Now come on, we need to go home, mum is waiting for us, and she doesn't look very happy!!!'.

'Right, we best go I suppose, come on boy' ordered Daniel to his pet as they made their way out of the den and off through the overgrown branches and leaves that covered their den when all of a sudden

Bucksy stopped in his tracks, lifted his head up into the air and began to sniff rather fast, Daniel turned round and saw what the dog was doing and questioned him jokingly,

'What's the matter Bucks??, Have you smelt a rabbit again?, come on let's g......'.

But before Daniel could finish his sentence Bucksy launched off over the ground and bolted straight through the bushes at such a speed as if he was tracking something, he didn't seem to care about how thick the bushes were, he just wanted to run,

'Where has that blooming dog gone now??' Lillie shouted to Daniel as he made his way through the bushes trying to catch a glimpse of where his dog had got to.

'Bucks....Bucksy!!, where are you??' He cried out as he could hear faint barking in the distance followed by a series of loud cracking and creaking noises, which sounded like the sort of noise you would hear if an army of people were trampling over ground littered with twigs and branches, then it all fell silent, Bucksy had gone deep into the woods this time, deeper than they had ever gone before as the light began to dim around them as Daniel, Lillie and Harvey all searched the woods around them for signs of the dog,

'Bucks...Bucks...' They all shouted, hoping for any sign but it was silent now,

'Where is that dog!!, we need to go Daniel' Lillie called across to him as he searched further ahead in the woods,

'I'm not leaving him here, what if he's hurt!!!, I'll search until I find him OK', Daniel angrily replied to his sister as he headed off deeper into the undergrowth in search of his friend,

They all headed in different directions and further apart from each other until Daniel heard something,

'What is that?' He said as he listened closely to the sound coming from just up ahead of where he was.

It sounded like a whimpering noise followed by a soft 'Bark',

'BUCKSY....' Daniel shouted out as he sped across the thick branch covered floor towards where he had heard what he thought was his dog, He shouted back to the others as he ran,

'I'VE FOUND HIM!!! He's over here, hurry u.....aagghhh'.

Daniel had fallen through the thick branches and twigs covering a hole deep enough for someone to get through, he seemed to fall for an age, arms reaching out as if him trying to grab onto anything to stop his descent into the darkness. His body hit the ground with a 'THUD' also whacking his head on the cold dark floor, as he started to feel dizzy he saw a fuzzy shape coming towards him through the darkness, eyes glowing in the distance as the figure walked towards him slowly but cautiously 'Bucksy?.....' he whimpered as his eyes shut and he lost consciousness.

Chapter Seven
The Journey 'Home'

As Daniel slipped in and out of unconsciousness he was always aware that someone or something was standing guard over him as he lay there stricken on the floor, hoping for someone to come to his aid, he felt himself being gently moved from the spot where he lay as if being moved to safety out in the open air, then for the last time he closed his eyes and it all went black.

What seemed like hours passed and eventually he started to stir, not before completely coming to, he heard a voice again calling to him, one that seemed familiar also,

'Home!!....Home!!....' It called out as he sat up gently, but all he saw as his sight came back were the faces of Harvey and Lillie who had seen the trampled bushes leading up to where he went through and had followed him down,

'Come on mate let's get you up and go home' Harvey answered, Daniel looked at Harvey wondering if it was his friend's voice he was hearing as he awoke or was it something else.

Lillie looked worried for the first time in a long time with her brother lying hurt on the floor,

'Are you ok Dan?...' She asked worriedly,

'I heard you shouting but couldn't see you, I was worried you were hurt!!' she continued.

'Daniel, still feeling slightly dazed was looking around constantly,

'Has anyone seen Bucksy?, I'm sure he was here a little while ago'

'No Dan..' replied Harvey, ' Not seen him since he ran off in the woods earlier, he'll turn up don't worry, now c'mon let's get you on your feet Dan, need to see if we can climb back up now' Harvey said as he helped Daniel get to his feet as Lillie put his arm around her shoulder and kept him steady,

'I'll go take a look and see what we can do, it wasn't that far in there I think' Harvey said as he looked back towards where they had climbed through and off he walked into the darkness of the cave.

Lillie was still holding her brother tight, looking a bit less worried now as he was standing beside her and seemed to be getting better with every passing minute,

'Are you ok?, you really scared me there!' she asked

'Yes I'm fine now I guess, bit sore but I'll be ok' Daniel replied as he brushed himself down while checking for any injuries,

'Errrm guys...' Harvey shouted from the deep in the darkness

'Think there's a teeny tiny little problem...' He continued as Daniel and Lillie made their way towards where he was standing,

'What's the matter Harv?' Daniel asked quizzically as Lillie and Daniel joined Harvey in the spot where he fell in.

'Well you see this bit here' Harvey was pointing up at the roof of the cave which was now covered over with earth and twigs, 'Well I'm sure that's where we climbed in!!'.

'Are you sure Harvey? How can you tell?? Its way too dark to see properly' Said Lillie questioning his reply,

So Harvey pulled out his small keyring torch which he took from the den and shone it onto the ceiling of the cave,

'Well that's where we climbed down, look!!' As he shone his light on the footprints he had made with his trainers as they were climbing down into the cave entrance, you could clearly see the imprint of his trainers disappear into the roof of the cave,

All three of them stared up at the roof of the cave not uttering a word as they all tried to guess what had happened,

'Well I reckon you must have caused the mud up top to fall in as you climbed in Harv....' Daniel piped up as he looked for the most logical solution,

'If I did that surely there would be signs of light coming in, that hole looks completely covered up as if it's not there!!' Harvey replied as he poked the roof with a stick he'd found on the floor,

'See....nothing... not even a bit of it moves, Bit odd I'd say'

Lillie had wandered off looking for any other signs of a way out of wherever it was they were,

'Nope...there's no way out over here either, that's just great, now mum's going to be worried even more, I told her I wouldn't be that long either'.

'I'm sure there's another way out of here, I'm getting hungry anyway so let's get a move on', Harvey said as his stomach rumbled inside the quietness of the cave which echoed around like a pack of growling dogs ready to pounce on their lunch.

So all three of them set off out of the cave, stopping just outside the entrance, looking for a route to take through the woods in front of them in the hope it may lead somewhere they recognise but where they were now wasn't the place they recognised at all.

Daniel was still feeling the effects of his fall and had to stop a few times as they made their way deeper into the forest giving him a chance to take in the surroundings which seemed to have a different feeling about it, the trees were bathed in a sort of golden glow which was different to the darkness of the woods near Daniel's house, the sky was filled with a bluey green haze which also buzzed with all sorts of creatures zipping around their heads as they sat there waiting for Daniel to gather his composure,

'This place sure is different to what I remember Harv...' Daniel quipped as he looked around at their new surroundings

'I'm sure this is all new to me, it's like we are in another world or something..' he laughed as Lillie emerged from the bushes ahead of them looking rather confused as she shouted to the boys who were ready to move on again,

'Errm guys I think we might be a bit lost...'

'What makes you say that Lillie, we can't be that far from where we need to be' Harvey shouted back as he made his way towards where Lillie was standing,

'Well....' Lillie replied 'I'm sure this hasn't always been in the woods otherwise we would've seen it!!'.

With that the boy's made their way through the bushes ahead of them, pushing back branches and making their way through the gap that Lillie had made in her search for an exit.

As they got to a clearing within the woods they were greeted with the most amazing sight causing Harvey, looking dumbfounded by what he was seeing, to pipe up,

'This definitely wasn't here before!!...Are we missing something?'

Just in front of the gang was the most stunning blue river which led down to a brook within the woods, just the other side of that was a small wooden cottage which was bathed in the most spectacular glow, the woods seemingly lighting the way for them to go with each step they took, as they stopped by the river's edge they stooped down and were met with the clearest water they had ever seen,

'Well this is weird isn't it!!' Harvey said as he turned to Daniel who was crouched down at the water's edge looking lost in his own thoughts,

'This surely must be a dream, this isn't our woods is it?' Daniel continued questioning his own thoughts, Lillie then turned to her brother and pinched his arm hard,

'OWWW, what did you do that for?' Daniel yelped as he rubbed his arm vigorously,

'Did that hurt then?, because if it did then this is all real!!' said Lillie as she sniggered at her brother being in pain from the pinch she had given him before attempting to be nice,

'I could have slapped you instead but I thought against that as mum would freak if you had a red mark across your face'

'Oh thanks a lot sis!!!' Daniel muttered as he stood up and stared at the cottage in front of them,

'Wonder if anyone actually lives there, I mean look at it, it's all old and rickety' remarked Harvey as he joined his friend by the side of the river, both looking in awe at what they were seeing in front of them, wondering if they should get closer to it to investigate the new surroundings they found themselves in.

Lillie being the more confident one had already made her way over to the cottage and was exploring the outside of it, looking for any clue as to where they were,

'Lillie….Lillie' whispered Daniel as he scouted the area around the cottage in case anyone came back,

'Be careful, you don't want to get caught do you?, someone might be on their way back or something' Daniel carried on as his sister became more inquisitive and started trying to open the door to see if she could get inside, but it was bolted shut from the inside by the feel of it.

'Harv...see if you can see anything round the other side, I want to find out what the heck is going on' Daniel ordered his friend to scout around the other side of the cottage to look for any signs of anyone living there, so off he trudged around the back of the cottage still muttering that he was hungry and how he needed to get home for tea but it seemed home was a long way away now.

Daniel head turned as he heard what sounded like twigs snapping just ahead of the cottage, he gestured for Lillie to be quiet as they slowly crept off away from the cottage to hide behind a collection of logs which were stacked up neatly by the water's edge,

Suddenly Harvey came charging round the corner yelling,

'Someone's coming, hide quickly!!' just as he said that he ran towards where Lillie and Daniel were hiding and slipped on the grass just by the logs which sent him sliding off into the river with a 'splash',

'Harvey!!!!...Keep it down will you!!' Lillie angrily said as Harvey dragged himself out of the river up alongside Daniel and they all sat quietly as a figure made its way through the undergrowth, It seemed the person was wearing a long cloak of some kind, it wasn't a very tall figure but seemed to be looking strong due to what it was carrying in its arms, the figure kept whistling as it made its way to the door, opening it slightly throwing it's 'catch' inside the door before stopping in its tracks, head turning to the side slightly and in a soft voice the figure called out,

'I know you're there...you may as well come out...I can see you behind the logs you know'.

All three of them looked at each other hoping that the person wasn't talking about them and by some miracle another three people would stand up and come out of hiding but there was no chance of that.

'Sounds like an old woman!! What do we do?' asked a rather scared Harvey as he thought about making a run for it,

'I vote for staying here, I'm sure she will get bored and walk off soon' replied Daniel as they sat tight against the logs, but the woman stayed silently still, waiting patiently for something to happen in front of her cottage

The woman turned fully round but her face was covered by the hood of her cloak, the clothes she were wearing were fairly oversized and dragged across the floor as she walked forward slowly onto the path in front of her, they were covered in the dust of the forest floor and the twigs from the trees as the cottage was fairly well hidden from sight which meant she had to do a lot of track walking to get home,

Lillie, who had been quiet this whole time, decided she would be the one who would go out. As she went to move Daniel grabbed her arm as if to stop her going but in doing this he fell back into Harvey which pushed him out from behind the logs.

'Woah.....Well done you two' Harvey scolded them both as he lay on the floor beside the logs now, feeling a pair of eyes burning into him, he turned his head to face the woman in front of him as she replied,

'Stand up boy, I presume you are a boy...your hair is very...ladylike!!, and tell me who you are and why you're here. You're trespassing on my land..',

81

'Oh just thanks for that!!!' Harvey said 'Ermmmm. Well you see….my name is Harvey Jones and I'm from a town called Lullington Mulch, which I think is that way' He said pointing off into the distance far into the woods.

'And what are you doing here in MY part of the forest?, I don't like trespassers you see, always hunting for things that have value to me, that's why I'm hidden far into the trees', the woman replied in a soft but authoritative tone,

'And who else is in your party?, I see two more sets of tracks coming this way, and I'm sure you don't have six legs hidden in those small garments you are wearing' the woman stared past Harvey as she spoke, waiting for Lillie and Daniel to appear.

Lillie then stood up as straight as an arrow and introduced herself seeing as she felt this woman was no threat to them,

'I'm Lillie Carter, very nice to meet you, sorry for stumbling onto your land but we seem to be lost and we are just looking to pass through from wherever it is we are!!'

'You look rather familiar to me….Hmmm…..Your face looks like someone I have seen somewhere before , but from where!!' the woman seemed to be racking her brain to search for the answer but stopped as Daniel rose up too and stepped out into the open.

The woman gasped as she set eyes on Daniel for the first time seemingly dumbstruck by what she was seeing,

'Can it be?….no surely not….if it is, why is he here??,' the woman said silently before carrying on asking the question she felt she needed to ask,

'And what is your name young boy?. If you are who I think you are then please accept my apologies for being so abrupt'

'D..Daniel Carter..' He replied nervously as the woman moved closer to where he was standing and looked him up and down muttering to herself as she examined him,

'Can I see you left arm please Daniel??'

Daniel thought this was a bit strange but seeing as he was too scared to say no he held it out anyway, the woman slid his sleeve up and upon seeing his birthmark on his forearm her eyes widened and she muttered something about him having 'The mark'.

Harvey looked confused as the woman fell silent for a second,

'What's she doing?, bit weird if you ask me' he whispered to Lillie who was standing there wondering why his brother was getting special attention from this old woman,

'Errm hello....can you tell me why you are looking at my brother like that please, it's kind of strange' Lillie piped up as the woman turned to her and replied,

'Sister!!! Why yes, of course I thought you both looked familiar, tell me please is this a relation of yours??', With that she pulled out a picture from beneath her robes and showed it to them both, the picture was of a woman all dressed up in what looked like a long flowing cape adorned with a familiar crest which the children had seen before somewhere, and behind her was the image of a man who looked like the one Daniel had seen in his dreams.

'That looks like the one on my diary!!!' Daniel exclaimed as he grabbed the grainy photograph from the clutches of the old woman,

'More to the point that looks like mum!!!' Lillie blurted out as she stared long and hard at it,

'Why is our mum in this picture?, Who are you and where are we??' Daniel had decided that they needed answers considering they were in a place where they didn't know and with a woman who seemed to know who they were,

'If the prophecy is correct then this is where it starts...You have come home!!!' the woman seemed excited by what she was thinking as she turned towards her cottage, beckoning the children to follow,

'Follow me and I will do my best to explain'.

Harvey grabbed Daniel's arm before he could move, warning him about following her, 'What if she's some scary witch woman who feeds on young children!!, I don't want to go in there, who knows what she's going to do to us!!'

'Shut up Harv...Look she's got a photo of mum in her hand, the cape she is wearing has the same emblem that my diary has and she seems to know who we are and where we are!!' Trying to reassure Harvey that it was all going to be ok, Daniel took his hand away and smiled at his nervous looking friend as he carried on talking to him,
'Trust me mate, I have a good feeling about this',
Lillie had already walked off towards the cottage as the old lady disappeared inside, she stopped at the entrance and waited for her brother to follow,
'If you're that worried why not wait outside then' said Daniel trying to calm his friend's nervousness down.
'Out here??...With who knows what watching me...no fear!!, I'm safer in there with the crazy old woman!!' Harvey pushed ahead of Daniel and they all stepped inside the cottage as Lillie shut the door behind them.
'Urrgh...what's that smell' Harvey commented as the scent of something being cooked wafted its way through the cottage as the children walked carefully through into a larger room at the back of the wooden cottage,
'Smells like old socks!!..That's nasty, wish I'd of stayed outside now!!' Harvey was still moaning as they were greeted by the sight of the woman standing in front of them, poking at her fire which had a pot sitting above the flames with something cooking inside,
'See I told you she wants to eat us!! Look at the size of that pot!!' A suspicious Harvey had gathered that the smell was whatever it was that was cooking inside,
The woman turned round to them with a burning stick in her hand which she had used to stoke the flames under the giant pot, stared straight at Harvey who was now rather freaked out by the attention he was getting and smirked as she looked him up and down and spoke in a soft tone as not to scare him,
'I have no intention of eating you boy, First of all I live off the fruit that the forest provides, no harm has come to any animals as I let nature take its course, I have been living out this far in the woods a very long time that I
84

have learnt how to use nature as my food supply, I set no traps in the woods to catch my food and I only catch a few fish in the river but I replace them with the same kind , I only venture to the town nearby to buy my bread and milk, so as you see I have no intention of cooking you in this pot, also I think you would taste funny and probably wouldn't fit!!', She cackled as Harvey backed away slightly behind Daniel who was sniggering at the thought of Harvey stuffed in the giant pot.

'You said there was a town nearby, How far is it away?, We really need to get home you see!!', Lillie interrupted the laughter that was filling the cottage as she felt slightly uneasy about where they were,

'Yes there is a town nearby, maybe half a day's walk through the woods I would guess, all in good time though, Where are my manners, I forgot to introduce myself' replied the woman who seemed focused on Daniel again as he stood there looking even more confused as she continued,

'My name is Lydia Wren and this is my home in the depths of the Sacred Forest of Pertania, So as I was saying, the woman in the picture I showed you earlier you said that was your 'mother'?'

'Yes it was..I mean is, where did you get a picture of her??' Lillie asked politely as not to show any kind of anger that someone else has a picture of her family,

'Well you see the woman standing there was known as Lady Runsfield, a truly wonderful woman who I felt very close to a long time ago. We grew up together, lived close to one another in the town. She went on to marry Lord Casborn and lived in 'The Castle' deep in the hills of Scandor, it was rumoured that she had two children, who were targeted by Dark Forces from the moment they were born as they would inherit all this land, then one day she just vanished with the children to somewhere unknown to everyone, even Lord Casborn was kept in the dark as to where they had gone as if he was captured then he may give away their whereabouts. This caused Lord Casborn to seek out those who wished harm upon his family, and the 'Battle of the Fourteen Bells' was rumoured to have begun'.

Lydia looked sad as she recalled what had happened to her friend but Daniel seemed intrigued now as to why his mum was in that picture,
'So now I'm totally confused!!, What's the Fourteen Bells thing all about??' Harvey said as he struggled to take it all in, while Daniel listened intently to what Lydia was saying and pressed her for more answers.
'So THAT'S my...I mean OUR mum in that photo??, I knew she was different Lillie!!!' Excitedly he grabbed Lillie by the arms and squeezed her tighter,
'I knew I'd seen that shield thing before, the one in the picture on mum's cape....That's the same on as on my arm!!, So all along I've had something that meant I belonged somewhere else, a clue to my past!!'.
'Lillie seemed taken aback by what she was hearing and decided to dig a little deeper so she could work out for herself what was actually going on,
'So, the man in the picture...who is that?? Is that our father?'
'That man in the background is indeed your father, Lord Aramel Casborn..' Lydia explained confidently,
'Personally I don't know too much about him but from the stories I have heard from the people in the town he seems to be a fearless warrior who is always on guard as their protector from whatever evil is lurking nearby, so I can't help you with anything other than that, I'm sorry'.
'So what's the Fourteen Bells thing you said about then, you haven't answered!!' Harvey was still looking for an answer to his question but was continually ignored,
'Is he here??, In....wherever it is we are!!. I still haven't got a clue where we are and it's getting late, we really need to get back home...' Lillie was sounding more desperate to learn more but realised that they also needed to get back where they came from, 'Home....My dear girl.... you are home, This is where you belong you see, your past is no more a secret, since you returned there seems to be a different feeling in the forest and beyond, even though you have only been here a small amount of time your life is in danger already, your presence has awoken something deep in the heart of the land to which all life on this planet is connected to, so now seeing as

you have no connection to the land then you have all been recognised as intruders of the land meaning that the hunters are aware of your whereabouts.' Lydia's warning spooked the children who seemed rather panicked by what they were being told.

'What do we do? Where do we go, we have no idea where we are or what we are supposed to be doing, I just want to go home!!' Daniel muttered loudly, his mind was racing as he tried to take it all in but he seemed slightly scared.

'Fourteen Bells?, Battle?' Harvey pitched up, seemingly less scared by what Lydia was saying to them all, still waiting for an answer to his question but he soon realised he was being ignored by everyone in the room.

'You are close to the town known as 'Erwin', located deep in the heart of the province of Vaymia' Lydia proudly told the children of where they were,

'And the only way I can see you all staying safe is to seek out your father, Lord Casborn, But I must warn you that it won't be easy finding him'

'Why is that?, We really need to meet him!!, we've dreamed of this all of our lives' said Daniel as he listened intently again to Lydia who was busy tidying up part of the cottage as if waiting for someone to arrive,

'Well..' She added, ' The journey is long and rather perilous you see, as I said earlier you are at least half a day's walk to the city of Erwin, but once there I have some people who will be able to take you in for a while so you can rest, but DO NOT stay too long...' She warned ' As the longer you are at rest the easier it will be for you to be tracked down so you MUST reach the castle in the Hills, It's best you travel by dark but I will guide you, When you reach Erwin you will need to look for 'The House of a Hundred Lights', Knock three times and you will be met by the keeper of the house, Lucas, who is a dear friend of mine.

He will look after you, I will send a message on to him and explain what is happening'.

So Lydia went on to explain to the children how to get to the town, making sure they stuck to the safety of the shadows and not to deviate from the path she was sending them on as the woods were patrolled constantly and now there would be even more men out looking as word spreads of Daniel's return to the City.

'I'm also missing my dog Bucksy, he's black and has odd coloured eyes, I followed him into this place but can't find him, have you seen him?' Daniel asked Lydia in desperation about his whereabouts as he was now getting increasingly worried about his other best friend,

She paused for a second to think if she had seen his dog but the look she gave Daniel seemed to show him that he wasn't seen by her,

'I'm afraid I haven't seen any such creature around here since I have been out collecting food, I'm sorry Daniel, I'm sure your friend will turn up soon, I'm sure of it' Lydia said, trying to reassure him that it will all be ok.

'Bells?? Any chance of telling us about them??' Harvey tried one more time for an answer to his question which Lydia finally decided to answer,

'Ahhh yes, The Fourteen Bells...Well they play a big part in the safety and security of this land, you see.....' She stopped suddenly as she was distracted by what sounded like footsteps outside the cottage in the surrounding woods,

'Well?? do carry on!!' Harvey muttered.

'Shhh Harv', Daniel lifted his finger to his lips warning his friend to be quiet,

'What??, I'm just trying to find out something that interests me but you won't let me sp.....', Harvey didn't get to finish what he was saying as Lillie had leapt behind him and had clamped her hand across his mouth, holding it tightly so he would shut up.

Lydia slowly opened the curtain just enough to peer out and not be seen and she could see what looked like burning torches surrounding the cottage, the figures loomed ever closer, their footsteps grew louder and louder as they reached the cottage door, heavy breathing could be heard, filling every inch of the cottage with a feeling of complete fear and dread by what was waiting outside,

'BANG BANG BANG',

Whatever was outside rapped on the door so hard that the whole cottage shook to its wooden foundations, followed by a sound that chilled them all to the bone but scared the children so much that they all froze on the spot.

'AAARRWWOOOOO' The sound shuddered through the cottage causing them all to cover their ears to shield it from the ghastly noise outside the door.

'What....was....that??' Harvey's voice trembling as his imagination thought of all the things it could be waiting to pounce on him,

'I'm too handsome to be eaten!!' He continued as Daniel was looking for something to defend himself with when he spotted Lydia over by the big pot on the fire.

'So what do we do now??' He asked, his voice sounding ever more panicky as the seconds ticked by.

Lydia was tugging at the side of the big pot which eventually swung outwards to reveal a hole underneath it and what looked like a ladder leading into the darkness below.

'Quick children, in here, this is the only way out now, the soldiers must of tracked you here' She gestured the children forward,

'This will lead you to safety, It will bring you out by the edge of the forest, but then you will be on your own, '

'How can we trust you??' Harvey sneered as the banging continued on the cottage door,

'You must believe me that all I want is peace for this land and you children are the only thing that can help us, if the prophecy is true then you MUST find your father and you must complete the circle, remember to stick to the paths I showed you.' Lydia became more desperate for the children to leave,

'Now please go and remember, find the town and the house but please stay safe, you are the future!! '.

'Thank you' Smiled Daniel as the children made their way into the hole beneath the pot, Daniel was last in as he took one last look up at Lydia and in a hopeful voice said.

'I'll do my best to help'.

And down the children descended, one by one into the darkness as the pot was pushed back into place just as crashing and the cracking of wood could be heard from up above them,

'I hopes she's going to be ok' Lillie said as she reached the bottom first followed by Harvey who still had the small torch in his pocket which he turned on to reveal the path ahead,

'I'm sure she will be fine sis' Daniel tried his best to reassure his sister as they all started off into the unknown,

'Now come on let's go, we've got a bit of a journey ahead and I want to find Bucksy before it gets too late' Daniel seemingly more confident now as they all made their way along the path towards the unknown.

Chapter Eight
The Search For The Town

As the group finally emerged from the tunnel, they were met by the sight of the most brilliant bluey white light cutting through the forest from up above them, everything glistened and sparkled as the light shone off every tree and through the bushes within the woods, Harvey turned off his torch and stared straight up from where it was coming from only to be met by something he wasn't expecting to see,

'Now that's amazing!!, stop guys' he said pointing up at the sky

As the trio stopped dead in their tracks they all took in the beauty surrounding them which was bathed in the glow from the gleaming light high up in the sky,

'Look guys, two moons!!!, now I know we aren't at home!!', Harvey exclaimed as they made their way slowly along the darkened path which stretched off into the blackness of the night,

'Shhhh Harv. We need to keep quiet from here, I don't fancy being caught by whatever those things are back there!!' Daniel gestured to his friend to keep a low profile as they made their way deeper into the forest and further into unknown territory,

The trio had been walking most of the night now and slowly the noises they had been hearing within the forest had quietened down which meant that they must be somewhat safe for now so Lillie stopped walking to rest against a tree as she called out to her brother,

'Daniel...We must stop, I need to rest'

'Yeah come on mate let's stop for a bit!! My legs are gonna fall off if we walk any more' Harvey panted as he collapsed against the nearest tree rubbing his tired legs,

'Ok, but not for too long, we need to reach the town before it gets too late!!', Daniel replied while searching the area around them for somewhere hidden to rest and recuperate.

'That'll do there!!' he pointed to a cluster of trees which together looked like a high enough hideout for them to rest.

So they started to climb the branches which led to a fairly flat part of the tree high up and good enough for them to rest.

They all slumped down, tired and starting to feel hungry as Harvey kept reminding anyone who would listen to him,

'I need food!!!...my stomach is talking, think it's going to eat me from the inside out' Harvey was holding his stomach tight to try and stop the pain he was feeling,

'Hmmphh, I'll go then!!' Lillie stood up seeing as no one wanted to leave the safety of the tree, 'But this is the only time I'll do it, oh by the way do we know what's food and what isn't here??'.

'Not a clue, it's a bit dark to see, durrr!!' Laughed Daniel as in that instant he felt a stinging pain as Lillie had swung an arm at her brother and connected with his head.

'OWWW what did you do that for??' He said rubbing his head as Lillie laughed the sort of laugh that echoed through the trees like the chatter of a primate as it swings from vine to vine.

'That's for being a smart ar........alec!!, I'm going back into the woods to look for food seeing as you two are too scared!!' As Lillie slowly descended the tree Daniel called down to her from the safety of the tree,

'See if you can find some fruit, oh and Lils....Please be careful, I need you safe'

'Don't worry I'll do my best, just stay hidden you two', she smiled at Daniel, Then with that Lillie tentatively stepped off the tree and scurried off into the darkness of the undergrowth to search for some food for them all.

Daniel sat back down and huffed as he had time to think about where they were and why they were here.

'I really miss home Harv, I wish we could just go home but it's looking like that's a long way off, plus I'm missing Bucksy, I just hope he's safe Harv, he's my best friend and I'm worried he's out here somewhere all alone and scared'.

'I know mate I'm sure he will turn up, that stupid dog always does and then it will all be ok, but let's just get through tonight and see where we get to, If you 'Dad' is who that crazy old woman says he is then we should be ok, maybe he can get us out of here and back home' Harvey reassured his friend,

'Come on Dan let's get some rest, I'm sure Lillie will be back soon'.

So the boy's drifted off for a while when their sleep, was interrupted by the sound of crashing branches and shouting in the distance,

All of a sudden Lillie appeared from the undergrowth clutching some sort of strange food looking things. She almost launched herself up into the tree she was looking that scared.

'Li….' Daniel mouthed, but he was cut short by his sister jumping on top of him and Harvey and telling them to be quiet as the forest lit up with the sound of something not seeming that human making its way towards where they were hiding out,

'ARRWWOOOO' came the screeching cry from something deep within the forest.

Lillie whispered to the boy's to keep their heads down as the creature crashed through the woodland and could be heard scratching and gnawing at the base of the tree, Lillie peered just over the edge of the tree branch only to be met by the sight of a dark skinned creature with huge powerful claws grappling away at the base of the tree, snarling as it could sense something was close to it, the beast was about the size of an elephant, had two huge rear muscular legs while its front legs seemed to be much more human like in their appearance which helped it to climb large objects, its tail was long and spiky at the end but it suffered with poor eyesight otherwise

93

they would have been found earlier, its screeching cry caused the trio to cover their ears as it constantly called out its location.

'What the heck is that!!' Harvey quietly mouthed as the creature kept calling out to whoever was with it,

Shhhh...We need to be quiet, I don't fancy being that things tea!! Look at it, it's nearly as bloomin' ugly as you Lillie, haha' Daniel had joined Lillie at the edge of the tree branch where she took offence to the insult from her brother and wrapped her hands around his mouth to stop him talking,

The next thing the children saw was a huge figure crash its way through the bushes and straight to where the beast was now circling the base of their hideout. The beasts handler was just as ugly as its pet standing well over eight feet tall, the darkness of the forest hid it's features but the stench from it was so foul that plants instantly died away whenever they roamed through the forest in search of prey.

It clapped eyes on the hiding place of the children high up in the treetops and started to climb up, the children scuttled to the back of the treetop where they were hiding,

'Oh god it's coming!!..What are we going to do?' Harvey whimpered as he felt the tree shudder with every step the beast took up it,

'I don't know….there's no way out…..Daniel I….' Lillie turned to see her brother stand over them both, they were frozen by some kind of force chanting the same thing he had done back at the school over and over again,

'Eramosa...Vin Sarmo Eramosa….' He chanted as the beast was now standing right in front of them looking right at the space where they all were gathered, it was staring long and hard all around the tree, but…….. nothing happened, the beast looked around some more, snorted in a sort of annoyed way then descended the tree back down towards the ground, the strange dark skinned creature was still snarling at the tree as its handler slapped it on its head as it walked past and beckoned it to its side, the beast just stood there for a few seconds before it's handler muttered in its strange language and stomped back over to the creature and dragged it by its neck away and off they stalked into the bushes, the handlers odd voice becoming more muffled as they made their way further and further into the distance.

Lillie and Harvey managed to break free from whatever had a hold over them and Harvey smiled as he patted Daniel on the back smiling as he said,

'Nice one mate, see you done it again!!, Blooming lucky I'd say!!'

'Wh...What just happened Daniel??, What did you do to us??' Lillie stared deep at her brother as she tried to make sense of what just happened,

'I...I think I might have some kind of weird power...It happened at school the day we went to sneak out' Daniel replied.

'Blimey mate, that was way too close, worked better than the last time!, what's next?, are you going to sprout wings and fly?, haha' Harvey seemed less fazed by his friend's seemingly new type of power as he scouted the forest floor for any sign of the beast or its handler.

Lillie on the other hand was slightly worried about what she had just witnessed,

'B..But how did you get it??, how long have you been able to do that??, you were chanting the same thing over and over again, how on earth did that thing not see us??'.

So you remember that day we left school, Harv and me I mean, well we hid in a small hiding place in the wall just as Mr Proctor and Mr Lint walked towards us, then the next thing I remember Harvey was asking me what I had just been chanting, seems the teachers stopped right by us but we were both sort of invisible to them, That was the first time I felt a bit weird' Daniel still didn't know how he had come across this kind of power he was experiencing.

'The first time???...' Harvey laughed, 'You've always been a bit weird Dan.haha'

'Shut up Maximus!!' Daniel laughed as he recalled his friend's funny middle name causing Harvey to snap a twig off the tree and throw it straight at Daniel which bounced off his head and dropped to the floor below.

'Yeah yeah laugh it up Dan!!, I'll get you back don't you worry', Lillie sat back against the tree still wondering what was going on and her mind began to wander,

'So, if you can do that, I wonder what us two will be able to do, It must be something good seeing as I'm the older one of us'

'Well with your scary looks people will probably turn to stone or something!!' Harvey said as he scarpered down the tree laughing and being chased by an angry looking Lillie who seemed rather speedy descending the tree compared to Harvey who was huffing and puffing his way between the branches as he fell to the floor gasping for air as Lillie jumped down the last few feet and landed standing over Harvey like a lion ready to pounce on its meal.

'WHAT...did...you..say??' staring down at Harvey all helpless on the floor Lillie felt the urge to drag him to his feet and show him who was boss but she stopped short of doing that as Harvey apologised for what he had said and seemed totally scared by her.

By this time Daniel had dropped down beside his sister and told her to leave him alone then realising they probably weren't safe anymore whispered to them both,

'Look guys we really need to get away from here now seeing as those things might come back soon and I don't know if that thing I do will happen again so I think we need to keep moving'

The trio all realised that the safest thing to do was to keep moving along the path until they got out of the forest and hopefully onto safety,

'Guys let's grab a bit of food then we can make out way to wherever this town is, ok?'

'Sounds like a good idea Dan, I'll see if that food Lillie got is ok to eat'. With that Harvey climbed up the tree to where they had been sitting and gathered up the food before carefully climbing down again so he didn't drop any,

'I guess its food, this one looks like an odd looking apple with spikes stuck on it' Harvey held out an object that looked like it was fruit and showed it to the others,

'Who's going to try it then?' He gestured for one of the others to take a bite,

'Not me that's for sure!!' Lillie turned away in disgust at the sight of the odd looking fruit,

'I think you should try it Harv' Daniel pushed the fruit back towards his friend, 'seeing as you were the one moaning that you were hungry'.

Harvey eyed up the strange fruit, wondering how he was supposed to get past the spikes on it,

'I guess I need to pick them off, here goes' so Harvey tried to snap the spikes off but they wouldn't budge, they were seemingly solid,

'Ok then, plan B' and with that Harvey launched the fruit at the tree but it stuck in the trunk with a THUD.

'Ahhh, is someone trying to tell me something?' Harvey moaned as his stomach let out a huge rumbling noise suggesting it was desperate for food now.

Just as Harvey began to think that he was never going to get any food then he turned to where he had thrown the fruit to see that it was slowly losing its spikes one by one, then a CRACK as it began to split in two revealing whatever it was that was inside.

'Look...' Lillie pointed to the inside of the fruit, ' It's.....ok to eat?' she added as Harvey had already shot over to the tree and had pulled the fruit open to reveal what looked like an apple shape inside the outer shell but there was no skin around it, it looked juicy and ripe so Harvey being Harvey didn't care about the danger of eating something that might be bad for him.

He took a big bite out of it and his shoulders instantly dropped in relief when he realised it was the most amazing thing he had ever eaten,

'Mmm, wmmmfff' trying to speak but his mouth was full of this strange but delicious fruit,

'Eh??, What are you talking about Harv?' Daniel tried to make sense of what he was mumbling but gave up when he saw that his friend had

97

grabbed another couple of these fruits and was launching them at the trees again.

'For you....' He managed to splutter out as Daniel and Lillie took it in turns to remove the fruit from its outer layer, slowly peeling back the outer layer, Daniel was slightly unsure about it so he held it in his hand and put out his tongue to prod at the strange fruits centre,

Then he licked the fruit which was dripping with the juices surrounding it,

'Tastes like.....bananas' Daniel's eyes lit up as he then took a nibble of the fruit which made his eyes widen as he smiled and said,

'And.....toffee!!!!'

Lillie stared at her fruit as she thought about taking a bite but said to the boy's,

'Are you sure these are ok??, I mean...well....we aren't at home now, I'm just a bit worried we might get poisoned or something'

Harvey wasn't listening to anything she was saying as he was busy stuffing his face with more of the strange fruit,

'The taste is different every time!!!' He shouted as he took another deep bite from the fruit, 'Strawberries!!!!....oh my gosh!! This just got even better, now I can taste chocolate. Mmm, I think I'm in love!!' Harvey exclaimed as he sank to his knees holding about a dozen of the fruits in his hands,

'My new best friend's...' He smiled as he held them close to his chest and holding them as if they were a baby,

'I'm not letting you go ever!!'.

'Get a grip Harvey!!' shouted Lillie, 'They can't be that goo.....'

She stopped mid-sentence as she took a small nibble of the fruit and immediately took another as a taste filled her mouth that was familiar to her from home,

'Oh wow that's amazing!!, That's blackcurrant jam and caramel!!' she spluttered as she kept eating the fruit like someone was going to steal it,

'This can't be real, surely not!!, this is heaven!!' She said smiling as she helped herself to one of the fruits Harvey had dropped on the floor.

'Oi that's mine!!' Harvey shouted to Lillie who was teasing him by holding it up high enough so he couldn't reach it,

'Not anymore!!, Finders keepers, hahaha' she laughed as she held it close to her body so Harvey couldn't steal it back,

'What is this place?' Daniel asked as he stared at the fruit in his hand which just looked like a plain round piece of fruit with no colour to it but a taste that was individual to everyone who tried one.

Lillie took one last bite of the fruit before snapping back to reality and remembering where they were supposed to be going,

'Look, you two we really need to keep moving I think, it's all good and well stuffing ourselves stupid with this food but we need to get to the town before it gets colder here, something doesn't feel right again'

Harvey smugly smiled at Daniel as they totally ignored what Lillie was saying and they talked about how amazing the fruit tasted, hoping that they could find some more as they wanted to search the area in case they needed to stock up before they carried on,

'Come on Dan let's go have a look for some more, I've got a right hunger on!!' Harvey scrambled round the area to see if they could find any more to take with them,

'Daniel held up what looked like a small fabric sheet and shouted to Harvey,

'We can use this to carry them mate, saves you eating all of them while we go'

'Like I would do that, what do you take me for!!' Harvey smiled as he licked his lips, tasting the last remnants of 'coconut and raspberry' from the fruit.

So the boy's scoped up the fruit from around the floor and placed them in the sheet and wrapped it up, attaching it to a stick, placing it over Harvey's shoulder to carry,

'Oooff....It's a bit heavy Dan!, can't you carry it?' he whined as the weight of the stick and fruit dug into his shoulder causing him to topple to the side slightly.

'No way, at least if you're carrying it you can't be tempted to eat any of them as we walk', Daniel laughed as Harvey struggled to regain his balance 'Plus I'M in charge here so you do as I say',

'Who died and made you king!!' Lillie laughed as she shot her brother a scorching look, 'I'm the oldest so I'M the one in charge thank you very much!'.

Daniel pushed past his sister muttering to himself as he went, just quiet enough for her to hear but not loud enough for her to hear what he was saying,

'Sorry?? , I can't quite hear you Daniel, do you have something to say?' Lillie cupped her hand around her ear as she waited for some kind of smart reply from her brother,

'Whatever sis….we will see soon enough, Come on let's go, Need to find this town and I must find Bucksy', Daniel couldn't be bothered to come back with a smart reply as he just wanted to get going as he felt totally creeped out by the forest.

As the beautiful moonlight shone through the forest like a torch, the trio kept to the path that they were given, still searching for the town they had to get to, This gave Daniel a chance to think about what was going on, his mind was wandering all over the place and he seemed to be struggling to take it all in as the trio walked further along the moonlit path, stopping whenever they heard the snapping of twigs or the grunting of some kind of animal,

'Wh..what was that?' Harvey suddenly jumped onto Daniel as a loud crashing noise could be heard to the side of them,

'I don't know Harv...why don't you go and have a look' Daniel scornfully replied as Harvey was becoming more and more agitated by every kind of sound resonating through the forest

'M..me..out there?, stuff that, I'm not going anywhere else apart from this way with you guys!!, Today is not a good day to get eaten Dan' Harvey trembled as he kept jumping even more with every step.

100

Lillie on the other hand was focused on the path ahead as the beautiful moonlight lit up the path like spotlight guiding them to safety,

'Come on guys keep up' she spoke back to the boys who were lagging behind slightly 'It can't be that much further to this town, surely'

'Blame Maximus back here sis, he's the one who's scared by his own shadow at the minute' Daniel was getting tired of Harvey's scared antics as he was getting tired again from all the walking,

'Shut up Dan, Look it's not my fault I don't like being scared by ten foot monsters with pets who have sharp teeth ready to eat me, I'm sorry if I'm a little jumpy but I don't like all this and I just want to go home'

'And you think I don't!!' Daniel turned round answering his friend angrily, stopping dead in his tracks in front of Harvey who dropped the fruit he was carrying to the floor ' All I want to do is go home but we are stuck here for now until I can figure out how to get back My dog is missing and I want to see mum but we can't right now, I don't need you whimpering and whining at every chance you get, so for once please just SHUT UP!!'.

Daniel's anger had caused his sister to stop and turn round as she had never heard him talk to Harvey, or anyone else for that matter, like that.

'Woah where did that come from Daniel?' she said, surprised by the tone in which it was said but could see he was getting slightly upset

'I've never heard you talk like that before, even to me and I'm your sister and we are supposed to not like each other that much'.

Harvey didn't know whether to laugh cry or just turn and run as he was frozen to the spot trying to take in the explosive response his 'best friend' had given him,

'Alright Daniel there's no need to talk to me like that ok!!, I'm sorry but I'm just as desperate to get home too, mum will freak when I see her I just know it' Harvey's voice trembling slightly as he tried to act cool about him having his head bitten off but his voice wobbled up and down as he spoke.

'Look we are all in this together, we just need to stick together and I'm sure we will be ok, let's just keep moving ok?' Lillie felt like she needed to act as a peacekeeper as the trio were in a place they didn't know, on a path they weren't sure where it led and to top it all off struggling to deal with all the news they had been given but they all had one thing in common on this night, They all needed to find a way home.

As the forest thinned out slightly Lillie could see a collection of bright light seeping through the last few trees in the distance which grew brighter with every step they took,

'Come on guys I think we might be near the town' She said excitedly as they all started to pick up the pace, all eager to see where they were heading and what they were heading into,

'Mmmm, I can smell food...and it smells amazing!! Harvey, who was led by his stomach once again, pushed past Daniel and shot off towards the edge of the final few rows of trees where they were met by a distinct warm looking glow from the lights which were shining like a beacon in the night sky.

As they made their way single file through the last bit of hedgerow that was shielding them from whatever was outside, they stepped through the final gap one by one and out into the open they were met with a collection of sights and smells they had never come across before,

'Wow...this place is massive!!' Harvey mouthed as they stood there trying to take in the sight in front of them,

'Come on guys let's go...' Lillie took the lead as she made her way towards the fencing which surrounded the edge of the town, Daniel was just stood there in complete awe of what he was seeing, 'Erwin!.....' He muttered as Harvey grabbed his arm and pulled him along.

Chapter Nine
The Town Of Erwin

The Town of Erwin stood silently in the peaceful province of Vaymia like a sleeping giant across the land waiting to come to life at the first sign of sunrise, By its size you could tell it is normally a bustling place to live with plenty to keep the townsfolk from steering too far away from the city, housing plenty of locals who were born here, it seemed that this town was a central hub for plenty of visitors wanting to buy whatever the locals were selling but this was the time of night when all was silent across the town and only the sound of the occasional animal noise filling the night air followed by a rumbling roar from in the distance which echoed around filling the night air like a blanket of fog descending deep into the streets.

The only lights to be seen across the sprawling mass of the town were the lights coming off of the buildings with lanterns burning brightly outside each door, it seemed that every house as decked out with at least one light source, only a few had lights coming from inside the houses with inaudible conversations being heard from behind the closed doors of many of the houses, it seemed the layout of the town was purposely built in such a way that the streets resembled what can only be described as looking like a maze, winding purposefully through the streets, each turn different to the last, such a layout was performed to confuse anyone who tried to attack the town by making each turn of a corner different from the next, making it harder to reach the parts of the town that seemed to house the most activity.

The residents were normally very friendly and peaceful which made it easier for their town to be attacked, which unfortunately was becoming more and more frequent as the years have passed, the residents would seek shelter in their houses at the slightest whiff of trouble, no one wanted to be involved in the protection of the town as their safety was a priority to the army who were sworn to protect them all.

The town itself seemed to house some sort of special secret that only a few elders seemed to know about and had taken a vow to never reveal what it is, which was why it was being attacked more and more these past few years causing some of the townsfolk to flee, never to return.

Army after army would descend onto the town but time and time again it would stand firm helped by the protection they received, the main reason being that looming over the Town like a protecting shadow was the Castle Erwin which stood at the far end of the town high up in the Whispering Hills of Scandor, seemingly silent until the alarm was raised where all sorts of activity could be heard as the Castle seemed to ready itself for its next battle.

But tonight all seemed quiet in the town as the trio stood at its edge, looking round for any signs of life, hoping that they wouldn't be spotted by whatever type of people lived here.

'Can anyone see anything?' Daniel's voice just higher than a whisper but low enough not to be picked up if anyone were in the vicinity.

'Nothing over here, think they must all be asleep or something' Lillie was on full alert as she crept back over to where her brother was standing, both of them still straining to see into the town for movement when all of a sudden Harvey appeared, trying to be as quiet as he could but it seemed even that was a big ask for him as he clattered into a metal bucket and what looked like a small trowel and rake propped up against the fence, sending him tumbling over followed by the tools being somehow wrapped up in his legs which clanged and banged around him as he fought to get them off.

Harvey ended up lying on his back right next to where Daniel and Lillie were standing, both leaning over him with faces like thunder at the noise he had just created,

'Well done Harv!!' Daniel sarcastically clapped his stricken friend as he lay there on the ground looking slightly dazed,

'Wake up the whole town why don't you. Only you could make THAT much noise, typical of a Jones boy!!' Lillie had decided to join in with having a go at him too.

'What do you mean by that Lillie?' came Harvey's reply as he struggled to get to his feet, still trying to kick off the tools that had become attached to him like a pet that wouldn't let go,

'It's not MY fault some idiot has left their stuff just lying around out here, could of had my eye out too!...and what do you mean typical of a Jones boy?' Harvey finally kicked off the tools which clattered against the post for the final time as he confronted Lillie over her comment.

'Well...' Lillie started 'Let's look at the facts. First of all you are a walking disaster area, everywhere you go you seem to get hurt, or fall over, or bring attention to yourself by being able to make the most amount of noise possible out of very little, You're clumsy, and to be honest I don't see why Daniel puts up with you'

Daniel sniggered to himself as Harvey just stood there listening to the savage mauling he was getting from Lillie,

'Oh gee thanks!, anything else you've forgotten?' came the reply from Harvey as he seemed rather taken aback by what he was being told,

'I'm sure you'll muck up in some other way before we get out of this mess so I'll wait until that happens then remind you', Lillie whipped her head round almost whacking Harvey in the face with her ponytail as she done her best turned up snooty expression.

Harvey turned to Daniel who was still sniggering to himself and with a look that seemed like he wanted to cry asked him,

'Is that what you think of me mate?, am I really that bad?'

'Well you are a clumsy idiot mate but that's why I like you so much, you're easy to control and make you do what I want you to do, I wouldn't change you for anyone else....Well apart from Bucksy I mean but he's not here so I guess I'm stuck with you. Haha'

'Thanks Dan, now I feel so much better!!' he replied, still sulking from Lillies scathing comments earlier.

105

'Right you two numpties, we need to somehow find our way to that house with the lights on it...What was it called again?' enquired Lillie as she readied herself to leap the fence and make her way towards the town,
 'Err it's called the House of a Hundreds lights sis, lucky I'm here isn't it or you'd be knocking on anyone's door hoping they would let you in!!'
 'Whatever Daniel...anyway we need to go, I'm getting a bad feeling about being here too long' Lillie shuddered as she thought about what could happen if they were caught.
 Just as she was about to make her way over the fence and down towards the town itself a few of the house lights lit up just ahead of where they were standing, It seems the noise from outside had awoken a few of the townspeople, Door after door was flung open as a few of them made their way outside to see what the noise was and where it had come from, Lillie quickly grabbed Daniel and Harvey by the arms and dragged them along the fence line further into the darkness, they jumped the fence and hid behind one of the dark houses on the edge of the town, peering into the blackness of where they had just left only to see a couple of the townspeople inspecting the mess Harvey had left by the fence, both muttering to themselves, as Lillie strained her neck out to try and catch what they were saying, all she caught were the words 'Twinnies' and 'Bulger's must of done this'.
 They then made their way back towards the safety of their homes, followed by every door slamming shut and what sounded like hundreds of locks being turned, then it all went dark across this end of the town.
 'Phew that was close!!' Daniel rubbed his forehead as he turned to Harvey smiling.
 'Too blooming close mate, what do we do now?' Harvey replied as he stood completely still so as not to make any more noise.
 'We wait....just in case they decide to come out again for some reason, then when it's clear we make our way into the town to find Luther and that house with that light on it' replied Lillie who was still on guard in case anything happened while they were hidden out of sight.

'It's the House of a Hundred lights and the man's name was Lucas. Don't you ever listen properly? Such a plank!!'. Daniel corrected his sister which made him smile as it wasn't very often he got one up one her.

'Whatever boy wonder. Come on I think we are clear, let's go before Hurricane Harvey strikes again' chuckled Lillie as she carefully made her way round the darkened edge of the house, she stopped right at the end of the wall watching as the last light flickered then went out on the house ahead of them,

'Right you two follow my lead but this time be quiet, especially you Harvey!' Lillie scowled at Harvey who put his head down as he knew he was mainly to blame,

So the trio made their way through the first part of the town, the streets twisting and winding round every corner they took, occasionally leading them down a dead end causing them to backtrack and try to find a new path through the town.

After what seemed like an age just as they felt like they were making progress through the maze like streets as if Lillie almost knew which turns to take their progress was halted by the banging from inside a house just ahead of them, so they slowly crept up to the side of it, leading them into the dark alley beside it which was blocked off like so many of the streets they had encountered so far.

They crouched down enough so they could pass under the window above them just as it swung open, spraying the alleyway ahead with light from within which scared Harvey and Daniel to almost give themselves away to whoever was inside.

'Hhhuu....' A scared sound Daniel was seemingly frozen in fear as he waited for whatever was inside to pop its head out, Lillie had spotted Daniel was looking very scared and nervous that she reached across to him, lay her arm across his chest and mouthed,

'Shhhhh' putting her other finger to her lips, Daniel instantly calmed down as he realised that the person inside must of just opened the window for air, but just as he breathed a sigh of relief a plate of eaten food was thrown out of the window which slopped against the house next door with a 'THUD', luckily Harvey was at the darkest end of the alley as he would of probably screamed out in terror at seeing food fly past his head.

All of a sudden as the trio crouched in total fear the alleyway darkened as a figure revealed itself against the wall opposite, looming out like a giant ready to pounce, arms stretched out wide then.... it let out a rather large 'YAWN' followed by a 'BUURRP', the figure stood there just looking out of the window for what seemed like a lifetime with Daniel and Lillie still stuck underneath the opened window.

Then, before the figure turned and closed the window, it spoke,

'Well that's the last of that I guess, see told you there was nothing to worry about, probably just those blooming animals again, this will stop them rummaging through the rubbish!'. And with that the window slammed shut and all was dark again.

Lillie and Daniel both looked at each other with a look that shouted 'We need to go!', but as they turned to Harvey they realised he wasn't there anymore,

'Harvey....Harv!!' whispered Daniel into the thick darkness at the end of the alleyway, waiting for a reply which never came.

'Where is that boy?' Lillie quietly muttered to Daniel as they searched the end of their hiding place but couldn't feel a thing down that end of where they were standing, then suddenly Daniel felt a hand grab him on the shoulder causing him to spin around in panic only to be met by a hand straight over his mouth and a voice shushing him.

It seems Harvey had somehow appeared as if from nowhere,

'What are you guys still doing here?, look what I've found!!' Harvey said getting slightly over excited as he finally felt he was being useful for a change,

'I've found a sort of passage thingy right in the corner here, look!!'. Lillie and Daniel crept along to where Harvey was standing, right by the corner of the wall which seemed to be at a dead end,

'What are we looking at Harv?' questioned Daniel as he felt Harvey was pulling his leg,

'Watch this guys!' as Harvey gently felt his way along the wall into the darkest part of the alley. He pushed the end of the bricked wall until he heard a 'CLICK' from behind the wall itself and what sounded like numerous locks moving and clanking, it seemed like there was some sort of secret panel which was big enough for them to get through completely hidden out of sight and only known to the people of the town by the looks of it, their eyes adjusted to the darkness as they peered into the darkened passageway which had opened up before them, they moved slightly along towards the edge of the tunnel to be met with what looked like some sort of escape route stretching as far as the eye could see in both directions.

'It seems to go right towards the centre of the town guys, right along the back of all the houses, it's big enough for us to all get down!, I wonder where the other end goes to?' Harvey said as he had already started to explore the tunnels before he jumped out on the other two.

'Are you sure it's safe in here?, seems a bit odd that there's this tunnel thing hidden away, what's it hidden away from? And I hope we don't get caught!' Daniel nervously feeling his way along the walls in the heavily darkened tunnel, with Lillie not too far behind him, holding onto his shirt as they edged their way further into the passageway,

'Where do you think this leads guys?' asked Lillie, hoping that someone would be able to give her an answer.

'Who knows but I bet it leads somewhere cool!' Harvey laughed as the sound echoed all around them,

'I wish there were some lights in here, I'm sure I've just trod in something nasty, Urrgh' Lillie groaned at the thought of what was in the tunnel with them, Then all of a sudden as if a switch had been flipped a stream of wall lanterns lit up along both sides of the passageway walls, creeping past them like a snake sliding through the grass and off into the distance.

'Whoa, who done that?' Daniel asked inquisitively as he turned to Harvey, who raised his upturned hands and shrugged his shoulders knowing it wasn't him,

'Wasn't anything I done Dan, maybe ask your sister, maybe she's a witch!, haha', He said to his bemused friend who then turned to Lillie who was now scowling at Harvey with a look that could taken down a large elephant.

'Did you do this sis?, What did you say?' Daniel had to ask as he knew it wasn't him,

'All I said was that I wished there were some lights in here, and then those lanterns lit up all around us'.

Harvey had heard enough and was making his way along the passageway as he shouted back to the others,

'Come on guys, let's see where it goes' and off he shot leaving the others in his wake.

'Harvey...wait for us!!' shouted Daniel as he set off in pursuit of his friend closely followed by Lillie.

The passageway seemed to go on forever until eventually it came to a dead end with Harvey pushing the wall like he did to get into it.

'Oh come on just move!!' puffed Harvey as he used all his strength trying to move the wall,

'Let's try together you two, see if we can get out of here before we are heard in here' Lillie said as they all faced the wall, hands spread wide, they began pushing with all of their might but it wouldn't budge an inch. They all stopped eventually and sat down against the wall totally worn out,

'Harvey was panting heavily, trying to get his breath back as he moaned,

'Why won't this thing just OPEN!!' no sooner had he finished what he was saying then all of a sudden the wall swung open the other way leaving the trio lying on their backs upside down in some kind of underground room somewhere in the depths of the town,

As their eyes became accustomed to the darkness and the dust from inside settled they were met with the sight of a darkened room, wider and much larger than the passageway they were just in, cracks of light were shining in from between the floorboards above them, lighting up unopened boxes stacked against the wall, ripped and ruined pictures were scattered around the room, some hanging half off, in the corner of the room a set of wooden stairs climbed up towards a heavy looking wooden door, as the trio ventured forwards further into the room all of a sudden the wall behind them swung back shut with a 'THUD' followed by the sound of locks clicking back into place.

As they stood in the middle of the room totally confused with where they were now no one dare speak a word at first until Lillie thought she would see if what happened in the passageway with the lights would work again,

'Lights….' She muttered, closing her eyes tight as if too afraid to look, hoping that her words might light up the room they were all in.

Harvey and Daniel looked at each other and shrugged their shoulders as they were still standing there in the darkened room, then one by one, in the cracks of the wall lights started appearing from everywhere, bathing the trio in a brilliant white light, their shadows appearing on the walls as if dancing with every new light that appeared,

'I think I know where we are guys!!' Daniel broke the silence as Harvey stood there in awe of their surroundings,

'I'd say we have found the House of a Hundred Lights!!, Ahhh maybe we were looking in the wrong place, This must be where we can find that Lucas guy!!'.

Harvey was too busy counting the lights he could see to hear what Daniel was saying,

'Sixty five, sixty six, sixty seven…' He counted slowly pointing at each one individually,

'AWWW great, I've lost count now!!', Harvey went to start again but Daniel gestured at him to stop,

It's ok Harv, I think this is the right place so no need to actually count them!!'

'So how do we get out of here without being seen?' Harvey enquired as he looked to the stairs,

'Well let's try the door up there first then eh, might lead somewhere', Daniel pointed to the door at the top of the stairs, just as he said that they heard a clicking sound coming from the door, his head swung round so fast almost causing him to fall over, then followed the sound of someone banging at the door hard, it seemingly stuck in position as every part of the door creaked and groaned as whoever was behind it was trying to force it open, the trio looked at each other in total fear as they searched the room for somewhere to hide but the only places were the small boxes leaning against the walls that had no chance of hiding them all, Harvey had the idea of trying to get back into the tunnels, so he ran to the wall, as the door upstairs was still stuck shut and now being banged against,

'OPEN' Harvey confidently shouted at the wall but nothing happened, the wall stayed exactly how it looked, not one part of it moved or looked like it was going to,

'Open....please!!!' Harvey tried again this time sounding more panicky than the last time, once again the wall didn't budge or make any kind of sounds so Harvey turned to face the others who were standing there hopeful that he could get them into the passageway beyond the wall but nothing was happening,

'Guys...I don't know what to do now!!' He continued now sounding ever so scared, just as he went to move the door at the top of the stairs flung open, banging hard against the bricks on this side of the door with a 'DONNGGG' as the metal handle slammed hard against wall. Lillie, Daniel and Harvey all screeched out loud and jumped back in total fear as the sound and sight of footsteps could now be seen and heard clomping down the wooden stairs, they scattered to the nearest boxes, trying their best to not be seen...but to no avail,

'Children...I know you're there, there's no need to be afraid, please...step out from behind the boxes, I can see you' the manly voice called out to them as the children stayed silent, hoping that whoever it was would go away thinking that there was no one down there but the voice carried on talking to them,

112

'My name is Lucas Deverill keeper of the House of a Hundred Lights, I'm presuming you are Daniel, Lillie and Harry...'

'Harvey!!!!!' Came the squeaky reply from behind one of the boxes at the back of the room,

'Ahh yes Harvey, that's it, Lydia told me all about you all, please step out I promise you that you are safe here with me for now, But if I may I'd like to ask a few questions myself', Lucas corrected his mistake as the children all stepped out from behind the boxes that almost hid them to be met by the sight of a slightly oversized man, beard hanging down past his stomach which was neatly trimmed and sporting coloured rings down his beard, his clothes were hidden by a cloak and his face was out of sight slightly due to his hood covering most of his head, but his voice had a warming tone to it which made the trio feel slightly at ease in his presence seeing as he seemed to know all about them.

'Come. Please, I've been expecting you all' the man gestured to the children to follow him up the stairs into the safety of the main house,

'But I must warn you, there is every need for quiet up here as I wouldn't want you caught up in any danger whilst you're here' Lucas warned the children of the importance of silence whilst he prepared a room for them to rest.

So off Lucas stomped up the wooden stairs and out of sight into the house above where they were standing, the sound of doors being clunked shut and window blinds creaking as they were pulled inwards to hide the escaping light.

'What do you reckon Dan?' Asked Harvey inquisitively, hoping for an answer that would put him at ease,

'Well...' Daniel replied 'Seeing as he knows exactly who we are, I think we best do as he says and follow him'.

'I'm with you Daniel, I don't get any kind of bad feelings from this place, but let's be ready just in case ok?' Lillie's answer put the slightest bit of caution into Daniel just as he was about to climb the stairs leading up into whatever was up there,

113

'Come on guys, there's only one way we are going to find out what's going on, let's ask the big guy!!' Daniel sighed as he gestured to the others to follow him as he made his way quietly up the creaky wooden stairs and through the door into the room above.

As they all stepped through the wooden door they were met with what looked like some sort of small bedroom, a basket with a blanket sat in the corner of the room housing a large bone off an unfortunate animal, a small bed sat proudly against the wall covered in warm looking covers that had been stitched together lovingly, a simple candle sat in its holder, the flame flickering in the smallest of breezes that whizzed round the room, a lone window had been covered up by a sheet draped over the blinds, stopping any light from escaping the room and out into the town around them

'What is this place?' Harvey asked as if Daniel would have the answer,

'Looks to me like someone's bedroom, and that looks like a pet's basket' Daniel pointing at the round wicker bed in the corner which then reminded him of his own loss since they came into this world,

'Bucksy…..' he muttered to himself as he stood there thinking about what had happened to his beloved pet Labrador.

As he turned round he noticed that Lillie and Harvey had made their way out of the room and had found a door that had led them outside into a small courtyard area, so he followed them outside into the night air.

'Woah...Look at all these lights Daniel, so beautiful!!' Harvey was mesmerised by what he was seeing in front of him.

The small courtyard they were standing in housed the most beautiful of sights, in the middle of it stood a tree, not a single leaf hanging off it but every branch was covered by countless small lanterns of light spinning and flickering in the night air, each corner of the courtyard was joined to the tree by a barely visible string which housed even more lanterns glowing with enough light not to be visible from outside.

'This...is...beautiful' Lillies eyes sparkled as brightly as the lanterns decking out the tree in front of her, she stepped closer to inspect them and as she did the light on the one nearest to her dimmed to almost nothing,

114

'What did I do??, why has it gone out?' she looked worried as if she had caused this to happen.

As they tried to make sense of this Lucas had made his way out of the door at the far end and was standing there watching them, listening to the panic in their voices as they thought they had broken one of the lanterns.

'It wasn't me this time thank god!!' Harvey puffed his cheeks out happy in the knowledge that he had played no part in what was happening,

'AHEM....' Bellowed Lucas causing the children to swing round to be greeted by the man they were supposed to be following but now he had removed his cloak and was standing there in front of them all,

'He's a bit ugly isn't he??' Harvey nudged Daniel who was now trying not to snigger at the sight of this slightly oversized man standing before them stroking his long greying beard.

Lucas had changed his clothes for something more comfortable for him, his beard was still decked out with the coloured rings keeping it together, his hair was tied back in a ponytail and he was sporting a pair of glasses which looked as big as Harvey's head,

'Jeez Dan look at those glasses he's got on too!!, they're huge, I hope they don't fall off his face and onto us otherwise we will be crushed!!' Harvey was doing his best to make Daniel laugh out loud but he was still just sniggering, barely taking his eyes of Lucas who was now making his way towards the children, Harvey gulped as Lucas towered over him like an enormous tree.

'Those lanterns are called 'EXTERIO ILLUMINUM'....or dimming lanterns to you and I' Lucas proudly explaining to the children about the wonders of the world around them as he continued telling them about the lanterns,

'Whenever they feel threatened by something they extinguish their light so as not to attract nearby enemies when they are in their group, just as they are now, but...they can act as a powerful ally if they are treated right and looked after as if a pet'

115

'In what way do you mean??, Now I'm totally confused' Laughed Harvey as he kept making the lanterns lose their light by reaching out to touch them, 'Now Henry…..Don't tease them or you'll regret it' boomed Lucas as he knew what was going to happen if Harvey continued to prod at the lights. 'Ermmmm my name's Harvey!!, Can't you ever get my name righ…..' Harvey moaned as he became frustrated with Lucas not getting his name correct so he swiped at one of the lights which extinguished its light instantly like a light bulb being turned off, what followed next took the children by surprise, none more so than Harvey as the lantern up a brilliant blinding white colour which seemed brighter than the sun, the light shone right onto Harvey's face and he shrieked out as his vision became just a blur of light,
'AHHH WHAT'S GOING ON!!!' He shouted out as he bumbled around the courtyard and fell against the tree clutching his face.
'I told you not to annoy them young man' Chuckled Lucas as he watched Harvey covering his eyes, unable to make any sense of what was going on around him as Lillie and Daniel just stood there looking rather shocked.
'That's what I was trying to explain to you all, Don't worry Hugo your vision will return soon just relax and in a few minutes you will be fine I promise' Laughed Lucas as he helped Harvey to his feet,
'IT'S HARVEY!!!!, How many more times do I have to tell you!!' Harvey whined as he was still rubbing his eyes heavily hoping for his sight to return, 'All I can see is a big white blur now!'.
Lucas smiled as he turned to Lillie and Daniel, clasped his hands together which caused the children to take a step back just in case something bad was happening,
'Now you two, as I was saying these lanterns aren't just any kind of normal lanterns as you have just seen, they possess the ability to emit the brightest of lights into the face of anyone or anything they feel threatened by, such as Horace over there….'
'HARVEY!!!!' came the rather snappy, angry reply from Harvey who was still stumbling around, looking for some water to wash his eyes out,

116

'But they also have the ability to light up the path ahead of whoever is holding them, namely their 'trainer' as we call them, but the light is invisible to everyone else around them so only the holder of the lantern can see where they are going, guided by an invisible light, which comes in handy when you don't want to be seen I can tell you'.

Lillie was looking a little confused by this so decided to speak up,

'So what you're telling us is that these 'lights' are lights but invisible lights'

'Well....yes, but also be warned when they sense danger the light inside them begins to pulse, they act as a distress warning to whoever is close to it ' Lucas said confidently

'Oh...alright then....as if this world couldn't get ANY stranger!' Lillie tried to take in what Lucas was telling them but it seemed so strange to her so she just huffed and went to help Harvey find what he was looking for. Daniel took a few steps back so as not to stumble into the lanterns for fear of him suffering the same fate as Harvey who was now blinking his eyes constantly in the vain hope it would help him see properly.

So Lucas walked off towards the door he had appeared from earlier, struggled to climb the steps slightly letting out an 'OOOH' every so often, Lucas wasn't what you would call a young man but he never revealed his true age to anyone, he turned round to face the children who were scattered around the courtyard, still engrossed by the lanterns and what they could do if treated right and with his booming voice summoned the children to him.

'Ok then you three young Boglins, follow me please, let's get you rested up and then we can have a nice little chat over a pot of Crub Juice.

So off the children went, Harvey being helped up the stairs by Daniel, following Lucas through the oversized door which gently shut behind them as they entered the house, clicking away as a lock could be heard turning inside it.

Chapter Ten
The Truth

As the children caught up with Lucas who had made his way into a darkened room lit by only a single candle, he had sat himself down in his favourite chair covered in the fur of some kind of rather large ugly creature, its head draped over the back of the chair and its jet black fur completing the darkness in the room.

The room itself was full of what looked like family pictures, row upon row of plates, cups and small trinkets sat on top of an overcrowded cabinet resting up against the wall looking like it would topple over at any minute, there were a couple of very large wooden doors at the far end of the room, leading off into bedrooms and other storage rooms.

Lucas beckoned the children into room but they were too busy getting their eyes to adjust to the darkness to see properly,

'Look at this place….It's so….dirty, urrghh!!!' Came Lillies response as she scrunched up her nose as a waft of something bad filled her nose,

'And what's that smell!!!' she said holding her nose tightly so no more of the smell could penetrate her nose.

'Please come in and sit down on the bench over there' Lucas smiled as he watched the trio stumble their way through the darkened room, Harvey slamming his shin into the bench with a 'THUD' as he walked forward, trying to find where he needed to sit,

'OUCH!, Now that's my leg broken, what's next?, attacked by a pack of dogs maybe?...or eaten by a group of sharp toothed butterflies!!'

Daniel laughed at Harvey's over the top reaction to hitting his shin and told him to shut up as he needed to find answers to why they were all here,

Lucas knew that Daniel would need to know about why they had ended up in a strange new world and spoke to him before he had a chance to ask, 'I know what you want to ask young Daniel...' Lucas started 'And I promise I will be as helpful as I can in the time we have but time is very limited for you all here, in this house I mean, as even as we speak you are all being hunted for who you are related to, so I will allow us to have some time together, for you all to rest and for me to help you understand why you are here but by first light I must send you on your way so you can complete the final part of your journey'.

'I do have a lot of questions I need answering Lucas so thank you for helping us' Daniel smiled as he knew they weren't far from finding out the truth about what was going on here,

'But first I just need to give us the time I need to be able to explain to you what is going on, so if you'll excuse me I'll be back in just a minute..' He stood up from his oversized chair and off Lucas went into the room at the far end of the room, grumbling as he went, moaning about his knees and back.

'What the heck is going on now!!' Harvey asked as he knew his sight had returned now and he was able to see where they were and what was in the room,

'I hope it's to make food, I'm starving!!' He moaned again as his stomach rumbled in the quietness of the room. Lillie just sat there seemingly frozen to the spot, not daring to move in case anything jumped out on them, which in this world they didn't know could actually happen

'I don't like this Daniel...You know how much I hate the dark, He needs more lights..' It seemed if Lillies words had been heard once again as one of the lanterns that had been left inside the room by Lucas lit up at the sound of her voice.

'Look at that...it's happened again' Smiling as her words seemed to bring light to even the darkest of rooms which made her slightly more at ease with her surroundings as she could now see what was in the room with her, which wasn't very much apart from some darkened photographs which sat

119

alongside her on a table made out of a fallen log, she couldn't make out the other faces in the picture as they seemed to have been faded by time but she could make out that Lucas was in the picture with two other people, she picked it up to take a closer look, it seemed that one, if not both of the people in the picture must be a relation to Lucas as they were all huddled together as you would expect when having a picture taken, she smiled as she could see how happy Lucas was in it, but her attention was broken by Lucas standing close to her he knew what she was looking at so he decided to let her know about the picture,

'That's a picture of my family Lillie, it's the only one I have now...' He sighed as he took the picture out of Lillies hand and stared lovingly at it,

'You see they were taken from this town, and me, many years ago during one of the most brutal wars we had ever witnessed here, In this picture are my wife Tira and daughter Sula, I do miss them so much, I don't know what has happened to them and I'd give anything to find out whether they are alive or.....' He couldn't bear to carry on the sentence for fear of showing weakness in front of his young guests.

'Anyhow.....' Lucas pulled himself together, put the picture down beside the chair and turned his attention back to the children,

'Right younglings I'll do my best to answer any questions you may have, I might not be able to answer every question you have as my knowledge is somewhat limited but remember time is short and you must rest also'.

Harvey's inquisitive mind meant he was first to ask Lucas a question about where they were,

'So as you know already we have been brought here by goodness knows what to find whoever it is we are meant to find and I know it has something to do with their dad but I do have one question I'd like answering...What are these Fourteen Bells all about?? I asked that lady in the cottage but she didn't answer my question so maybe you could help'

'Ahh yes, 'The Fourteen Bells of Peace', well there isn't much can tell you about them for the safety and protection of them but they are the key to peace in this land...' Lucas carefully choosing his words as all three of the children edged closer to him, listening intently as he carried on explaining about the origin of the bells,

'You see the 'Fourteen Bells' had been hidden on this land for as long as anyone can remember, well I say Fourteen Bells as that was their original name.

Over the centuries their numbers have diminished from the wars which have plagued our land, there is now only four left.

Inscribed on each of the bells is a passage written by the original founders of Erwin, a group of peacekeepers who swore that no harm would come to such a beautiful world while the bells still hung, but as the founders were a peaceful race they swore that if they ever fell, all fourteen of them, then the land would become lost to the dark, and whatever evil forces roamed this peaceful land would be able to wreak havoc on who or whatever was here at the time.....'.

Daniel was listening intently to Lucas's explanation waiting for his chance to ask some questions but Lucas was still talking and explaining the history of the Fourteen Bells to Harvey,

'...So the bells had to be protected from harm in the only way the founders knew, they constructed a mighty army made of stone, faceless warriors who stood as high as the tallest trees in the forest, ready to protect the secrets of the land, their numbers hid the entrance to the caves where the bells hung, forming a shield of stone so nothing could penetrate them. They would stand dormant for many years, standing guard, never moving, until an act of war triggered the keepers of the 'Book of the Silent', which was the statues are known as 'The Silent' to them but to us we know them as 'The Overgaard', to use the book to bring the surviving Protectors 'alive' and ready to stop whatever forces were trying to gain control of our world, the book controlled the statues themselves. Whoever read the sacred script held within the pages of the book would then be in complete control of the stone army but the book couldn't be read by just anyone, you see for anyone who actually gets to read from the book will be met with blank pages as it's said that the book has to read you before it can be read, that's

121

why no one knows where the book is hidden so as to keep peace on our land'.

'Wow that's a bit of a long story, but what does it have to do with us, and what do you know about my father?' Daniel felt the need to step in now as he was desperate to find out some answers for himself.

'Well, master Daniel, I was just getting to that part, as the legend goes the Peacekeepers predicted that if the number of bells ever dwindled to almost none then 'The Leader of Three' would appear to oversee the protection of the land, any of these 'Three' could access the book and use it for good, so just after the first real big war your Father was paraded through the town with two other people.

These three were chosen as our protectors, one I'm told was his brother and the other one is still unknown to this day, but it seems they weren't able to work together as a team and eventually there was a fall out between them which sent them in different directions, they never heard from each other again and the land was once again waiting for the arrival of another 'Three' but we have been waiting years for them to come along until….' Lucas looked up at the children who were hanging on his every world until the penny seemed to drop for Daniel who looked up at Lucas, a twinkle lit up his eyes knowing there was something good about all this,

'Oh you mean us!!....We are 'The Three' that's what you're saying, but we don't know anything, how are we supposed to help?'.

Daniel seemed to be struggling now with this new information but Lucas tried his best to reassure Daniel, Harvey was too busy looking round the room watching some sort of flying insect looping it's way in front of him which caused him to laugh out loud,

'Have you seen this fly thingy?, It's going nuts here!!...' Harvey was too distracted to hear the news that would shape their new future so Lillie slapped him on the arm to get his attention back,

'Will you listen Harvey, have you not heard anything Lucas has been telling us? We are supposed to be the ones to help keep peace here'

Harvey's eyes lit up as all he could think of was holding huge weapons and fighting off dragons and whatever else was out there, a smile spread across his face as his head shot round to Daniel, he couldn't stop grinning as he was hitting Daniel's arm constantly,

'I told you something was special about us!!....and you never listened, I was right all along Dan!!'

'Stop hitting me Harv, something doesn't feel right to me, So Lucas what can you tell me about my...sorry OUR father?, I don't feel we know enough to understand what's going on here' Daniel felt he needed to ask as a lifetime was passing him by without him really knowing about his father,

'Well unfortunately I personally don't know much about your father...' Lucas felt slightly sad that he couldn't answer some of the questions Daniel was asking him,

'...but I do know that he is a most fearsome warrior of immense power and strength who will stop at nothing to protect this town and it's people, he has rarely been seen here, only during battle does he ever show himself, it's like he has to stay in the shadows, only appearing when he senses that the tide is turning in the battle of the town. I was personally picked by him to stay here in this house and make sure that the secrets of the land stay out of the clutches of evil, this house is central to the safety of Vaymia, I have been sworn to protect this house and the secrets it holds deep within, and I will fight for it with my last breath' Defiantly Lucas pumped his fist to show his loyalty to protecting his home and the land he loved, Harvey sniggered behind Daniel's back before whispering to him,

'Blimey Dan...Bit over the top that wasn't it?, is he for real?'

Daniel wasn't concentrating on Harvey as he felt that Lucas wasn't telling him that much about his father.

'So how do we find our father then Lucas?, We've come this far without actually knowing why we are all here so I just want to meet him'.

Lucas sat back in his chair clasped his hands together and sighed as he knew he must help the children reach their father but he didn't want to give them too much information about him and where he was as he felt it would affect them and their development, him knowing just how important they were to the safety of Vaymia.

He knew they needed to find their own way to prove him right that these children were the next of the 'Three' that would become the ultimate protectors of the land alongside their father, he had to tread carefully as too much information wouldn't allow them to fulfil their destiny,

'As I said Daniel I can only offer you all shelter for just this night only, you see I have had to cast a spell over this house to cover your presence here but it will only be active until sunrise then you must all leave otherwise bad things will descend here'

'But I need to know more Lucas, what are you hiding from us?, I want to know more about our father' pleaded Daniel but it fell on deaf ears as Lucas bluntly replied,

'I can offer you no more information Daniel, it is now up to you three to decide which path you must take'

'What do you mean 'path'?' Lillie replied looking extremely puzzled by what they were being told now,

'The paths I speak of are the paths for your individual futures, there will come a time when a choice will have to be made by all three of you, you must all come to the same result though'.

Lucas's tone became one that sounded like a warning to the children which made them all shoot back into the seat they were on as he carried on,

'But for now my young friend's you must rest, and by sunrise I will help you on your next part of your quest, I will provide you with things that will help you find what you are looking for but that is all, only you alone can find the right path'

'I have so many questions still though Lucas..' Daniel almost begging for answers now as he could see Lucas was getting slightly uneasy 'that's enough questions now Master Daniel!!' Lucas almost bellowed as he let his calm guard slip slightly,

'I'm sorry for my outburst children but from here on in I cannot interfere with your quest otherwise it may lead to an outcome that would endanger us all', Lucas hung his head slightly knowing that he shouldn't of reacted that way,

'You will get all the answers you need when you find your father, I promise you, but I cannot help you other than show you the direction you must travel in, I'm sorry, please when you get to where you need to be do not mention what you have seen here' Lucas pleaded with the children one last time,

'Why not?, Now I'm totally lost...' Harvey threw his arms up in the air and sighed,

'Because master Hugh if anything ever happens to any of you three then the information you have now would be dangerous for this place and for Vaymia itself'

'HARVEY!!!...It's Harvey....for the love of all things right can't you just get my name right just once' Harvey had had enough of being called by every name but his own and went to storm out, but the doors were bolted shut.

'What's going on here then?, I want to get some air, why are the doors locked!!' Harvey turned round to face Lucas who was striding towards Harvey who was now looking rather scared as Lucas towered over him, inhaled sharply, then gently pulled him away from the door as he explained why they were locked,

'Well, if you must know, the reason why they are all locked is for your safety and protection...',

'Protection from what?' Harvey replied looking confused as Lucas drew breath to speak again,

'If I may continue...protection from the Graxx Army, an army so evil that they would stop at nothing to destroy this once peaceful land, they wouldn't think twice about killing their own people if it meant they would rule this land',

'But what does that mean for us Lucas?, I'm still confused..' Daniel questioned Lucas once again to find out why they were locked in here,

125

'Well...as I said earlier I had to cast a spell on this room, a spell that has to protect you, one that surrounds you all which hides you from the vision of the people connected to the land...'

'Kind of like us being invisible you mean....' Lillie felt she understood what was going on now and felt happy enough to continue speaking over Lucas,

'Just like what happened with all three of us after we left Lydia's house in the woods you mean...'

Now Lucas looked confused as he turned to Lillie, tilted his head slightly to the side and felt he needed to ask the questions now,

'What do you mean Lillie?, What happened in the woods!!'.

So Lillie went on to explain about how they had hidden up a tree in the forest as something chased her, and about how Daniel seemed to be able to make them 'invisible' just by some sort of chant and how it wasn't the first time he had used it,

'Hmmmm, interesting....' Lucas stood there stroking his beard as he thought for a minute or so before replying,

'So it seems that you DO have the 'gift' Daniel...., and it seems strange that you were able to use it in the other world, it must be stronger than first thought',

'What gift Lucas?, I'm totally confused' Daniel stared blankly at Lucas, trying to make sense of it all,

'The Non Seeing gift Daniel, It allows you to hide yourself, or anyone who is in contact with you at the time, so that you are kept out of danger. It cocoons you in a sort of protective bubble so you cannot be detected by anyone or anything. It must be strong in you considering where you used it and how powerful it was for you'. Lucas could sense that Daniel wasn't sure of how he used it but he knew just how powerful it would become as long as he learn to use it in the correct way,

'Trust me Lucas it really works!!, he has used it twice now and both times we weren't spotted, is he some sort of wizard or something?' Harvey had let his imagination run away a little as he got excited at what his friend might become,

Lucas smiled at Harvey as he could see him imagining all sorts of things about Daniel,

'I assure you Harvey....see I did get your name right!!, He will become whatever he needs to be but as long as he stays connected to the right path'

'Oh right that's easy then!!' Laughed Harvey as he smiled in Daniel's direction,

'I'm sure I can help him with that' he continued but Lucas's words came with a warning too,

'Do not take this journey lightly....You must follow your own paths in this land and not let any harm come to one another, your actions will be judged which will affect the outcome of the final choice you have to make so please make sure your actions are true and correct, my hopes for you are high and we are living in a land of hope now'

'Well whatever happens we will do what we need to do and must do I promise Lucas' Daniel smiled as he stood up, looking at Lucas and held out his hand for him to shake, just as he did he remembered something else which seemed to have completely slipped his mind since the three of them ended up in Erwin,

'But I do have just one more question Lucas if I can ask it'

'Of course Daniel but then you must eat before you rest for the remainder of the night' replied Lucas as he leant back against the door frame waiting for whatever Daniel was going to ask him,

'Well, when we all came through here I didn't actually come here on purpose, you see I was searching for my dog, Bucksy....'

'Dog???....what is that?' a puzzled Lucas replied stroking his beard as he racked his brain to try and think of what Daniel was asking him,

'It's my pet Lucas, He's what we call a dog where we come from, he's black in colour and has different coloured eyes, he walks around on all his legs too. I was chasing after him and then the next thing I remember was waking up in this place' 'Hmmmm, I'm not sure I've seen any such animal

127

come through these parts Daniel, well….nothing that looks like the animal you've described any way' laughed Lucas,

'But if I see anything like what you have described then I'll be sure to direct him you're way I promise, but for now I have prepared a feast fit for a King', Lucas disappeared for a few seconds before bringing in tray after tray of all sorts of food in, placed it on the table in front of them before taking a step back.

'Please eat children, you have a long journey ahead of you, you must keep your strength up'

None like the children had ever seen before but that didn't seem to stop Harvey who had already tucked into what looked like the biggest chicken leg ever seen,

'Oh wow guys!!...You have to try this food, it's amazing' Harvey said, spitting food out as he spoke to his friends who were standing there just watching him devour his food without pausing for breath.

'I think I'm going to be sick!!' Lillie had to turn away so as not to watch Harvey eating in the way he was,

'You're such a pig Harvey!!, How can you eat like that, it's disgusting!!' she continued but seemingly put off eating the food which had been prepared for them all,

'I'm sorry if my eating makes you feel sick Lillie but who cares anyway I'm starving!!' Harvey replied still shoving food into his mouth without asking what it was,

Daniel picked up a piece of two legged meat, took one sniff of it and took a small bite out of it,

'Mmm, not bad Lucas, what is it?' He asked inquisitively,

'It's a local animal, Daniel, called a Groggle, we only breed them for a means of food, they are a delicacy to these parts, do you like it?' Lucas smiled as he saw Daniel's face light up knowing he seemed to be enjoying it.

'Well it tastes amazing, come on Lillie try this!!' He beckoned his sister over but she was having none of it,

'No way, I've turned vegetarian now!!' she turned her nose up at the food she had been offered,

'Since when?' questioned Daniel,

'Since about one minute ago, watching that disgusting friend of yours eat his food like a pig!!' Lillie answered back angrily turning her nose away and up into the air at the sight of the food on the table
'I'll stick to this fruit, it looks far more appealing anyway'.

So Lucas stood up, walked towards the door and just before he opened it to walk through he turned to the children and spoke softly,

'Remember children, when first light arrives I'll be back to help you on your journey so get plenty of rest, but DO NOT leave this room otherwise the spell will be broken, all you need is in here, I won't be far away so please relax and get ready for tomorrow'

'Good night Lucas and thank you for this, I wish we could of found out more about my family but I think I'm beginning to understand this place now and I understand what I need to do, I hope we will meet again sometime in the future' Daniel thanked Lucas for all he had done for them,

'It has been my pleasure Master Daniel, I'm sure our paths will cross again after tomorrow, but now rest and I will come for you in the morning'.

And with that Lucas walked out of the door, he turned round just before shutting it wondering how the futures of these three children would turn out, he smiled, shaking his head as the door slammed shut, he locked the door and walked out across the yard muttering to himself as he went,

'I'm sure it will all work out..' he said as he reached the other door and walked through it, closing it solidly behind him.

Chapter Eleven
The Final Journey

Bucksy's tail was wagging as him and Daniel were standing in the middle of a field surrounded by the tallest trees that reach up to the heavens as far as the eye could see, the sun shining brightly casting shadows across the ground as the wind blew through the grass gently almost as if it were dancing to the beat of the earth itself, Daniel was at the edge of the field looking like he didn't have a care in the world as he was throwing his favourite ball to Bucksy who barked with happiness at his toy being thrown for him to catch.

'Good boy...Go on fetch this one' Daniel threw the ball as hard as he could across the field as his friend ran off into the distance barking as he chased his ball.

'Bucksy....Bucks...come back...here boy come on' shouted Daniel as he could hear Bucksy barking from the other side of the field, he picked up the ball in his mouth, tail still wagging as he chewed down on it, Daniel kept shouting to his dog to return but Bucksy just sat there facing the other way, still wagging his tail, so Daniel set off across the field towards him but the more he walked he could see he wasn't actually getting anywhere, he started to run as fast as he could but Bucksy got further and further away, now Daniel was panicking as he couldn't reach his friend shouting as he went,

'BUCKSY....BUCKS...please come back...Please.....' His words had no effect, then everything went black around him as a voice came through the darkness, it spoke only a few words in a wispy way,

'Choose the path…...reveal the power…' then it was gone and blackness fell completely.

Daniel sat bolt upright in the chair where he had fallen asleep looking rather bleary eyed as he searched the room for the other two,

'Bucks…' he murmured as he realised it was all a dream, he was back in Lucas's house with Lillie asleep in one corner, laying on top of a pile of warm looking sheets, and Harvey snoring his head off in the other corner occasionally talking in his sleep,

'Mummy...bacon….yeah' he mumbled as Daniel just stared at him trying to contain his sniggering as he turned to Lillie who was stirring from her sleep,

'Morning sis' greeted Daniel, he kind of guessed it was morning by the most brilliant rays of sunlight streaming through the cracks in the curtains and blinds covering the windows, feeling the warmth on his face as he sat up and stretched,

'Morning Daniel, are you ok?, you look like something's happened, bad dream?' she asked as Daniel sighed and smiled weakly in Lillies direction,

'Dreamt about Bucksy last night, I miss him so much, it's the first time I've thought about him properly since we've been here, guess I've been kind of side-tracked in some way' He explained, sounding heavy hearted as he told Lillie about his dream,

'Oh plus I heard another voice just before I woke up, it was to calling me, something about 'choosing a path and revealing the power', bit weird I'd say'

'I wouldn't call anything weird in this place Daniel, that's probably the most normal thing that happens here, Keep it to yourself though, Let's not tell Lucas about it' Lillie sort of warned Daniel about sharing the contents of his dream in case Lucas wasn't all he claimed to be.

'Yeah you're right sis, this is just between us and Harv…' He trailed off as he turned to Harvey who was still snoring his head off, a drool patch covering his pillow, the occasional smile spreading across his face,

'Wonder what he's dreaming about?' Laughed Daniel as he looked towards Lillie once again,

131

'My guess is food' Lillie laughed as she stood up from her makeshift bed walked around the room towards the door and stretched her arms out wide before yawning away rather loudly which seemed to cause Harvey to wake up from his sleep.

Harvey looked still half asleep as he spread out across the chair, his body going as stiff as a board as he stretched,

'What did you wake me for?, I was having such a good dream' He moaned as he stretched for the last time before sitting up, his hair looking all over the place, he wiped the wet patch from around his mouth before looking around the room for something to eat,

'Is there any food in here?, I'm starving' he asked as his stomach rumbled louder with each passing minute,

'Is that all you think about Harvey? you're a pig!!' Lillie moaned at him as all she had heard recently was about how hungry he was,

'Takes one to know one Lillie' Laughed Harvey as he felt the full force of a pillow whack him round the head from behind,

'Ow...' He cried, 'What did you do that for?, I was only messing'

'You deserved that, trust me, I wanted to do that to you during the night to try and stop you snoring, and you're so loud!!' Lillie barked at Harvey, knowing it would only wind him up further before he would get angry and accidentally break something,

'Whatever Lillie..' snarled Harvey as he turned away to grab a pillow, he swung round in a flash and threw it as hard as he could towards Lillie, she moved like lightning to avoid it just as the door opened and in walked Lucas who took the full force of the pillow right in the face,

'OOFF' Lucas winced as he was hit square on the nose.

Harvey's mouth dropped as he realised what he had done, Daniel on the other hand burst out laughing at the sight of Lucas standing there looking rather annoyed at what had just happened.

'I hope that wasn't really meant for me Harvey otherwise I'd of made you go eat with the Groggles outside my boy, come to mention it you do seem to look like one of them, I think I'll name it after you!!',

'It was meant for Lillie but she was too quick, I'm sorry Lucas, totally my fault' an embarrassed Harvey replied hanging his head in shame as Lucas towered over him shaking his head,

'You must learn to tolerate each other as a three otherwise you may not end up on the right path, learn to accept each other's failings and embrace your future' Lucas said wagging a giant finger at all three of the children who were just standing there looking at him as he spoke,

'We will do our best Lucas, I will try to keep us all together, I just hope Bucksy is safe, I need to find him now, he's the reason why we are all here' Daniel felt a sense of sadness as he spoke of his most loyal companion but also hope, hope that they would be reunited soon, he knew he couldn't be far away now, Lucas sensed the sadness Daniel was feeling so he felt the only way was to distract him,

'Right my young friend's, it is time...'

'Time for what Lucas?? Breakfast?...I'm starving!!' Moaned Harvey as he held his stomach,

'I mean it's time you three went on your way, the spell is close to ending and once it does you will be visible to everyone in this land, so please you must follow me to the UnderLand' Lucas was now looking slightly agitated as he knew they must go now otherwise their presence would bring all sorts of evil to Erwin,

'What's the UnderLand?, sounds horrible' Lillie asked as all these new places seemed to confuse them all,

'The UnderLand...' Lucas explained ' is the network of tunnels created under this town, we have used them on many occasions to flee the wars, there are three routes, one leads to the edge of the other side of the forest, the second goes deep into the heart of the mountains, and the third.....well it can only be accessed by a few special people',

'Why is that one so special?' Daniel asked, looking quizzically at Lucas,

'Well Daniel that tunnel leads deep into the belly of this town, it descends thousands of feet below Erwin then spreads out across the land in all directions just in case anyone evil manages to somehow find a way in, it is rigged with all sorts of traps and challenges and there are numerous tunnels leading off into nowhere, but only the few can walk straight through each one as it leads to the Bells, It's a hazardous walk that only a few have made and lived to tell the tale' explained Lucas,

'But now children no more questions as it's time...I have packed you each a small sack with enough food to keep you going on the rest of your way, I have given you each one of the Lanterns from the courtyard but they are just normal lanterns to you as you need to learn their characters and let them become attached to you, I can give you no directions on where you need to go but can only ask that you make your own choices from now on and please above all else....choose the right path'.

'That easy then!!' Laughed Harvey as he felt they were on an impossible journey and likely to come into harm,

'Shut up Harv...' hissed Daniel as he stepped forward towards Lucas and thanked him for everything he had done,

'Please follow me now children, the UnderLand awaits and you must go now, follow me and I will lead you to the beginning of the final journey' Off Lucas strode to a side door in the room, he tugged it open and walked down the stairs into the darkened room below, beckoning the children forward to follow him as he lit a lantern which shone his shadow onto the wall making him seem even larger, he pulled back a group of boxes stacked against the wall and whispered at the wall not loud enough for the children to hear and the wall groaned, creaked and clicked as it opened up in front of them all to reveal the start of a tunnel which stretched as far as the eye could see,

'Welcome to the UnderLand children...' beamed Lucas as he gestured the children to the entrance of the tunnel.

'Y..you want us to go in there??' Lillie asked nervously as she didn't feel safe seeing how deep it went and just how dark it seemed,

'It's fine...' Lucas said, doing his best to reassure the children, 'I promise you...These tunnels are as safe as any other place in this land, No one knows they are here, Now you must go inside and begin what must end',

'Are there any dangerous creatures in the tunnels though?, I don't fancy being somethings dinner!' Harvey said in a scared but jokey tone,

'There may be a few creatures down there but nothing that will harm you, you have my word on that' Lucas smiling as wide as his mouth would allow him, revealing his oversized teeth to the children who just stared at him in amazement,

'Blimey Dan have you seen the size of those!!' Harvey sniggered at the size of Lucas's teeth which to him looked like a row of dirty old spades.

Daniel told Harvey to be quiet as he just stared straight ahead, looking deep into the blackness of the tunnel in front of him, he turned to Lucas who was trying to move the children along, knowing this might be the last chance he had to speak to him felt he needed to ask one more question,

'So we just need to follow the tunnel to wherever it takes us and it will lead us to my father?'.

'It will lead you where you need to be Daniel, as I said the path can only be chosen by you and you alone, please children I must insist you go now, every second longer you are standing here means your presence is felt more and more'.

So as the children made their way one by one into the start of the tunnel they each said goodbye to Lucas as they went past,

Lillie smiled as she turned towards the entrance, looked straight into Lucas's eyes and said,

'Thank you Lucas, for all you've done, I hope we will see you again soon'

'I'm sure our paths may cross sometime in the future Lillie, and may you find what your heart is showing you' Lucas smiled and waved at Lillie as she stepped further into the darkness,

'Yeah, what she said…' Harvey didn't bother looking back but just threw an arm up, kind of waving as he set off after her,

'Goodbye Henry…' smirked Lucas, softly replying to Harvey as he drifted off into the blackness of the tunnel,

Daniel just stood inside the entrance looking at Lucas, kind of knowing they may never meet again,

'Thank you Lucas, it's been a pleasure meeting you, and thank you for the help you gave us last night, I'm so glad Lydia was right about you',

'The pleasure was all mine Master Daniel, now go and become your future, I just hope that you fulfil your potential' Lucas gestured Daniel towards him and placed his hand inside his pocket, pulling out a small bottle with some sort of powder inside it,

'This is for you, the contents of this bottle are designed to cause a distraction if you ever come into any harm, please take care and good luck on your journey Daniel',

'Thank you Lucas….I..I just hope that what we find from here on in is right for us, I need answers...so many questions to ask' He added as he started the journey into the darkness of the tunnel.

'Hold on Bucks I'm coming..' Daniel said as he walked further into the tunnel looking for Lillie and Daniel, Just as he started he heard the clunk of the locks in the wall turning, he turned round and was met with blackness as the hole in the wall was no more.

Daniel raced off into the tunnel, hearing Lillie and Harvey talking to each other, Lillie had lit her lantern now and was shining the path ahead so they could see what was in here, they were surrounded by nothing but stone walls, constructed in such a way as to simply show the path forwards.

On the walls were drawings of what looked like locals from Erwin and beautiful paintings of the town, seemingly drawn from memory.

It seemed that no one had been down here for a while as webs filled the corners of the walls, as the children moved further on dust from the floor swirled round their ankles like a dancing ballerina.

'Have you seen these drawings??, they are beautiful aren't they' Lillie ran her hand over them to see how fresh they were,

'What are they supposed to be of do you think?' Asked Harvey as he stared at the paintings long and hard,

'Well they look like the town to me, from what we have already seen I mean....'.

'In the middle of one picture which was of the town itself, you could clearly see the House of a Hundred Lights, all its features visible to the children, the courtyard surrounded by the numerous rooms there, the shape of the building itself looking like a triangle surrounded by the circle shape of the town.

'It's so beautiful...wonder who painted these' Lillie smiled at the sheer beauty of what she was seeing.

'Whoever it was must have been down here a very long time!!' Daniel looked at each painting very closely when he spotted the initials S.R on every one of the paintings.

'Someone's put their initials on here guys, S.R, I wonder who they belong to?'

'Dunno Dan, I just want to get out of here..feeling a bit claustrophobic now' Harvey kept close to Daniel as they made their way along the tunnels beneath the town, every sound was amplified by the walls of the tunnels which scared Harvey just a bit more with each noise.

'Can you hear that?....and there it is again, sounds like someone whispering to me!!' Harvey stopped dead in his tracks, pulling Daniel back with him,

'Get off Harv, I can't hear anything apart from you moaning and whining, Lillie can you hear anything?' asked Daniel as he was now getting slightly fed up of Harvey and his chattering teeth behind him.

Lillie then all of a sudden stopped walking, held up her lantern and squinted to look into the distance,

'Shhh....' Lillie waving her hand at both of them to be quiet,

'W..what is it....is something there?' Harvey backed up against the wall as if he was part of it,

'Shhhhh, can't you hear that, because I can!!' Lillie continued,

'What can you hear Lils??, Is something going to eat us?' Daniel bravely stood beside Lillie, ready to defend her from whatever it was she was talking about,

'I said quiet....It's definitely saying something.....sounds like.....Harvey..is..a..big..useless..idiot' Laughed Lillie out loud as Daniel smirked at her playing a trick on Harvey who was stood against the wall still trying to hide until it sunk in that Lillie was winding him up,

'Oh ha blooming ha Lillie, thanks for scaring me like that!!, you're so going to get it back I promise you!!!' Harvey angrily said as he stormed past Lillie, barging her as he went along the tunnel, muttering to himself about revenge.

Daniel and his sister were laughing at Harvey as they carried on through the tunnels. They started talking about meeting their father and what might be happening with them,

'I hope our father wants us around sis, and I hope Bucksy is safe, I miss him so much, hope he isn't injured or anything' Daniel hoped that maybe Bucksy was safe and had found his way to his father's side,

'I'm sure we will be fine Daniel' Lillie replied, trying her best to reassure her brother, 'I have a good feeling about this, don't know how but I just do, as for that dog of yours I'm sure he's ok, he's big and strong and too much of a scaredy cat to want to get into trouble here, now come on let's go find that idiot friend of yours before he hurts himself'

So as they picked up the pace they could still hear Harvey's voice muttering to himself somewhere in the distance so Daniel, who was a bit worried Harvey might get lost, called out,

'Harv...Harvey...slow down mate, we don't want to get lost in here'

But Harvey didn't answer back, he must of been too far ahead to hear Daniel shouting, a rushing sound could be heard ahead of where they were which may have been the reason why Harvey couldn't hear them,

Lillie turned her head to the side and craned her neck forward slightly trying to guess what the noise was and where it was coming from

'That sounds like water Daniel...maybe a waterfall or something, this way....come on let's go',

'A waterfall inside here?, that sound odd to me sis...hope Harvey's ok and not fallen in, he can't swim!!' Daniel scurried off after his sister who seemed to be running rather fast lately,

'Lils...stop!!' panted Daniel as he eventually caught up with his sister who had stopped sharply in front of him by what seemed the edges of a pool of water, he put his hands on his knees trying to catch his breath, Lillie was standing there with her mouth open wide as she was met with a sight as stunning as anything she had ever seen.

They had come across a large opening in the tunnel, bigger than any of the tunnels they had been in before, the room was round in shape with tall warrior type statues curving round the sides of the pools of water which were directly ahead of them, as if watching over this place.

'Look at this Daniel...' she gasped as the sight of not one but two waterfalls in front of them, completely see through and glistening from the light her lantern was giving off.

The waterfalls seemed to be coming from high up above them from two separate holes in the roof of the tunnel, cascading down into its own pool of water, a small path went between the waterfalls which meant that this was the way they were meant to go. It seemed to be hiding something behind each of the streams of water.

As they made their way along the small path laid out before them Daniel reached out his hands and ran them through the water,

'Oh wow this water's so warm Lillie...It feels strange to me, like no water I've ever felt before' Daniel let the water run over his hands then pulled them out, the water itself ran off his hands slowly unlike the water back home, and when there was no more left on his hands they were bone dry,

'How strange...it does feel kind of...a bit slimy?' questioned Lillie as she examined the water running off her hands now,

'My hands are dry...not a trace of water on them, best not drink it though Daniel, who knows where it came from'

As they got closer to the other side of the pathway they both looked down into the water and were met with the most crystal clear water they had ever seen, a seemingly bottomless hole which held no signs of life.

They both stopped to admire the beauty of the water, crouching down beside the water's edge when Daniel all of a sudden saw his reflection change to that of an older man dressed in what looked like the clothes of a warrior, within a few seconds it had changed back to his present self.

'Woah!!!...Lillie did you see that?, My reflection in the water changed...I just saw what looked like me but a lot older, then it just vanished' Daniel was reaching out to grab his sister who was reaching for him also,

'Mine changed too Daniel...I saw myself in the most beautiful clothes, and holding a child. What is this place??'

'I don't know sis but let's keep going, I'm sure we'll find out soon enough, we need to find Harvey before he gets even more lost' Daniel snapped back into reality as he knew Harvey couldn't be that far away.

As they walked past the end of the waterfalls they were met with three paths, they all looked exactly the same.

'These must be the paths Lucas was telling us about, and how we must choose our own path...But which one??...and where is Harvey??' Daniel stood there trying to think about which path he felt the strongest pull towards,

'HARVEY....Harvey? Can you hear me??' shouted Daniel at the top of his voice.

A very faint shout of 'YES' could be heard from the tunnels ahead of them.

'Harv...which one are you in?? Stay where you are and we'll come to you mate, don't touch anything either' Daniel gestured to Lillie to listen at the first tunnel,

'Harvey are you in the first one??' she shouted as loud as she could,

'First one....trouble...wait....' came the faint reply from what sounded like Harvey some distance in the tunnel.

'What did he just say? Is he in trouble?....Daniel, sounds like he's in this one...come on let's go' Lillie shouted as she started off into the first tunnel after Harvey.

'Lillie wait for me!!' shouted Daniel as he knew he couldn't let anything happen to Harvey, he shot off in hot pursuit of his sister, he could hear faint shouting coming from in the distance, he caught sight of Lillie's lantern just up ahead, she had stopped because the tunnel split off in two separate directions,

'Why have you stopped??' Daniel asked

'Quiet...' Lillie added quickly,

'Why??...what can you hear?' Daniel was tugging at his sister's shoulder, trying to get her full attention,

'Shhhh...I can't hear anything now...I don't know which way to go Daniel' Lillie stood at the entrance to the tunnels in complete silence hoping for a sign of some kind but not a thing.

Only the faint dripping of water could be heard coming from ahead of them.

All of a sudden what sounded like loud voices in the first tunnel drifted up to Lillie and Daniel followed by the sound of a high pitched scream,

'Yaaaaaa..leave..help...' Lillie couldn't make out what was being said but it sounded like trouble.

'Come on let's g.......' Lillie went to move, what followed was a loud 'BOOM' as a flash of light and a rush of wind tore through the tunnel towards them, then it all went black.

Chapter Twelve
A Detour To Safety

Staggering to his feet slowly Daniel felt uneasy as he searched for something to help him get to his feet, as he did his vision was slightly blurry and his hearing was fuzzy.

He sat against a pile of boulders that had come down from the tunnel wondering what had just happened then he remembered Lillie was there with him, she was lying face down on the floor of the tunnel not moving so he sat down beside her and turned her over.

'Lillie...wake up..please' he begged as he lifted his sister's head up onto his legs, looking down at Lillie's face which had a few scratches all over it but no signs of anything worse than that,

'Please sis...I need you, don't be hurt too bad' almost in tears now as he held her tight in his arms,

'Mmmbbhhhh...' came the sound from under his arms as Daniel looked down at Lillie, he took his arms off her head in surprise as she opened her eyes,

'I said...get off my face you lump....' Lillie sat up, gasping for air as Daniel had nearly suffocated her with his arms covering her head,

'Are you ok?' he asked looking for any other signs of injury,

'No I think I'm ok, what about you?' Lillie spun her brother round so she could check he was ok also,

'Apart from a pain in my arm I think I'm ok sis, I'm more worried about Harvey being ok...OH NO...he was on the other side of that blast!!!, we need to get to him' Daniel was panicking now as his best friend was somewhere on the other side of the wall of rock in front of him with who knows what.

He started scrabbling at the rocks, trying to move them but there were far too many for him alone, Lillie on the other hand had found what seemed like some sort of escape route caused by the blast, a beam of light shone into the tunnel lighting it up as if showing them the way,

'Daniel...come over here quick, I think there's a way out of here' she shouted to him as further rumblings could be heard all around them now,

'Where does it go sis?, does it lead out?' Daniel's eyes slowly adapted to the light as he could see that the escape route seemed to lead them up to the surface but it was quite a climb,

'I don't know where it actually goes but it's better than being down here, plus Harvey is up here somewhere and we need to find him' Lillie had already started the long climb up the mountain of rocks that seemed to be acting like a ladder for her as she shouted down to Daniel to hurry up,

'Come on Daniel...we need to go now, its safe I promise you'

Daniel stood there for a minute or so looking around to see if he could spot any other way out apart from climbing up what looked like to him the biggest mountain he'd ever seen,

'Errr I'll be up in a minute sis...' He nervously called up to his sister who was making good ground on the climb up,

Lillie stopped to look back down at her brother who seemed to scared to move,

'Daniel come on. Please, before this whole place collapses' just as she said that the ground around Daniel started to shake and rumble,

Daniel leapt up onto the rocks like a rock climber, climbing as fast as he had ever done, he caught up with his sister who was waiting on a small ledge for him,

'Told you to hurry up' she laughed as she could see the sheer look of terror on his face now,

'Shut up you!!' he replied, shaking slightly from what had just happened,

'We should be out soon Daniel, just follow me, do exactly as I do and we will be out of here in no time' Lillie slowly started to climb again, slowly this time so that she could see how close her brother was,

'I'm right behind you, not the best view so keep going please' Daniel said, looking for the same place to put his hands and feet that his sister had just done,

'We're almost there Daniel...Just a little further now' Lillie climbed up the last few feet and out into the brilliant sunlight which was beaming down on them, she turned round to look for her brother who was almost at the top, when one of the rocks he was standing on gave way and he lost his footing causing him to start slipping downwards into the darkness below,

'WOOOAAAHHH' he cried but quick as a flash a hand reached down to stop him from falling.

'Got you bro...' Lillie smiled as she had reached in to grab hold of her brother's arm just as he slipped, she pulled him up and out of the hole and they fell back onto the safety of the grassy field they had now found themselves in.

'That was close!!, thanks sis, I owe you one' smiled Daniel as looked at Lillie who was puffing away,

'You owe me more than one Daniel trust me. She laughed as they both tried to catch their breath for a moment, then it dawned on them that there was no sign of Harvey,

'Sis, get up!!!, where's Harv??, did you see him up here when you climbed out??' Daniel was panicking at the thought of losing his friend,

'I was too busy saving you to worry about him, he can't be far, I am a bit worried about the noises I heard from the tunnel though, I hope it wasn't him shouting' replied Lillie who was now scouring the woods around them for a sign of Harvey.

'Look Lillie, over there' pointed Daniel who had seen something dangling off of a branch at the entrance to the woods,

'It looks like his jacket to me!!' Daniel pulled off the piece of clothing that was attached to the tree branch and read the label,

'Harvey Jones, aged twelve years.. This is his alright sis!!, where is he? This is all we need!!'.

'Come on Daniel we have to find him, I have a bad feeling about this...'
Lillie grabbed her brother's arm as them slowly made their way into the
woods on the hunt for Harvey,

'HARVEYYYY....HARV, ANSWER ME' shouted Daniel as they searched
the path in front of them for any more clues on what had happened to him,

'NUMBSKULL....WHERE ARE YOU HIDING NOW??' Lillie shouted then
told Daniel to shush so she could listen for any noises that might sound like
Harvey's voice, but no sound came back.

Daniel spotted something just up ahead and raced off to pick it up,

'It's his shoe!!' exclaimed Daniel as he held it up,

'How do you know it's his shoe Daniel?' asked Lillie,

'Because it blooming stinks, he has a strange smell about him!!',

Lillie laughed at Daniel's response, as she did she then saw that the path
ahead had been disturbed recently,

'I think he's gone this way...but what has got him?, come on Daniel let's go
find him' Lillie felt that this was the way forward but caution was needed in
case anything was going to take them too, and off they went, following the
path of broken branches in front of them, hoping that it would lead to
Harvey.

Harvey felt rather odd as his eyes slowly opened, he felt his head spinning
and his face felt puffy, he could hear voices in front of him but could only
make out blurred faces, they were speaking to one another about him,
muffled sentences as Harvey was still feeling groggy,

'Is this him?' one of the voices asked,

'Not the one we want but a good replacement, boss will be pleased!' said
the other voice, then footsteps were heard coming towards Harvey, he
could hear a tapping sound and someone breathing heavily, he could just
about make out the outline of a hooded figure standing what seemed close
to his face, his breath smelling foul like a thousand year old sandwich,
Harvey kept falling in and out of consciousness, waking every so often to
the sound of more voices all around him,

'Have you done it to this little one?' a voice excitedly asked, a deeper voiced replied sounding rather content now,

'Yes it is done, the spells have been added…remember that we have to stick to the plan', Harvey felt even more strange as he tried to fight off whatever it was that had been done to him,

'Now...Let's clear his mind, so he can't remember this...' the deeper voice cackled, then just as Harvey was about to blackout he heard some sort of spell being cast and at that point it all went dark.

He woke a while later, opened his eyes again, rubbed them but this time he could see clearly, he was stuck in some sort of cage in the middle of some woods, looking around he could hear some sort of animal noise, a barking sound which he hadn't heard before,

'Where the heck am I?....How did I get here?' He muttered to himself as he sat there trying to figure out what was going on and where he actually was. In front of him was the embers of a fire, surrounding that were logs that had been placed as if made for seating, Harvey tried tugging at the cage door, hoping it might swing open and he would be free but it wouldn't budge.

He swung around when from somewhere in the distance he could hear the same voices talking to each other that he had heard earlier but he couldn't make out what they were saying this time, he could hear a lot of laughing coming from their direction,

'I need to get out of here…' He began panicking slightly at the thought of whoever it was coming back to do something terrible to him,

He was trying everything he could to get the door open but it still wouldn't budge, then he noticed something shining from just outside the cage on the floor in front of him, it was slightly hidden by some leaves.

Harvey reached his arm out of the cage, stretching every part of him to make his arms as long as they could go then he managed to grab it,

'It's a key!!..' He breathed a huge sigh of relief as he held it out in front of him, glistening in the light shining through the trees onto his prison,

'This has got to open the door!!' Harvey excitedly said as he slid his arm out of the cage and onto the lock that was holding the door shut, he fumbled with the key as he tried to slide it into the keyhole, dropping it every few seconds,

'Oh come on!!!... just get in there will you!' starting to panic slightly as he could still hear the voices talking some way off in the distance, worrying all the time that they might come back to find him escaping.

Harvey was still trying to release himself from the cage but unbeknown to him he was being carefully watched, In the bushes far behind the cage a figure could be seen buried deep in the middle, a pair of eyes could be seen, yellow in colour, almost as dark as the setting sun.

They didn't move their line of sight from what Harvey was doing as he battled to free himself, then the figure whispered quietly while waving its bony hand in Harvey's direction.

'Te Libero...', The figure then slowly disappeared out of sight back into the blackness of the bush.

And with that the lock sprung open with Harvey still holding the key in it, unaware that it wasn't actually him that had undone it, he swung the door open but quickly grabbed it before it banged against the side of the cage,

'I'm free!!!' he said happily before realising he might still be heard, then turned his head to scout the surrounding area to see if anyone had heard him, but nothing could be heard now even the talking he had heard in the distance had stopped.

Slowly and ever so quietly Harvey crawled out of the cage door spotting what looked like a path between the trees in front of him now and leading out of wherever it was he was in, he stood still for a few seconds until he felt it was safe to make a dash for it, took one last look around then he set off at such a pace into the undergrowth and down the makeshift path hoping that it might lead somewhere safer than where he had ended up.

Back at the area where Harvey had been held the hooded figure suddenly appeared from the back of the bushes cackling away to itself, it's hood hiding whatever evil face lurked underneath, standing there just staring as he could see in the distance Harvey running away,

147

'Ahh excellent...' The figure clasped its hands together, rubbing them in such a way as if it was pleased,

'The plan has been put into place....the spells have started...soon we will know everything we need to know about their whereabouts...Master will be so pleased' The hooded figure seemingly floated off past the bushes and into the distance still cackling to itself as it disappeared out of sight.

'HARVEY.....WHERE ARE YOU?' came the cry from Daniel as he stood at the edge of what looked like a thick part of the forest, he could hear what sounded like whispers coming from all around him but none of them sounded like Harvey's voice,

'Turn back....' said one whisper

'Too much danger....' another one floated around Daniel's head and seemed to float away,

'Where are we?' Daniel asked himself, looking for any sign of where Harvey had disappeared to, just as he went to move off Lillie came stumbling through the trees behind him, her clothes ripped slightly and her hair all over the place,

'Have you found him sis..?' asked Daniel hopefully,

'No sign of him Dan...I've been all over these woods and can't see any trace of him now' Lillie puffed as she tried to catch her breath,

'But I have been hearing lots of what sounds like people whispering to me..' she continued

'Me too Lillie. The whispers seemed to be warning me about this place' Daniel's shoulders seemed to drop at the thought that something bad had happened to his friend.

Lillie tried her best to comfort her brother who she could see was getting slightly upset, she stood next to a group of bushes with a tree beside them which she had to rest against after her exhausting search earlier,

'Don't worry Dan I'm sure Harvey will turn u.....' her sentence hadn't finished when all of a sudden something came crashing through the bushes right next to she was standing taking her completely by surprise, the person collapsed in a heap on the floor gasping for air.

148

'Harvey!!!' shouted Daniel as he realised his best friend had just landed right by his feet huffing and puffing away, Harvey just lay there looking up at the sky for a few seconds then suddenly sprang to his feet still panting and trying to speak,

'Huuu..Huuu...have to go...Huuu...being chased....' he managed to get a few words out before struggling for air again,

'Eh?, Chased?, by who Harv?, who's after you and where have you been?' Daniel quizzed his friend hoping he could tell them what was going on,

'The woods....cage...Huuu Huuu...people...got to go...now!!!' Harvey frantically waved his arms as he knew he was struggling for air so Lillie decided that the best option was to get out of there,

'Let's do as he says then Dan, we will have to help him though, you get under one arm and I'll get under the other one' and with that they both hoisted Harvey up off the floor and made their way back along the trail they had just came from until the eventually came to a path that split off in two different directions,

'Oh great...which path is it sis?' Daniel asked as if Lillie would know where to go,

'I don't know!!, weren't you paying attention to where we had come from when we came through here earlier?' she replied angrily

'Jeez I was only asking Lillie!!, Ok then we'll go this way' Daniel pointed to the path that went off to the left and they made their way along it, pushing branches and twigs out of the way as they battled their way along it,. Hoping that this was the right path.

The path they had chosen seemed different to the one they were on before, all the while they could hear whispers making their way through the woods, swirling around them like wind,

'So close.....be wary...' came on whisper which blew straight through Daniel's ears and off into nothingness just as the others had done before,

'Follow...follow' came another which swirled between the group then vanished.

149

Harvey was still feeling the effects of whatever it was that had happened to him earlier but he needed to stop for a sit down.

'Stop...Please guys...I'm shattered' He begged with them as they came into a clearing some way up the path, they helped Harvey sit down on a fallen log before feeling the need to question him.

'Did anyone else hear that?...sounded like someone whispering to me!!' Harvey looked at Daniel and Lillie who were both standing there, arms folded looking straight at him,

'Wh..What are you guys staring at??' he answered them quizzically as if nothing had happened,

'Never mind that Harv, we want to know what happened to you, you were babbling about a cage or something.' Daniel needed to know what had gone on earlier, Lillie on the other hand just knew something bad was happening,

'More to the point, what happened to you after the explosion in the tunnels, I could hear your girly screeching then the next thing I know some kind of bomb had gone off and we were nearly buried back there',

'I don't remember any of that at all!!, I only remember being in a cage in the woods, don't know how I got there or anything!!' Harvey racking his brains to try and answer Lillies question but whoever it was who held him captive had wiped his memory, for a reason.

'So you're telling me we were nearly buried alive in the tunnels and I seemed to have been taken by someone for them to do heaven knows what to me!, Urrgh I feel so nasty!!' Harvey's face dropped at the thought of someone possibly hurting him while he was in the cage in the woods,

'Let's hope they knocked some sense into you then Harvey!!' laughed Lillie as knew it would annoy him.

'Leave him alone sis!!' barked Daniel as he sat next to his friend now, 'Any way, what is it we are doing here?, I'm having a hard time remembering anything, my brain is still spinning' Harvey sat with his head in his hands trying his best to piece together the events of the day,

'Don't you have to have a brain for it to be able to spin!!' laughed Lillie again and watched as Harvey became more annoyed by her comments, a glint of rage burning in his eyes as for a split second he wanted to have a go at Lillie, he felt the urge to try and stand up to confront her but something was stopping him, a small voice whispering inside his mind 'Soon....' came the sound from deep inside Harvey's head, he didn't flinch when he heard it as if dismissing it completely from his thoughts,

'Once again...shut up sis!!' Daniel was now getting fed up with his sister constantly going on at Harvey,

'You can see he's still not with it properly, so just leave him alone OK!!!' Daniel's words were filled with a tinge of anger towards his sister, he was getting more and more fed up with every passing second,

'Blimey Daniel...don't go over the top, I'm only messing around!!' the blunt reply from Lillie caused them all to stop speaking to one another.

Daniel was focussing on making sure Harvey was ok now, sitting next to him on the log asking him any question to try and jog his memory, Lillie had decided to go off for a wander to clear her head muttering to herself as she strode through the woods, disappearing from sight.

'Wonder where she's gone' Harvey asked Daniel as they had both watched her walk off without even bothering to call her back, knowing there was something sinister out in the woods,

'Dunno Harv...and at the minute I don't really care, she's always on your case and I've had enough, so as far as I'm concerned she can get herself lost!!' Daniel's answer threw Harvey aback slightly as he hadn't really hear him talk about his sister with such anger in his voice.

'Don't get too upset with her Dan, if we are going to get out of here we all need to stay together. Three heads are better than one I'd say' Harvey smiled as he looked straight at his friend who seemed to have a slightly worried look on his face now, knowing his sister was out there somewhere without him by her side.

'I just hope we find what we are looking for Harv, I mean, as well as hopefully finding my father, I want to find Bucksy....It's strange though as I haven't really thought about him that much lately. It's as if I'm meant to forget about him but I can't.' Daniel was now sitting bolt upright with all these thoughts running through his head now like someone had turned a tap on inside his mind, pictures of people he had forgotten about, people he had never met and images of places he had never seen before.

'It's odd...' He continued, 'since we've been here I've started to feel like this place is growing on me...I mean like I'm starting to feel part of this place',

'Come to mention it Dan, I've been having odd feelings lately too, it's like the longer we are here the more we feel accepted by the land, it's hard to explain but that's the only way I can put it' Harvey knew exactly how Daniel felt and they both felt a sense of safety for the first time. Just as Daniel was about to speak Lillie came crashing back through the woods to where they were sitting.

'You both need to come see this!!!' She smiled excitedly, barely able to contain her excitement,

'What is it now sis...I'm not really interested by whatever it is you've found now!!' Daniel dismissed his sister but she knew he would want to see what it was that she had seen.

'No trust me you'll really want to come see this, I think I might have found what we are supposed to be looking for!!' Lillie pulled Daniel to his feet tugging at his arms, wanting him to follow her.

'You've seen our father?, Bucksy?' Daniel questioned Lillie constantly knowing it was something important enough for her to want to come back to find them,

'Not quite but I think it's the next best thing Daniel!!, Come on we must hurry, I promise it will be worth it' Lillie helped Harvey to his feet so it must of been rather important for her to want him to see this too.

'Can't you just tell us please, I'm fed up of walking now, my feet are killing me..I'm hungry...I smell..' Harvey moaned as he was pulled along through the woods, crashing through branches as Lillie pulled him along at such a speed that his feet nearly left the floor,

'LILLIE WAIT!!' shouted Daniel as he struggled to keep up with his sister, then as Daniel spotted Lillie and Harvey standing right at what looked like a flight of huge steps in front of them they were met with the sight of a huge looking building looming over them. They all gasped at the same time as they realised they were one step nearer to the truth.

'Castle Erwin!!!' Daniel shouted excitedly, they reached the edge of the steps and as they started to climb up Harvey was just behind them looking up, all of a sudden a strange purple looking colour filled his eyes completely.

Chapter Thirteen
The Home From Home

Looming over their heads stood the Castle Erwin, a huge battle scarred looking structure that took their breath away.

As they climbed the huge steps which led directly up to the castle it seemed that it was tall enough to reach the sky and beyond, its sheer size cast a huge shadow over the surrounding land and over the town of Erwin which sat there like speck on the landscape due to the sheer vastness of the castle. Five broad, round towers can be seen surrounding the castle, they seem to reach twice the height of the castle walls and are connected to them connected by reinforced thick heavy walls made of silver stone.

Large looming windows were scattered generously around the huge walls with smaller windows around the lowest part of the castle, along with what looked like small holes set at different areas along the walls, possibly lookout posts of some kind.

A great gate with enormous wooden doors and large protects those in need of aid in this hard to get to mountain pass. Across the gate was the shape of a huge shield which would split in two when the gates were opened, and on the shield there was what looked like the figure of a huge winged bird stretching across its width of. The castle doors seemed like the only way to access the castle but it's not the only way in as with most castles of this size there would normally be secret passages used by those inside the castle for whatever they were needed for.

Carts, boxes, tents and various trade goods are stacked were packed outside the castle, ready to be moved on. This castle has stood the test of time so far and despite knowing some very rough times which were getting more frequent as the years rolled by but the castle still stands as proud and protected as it has done, it looks like it will do so for many years to come with aid of a little more new protection.

'Are we there yet guys?. I'm shattered!!' Harvey moaned as he knew he couldn't go much further,

'Come on Harv it's not that far really, time we started working off some of that food!!' laughed Daniel who was almost bounding up the steps ahead of him, desperate to get to the castle,

'It's alright for you Mr 'I'm Number One', we can't get up there as fast as you so I'm sorry if I'm stopping you from getting there any quicker!!' Harvey seemingly getting slightly annoyed with Daniel with every step the trio too.

'Oooo what's up with him?' Lillie laughed as she knew Harvey wasn't the best climber in the world,

'You can be quiet as well Lillie!, Not everyone is as good at stuff as you, jeez you're both getting on my nerves now!' Harvey sniffed as he struggled to climb the huge steps upwards, not letting Daniel or Lillie see his face which was seemingly buried in his top, his eyes still an odd looking colour.

'Let's just stop talking to him sis...at least we can't annoy him if we don't speak, anyway it's not that far now, I can see the top!!' Daniel pointing to the top of the steps which seemed to level out onto grassland and on towards the castle itself,

'Good don't speak to me!!!' came the whimpering sound from behind them as they both decided to push on ahead and wait for him at the top.

As they finally reached the last stone step they sat down together, watching as Harvey struggled with each step but the land itself caught their eyes, they could see over to the woods where they had just come through and down to the town of Erwin which looked so small in comparison to when they were actually there, it looked so silent from up by the castle too.

A stunning sunny haze filled the sky, bright colours bounced off of every part of the land, their faces filled with a warm feeling making them forget about the climb they had just had to do,

'Wow Lillie this place is so beautiful!!, look how far you can see!!' Daniel pointing out to the horizon where what looked like the sea sitting there like a painting on a canvas,

'It's stunning Daniel...I hope it stays like this though, from what Lucas told us this place is getting worse, I feel like we are here for its protection' Lillie smiled slightly at the thought of staying here for whatever purpose they were needed for.

'Think we need to get a move on though, let's help happy up the last steps then we can get going' Daniel leapt up from the stone step and thrust a hand out to Harvey who was now up with them,

'Thanks mate, I thought I was going to fall!!' Harvey laughed as they pulled him up the last step, Daniel and Lillie both looked at each other puzzled at the way Harvey was with them now,

'So what was with the attitude towards us a minute ago Harv?, thought you didn't want to talk to us'

'Eh?, what are you going on about Dan?, I don't remember saying a word to you!!' Harvey puzzled look seemed to confuse them both as he stood in front of them smiling away now,

'You had a right go at us!!' Lillie said as Harvey looked even more lost now,

'Still not got a clue what you're on about Lillie!!!' Harvey replied as he marched off up the slight hill towards the castle doors whistling to himself happily,

'Come on then...' he shouted to the other two, waving his arm at them, gesturing them to join him at the top of the hill,

'Let's go see what's inside here then!' Harvey said as off he strode with Lillie and Daniel just staring at each other in utter disbelief at Harvey who seemed to have forgotten the attitude he gave them earlier.

As Daniel and Lillie eventually joined Harvey at the giant doors to the entrance of the castle they stood there in disbelief, the sheer size of the doors had them lost for words, Daniel took a few steps back as he thought he could see something familiar to him,

'What's the matter Daniel?, where are you going?' asked Lillie as she turned around and noticed a strange look on her brother's face, Daniel had pulled up the sleeve on his arm also and was looking at his birthmark then up at the giant doors then back again to his arm

'Ermmmm, I think you need to see this Lillie…' Daniel beckoned his sister over to look at what he could see.

'What is it?, what do you see?' she asked as Harvey also bounded over now,

'Well take a look at the birthmark on my arm..' he thrust his arm out so his hand was pointing upwards, held it out so they could all see it,

'Wow you've learnt how to point upwards Dan!!' laughed Harvey not really knowing what he was supposed to be looking at,

'Shut up Harvey..' Lillie reacted angrily, 'Yes Daniel, I can see your birthmark, but what else am I supposed to be seeing?'

Daniel tensed his arm as if to say 'look a bit harder',

'Look closely at the birthmark on my arm then look at the symbol on the doors..' hoping that Lillie would spot it.

Then finally the penny dropped, her eyes lit up brighter than ever before and a broad smile spread across her face,

'It matches!!!!, Oh Daniel I'm guessing we are where we need to be now!!, we've made it!!'

Harvey strode up, grabbed Daniel's arm hard, looked at it for a few seconds then without a flicker of emotion said,

'Looks like something my baby cousin would draw with a crayon!!...I mean it almost looks like that bird thing on the doors but to me it looks like a big splodge',

'Well thanks for that amazing input Harv!!' Daniel felt hurt that his friend couldn't see something so obvious, seeing as they were supposed to be the best of friends.

'So how do you think we get in there then?, I can't see any other way past those doors' Lillie scoured the entire front of the castle for signs of

157

another entrance just as Daniel walked towards the doors and banged on them as hard as he could.

Harvey ran to his friend shouting, trying to stop him from what he was doing,

'What are you doing that for??, what if they want to eat us or something!, I can't face being thought of as someone's free lunch again'

'Shut it Harv...I can't hear anything...' putting his hand over Harvey's mouth was never the nicest thing but he was desperate to listen for any kind of movement behind the doors,

'Well it looks like no one is home Dan, come on let's go, this place is giving me the creeps now, it's so eerie!!' Harvey tugged at his friend's arm hoping he could pull him away but Daniel was rooted to the spot, ear pressed up against the door, when all of a sudden a large 'clunking' sound could be heard from behind the doors, what sounded like a rusty lock of some kind turning itself until it opened with a thud, there seemed to be movement and noise now coming from deep behind the castle doors, the sound of footsteps filled the silent air now, the children slowly backed away from the doors as they heaved open little by little, a blinding light shone out from within which caused the children to shield their eyes from it.

They hadn't noticed that a soldier was walking out from between the open doors directly towards them, it was a soldier of double their size wearing what looked like full battle armour, a metal mask with deep dark eye holes hiding glowing yellow slit eyes covered its face as it stopped within a few feet of them, it's eyes seemingly slicing through them as they stood just staring right back not knowing whether to try and run or just accept whatever was going to happen,

'I...I...errr...th..think we are in trouble now!!' Harvey said as every part of his body was trembling at the thought of what this soldier might do to them.

Daniel just stood open mouthed staring at the soldier whose armour was glistening in the sun, It's mask bore the scars of many a battle by the look of it, deep scratches and dents covering the surface of the mask, Lillie, on the other hand, wasn't in the mood for any more games and stepped in

158

front of Daniel and marched up to the soldier not in the slightest bit scared, the soldiers head look downwards to where Lillie was now standing

'Look...whoever you are!!, We have been sent here on this journey by lots of people we have met along the way, we are all hungry, tired and above all else totally fed up!!. People are supposedly after us wanting to hurt us and all we want is answers. We didn't ask to come to Erwin, it just happened, so if you could please just tell us what you are and what you intend to do with us then that would be just....well super!!'

'Go Lillie!!!' Harvey shouted from his hidden position behind Daniel as he watched her wagging her finger at this giant person standing between them and safety.

'Is she trying to get us eaten or something?, Daniel go get her back before she gets hurt',

Daniel shouted to Lillie to step away from the soldier but she wouldn't listen

'Lillie please...I don't want you hurt, let me try' Daniel pleaded with his sister to get behind him but she refused so Daniel stepped in front of her and tried to grapple her away, in the scuffle Daniel's sleeves pushed up his arms to reveal his birthmark on his arm.

The soldier stooped down when he spotted it, wanting a closer look at what it was on Daniel's arm, then in a booming voice shouted as he turned back towards the castle doors,

'He has the mark!!!!, the boy has the mark' the soldier said rather excitedly,

'What's he going on about Dan? What mark?' came Harvey's reply as he stood there now totally confused by what was going on,

'The mark on my arm you plank!!!, you said your baby cousin could've drawn, this mark!!' as he thrust his arm right into Harvey's face to show him that the mark actually meant something to the guard standing before him.

'Ohhhh that one!!' as his cheeks flushed a crimson colour through embarrassment Harvey finally realised what all the fuss was about and smiled awkwardly at Daniel who now turned away from him to once again face the giant soldier standing there waving to someone in the castle doors to follow him out.

As Lillie and Daniel stood there slightly stunned with what was going on, through the mist coming from within the doors to the castle the figure of an older man appeared, limping slightly as he walked, a large cane in his hand helped him to balance himself.

'Who's this?..' questioned Harvey as Daniel's eyes were transfixed on this figure coming towards them

'Maybe this is your dad Dan….' he continued,

'Thought he'd be much younger, looks like he's been beaten up a lot too!!' Harvey had noticed the fact he was struggling to move properly.

As the figure drew closer they were met with the sight of an older man now standing in front of them, his face was shielded from them slightly by a hooded cloak but they could see that he was a lot older as his hand holding the cane was wrinkled and boney.

His long greying hair draped down past his chest from behind the hood and his breathing was shallow and rattley.

'Come...come forward boy…' the old man beckoned Daniel to step forward, he turned round to look at his sister who was urging him to go, 'Don't be shy boy...', he continued

'Go Daniel, see what it's all about, I seem to be getting a good feeling about this' Lillie smiled as she slowly stepped forward too, just behind her brother who slowly stepped up towards the old man.

'So...My soldier here seems to think you have the mark…' The old man smiled as he pulled his hood back slightly to reveal more of his face which was scarred and weathered,

'The mark?, you mean this thing on my arm...my birthmark' Daniel peeled back his sleeve to reveal what he thought was his birthmark and showed the old man who took his arm in his hand and looked at it in detail, his eyes squinting occasionally as he did so,

'Ahhh yes, this is definitely the mark…' smiling as he looked straight at Daniel,

160

'So what does this birthmark mean to you?, to me it's just a mark that's always been there' Daniel asked politely as the old man took a deep intake of breath before answering,

'This 'birthmark', as you call it, is a mark that is given to all young boy's after they are born, it's the emblem of Erwin, only a select few will have theirs still visible over time' The old man pulled the arm on his cloak back to reveal a slightly faded but still recognisable mark on his arm that was the same as the one on the doors and just like Daniel's also.

'The mark represents Power, Freedom and Knowledge..., you see there have only been a handful of people who possess or have possessed this very special mark over their entire life, and as you can see I am one of those people', the old man smiled at Daniel as he said this with the kind of look only a family member could share with you,

'And who might you be then?' Harvey piped up from behind the shoulder of Lillie who turned around glaring at him,

'Ahh yes...please forgive me' the old man cleared his throat before continuing,

'My name is King Tahlid Casborn, Ruler of the realm of Dioshea and Overseer of the Last Bells'

'Bit of a mouthful that' Harvey laughed, Lillie elbowed him in the ribs to stop him talking as she was getting fed up of his attitude now,

'Keep quiet Harvey!!, any more of that and I'll brain you' she warned him,

'Oooo, sorry!!' Harvey screwed his lip up as if to mock Lillie, followed by a rueful smile as if something strange was happening to him again,

'Please do go on, I'm sorry for our idiot friend at the back there' Lillie turned and threw Harvey the kind of glance that would normally bother him but he seemed slightly vacant,

'Well you see...' The old man cleared his throat once again 'it seems as if we have been expecting all three of you here at the castle, as I said before the mark is one that runs through our family...'

161

'Our family?..' Lillie screwed up her eyes slightly as if taken aback with what she was hearing,

'Yes...Our family...' the old man beckoned Lillie closer to him,

'You see I know who you two are now, in the past few days I have felt something strange within this land which made me aware of your being here, it's a feeling I hadn't felt in a very long time!!'

'So YOU'RE our father??' Daniel's face suddenly lit up as he had known there was some kind of connection here now, a feeling of them belonging in Erwin, a feeling that they were part of a bigger family,

'Not quite my boy, although you are part of this family along with your sister...Yes I know that you are both related my girl, I would be known to you as 'Grandfather' where you are from..' And with that he pushed back the hood of his cloak to reveal his face to the children, a huge smile spread across his slightly withered face.

Daniel took a step back as if wanting to take it all in, he was totally expressionless, not knowing whether to run away or run forwards, Lillie on the other hand let out a huge sigh of relief and smiled one of the biggest smiles she had ever shown, the old man beckoned her into his arms which she accepted and squeezed him so tight,

'Well young girl, you are a strong one aren't you!!' The old man laughed as he felt a tight grip around his waist which didn't want to let go, Lillies eyes filled with tears of happiness as she thought about all they had gone through to get here, not through choice though.

Daniel slowly walked towards the old man still a bit unsure of what was happening, so many questions filling his head right now, he stopped short of who he was told was his Grandfather,

'S..so that means that our father must be here somewhere...' Daniel's shoulders stiffened as he spoke,

'Well yes...you are correct...Lord Casborn, Your father and my son, does live here my boy, He has been ever desperate to find out where you disappeared to, It has been something that he has been hoping for ever since you were both young, a search that has taken its toll on him',

'You mean...It's actually him?...Our actual father?' Daniel seeking an answer to confirm what he was hoping for which the old man duly gave him,

'Haha, yes he IS your actual father my boy, and you will get to see him very soon I promise, but first we must go inside and I will explain further ok?' the old man put his arm out for Daniel to get under which he happily did, letting a smile fill his face and tears welling in his eyes,

'Errmmm...hello!!' came a voice from behind, 'what about me??, do I get to come in?' Harvey was standing there, hands on hips looking rather annoyed by them walking off and leaving him stood there alone,

'Ahh yes, the foolish friend...' the old man turned round laughing as he seemingly knew of Harvey and what he was like,

'Of course young man, please follow us but please be careful inside, this place is centuries old and isn't ready to fall down just yet'

Lillie let out a roar of laughter when she heard this making her hold her stomach tight,

'Haha it seems everyone here knows of you too Harvey, I bet this isn't the only place that sees what we see!!' She mocked Harvey even more as he just stood there looking red faced and angry,

'Do you know what..' Harvey said 'Think I'll stay out here instead of coming in with you, don't want to cramp your style or anything!!' 'Then stay there then you oaf, see if I care what happens to you!!' Lillie replied as she turned on her heels to join her Grandfather once again,

'No I'm only joking My dear boy, please join us inside, this does concern you too and anyway you don't want to stay out here too long in case something decides to have you as its lunch, there are a lot of roaming creatures here, all hunting for that one big feast!!' a glint appeared in the corner of King Casborns eye as he tried to scare Harvey into moving which he duly did.

Daniel had never seen his friend move so fast as he shot past them towards the open castle doors muttering to Daniel as he went past,

'Errrr I'll meet you in there Dan, bit of a toilet situation going on now!!'.

163

Daniel laughed at the sight of Harvey running off, Lillie just muttered how embarrassing he was as they made their way towards the doors of the castle, the winged bird emblem sitting proud on the doors as if on a constant look out for trouble.

As they got closer to the castle Daniel had to ask his grandfather a question about his family though,

'So I'm...sorry WE are going to meet our father here?'

'Yes my boy, and on his return here his endless search will be over, you see he has always dreamed of this day, the day he would get to see his children again, then the circle would well and truly be complete, nothing would ever break it apart again!' King Casborn smiled at the thought of his son being able to finally rest properly,

'You mean he isn't here right now?' asked Lillie

'I'm afraid he's out on...shall we say...castle business, but he should be back tomorrow by dawn, he has no idea you are here so I think a little surprise will be in order!!' laughed the King as they reached the doors to the castle.

'Oh, I do have one last question though' Daniel said as he stopped in his tracks,

'And that is?' The King replied,

' The reason we ended up here was because I was chasing my pet who I thought fell through some kind of hole, and now I can't find him, His name is Bucksy and he's a dog, black in colour with strange coloured eyes and he's my best friend, Have you seen him anywhere here?' Daniel asked inquisitively.

'Hmmm...' The King screwed up his eyes and tapped his bony finger on his hairy chin as he seemed deep in thought at what Daniel was asking,

'I think I might be able to help you there...I think I know who you are talking about, let's get you all settled here first though, then I can give you anything you need'

'So you have seen him??, you don't know how long I have been looking for him!, He's the only reason we are here' Daniel said excitedly at the thought of being reunited with his faithful friend after such a long time.

'Haha...Ok ok my dear boy, let's take that excitement down a little, we have much to talk about first, I promise you that you won't be disappointed. Come on let's get you both inside...now where has that friend of yours gone??' asked the King just as Harvey's head poked round the castle door looking rather distressed,

'Ermmmm, King...I really do need the bathroom now!!, where am I supposed to go, and please hurry!!' Harvey's face was turning a brighter shade of red as he was getting more and more desperate.

'Yes yes my boy, the guard will take you where you need to go and we will all meet in The Great Chamber after you have done whatever it is you are needing to do' The King smiled as they all disappeared off inside the castle doors which creaked and groaned shut behind them, all sorts of locks could be heard clicking into place from inside the doors, the castle was now locked down tight once again.

Deep within the forest below at the place where Harvey was held captive the cloaked figure stood totally still as if deep in thought, it seemed that whatever had been done to Harvey in the cage meant they had some kind of link to his mind, the figure was able to access Harvey's mind and see where he was and slowly manipulate his mind.

'Good...Good..yesssss, VERY good..' the figure cackled as it seemed as if he had seen something of importance from within Harvey mind.

With that it disappeared off into the dense woods before vanishing out of sight.

Chapter Fourteen
The Meeting

Inside the castle walls Lillie and Daniel were taken aback by just how big the grounds of the castle were, it seemed to stretch on for miles with plenty of buildings scattered around the edges of the walls bustling with chatter and laughing from within them. Heads could be seen poking out from around most of the doors as the King walked by with the children in tow.

In the middle of the castle grounds stood what looked like an open oval area with seating spread all around it, flags stood proud and flapping in the wind as if watching over what was inside, shouting could be heard from behind the closed gates which stopped anyone entering without permission, Two very large looking guards dressed in armour stood either side of the gates not moving a muscle.

'What's in there?' asked Daniel as they walked past the arena just as a loud roar went up from inside,

'That would be what we call the 'Proving Grounds' for our latest batch of new warriors….but that's nothing you need to worry about yet my boy, you see we aren't just a castle that protects this wonderful land we live in but we are providers of what you would call 'schooling…..',' Harvey groaned as he thought he had got away from trying to be taught about things he had no interest in, the King stopped, looked straight at Harvey as if to say 'stop talking',

'Sorry!!!..' mouthed Harvey who had now gone a nice shade of embarrassed red, The King continued what he was saying to the children who were seemingly very interested for once,

'As I was saying before I was rudely interrupted, every youngling here has to progress through our system to see how their future will turn out. Every person here has a purpose and will either stay here in some capacity, whether it be as a Guard, Warrior or even down to the task of cooking for all the people who live within these walls, depending on their outcome they could end up working down in the town at the bottom of the hill'

'Oh so it's like a city within a city!!' Lillie called out as the King smiled at her understanding of the castle and what goes on here,

'Yes my girl, we like to make everyone feel as valued in here as they would anywhere else but we do believe that every child has to go through the same process as everyone else to realise how important they are to this fine place' The King had a feeling he was getting through to the children now as they took in all that the castle had to offer,

'So if we are to stay here then you want us to go to school??' Asked Lillie as once again Harvey groaned out loud in unhappiness at the thought of having to go back to school.

'Oh fantastic!!, just when I thought we were free from school you go and throw this at me!!' Harvey threw his arms in the air with a distinct lack of respect towards the King and their culture,

'My dear boy...' The King put his hand on Harvey's shoulder and smiled 'This place provides a safe and structured learning for all the younglings to come away with the best possible future they can achieve. It keeps them safe from evil and allows them to learn about our past and what it means to us all, is this such a bad thing?'

'N..No..sir..I guess not' Harvey stared at the floor as the King carried on,

'Well then I hope you appreciate what I have tried to build here since I became King of Erwin!, I would give my last breath protecting this castle and all the people inside it and with the learning they are getting here I hope. No I KNOW they would do the same for each and every person behind these walls and beyond. So please afford me the respect that I deserve otherwise your stay here will be short lived, do you understand', Harvey was taken aback by the tone of which the King was talking to him, he started to feel slightly awkward with everyone staring at him, then all of

167

a sudden his whole personality changed, his eyes flickered as if some sort of spell was taking him over,

'Oh I'm so sorry that I might not be able to stay here and learn about whatever rubbish it is we are supposed to be taught, I'm sorry that I'm not Daniel, we can't all be perfect now can we, I'm sorry I'll never be a great warrior and I'm sorry we ever came to this place!!' with that Harvey shrugged his shoulders in anger making the King's arm fall to his side and off he ran towards the nearest open door slamming it behind him as he did so,

'Har....' Daniel shouted in anger at his friend showing a complete lack of respect towards his new found family, he went to set off after him but the King put his hand across Daniel's chest to stop him,

'It's ok my boy, just let him go, I can understand how this must be affecting you all differently' Daniel sighed and stepped back not noticing that the King was deep in thought, his eyes squinting slightly like he knew something didn't feel right, stroking his greying beard as he stood there. Just as he was about to say something the door which Harvey went into swung open with a bang against the wall and a sheepish Harvey walked out looked straight at Daniel and sounding rather embarrassed said,

'Th..that's a storage cupboard...',

'Harvey!!....' Daniel confronted his friend finally 'What's the matter with you??'

'What do you mean?' He answered back

'I can believe how disrespectful you're being to them, It's not the first time either, I'm getting fed up of all this now, It's about time you grew up a little' Daniel prodding Harvey in the chest in anger,

'Ow!!!!...That blooming hurts, why are you doing that!!' Harvey pushed Daniel's hand away from him hoping to reason with him,

'Because of what you've just said you idiot!!, don't you remember?, or are you acting stupid again!' Daniel replied getting angrier by the second at Harvey's seemingly awful lack of memory,

168

'Eh?? I'm so totally lost mate, I just remember standing in that cupboard thing for some reason, I haven't got any clue what I'm supposed to have said so get off my back OK!!' Harvey pushed Daniel out of the way and stormed off again straight through the same door he had just walked out off. Sheepishly he walked straight out with everyone watching him before Lillie burst out laughing,

'Haha what a plank!!' she snorted as Harvey then looked for the next available door to walk off to, The King had decided that Harvey may need a little help so summoned the closest guard over to him and spoke,

'Please take the boy to the Great Chamber for me, don't let him wander off and for goodness sake DON'T let him touch anything, do you understand!!'

'Yes My King' the guard replied, who then saluted before turning on his heels and ushering Harvey away from the group,

'Wh...where are you taking me?' Harvey cried as he was led away from his friend's 'Daniel....Helpppp!!!' he shouted back, The King reassured them that he was going to be fine,

'My dear boy don't worry about your rather odd choice of travel companion, I've sent him off ahead and we will be joining him very soon, I want to share something with you and your sister before we meet up, I've told my guards to watch him very closely until we are finished here'.

So Daniel and Lillie followed the King across the castle grounds asking more questions than he had ever heard from anyone before, all the doors scattered around the grounds slammed shut one by one as the King walked past each of them,

'Where are we going now?' asked Daniel as he hurriedly walked after the King who was striding off towards the end of the courtyard straight towards a tall wooden door adorned with the same symbol as the one on Daniel's diary.

'Inside my boy, I have a few...surprises to share with you' The King smiled as the door was pulled open from inside and they stepped through into the unknown.

As the children walked down the castle halls they couldn't help noticing the grand pictures which were hanging on the walls looked remarkably like the ones hanging in the corridors at Longmeads,

'Lillie...are you looking at the paintings on the walls??, I'm sure that one looks like the old headmaster Mr Crumble, it's even got that weird scar he had on his cheek!!' Daniel blurted out as the guards looked at him strangely as he seemed to get excited by what he was seeing, Lillie had noticed something at the end of the hall and shouted back to Daniel,

'I know Daniel!!...this one looks like our first headmaster...you know...the one who opened the school...Mr.....whatshisname?'.

'Fleetch!!...' Daniel said after racking his brain for a minute or so,

'He was the one headmaster that all of the first pupils at the school were the most scared of, he was supposed to have some sort of magic powers, or so the story goes'

'What story? let me guess it's one of your stupid made up ones again!!' Lillie tutted as she waited for some sort of made up story that her brother always came up with.

'No honestly it's true, you know Archie Davies in the second year...'

'No..but do go on..' Lillie added

'Well...'Daniel started 'his dad said that HIS dad used to be a pupil at the school and in his class there always seemed to be a lot of his classmates missing from lessons, so one day he got sent to the headmaster's office...knocked on the door but there was no answer, so he opened the door and crept in, still no headmaster, he noticed that there was a secret door open in the corner of his office hidden behind a bookcase with steps going down into the bottom of the school, so...he sneaked down the stairs until he reached a dimly lit room...'.

'Yes...' Lillie now seemingly engrossed in what Daniel was saying

'So, he crept silently into the darkness, feeling his way along the cold stone walls until he saw something move in the corner of the room that turned his hair white and stopped him talking ever again...'

'Which was??' Lillie shook her brother's arms as she was desperate to find out,

'Well...We don't know as he never spoke again!! But I bet it was scary!!' Daniel smiled as he left Lillie hanging like a worm on a fishing hook,

'Oh come on!, you can't leave it like that Daniel' Lillie said as she threw her arms in the air knowing that her brother had nothing else to tell her,

'What more do you want me to say sis?, that was it, let's just imagine how bad it actually was!!' laughed Daniel as he caught a glimpse of the King laughing to himself,

'These are the finest Kings ever to have ruled over this land' The King smiled as he recalled his lands fine history 'The last picture is of MY father, King Loran Casborn, our lands finest ever warrior, he taught me everything I know and there isn't a day that goes by when I don't thank him for all he gave to me and your father' The King stood right in front of the painting of his father and smiled, seemingly lost in thought, 'Anyway...as I was saying I think I may have a little surprise for you in here', they stood outside a large door and the King knocked.

The door creaked open and they were met with the most dazzling room they had ever seen, it was filled with the finest furniture and statues which were sitting on a marble floor, a large table sat in the middle of it surrounded by fifteen overly large chairs, the children stood open mouthed at the sheer beauty of this room they were all standing in,

'Welcome to the Great Chamber, children, My sanctuary from the outside world' the King stood smiling at the end of the table, arms spread wide as if to say 'this is me and this is who I am', Harvey then appeared from out behind one of the chairs looking a little worse for wear after whatever it was he had been up to,

'Hi guys' Harvey said as he softly raised his hand and waved at Lillie and Daniel who were staring back at him confused about his strange behaviour lately,

'Alright Harv...feeling ok now?' Daniel said awkwardly as he felt something was happening with his friend,

'I'm ok Dan...Feeling a bit odd lately but I thinks it's just this place messing with me a little' replied Harvey, looking a little embarrassed now,

'Just stop being an idiot Harvey...' Lillie stared deep into Harvey's eyes with a burning rage 'We are all a little different here and it doesn't help that you're acting all crazy again'. The children were arguing amongst themselves so hard that they didn't notice that the King had disappeared through a side door which led to his private study room,

'Guys...guys...GUYS!!!' shouted Harvey 'Where's your grandad gone?'

'He was here a minute ago I think..' Lillie scoured the room looking for the King but he was nowhere to be seen.

All of a sudden the door swung open and through it came the King followed by another of his closest soldiers, this soldier stood as tall as the King, wearing body armour as shiny as the midday sun, his hair hung down across his broad shoulders and fell down his back covering his cape which was the same colour as the Kings and the same one that Daniel had seen in his dreams,

'Children....I said I had a few surprises for you so this seems like a good place to start, first of all I'd like to introduce you to...'

'Our father???...' Daniel shouted excitedly, clapping his hands as he jumped on the spot,

'Haha, not quite my boy but you may recognise him very soon...as I was saying I'd like to introduce you to my third in command and one of my most trusted guards, I haven't seen him for quite some time and it's so good to see him looking well...This is Garin Dell'. Lillie stepped forward to shake the hand of Garin as he leant forward to greet her, she then gasped out loud and took a few steps back as Garin smiled at her knowing that she had recognised something ever so familiar,

'Th...those eyes...I know those eyes' Lillie spluttered for words as she turned and looked straight at Daniel, Garin smiled softly replying to Lillie who seemed in total shock now,

'Lillie. It's so nice to see you again' he said as Daniel was looking totally confused now,

'How does he know your name sis??, and why is he saying it's nice to see you again??'

Garin strode forward as Lillie covered her mouth with her hands, he stopped just short of Daniel and crouched down slightly in front of him,

'Wh...who are you??' asked Daniel as he stared straight at the face of the guard who was waiting for Daniel to see the person he wanted him to see,

'Hello Daniel...' Garin stood up straight and took a deep breath and smiled at Daniel knowing he could now see the real identity behind what was standing in front of him now,

'N...No...it can't be!!!...B...Bucksy???' Daniel's head started spinning and the next thing he knew he was down on his hands and knees feeling slightly sick and lightheaded,

'Wha...Eh??...but...Errr....How...' Harvey had never been so confused before but even he was struggling and Lillie just burst out laughing unable to believe that this was their pet,

'Oh really!!, we are supposed to believe that this...man...is, or was our dog??, Why should we believe this', Garin knew that revealing who he actually was might not sit with some and he expected it to be Lillie so he reminded her of something that only they could know,

'Lillie...' He started 'Do you remember that day when you were up in your bedroom and you were singing at the top of your voice, not for the first time, then I came in and you saw me sniffing around so you threw that round thing at me and it hit me straight on the nose..'

'Yes I remember it well, Bucksy was constantly in my room' Lillie recalled,

'Yes, it was your favourite snow globe if I recall!!, the one with the snowman with the huge teeth, I still have flashbacks to that day' Garin winced at the thought of it hitting him all those years ago,

'Bucksy!! So it is you!!', declared Lillie with a wry smile 'How is this even possible?'

Garin gently picked Daniel up off the floor to check he was ok and held onto him fairly tight before giving the children the explanation they deserved,

'Well, the day you left this place, both of you, was the day your father was sent on his most dangerous mission which was to protect you all from harm. He knew that it wouldn't be long before the Graxx Army would find out your location and you were to be disposed of because you were, sorry, are the rightful heir to Erwin..'

'Go on, please' Daniel looking straight up at Garin as he knew he needed to find out the truth,

'So you're grandfather, the King, advised me to track you, your sister and your mother down and go with you away from this world as protection, so I set off to search for you, finally I caught up with your mother Stephanie and made her understand that I was to be your protection, but I knew that I would have to leave this place and stay by your side for as long as I was needed'

'But why did you turn into a dog??' Lillie asked

'I'm getting to that my dearest Lillie, so...as it turns out the King wanted your father to not know of your whereabouts as it would put you all in danger, meaning that you would be hunted constantly by the Graxx Army, He was distraught at losing you but he never gave up searching even though the King knew everything it needed to be that way, so I had to find a form of something that I knew would be able to be as close to you all without arousing suspicion so I found the one thing I knew wouldn't be seen as out of place, a canine, I knew I would be safe staying like that as I had carried out research of your world'

'I can never forgive myself for deceiving your father the way I did...' the King said '...But it was our duty to protect the future and this was something that had to be done otherwise evil would win and this whole empire we have built up over the years would be lost, YOU are our future Daniel...you are our blood, Your father never knew that I knew and one day I will have

174

to tell him but for now we must let this all die down then I will explain everything to him'.

'I'm so confused!!!' Harvey moaned as he tried to get his head round what was going on, 'So you're telling me that you are. Sorry were Bucksy??'

'Yes Harvey, as strange as it sounds, I was part of the family for all those years' Garin replied

'Nah, I don't believe you!!' Harvey said as he was sure there was something else going on here'

'I assure you I was, Harvey, how can I prove it to you?' Garin knew he could easily get Harvey onside,

'Do something only Bucksy would do' Harvey put Garin on the spot hoping to catch him out,

'WOOF…' laughed Garin as he mimicked his 'Bucksy' voice,

'Ha blooming ha!!!, Oh my sides are splitting here!!, Ok then tell me something that happened to us if you are who you say you are!!'

'Hmmm, let me think' Garin smiled at the story he was about to tell '…Ahhh yes, I have just the story, the day Daniel and I were on our way to your school and we went into the woods to hide from us…'

'Right…go on' Harvey was a bit unsure at what was about to be said so Garin continued,

'Well that day I remember we couldn't find you and Daniel was throwing that stick for me to chase, I remember sniffing something in the bush and sticking my head inside only to be met by the sight of your bottom staring at me, so I grabbed your leg and you let out a cry, then what followed was the foulest stench I had ever smelt from someone, It filled my nose like the fog, It smelt like po….'

'Yes, yes I totally believe it's you ok!!, Can we not go on about that then!!' a rather red looking Harvey turned his head to see Lillie and Daniel both in fits of laughter now,

'Oh shut up you two, it's not like I actually done anything!'

175

'Oh that's so funny, haha' Lillie laughed out loudest 'you must have more stories about him Garin!!'

'I think he has been embarrassed enough children' interrupted the King, 'Now I have news that your father is on his way back to the castle, one of the lookouts has spotted his men in the distance so I think we must prepare for his return, Are you ok you two?' The king put his hands on Lillie and Daniel's shoulders and smiled at them,

'I think so sir, it's just....something I have always dreamt of and I can't believe it's now coming true!!' smiled Daniel as he knew it wouldn't be long before their dreams were finally realised.

'Well let's go prepare for his return then children' the King smiled, his voice boomed as they strode off into the King's own quarters to ready themselves for the next part of the surprise, but there seemed to be something wrong as one of the lookouts came running into the office asking for a quiet word with the King, his face turned to one of anxiety as he looked back towards the children who had noticed that something wasn't right,

'What's going on?' Daniel asked,

'It's nothing you need to worry yourselves about children, just a little bit of an issue that needs my attention, please go with Garin and I will be back soon.....Garin I may need your assistance later' as the King strode off he threw a look at Garin which he had seen before and he knew it was not the best of news,

'Yes sir...I'll be along as soon as the children are settled' Garin turned towards the children giving the a smile to try and put them at ease but Lillie saw straight through it,

'What's actually going on Buck...sorry, Garin!!, I know something is up and we aren't going anywhere until you tell us'

'I assure you it's all ok children, just some business that the King must see to personally, so please follow me to the Chamber' Garin ushered the children away down the long hall to another part of the Castle, opening door after door before they got to the Chamber. The children went into the room first and were struck by the sheer size of the room itself.

Garin turned round to shut the doors behind him and just before they closed a huge amount of shouting was heard from the end of the hall ahead of the room as a group of guards ran past carrying a figure on a stretcher, shouting for people to move as they made their way hastily along the corridor and off into the distance, closely followed by the King who was as concerned as he had ever been and was heard saying '....and don't let them see!!'.

A look of disbelief spread across Garin's face as he knew exactly who it was but knew he needed to keep calm so the children wouldn't suspect anything, so as he clicked the doors shut behind him he turned to all three of them putting on his best 'nothing is wrong' voice and said,

'Right children let's get you settled in here ok, I shall have to go to the King for a little while but I assure you I will be straight back'

'I still don't believe you Garin...You're hiding something from us!!' Lillie pressed for an answer but Garin was too clever when it came to being questioned,

'Lillie...I know you think I am hiding something but It is nothing that concerns you or Daniel, I shall be back as soon as the King has attended to this' Garin smiled as he unlocked the door and walked off, he could be heard talking to the guards behind the door telling them to '...not let them leave', and with that his footsteps disappeared off into the distance until it was complete silence out in the corridors of the castle,

'Something isn't right!!' Lillie said as she started looking for a way out of the room without being seen,

'What do you mean by that sis?' asked Daniel as he stood there scratching his head, Harvey on the other hand had decided to sit down on the bed and stretch out flat,

'Yawn...let's just wait until Garin comes back, I'm sure it's nothing and anyway I'm far too comfortable on the bed!!'

177

'No something is definitely going on, I just heard one of the guards say something about someone 'normally healing quicker than that' but I couldn't make out who it was they were talking about' Lillie said as her ear was now pressed to the door listening to the chatter going on between the guards,

'The door isn't locked either!!' whispered Lillie to the others 'Let's go take a look around!!',

'Mmmm, I don't know if we should, we might get caught then who knows what would happen....' Daniel knew that they should actually stay in the room as he didn't want to annoy his new family.

'Oh come on Daniel, where's your sense of adventure!!, you know there's something strange going on here, let's go explore!!' Lillie excitedly said as she knew she could twist her brother's arm.

'Harv...what do you think??...Harv...Harv?' asked Daniel as he turned to see Harvey had fallen asleep on the bed and was snoring his head off.

'Typical!!' said Lillie 'Come on Daniel let's make a break for it, the guards have walked off!!'.

So Lillie grabbed her brother after he shook Harvey awake and dragged him out of the door and along the cold corridor in search of answers to whatever was happening here.

Chapter Fifteen
A Sons Love

Deep in the heart of the castle, way below ground footsteps could be heard running back and forth between the sound of slamming doors followed by the sound of shouts from one of the rooms, muffled voices saying '...never seen him like this before...' and '...this isn't the way it's meant to be...' could be heard, all sounded slightly concerned when all of a sudden the King came down the stairs looking deep in thought as he approached the room where the voices could be heard.

'So how bad is it?' asked the King as he approached the door to be met by the duty guard,

'Not too sure sir but he has been asking for you since he woke up' came the reply, the guard knocked on the door which then swung open with the creaking noise expected from such old doors, the King strode into the room and everyone inside bowed respectfully.

The King stood silently as he looked at the soldier lying on a bed looking very dishevelled and displaying what looked like wounds sustained during a fight, he placed one arm across his chest, resting the other one on it as he stroked his beard slowly, his face looking very anxious but also slightly confused,

'I want everyone to leave this room please...' the King said without even turning his head to look at his collection of soldiers and doctors,

'But sir...' said one of the doctors '..I need to stay with him for a while!',

'It's ok, I shall be in here with him, I am all he needs at the minute' replied the King,

'But sir...' the doctor trying to insist he stayed,

'OUT!!!!' bellowed the King 'We shall be fine, I need a few minutes alone with him',

'Y..Yes sir...' the door opened and all the guards and doctors scurried off as fast as they could out of the room, shutting the heavy door behind them, the King could hear muttering from outside the door but it didn't seem to bother him as his priority was the man whose eyes were now trained on the King.

'F...Father...is that you?' the soldier weakly asked,

'My son....' the King smiled as he lay his hand on the chest of the soldier, 'how are you feeling?, because you look terrible!!'

'I....I..feel...odd father' came the reply as the King looked his son up and down assessing his wounds,

'Hmmm...' the King said 'I've never seen your wounds take this long to heal son',

'What's happening to me?, I feel so weak!' the King's son tried to turn over but struggled,

'Rest my son, I'll figure out what's going on soon enough I'm sure, so I order you not to move!!' The King chuckled to try and hide his fear at what was actually happening to his son as he lay there stricken on the bed,

'Yes sir...' the King's son lay back down and closed his eyes as the medicine he had been given from the doctor started to take effect.

The King walked over to the door, carefully opening at and called the doctor back into the room,

'Safin....I need you to keep a close eye on my son please, I want you to keep me informed of any change in his condition, I need to find out why his body isn't healing as quickly as it normally does'

'Yes sir...I'll let you know if there's any change' Safin replied as he stood over the King's son looking at his wounds and taking notes,

'There's something happening here that I can't quite put my finger on....Hmmmm, I need to speak with the children...' Off the king strode down the corridor and round the corner his steps getting faster as he knew he needed to speak to the children at once but little did he know that the children had already left the room during the guard change and were searching the castle for information to what was going on. 'You found anything in there Harv?' asked Daniel as they opened yet another door in the castle,

'Nope, not a thing....errrr Dan....remind me what we are looking for again?' Harvey stood in the doorway of the latest room looking totally lost,

'Are you serious mate?' Daniel's jaw dropped as he stared at Harvey

'Are you telling me that since we started looking you have had no idea about what we are looking for??, you really are lacking in brain cells aren't you!!' Lillie felt her blood boiling as it seemed they had been wasting their time because of Harvey, Lillie turned away just as something seemed to click inside Harvey's head once again,

'Ohhhh I'm so sorry Lillie!!!, I don't really care about all this...whatever it is we are doing!!, And I'm so sorry that we haven't found enough answers for you and Daniel so far but I'm so happy that you're going to meet your dad soon, well YIPPEE....let me congratulate you both on actually getting to meet your father while I never will!!!',

Harvey slammed the door shut behind him as he stormed off down the corridor and in through another door just around the corner from where they had ended up, Daniel looked at Lillie and Lillie looked at Daniel with a look that they both knew something wasn't quite right with Harvey once again,

'What is going on with him now!!!!' asked Daniel as he clapped his hand to his head in despair 'I mean this isn't the first time he's been acting strange since we got here',

'I really haven't got a clue but I reckon this must all be linked somehow, come on let's go after him and see what's going on', and off they went, just as they rounded the corner the door opened and out stepped Harvey who almost bumped into them as they closed in on the door,

'Whoa guys...slow down a bit, you nearly knocked me over!!' Harvey smiled as he was met with the faces of two very confused children just staring straight at him,

'What is wrong with you Harv?' asked Daniel.

'What are you on about now?, and why are you both staring at me all weirdly!' Harvey stood there looking totally confused as usual as Lillie put her hands on her hips and huffed loudly,

'Look Harv...what is the matter with you?' said Lillie 'all you've done lately is have a go at us...what is your problem?'.

'Eh?...I haven't got a clue what you are on about!!, all I remember was leaving the bedroom and stepping through this door...come and see what I've found though, it's so exciting!!' Harvey said half confused and half excited, and off he ran back through the door he had just came out of, Lillie and Daniel stood there just staring in disbelief once again as they were totally lost with the whole Harvey thing now,

'Wha....' Daniel said, unable to finish his words,

'I know Daniel...Come on let's follow that lump wherever he has gone' replied Lillie as they flung the door open and followed the sound of Harvey's heavy footsteps to the end of another corridor until the came to a set of steps leading down into the heart of the castle.

'Do we...' asked Lillie looking at her brother for answers,

'I guess so sis, Harvey must be down there somewhere. I can still smell him!!' he replied not really looking forward to stepping into the unknown, just as a shout could be heard coming from the bottom of the steps,

'Come on guys...there's so much more stuff down here!!', Harvey was snooping round below them and had seen something that might be of interest to both Lillie and Daniel. The staircase dropped downwards like a coiled snake wrapped around its prey, the dimly lit walls feeling cold to the touch as they descended deeper and deeper into the heart of the castle when all of a sudden the steps ended and the children were greeted by the sight of about six doors, all identical and bearing the crest of the castle on them. As they stood there looking round Daniel realised he couldn't see Harvey anywhere,

'Harv...' he whispered gently 'Harv...where are you?' but no answer, it was creepily silent where they were standing, the only sound they could hear was what sounded like a dripping tap and the occasional moaning coming from behind the walls, Daniel and Lillie slowly stepped towards the first door making sure their footsteps didn't make any sound, Lillie reached out her hand to lift the latch on the first door to see if they could spot Harvey, just as the door creaked open...

'WAHHHH...' Harvey jumped out from the darkness and scared the living daylights out of them both sending them crashing to the floor.

'HAHAHAHA....' laughed Harvey who was doubled over in laughter, 'Oh that's so funny...you should of seen your faces hahaha', Lillie dragged herself up off the floor and lunged at Harvey grabbing him by the scruff of the neck, pressing her nose up against his,

'NOT...AT ALL...FUNNY!!!' Lillie scolded Harvey as he stood there looking deep into her eyes and could see the anger building inside of her.

'It...it was just a j..joke!!' Harvey felt his whole body go limp with fear as he had a feeling he had overstepped the mark this time,

'Oh yes. It's so blooming funny to have someone jump out on me in the pitch black and in a place we've never been to before, you've gone too far this time Harvey!!' Lillie's patience with Harvey had finally snapped and she felt he needed to be taken down a peg or two,

'I'm sorry!!!...' Harvey whimpered 'I didn't mean to scare you both that badly!!', Daniel dusted himself down and felt he needed to say something but knew that he needed to stay calmer than his sister was,

'Look Harv...You really are starting to annoy everyone here so please just stop with all the scaring, it's starting to wear thin and I'm not in the mood for your totally unfunny jokes now'

'Y..yes Daniel...I promise I'll stop it from now on, just call Lillie off, I don't fancy my good looks being damaged' Harvey tried to push Lillie off but she was far too strong,

'Lillie...Let him go please!!' Daniel said but Lillie was still burning her eyes into Harvey's scared face,

'Lillie!!!!, Leave him please, he's had enough!!' Daniel pulled Lillie's arms off his friend as she took a step back and angrily replied,

'Last warning Harvey...Last warning!!!', Lillie turned towards Daniel still looking angry so she didn't notice the evil glint that was present in Harvey's eyes and had spread across his face now, it seemed something had taken over him for a second as he heard a voice in his head saying 'good..good, it's working....', then it was gone and he seemed to forget about it.

Their attention was taken by a groaning noise coming from a room hidden deep in the darkened corner of the corridor,

'What's that noise?, where's it coming from?' Harvey asked,

'Sounds like someone in pain!!' Daniel answered back, as the trio made their way towards the corner and into the darkness feeling their way along the wall.

Inside the room the King's son was becoming restless on the bed, his body twitching with every movement, the doctor in the room noticed this and stood there scratching his head as he watched his wounds beginning to heal faster with every passing second,

'What is going on here now??' the doctor asked himself 'why are his wounds healing much faster?, I must go and find the King!!' He said as he made his way towards the door.

On the other side of the door the children were looking for a way in when they heard a noise like something unlocking right next to where they were standing, they all looked at each other in panic and scattered into the other rooms just as a secret door flung open and out strode the doctor who was now in search of the King, the doctor forgot to close up the secret door as he speedily climbed the stairs and off out of earshot.

Daniel was the first to slowly open his door followed by Lillie and finally Harvey made an appearance by accidentally slamming the door shut behind him which echoed through the halls and up the stairs causing Lillie and Daniel to stare at him angrily before their attention turned towards the secret door.

The three children stood there looking at the door wondering what lie inside,

'Sh...should we take a look inside?' Harvey's voice got slightly squeakier as he began to worry about what was inside, Lillie slowly stepped forwards, edging ever closer to the door which was slowly creaking on its hinges due to the light draught swirling around the room,

'Shhh...I'll take a look!!' Lillie gestured to the boy's to stay put,

'Be careful sis..' Daniel held his hands up to his face as he watched his sister edge ever closer.

As she reached the entrance to the hidden room she took a deep intake of breath and let out a small shocked noise as she noticed someone lying on the bed in front of her, she stood there just transfixed on the person who to her looked like they had been injured somehow.

'What is it Lillie?, what can you see?' asked Daniel,

'You better come take a look for yourself Daniel!!' she replied as Daniel crept over to where his sister was standing, followed by Harvey who was holding onto his friend for dear life.

'Be careful Dan..' said Harvey as they both reached the open door to be greeted by the same sight of a soldier lying wounded on the bed, weak moans could be heard coming from him as he lay there unaware of the children standing in the doorway just looking at him with shocked looks on their faces. Harvey whispered to Daniel about who it might be,

'Do you reckon he's an important soldier or something Dan?, I mean look at how he's dressed, all shiny and scary looking'. Daniel had noticed the symbol on the soldier's bare arm which was exactly the same as his,

'Wait...guys, have you seen this?' Daniel moved closer to the stricken soldier, trying to get a closer look at the symbol,

'That looks like yours Daniel!!' gasped Lillie as she stared at Daniel then back at the soldier's arm,

'Looks sort of alike Dan...' smirked Harvey as he stood there just looking around the room for somewhere to sit,

'Do you remember what the King said earlier...about only a select few having this mark on them and how important they were, do you think this is our fath...' before Daniel could finish what he was saying and as he held his arm close to the stricken soldier, the special marks they both had started to glow a light blue colour beneath the skin,

'Daniel...your arm!!! What's it doing?' Harvey stood there pointing at the glowing symbol on his friend's arm,

'Wh..what's happening!!' Daniel said as he was rooted to the spot now unable to move.

As their arms touched it was though they could see each other's thoughts and memories, Daniel was now seeing everything that he had seen in his dreams, The soldier standing on the hill, the dusty land far from the castle, he was also hearing the voices of all the people who had swirled round inside his mind before they had got to the castle. Then there was an image he hadn't seen before, a dark looking figure with his head covered by a cloak but a pair of eyes burning as bright as the sun surrounded by blackness.

Then as the images disappeared the soldier's arm gripped onto Daniel's so tight that it scared him senseless and he let out a scream,

'Yaahhhh!!!' he cried out loud

'Huhhhhh...' the soldier took the deepest breath like he had just been brought back to life and his eyes opened slowly, he was still laying on his back just looking up at the ceiling when all of a sudden a face appeared in his view,

'Hello' Harvey had leant in for a closer look, smiling as he stared right into the eyes of the soldier who seemed to be struggling to focus on anything,

'Wh..wha..Who's there?' came the reply, Daniel was still frozen with fear as the soldier was still gripping his arm tight and Harvey was waving his hand in front of the soldiers face.

'I don't think he can see me' laughed Harvey as he kept waving his hand across the face of the soldier like a demented lunatic when all of a sudden the soldier sat up dead straight causing Harvey to lose his balance and fall to the floor. He turned his head towards where the children were standing and stared intensely at both Lillie and Daniel, his eyes squinting as he tried to focus them, he inhaled deeply as if ready to speak then…,

'That really hurt!!...' moaned Harvey as he rubbed his backside gingerly ' and it's going to leave a mark!!' he continued whining as the soldier swung his legs round and sat on the edge of the bed carefully as he was still feeling a bit groggy. He lifted his head up, brushed back his hair, Daniel took a step forward and Lillie gently tugged at his arm,

'Be careful Daniel…' she said but Daniel had seen something that made him sure he knew who the mystery soldier was,

'I...I've seen his face before. I know him!!' Daniel said as he was drawn deeper into the soldiers eyes, they both leant in at the same time, Daniel staring at the soldiers face taking in every line, wrinkle and scar on his face. The soldier squinting his eyes took in every detail of Daniel's face as he too felt something between them, he opened his mouth as if to speak and small breathy noise came out, just as he was about to speak the silence was broken by the sound of doors banging behind them and what sounded like a small army clomping down the stairs,

'Children….come to me please!!' It was the King shouting as he raced towards the open door, both Daniel and the soldier looked away as the King appeared at the door,

'Why are you three down here?' he asked 'You were supposed to stay in the quarters until I came for you, Garin was under strict instructions to keep you there'

'It wasn't Garins fault, we sneaked out when the guards changed over, I wanted to see what was going on and I dragged these two with me' Lillie put her head on her chest as she knew what they had done wasn't the right thing to do,

'You can't just go wandering round the castle, especially without an escort' The King replied as he made his way over to the soldier on the bed and stared at him with a smile as Safin carefully lifted up the soldier's arms to look at the wounds,

'The wounds have healed your majesty, something must have happened!!', said Safin who seemed so surprised by the state of the soldier now. The King turned toward Lillie and Daniel, leant forward slightly, a smile stretching from ear to ear as he put his hands on their shoulders,

'Daniel...I know you know who this soldier is right here..I can tell by your expression, and Lillie...it's time you all found out the truth'

'So who is he then?' said Harvey as he pointed at the soldier, 'I'm totally confused now!!'.

The King strode over to the soldier and rested his hand in his shoulder,

'My son...I have been so worried for you lately, but things have been moved a little faster than I have anticipated, I haven't been totally honest with you and I feel the state you found yourself in is because of me keeping something from you for all these years, something that now I can see has had a serious effect on you and your health'

'Ohhhhhh, now I get it!!' a light seemed to click on in Harvey's head as Lillie and Daniel just looked at each other open mouthed,

'He's your......' Harvey was cut short as the soldier's head poked round from behind the King and he finished Harvey's sentence

'...Father, I'm your father' he smiled as the King helped him to his feet and held onto him, 'My...children...' The soldier smiled 'It's you!!, You have come back to me' He cupped the faces of Lillie and Daniel as he stared deep into their eyes, a tear rolling down his cheek,

'May I have a hug?' The soldier asked, hoping for the response he so desperately wanted. Lillies smile stretched right across her face as she knew it was the right thing to do now and she felt safe so she took a step forward just as the soldier bent down and embraced her tightly.

Daniel just stood there totally stunned by what was going on, the soldier opened his tear stained eyes and reached out an arm,

'My...boy, please' the soldier begged Daniel to come to him which he then shot forward and practically threw himself into his father's arms and buried himself deep into the body of his father, who then let out a huge sigh of happiness and relief as he realised his search for his family was over for

188

now, but the path ahead was going to be one to test even the strongest of bonds but for now this was time for family.

The King smiled and clasped his hands together unaware of the trouble that was heading their way, 'The Circle is finally complete!!' he said as the soldier rose to his feet gingerly,

'My children...You were my biggest wish and my whole world, I cannot tell you what I have gone through to get to this place, I want to hear and know everything. From the start, but I must also speak with my father. Please allow me some time then I promise I will be all yours, I won't let you go ever again'. So as the children were led outside the room the doors shut behind them and they were once again ushered up the dark staircase leading to the upper floors of the castle where they were once again greeted by Garin who had been frantically searching or them all around the castle grounds,

'Children, where have you been?, I left you in that room for your own safety and now I see you have somehow ended up here', Daniel smiled as he explained to Garin what had happened and how they had finally found their father, Harvey was less than impressed as he was standing there holding his stomach,

'Guys...I'm starving, can we please get something to eat, I'm wasting away!!'.

Garin looked at Harvey and knew that he would only start moaning more unless he was shown food.

'Yes ok Harvey, I have had a feast laid on for you in the Quarters so please can we go and this time try to stay in the room ok?'.

So the children were led off to the Quarters to feast on whatever delights they had been left with,

'Oh also...' said Garin '...we have placed the bags you had with you in the room also, they had been left out by the gate when you came in. one of them seemed to be glowing for some reason', Lillie sniggered as she knew it was one of the lanterns they had been given by Lucas,

'It's ok Garin it's just a lantern, nothing special'.

So as the children tucked into the mountain of food that had been prepared for them Lillie and Daniel smiled at each other across the table knowing that whatever had brought them here had helped them find their father after all this time, but the evil spark that had been implanted in Harvey began to grow stronger with every second.

Chapter Sixteen
Starting To Change

As the children sat there making their way through the feast that had been prepared for them Lillie and Daniel suddenly looked up and smiled at each other as they both realised just how big a deal this meeting was now that they had found their father but they weren't aware of just how crazy their future was going to become, Harvey wasn't really that bothered by what was happening around him though, something that wasn't lost on Daniel,

'Harv...how come you don't seem that bothered by what's happening here?, I mean...this isn't like you at all, you're the sort of person who gets excited by a free cookie and you can't wait to tell everyone but you seem...well really calm', Harvey looked up from behind his mound of food and raised his eyebrows slightly, as he was trying to swallow whatever it was he had stuffed in his mouth this time,

'To be honest Dan, I don't really care about the fact you've finally found your dad, I mean yeah...It's great and all but what about me?, It seems I've totally forgotten about my mum since we've been here and all you've banged on about is your dad and how much you needed to find him, but let me remind you that I didn't ask to be here in the first place remember!!, that was down to that stupid dog of yours and you deciding to follow it after he ran off, so now all I can think of is my mum!!'

'Whoa ok Harv!!!' replied Daniel looking taken aback slightly by Harvey's honesty 'I'm sorry that we have ended up here but look, now we are here and we've found somewhere that we actually belong...'

'YOU belong!!! Not me' Harvey replied,

'WE belong mate...' came the stinging reply from Daniel '..we might be about to have some kind of adventure or something, like when we used to mess around in your garden and that, all the times you wanted something exciting to happen and now something actually might be, so let's see what happens from here ok?'.

Harvey just stood there looking right through Daniel as if his mind was elsewhere,

'To be honest Daniel I just want to go home now, I've had enough of following you around and you telling me what to do, also that sister of yours constantly picking on me so I'm sorry but I'd rather eat worms than stay here a minute longer!!' Harvey stood up and shot out of the door as quick as he had ever moved, Lillie just shrugged her shoulders as the door slammed shut behind Harvey.

'BABY!!!' shouted Lillie as it seemed Harvey's attitude had finally made her patience wear so thin that she didn't want anything to do with him, 'Why do you still bother with that friend of yours Daniel?, he's totally holding you back still, and what the heck is going on with these mood swings!!',

Daniel huffed as he sat back in his chair seemingly thinking the same thing now 'I don't really know anymore Lillie, he's ruining all this for me, I wish he would just leave me alone for a bit!!'.

Harvey was making his way through the cold echoey corridors of the castle seemingly on some sort of autopilot, as he passed all sorts of castle inhabitants on the way they just stared right at him as if they could see something was wrong with him but daren't ask. He kept muttering to himself along the way too but barely high enough for anyone to hear what he was saying,

'Hooded man...hooded man...the woods…' he was mumbling so much to himself as he made his way to the castle doors, with a show of strength he hadn't shown before he managed to open the huge doors to the castle which weren't being guarded and off he went, his eyes still glowing an unnatural colour, as he descended the huge steps he seemed to know where he was going, his face had a huge but creepy smile on it as he made his way towards the woods.

Harvey stomped right through the woods crushing everything in his path as he went until after a while he came back to the place he had been held in a cage against his will, he stood completely still as if in a trance still muttering to himself 'Hooded man...hooded man...take what's yours...' his eyes glowing in the darkness of the woods as he stood there, when all of a sudden directly in front of him the hooded figure appeared, floating just off the ground as he reached out a gloved hand and placed it on Harvey's shoulder,

'Ahh it seems the spell is working as intended. Master will be pleased' said the figure 'Let me see what he has gathered so far!!', as the figure moved his hand up to Harvey's face he seemed to put him deeper into a trance as what followed was a sort of memory removal, all the things Harvey had already seen were being sucked out of his head and into the body of the hooded figure who could see every thought and vision Harvey had seen,

'Good..Good..' the figure seemed to be getting what he needed from Harvey's head, 'Ahhh just what I needed...now with this spell getting stronger inside you I need more!!, time is precious but we must not be found out...keep bringing me information boy, the Fall of the Bells will come and the Boy Prince will be no more', then the contact was broken and the figure turned on the spot and floated off into the woods again before disappearing completely, Harvey was still under the spell he was before but it seemed he was being controlled from another source.

As he stood there he heard a voice inside his head talking to him,

'Go back and gather more...help us to see...' and no sooner had it been said then it just disappeared and Harvey was left standing in the woods all alone and still stuck in a trance.

In the darkest part of Dansheer, a province deep in the darkest part of Vaymia stood the imposing figure of Castle Rondor, it was as wide as it was tall and surrounded by a river so black that nothing could survive in it, but what looked like huge eels could be seen swimming through the black waters, electrifying it, meaning nothing could ever get out if they fell in. The skies above the castle were dark like nothing you had ever seen before and filled with relentless which soaked the land from morning to night, the Castle itself was so crudely made that every brick that went into making it was jagged and broken, the walls were covered in moss meaning nothing could climb it and heavy doors, bigger than any that had been ever seen stood proud at the front of the castle and were covered in the armour of the enemy as a reminder that this place was evil. Inside lived the imposing figure of Emperor Aret Del, the most feared of rulers known across the planets, he rarely involved himself in battles unless absolutely required and he was the most feared warrior ever to set foot on this land, he wouldn't think twice about slaying an enemy or even one of his own if it was needed, even his own army, The Graxx army, were scared to put a foot wrong for fear of having their life ended in a truly horrible way in his purpose built torture room which had seen a lot of activity lately.

As the rain fell heavily the hooded figure appeared at the edge of the forest seamlessly floating towards Castle Rondor and up to the edge of the surrounding river where there seemed no way across but the figure just floated across the river, the electricity crackling below as it passed.

As it reached the other side the huge doors creaked and groaned their way open and the figure carried on inside where the castle grounds were so dark and had a damp feeling about them that you could tell this was a place where bad things happened, there was the odd light flickering in the distance but nothing else.

The figure silently moved through the eerily quiet grounds and up a small flight of stairs towards a door which opened wide with a flick of the figures hand, the figure floated in through the open door which then slammed behind him and along the darkened corridor he kept going, not a sound could be heard anywhere inside the castle as he approached what looked like a door made of the darkest most rotten wood but seemingly held together with all sorts of bones and skulls which made it look like a

194

door of some importance, the figure stopped outside the door as if waiting for something then slowly it opened,

'Master....' The figure said as he was met by a room decorated with such evil that it would make your skin crawl, 'I have news on the boy...'.

At the end of the room stood a huge window overlooking the castle grounds and in front of it stood a huge throne made from skulls, a voice came from the chair, a voice so deep it seemed almost unearthly, Emperor Aret Del had been alerted to Skaffs presence as he got closer to the door,

'I'm listening...' He boomed '...We need to move this plan forward and the boy is causing me problems, I have seen the change in him ever since we sent the scout into his world to shadow him, he has become strong but he doesn't know his true power yet'

'Yes master...but everything is falling into place slowly but we cannot afford to rush this, we cannot risk them finding out what we are doing' the hooded figure replied 'But I assure you that the last of the Bells will fall and we will be victorious, Erwin WILL be ours and the land will cease to be protected so you can rule once again!!'

'Make sure that NOTHING interferes with this plan, and I mean nothing, or else the consequences will be far greater than you can imagine, this land is rightfully mine and no one shall stop me!!' said Aret Del, still sitting at the end of the room facing towards the huge stained window, looking out over the castle where he ruled

'What of King Casborn though my master?, It seems that there's a significant change in his well-being, the land feels slightly odd, his presence seems to be disappearing with every passing day' The hooded figure asked,

'He shall be taken care of in due course Skaff, I shall be the one to end it, he has taken everything from me and only I can stop him' came the sharp reply once more

'Now Skaff, go and inform Commander Grogg of the latest news and make sure the Army is ready for the next assault on Mesita, we must see how far we can push this time, we need answers and we MUST find the Bells, we must finish what I started and the boy cannot find out....'

'Find out what Master?' came the slightly confused reply,

'He cannot find out the secrets of the land and the reason why he is truly here...The family must be silenced and the boy....well let's just say I have something rather special lined up for him'. Said Aret Del as a huge smirk spread across his face,

'Now go!!!' he barked 'I have some important business I must see to'

'Yes master' replied Skaff as he turned and floated off out of the open door behind him.

Aret Del just leant forward in his seat and watched as the rain fell heavily down across the castle grounds, lightning ripping across the scorched skies like an arrow and not a soul could be seen outside wandering the grounds.

Aret Del huffed as he stared outwards before talking to himself,

'The day will come…' he said over and over as he clasped his hands tighter and tighter until they turned a white colour, then he stood up straight and stormed out of the throne room and off into the corridor, his boots clomping along the stone floor as he strode along still muttering the same phrase over and over again, he reached a long set of stairs which led into the bowels of the castle, they stretched as far downwards as they did upwards and were dimly lit too, at the bottom sat a pool of dark water, as still as the calmest seas until Aret Del reached the bottom where the water rippled heavily then with an almighty splash a creature arose from it, snake like in its appearance, two horns sat in the middle of its forehead and row after row of sharp pointy teeth filled every space in its mouth. As the creature saw Aret Del come closer it lowered its head towards him like a dog would do when looking for attention and rested its head across the stone bricks, a deep purring noise filling the cold air as its tongue reached out towards its keeper,

'Ahh my faithful friend, how are you today Chikra?' asked Aret Del as he gently stroked the creatures face

The creature nudged itself into the body of the Emperor and let out a small but deep noise which seemed to suggest the creature was happy now it had met its master,

'Do not worry Chikra, it won't be too long before I can free you, when you are full strength I will need you...my pet you will have your revenge I promise you' he said still stroking the side of the creatures head as the rest of its body slowly raised out of the water to reveal huge cuts and scars along its body.

'Now my pet...' Aret Del said 'I must go...I have had a visit from an old friend, a huge smirk spread across his face as he knew something from his past was waiting for him below.

The creature disappeared back into the black water as Aret Del strode off through the door at the bottom of the steps, as he paced along the dark cold corridors of the lower bowels of the castle he could hear screams coming from behind most of the doors, these were holding cells for any enemy they had captured and it seemed every cell was full. At the far end of the corridor stood a lone door with a couple of guards standing outside, as the Emperor approached the guards bowed their heads out of respect and opened the door.

As the Emperor entered the room he stood still to let his eyes adjust to the darkness, a small window high up in the room was the only source of light, a dark light, that filled the room with a essence of evil.

Aret Del smiled as he caught sight of a figure chained up to the wall, hands raised above their head and feet chained up to the lower part of the wall,

'Well well well...Do you know how long I've waited to get you back??' Said Aret Del as his eyes were met with the sight of a familiar face,

'Aret Del...' The sound of a familiar woman's voice replied 'I was wondering how long it was going to be before you showed up!!'. The figure leant forwards slightly into the small source of light shining down on her to reveal who she was,

'My dearest Lydia....How I've missed you so!!' he cackled as he moved closer and saw the muddied face move closer to his, it's wrinkled appearance covered in a collection of small bruises, her clothing all ripped in places and dirty,

'I see you are keeping well Lydia...' laughed Aret Del as he took a few steps back in case Lydia decided to attack him,

'As well as can be expected, seeing as I'm being treated like an animal!!' She replied angrily 'I'm chained to a wall in the coldest darkest most horrible place ever, I've been here for a few days and you haven't told me why!!'

'It seems, my dear, that you have been rather busy I have been told' came the calm reply as Aret Del slowly paced up and down,

'I'm always busy, but I have no clue what you're talking about, and I'm angry at the way I was ripped from my cottage by your men!!' Lydia's voice began to raise slightly as she sort of knew what Aret Del was getting at but she needed to throw him off the scent,

'Well....' started Aret Del 'as you know there seems to have been a slight...shall we say...disturbance in the land lately, someone or some people who have stumbled into this land, whether by accident or on purpose....'

'And what are you getting at?' Lydia replied, knowing whatever she says may place the children in even more danger,

'It seems that two of them are related to Lord Casborn, one is the rightful heir to the Kingdom and the other. Well she isn't that important. But as it turns out they have made it to the castle and have been reunited with their father!!' still calmly speaking Aret Del paced even slower in front of Lydia,

'And?.....' Lydia tried to show she knew nothing of what he was talking about,

'And it seems..' replied Aret Del '...the journey would of been perilous for three people who have no place in this world of ours, but as I have been informed, they may have had a little help'

198

'And you think I have something to do with that?, do you really think I'm that stupid, you know where my loyalties lie!' Lydia replied angrily,

'So why did you disappear so suddenly all those years ago then?' came the scathing question right back at her 'One minute we are on edge of taking over this world, you and I, then the next thing I know is you have vanished into thin air, and Casborns wife and children have somehow escaped!!'

'I left because I didn't agree with what you had become!, Yes I admit I was taken in by you at first but my judgement became clouded and I felt more and more brainwashed as time went by, that's why I left' Lydia knew she was slowly putting him off of suspecting her involvement in what had happened all those years ago,

'I moved as far away from you as I could because I was angry and upset, you had changed..' Lydia said as Aret Del stopped right in front of her, 'You weren't the same person any more, power had gone to your head and I could see that nothing was going to get in your way of complete control, I knew nothing could stop you, not even me, and I feared for my own safety, you became withdrawn, you cared for no one but yourself, I knew if I stayed then you would harm me and I couldn't stay',

'I wanted total control so WE could rule this land together Lydia..' He explained 'I done all this for you, every battle I fought, every village I conquered, every life I took, It was all for you. But the day you left made me think that you had betrayed my trust'

'I'd never have done that, maybe it was a coincidence that they disappeared at the same time but you were becoming someone I couldn't trust anymore, that's why I went deep into the woods, I knew I would be safe there, I had to cast a spell to hide myself and the cottage as I didn't want you to find me!' Lydia had been getting her story together for a long time as she had a feeling this day would come, she knew what she had to do and was well aware if the consequences,

'Ahh yes your cottage..' he smiled wryly '..a place of safe haven, I wondered why it took so long to find it!!, my men always returned with no

199

news on so many occasions, My feeling was they weren't looking very hard so I had them disposed of for failing me…'

'Exactly what I'm getting at..' replied Lydia now knowing she was making Aret Del see she wasn't lying to him '..You didn't think twice I bet, now you know if I had stayed then how long before you done the same to me?'

'Lydia, do you really believe I would have harmed you in any way?, I'm quite upset that you would of even thought that about me..but with every passing day you didn't return made me more hateful and wanting to exact revenge on Casborn and his family as I feared you had turned' Aret Del sighed heavily as he turned away from Lydia,

'But I still have an inkling you are involved somewhere, a feeling buried so deep keeps nagging away at me with every passing second in your presence….I'm sorry Lydia'

'Sorry for what?..' she replied slightly confused now

'Sorry for it having to come to this, no mortal can unlock whatever secrets you are hiding....so let's try another way..' Aret Del laughed as he knew something wasn't right, Lydia was worried about what he was saying,

'Wh..what are you talking about?, please let me down, you know I'm telling the truth' as Aret Del started to walk out of the room Skaff had been waiting patiently outside,

'Skaff..' smiled Aret Del '...go do your thing, extract whatever information you can from her, spare her no pain!!'

'Yes master' Skaff replied as he floated into the room, Lydia had seen what was going on and began shouting,

'PLEASE!!, please not this….Aret Del let me down, I beg you..Aaaahhhh' as he made his way down the corridor he could hear the screams of Lydia echoing through the darkness, he smiled to himself as he walked out past Chikra who had surfaced and was waiting to greet his master,

'It's ok my pet...soon we will get what we want, then this land will be mine, once I get my hands on the Book of the Silent then I shall make them all fall!!' clenching his fist as knew that a sacrifice would have to be made to bring it all to an end, 'but for now we must keep searching, I can feel them...they are calling to me'. With that he patted Chikra on the head and smiled.

Aret Del walked up the spiral staircase deep in thought, plotting his next battle which would bring him one step closer to the Book of the Silent and total dominance over Vaymia, but he knew that one boy stood in his way, a boy who had no idea of the power he possessed, a boy who, if he didn't stop, would lead the army Aret Del feared most and then there would be no stopping him from keeping peace throughout the land.

As he emerged at the top of the staircase he was met by his most faithful of servants, General Grogg, a warrior so feared throughout the planet that Aret Del never needed to show his face in battle unless it was required,

'Sir...' General Grogg said as he lifted his arm across his chest and bowed his head slightly '..The army has been readied and are awaiting your orders'

'Excellent Grogg...' said Aret Del 'This time something feels different, I feel a greater pull towards the land, it's like it wants me to find the Book of the Silent...but why?,'

'Sir if I may...' said General Grogg as he moved alongside Aret Del,

'Go ahead Grogg, my most loyal of servants, you know I value your opinion' he replied,

'Well, in the past few years I have felt a change in the makeup of the land, a feeling I have never felt before...a feeling so strong that it felt like we were being pulled towards the source...with every battle I felt as invincible as I had ever done, I could see even more fear in the people than I had ever seen before. It was like they knew something big was happening and it scared them...every battle seemed to get easier, I can't figure out why but it seems the presence of the boy has somehow energised the land but taken its energy away from the people and directed it towards the boy...this battle must be carefully thought out sir. We cannot afford to let him defeat us'

'Hmm, that does make sense Grogg' replied Aret Del 'Skaff was right when he said we need to not rush into this, I see the bigger picture now. It all makes sense!!, we must use the friend to gain the information, as much as we can take from him, then when the time is right we strike!!!, take them all out and the Bells will fall'.

'Yes sir..' saluted General Grogg 'Address the Army and make this land ours'.

As General Grogg and Aret Del made their way through the castle towards the waiting loyal army that was assembled in the castle yard their laughter could be heard echoing along the corridors, the plan they had so carefully thought about was finally looking like it would work, everything that had been foretold by the ancestors was falling into place slowly but how it all ends was never written, but Aret Del was sure he knew that he would finish what had been started and his triumph would be felt throughout the land, he just needed to remove the final obstacle stopping his rise to ultimate power.

As Aret Deal and General Grogg pushed open the heavy steel doors that led out onto a balcony overlooking the castle grounds they were greeted by the sight of Graxx Army, stretching back as far as the eye could see, row upon row of the most evil collection of soldiers ever seen, anger and hate filling the air like a poisonous gas,

'LONG LIVE THE EMPEROR!!!...' the chorus of noise greeting him like a wall of sound as it made its way along the soldiers and creeping up the wall like ivy, Aret Del smiled as he stood at the edge of the balcony, arms stretched out in front of him, his head bowed slightly as he took in the constant chanting from his army of warriors, then as he lowered his left arm the chanting stopped. Aret Del lifted his head up slightly as all eyes were trained on him,

'My loyal Graxxians....' Aret Del said '..for so long now we have been fighting a war so big and so long that it seemed never ending...A war so vicious and so barbaric that we have lost a lot of our 'family' along the way. But I have never questioned anyone about their loyalty to me, you have all fought valiantly at my side without ever asking for anything...but I can tell you that the past few battles have seen a significant change in our quest...you should have all felt the difference across this land, but now it seems Casborn isn't the same man as he was before...but a mere mortal now thanks to the appearance of his...children'.

A low murmur buzzed through the troops as they had a feeling that something wasn't right now and with this latest news it seems the rumours were true, Casborns children had returned to carry on the name.

'But I have a plan which has been in place for some time now which has slowly turned the tide in our favour, a plan so effective that even his son won't be able to break free from our clutches, and yes we will find the boy and his sister, we will show Casborn we are the force he is so afraid of, we will destroy the last of the Bells and the Book of the Silent will be mine, we shall bring this planet to its knees, We shall be victorious and I shall have it all!!' Aret Del lifted his hands towards the darkened skies which were filled with thunder and lightning as if they themselves applauded his speech,

'ARET DEL, ARET DEL, ARET DEL...' the Graxx army chanted as one for their leader as they had bought into his plan of destruction,

'Now let us go...' Aret Del shouted '..We have many places to go, many villages and towns to take over, this is the beginning of the new world'. The huge gates creaked and groaned open as the Graxx Army made their way out of Castle Rondor, footsteps stomping across the muddy land as they made their way across the bridge and down the hill that led to the castle, their journey would last longer than normal as Aret Del knew he needed more soldiers to fill his depleting army and the only way to do that was to bring down every town and village along the way in search of people who must fight for him or face a life of pain and torture, this thought drove him on in his quest to finish Lord Casborn off once and for all and for his children to never be able to take the throne of Erwin from him.

'I must succeed Grogg...for too long I have waited to get my revenge on that family' said Aret Del as he banged his fist down on the stone railing,

'I will do everything in my power to make that happen' replied Grogg

'I know you will my most feared warrior' Aret Del smiled as he turned to face General Grogg 'now you have my total trust and respect, go do what you do best, lead that army and bring me new soldiers, we must be prepared for when the day comes!'

'Yes sir, we shall have you a new batch soon, that is my word' replied Grogg as he placed his clenched fist across his chest and bowed his head slightly, the off he strode out of the gates which then creaked and groaned shut behind him. Aret Del then turned round and walked back into the safety of the castle with the heavy rain beating down outside still.

Chapter Seventeen
Learning Curve

'Did you see where Harvey went to?, he's just disappeared again!!' said Daniel as he stepped outside their bedroom looking up and down the corridors for any sign of him, Lillie sighed heavily as she threw back the covers on her bed,

'I don't know and I don't really care Daniel' Lillie replied with a short tone 'if he's stupid enough to go running off on his own then that's his problem, his odd behaviour is really grating on me at the minute'

'Yes I do get it sis but he's still my friend and I do feel slightly guilty about you both being here, seeing as it was my fault and all' Daniel said as he came back in to the room and shut the door behind him,

'Look Daniel, there's a reason why we are all here and it's not your fault ok, as I look at it we were meant to find our family so no matter what you think I believe this was meant to be' Lillie doing her best to reassure her brother as he looked slightly sad,

'But what about mum?, It's weird as I haven't really thought about her much since we got here, I mean...it's like we are being made to forget about everything we had before here, I hope she's ok, I really do' Daniel looked out of the window in their room as the suns set over the land, a rainbow of colours filling the sky as they sank lower behind the castle walls,

'Daniel..' Lillie knew that she had to step up and look after him 'I totally get what you are saying but as I see it mum, if she is our mum I mean, was following orders to get us to safety, I'm sure she feels like you do now but I have this feeling deep inside of me that tells me she is fine ok, so let's try and figure out what we have to do while we are here',

'Ok sis I trust you, but I do need to find Harvey also, I'm worried about him, he hasn't been seen for ages now, I'll never forgive myself if he's hurt or something' said Daniel as he got dressed into his clothes, he grabbed his lantern from his bag and slowly opened the door

As he poked his head out of the bedroom door to have a look he noticed the castle corridors were quiet and dark so he knew he would have to be quiet as he wandered off, just as he was about to go he felt a tug on his arm, Lillie had got dressed too,

'I'm coming with you Daniel, If we stick together we should be ok, can't let Dad or the King find us since we are supposed to be in the room until he comes for us',

'Ok but remember we are looking for Harvey ok?, and please just this once don't upset him again, I just want us all to get along now' said Daniel as he took a few steps out into the corridor, he touched his lantern which turned on and lit the way ahead for him,

'Daniel...where are you??' asked Lillie as she felt her way along the corridor slightly,

'I'm right here sis, can't you see me?' he replied as he turned to face his sister who was still feeling her way gently along the wall, he stopped and was waving right in her face,

'I'm right in front of you Lillie!!, hellooooo, what's happened to your eyes!!' laughed Daniel, just as he was about to push his sister he remembered that he was using his lantern which showed only his location to himself,

'Oh yeah...just remembered I've been using the lantern Lucas gave us, no wonder you can't see me, haha' Daniel slapped his head gently as he felt silly about it,

'Well I still can't see..' replied Lillie as she reached out to her brother and grabbed his arm hard which caused him to yelp in pain,

'Be careful sis!!, your hurting my arm, let go'

'No way, that will teach you for messing with me' she laughed quietly to herself as she pushed him forwards along the corridor,

'Where's your lantern then? Asked Daniel as they walked along the corridor past a series of locked doors,

'Back in the room..I didn't have time to grab it seeing as you ran off!!' Lillie replied as she was still holding onto Daniel's arm tightly.

As they approached another corridor which looked exactly like the last one Daniel heard a heated exchange taking place at the end of it, the children slowly crept along until they reached the last door, it was slightly open and Daniel peered in to be met with the sight of his father and Grandfather the King talking about them both,

'...you know the rules of the castle son..' said the King as looked straight at Casborn,

'Yes father...but I cannot let anything happen to them, I insist they be excused from schooling, we know nothing of them yet and what they possess, let me have time with them' Casborn replied, pleading with the King,

'I cannot allow them to stay here without the proper schooling, just in case they are what we hoped they would be, I will have Garin keep an eye on them for you as I need you by my side but you cannot interfere with their development' The King knew that they must do things right, the prophecy didn't allow for any interference,

'Yes sir. But...' said Casborn

'No buts son...and NO exceptions!!! It has been agreed now, they will start the schooling immediately and let's pray the prophecy was right, I have a feeling we will need them eventually' the King had made the decision and Casborn knew he had to stick to it,

'Ok, but if anything happens to either of them....' he said

'If they are who we hope they are then they will be as strong as their father, I guarantee it' smiled the King as he made his way over to the window unaware that they were being listened to from outside the door.

Daniel backed up slowly and turned towards Lillie,

'What's the matter Daniel? What was all that about?' asked Lillie

'Errr, from what our father was saying it seems like we are being sent to whatever school it is they have here!!, I thought we'd got away from all that!! moaned Daniel quietly as they crept along the corridor and out towards an open door that would lead them outside,

'Really??' beamed Lillie in the semi darkness 'I can't wait for that, I've missed school so much' Daniel huffed at the thought of having to sit in a classroom again and having to learn about things he had no interest in,

'Oh great more boring lessons!!, I'm sure Harvey will just love being the butt of the jokes again....HARVEY...' said Daniel rather loudly as he remembered they were looking for his friend '..We have to find Harvey!!'.

Daniel shot off out of the open door and into the courtyard which was bathed in the lowering light of the two suns which shimmered off the castle windows and reflected in the small fountain which streamed water from its top.

The children encountered one of the castle residents on their way towards the door and stopped in front of the woman,

'Excuse me..' asked Daniel 'but have you seen a boy about my height, a bit wider than me with light brownish hair wandering around here?', The woman looked at Daniel and Lillie with a puzzled look,

'Your Lord Casborns son aren't you??, The one we have heard so much about in the past...you're actually here'

'I'm Daniel and this is Lillie, my sister' smiled Daniel 'but we are looking for my friend who has gone missing and we need to find him before he has an accident or something',

'He is an accident' laughed Lillie as Daniel slapped his sister on the arm,

'Ahh yes the other boy from your world. Yes he's right over there' the woman pointed at Harvey who had managed to find his way in and was looking rather sheepish as he wandered over to his friend,

'There you are Harv!!!, where have you been?, I've been looking everywhere for you' said Daniel as he grabbed hold of his friend by the shoulders, Harvey had a confused look on his face as he looked at Daniel,

'I..err. Don't really know Dan' said Harvey as he scratched his head, 'the last thing I remember was eating food, then the next thing I'm standing in the middle of the woods, I recognised the place as I think I'd been there before, I have a vision of a cage or something'

'What about the stuff after that?, you stormed off again after we were eating and you were saying horrible things to us' Lillie reminded Harvey of what had gone on earlier, a puzzled look spreading across her face as she seemed to have a feeling something was not quite right, Harvey just shrugged his shoulders heavily,

'I dunno...maybe it's this place messing with me' he replied,

'Ok Harv...any way let's get inside before we get cau....' no sooner had he started than he looked up to be greeted by the sight of Lord Casborn and the King,

'There you are..' said Lord Casborn '..first of all I don't appreciate you leaving the safety of the room, and second of all until you are aware of just how important you are to this place I will have Garin keeping an eye on you all ok??',

'I guess that's ok' said Daniel 'oh but may I ask you something else?'

'Yes son, go ahead' smiled Lord Casborn

'Is it true that we have to go to classes here?, I overheard you speaking earlier' Daniel seemed a bit embarrassed at telling his family he had been snooping in on them,

'Daniel..' started the King 'yes it is true about what you heard, we were actually just coming to tell you, but you see we have to get you all into our system so that you hopefully will become a huge part of our future, and that does include a bit of history and studying, oh and maybe a few surprises thrown in'

'Oh that's just great!!' Harvey moaned as he threw his arms up in the air 'I only wanted to bunk off school for the afternoon and now this happens, thanks Dan...No really thanks, more chances for me to be picked on!!'.

The King stepped forward and leant in towards the children, a smile spreading across his face as he spoke gently to them,

'I understand that you may find this a little....daunting my children but I assure you that there is a necessity for you to go through the process we have in place as it allows us to make sure you are where you need to be',

'We all have to do it? Even though he is our father?' asked Daniel,

'Yes Daniel, no one gets any special treatment here, this is our way and the way it has always been' replied the King 'Now let's get you ready for your new day children, Garin...please can you take the children to get their schooling clothes from the store please?'

'Yes sir' said Garin as he turned towards the children and smiled,

'Oh and Garin...do watch them closely for me please' the King smirked slightly as he knew how inquisitive the children were,

'I will do my best sir. But this one seems to be a bit more slippery!!' he laughed and he put his arms around their shoulders and moved them towards the door to the castle.

As the children walked off through the door and out of sight Casborn turned to his father, etched across his face was a look of unease,

'Do you think they will be alright father?, I mean they have no idea what is going to happen from here on in'

'Let's see what happens my son' replied the King 'if everything happens as it should then we must not interfere, just one intervention might be hazardous for our future, we need to follow the prophecy'

'Let's hope you are right father...and what of Stephanie? Replied Casborn 'will we see her again?'

'I don't know my son, but what I do know is that one day, if and when the prophecy has come true then the children will have to make a choice..' the King said as he turned away from Casborn,

'What choice father?' asked Casborn as he caught up with the King and placed an arm on his shoulder,

'I don't have any more information than that son' he said 'It is written in text that 'When all is silent and evil lay still, the one who won the battle must ascend the final hill. In front of them a choice is set, a change or stay

210

the same, but ever more for eternity live out their rightful name'. These are the words we must listen to if we are to move forward'

'I guess you are right father, but please help them stay safe if possible' Casborn said as they both walked off towards the door where the children had gone. 'I look like an idiot!!' groaned Harvey as he stared at himself in the mirror, looking at his clothes he needed to wear for classes,

'You look fine Harvey' smiled Garin as he helped Daniel on with his outfit, Harvey's clothes looked strange to him as it looked like he was wearing a dress, he was flapping his arms around like a bird,

'Why do I have this huge hood too??' he asked as he pulled it up over his head and seemed to get lost in it,

'It's so your face can't be seen that well if you are out of the castle grounds, making it harder for anyone to notice who you are and how important you might be' replied Garin

'And if you fall flat on your face then no one will see how ugly you really are' sniggered Lillie as she spun round slowly whilst looking in the mirror, her robes fitted her perfectly which made her smile,

'Shut up Lillie' Harvey scowled back as he went to walk forwards but trod on his robe and fell flat on his face landing with a THUD which caused Lillie to burst out laughing and Daniel to snigger to himself quietly,

'Told you it was too big!!' he moaned as he sat there on the cold floor, arms crossed and looking like he was about to explode,

'I'll get you another set of robes Harvey, Sorry it was my fault I just wanted to play a trick on you' laughed Garin as he helped Harvey up off the floor and made him take the oversized robes off,

'Here you go, these should fit you' Garin said as he tossed Harvey a new set of robes which landed on his head,

'NOT FUNNY…' Harvey said as he tugged the robes off his head and he put them on 'finally!!...these fit better!!' Harvey said sarcastically as he walked around the room almost marching so he didn't trip over.

'Right children, now you are ready we are going to see your father before I escort you off to the class for your first day' Garin said as he opened the door for the children to step through,

'Oh yippee!!' remarked Harvey as he kicked the floor in anger at the thought of having to go to classes again,

'Come on then children, let's go, best not keep your father waiting' said Garin 'and Harvey...you look fine and I promise you that everyone here is warm and friendly, you will be treated like one of us'

'Well if I end up outside the classroom again I won't be happy and it will be your fault!!' Harvey now storming off down the corridor ahead of them all,

'Where does he think he's going?' laughed Lillie as she stopped behind Garin who was opening a door just down from where they were a minute ago, Daniel noticed Harvey was about to disappear and shouted after him,

'HARVEY...Harv...where are you going??' he said as Harvey stopped dead in his tracks and turned to face Daniel,

'This way!!' came the smart reply from the other end of the corridor,

'I gathered that mate but I think we are supposed to follow Garin in here' Daniel said pointing to the open door which was filled with the figure of a soldier who could be heard sniggering to himself as he knew Harvey had walked off and held back on purpose,

'Yes I knew that...' Harvey replied 'but I was just making sure that we weren't being followed or something' he stomped back down the corridor and shoved past Daniel, his face as red as the setting sun, mumbling under his breath to himself,

'Yeah whatever Harv..' laughed Daniel as he followed his friend into the room and Garin shut the door behind them.

'Ahhh children..' smiled the King as he set eyes on all three of them standing there in their robes, looking slightly awkward apart from Lillie who was ecstatic at the thought of going back into school,

'I love these clothes!!' she beamed 'When do we start?',

'My my, you all look wonderful' the King said as he clapped his hands together in appreciation 'I have been waiting for this day for so long, Now my children, we must get you introduced to your new study group, I will go ahead and speak to your teacher, but I shall not mention the connection between us all, other than you are simply lost and in need of our help. Son, I will leave the children with you, when you have finished escort them to Lady Willo's class if you please'

'Yes sir..' replied Casborn 'I shall be along soon', and with that the King smiled as he walked past the children and off out of the door, his footsteps could be heard all the way up the corridor.

Daniel turned back to where his father was standing and seemed a bit hesitant,

'What's the matter son?' asked Lord Casborn 'you seem a bit lost, is everything ok?'

'I..er..I don't know really, It's just that it seems like we have been through so much since we got here but we have no idea about what's going on' Daniel said in a way that made him seem very down and looking for answers from his father,

'Well please ask anything son' replied Casborn 'you are here because it was meant to be, ALL of you were brought here to find something you were searching for, I cannot be more thrilled than I am already to be reunited with my beautiful son and my wonderful strong daughter, I cannot tell you how long I have been searching for you, my world now feels complete'.

'I have dreamt of the day that we got to meet you, it was the visions I was having that made me feel a strong pull towards you, I don't know how but it seemed that we just had to be here, but mum....' Daniel replied as his father knelt down in front of him,

'Your mother made the ultimate sacrifice in taking you from this place son, both of you, she knew there would be no way back from your world, I could not know where you had gone otherwise you would have been in danger and the King wouldn't allow that, that is why you had to leave me behind. Not a day has gone by that I haven't thought about seeing you

213

again.' Casborn smiled, tears filling his eyes as he finally felt a huge weight lift off his shoulders.

'We are all happy father' said Lillie as she moved in for a hug, 'I just wish mum was here with us to see this day'

'She is quite safe from harm children, you see from the moment you stepped into this world time froze on her side, she is in a place where she cannot be found or harmed in any way' said Lord Casborn doing his best to reassure his children while Harvey just stood there silently, a glazed look spreading across his face which went unnoticed by everyone else, he was scouring the room for something, eyes squinted slightly, a voice in his head kept calling to him,

'Look around...bring us more...' the ghostly voice was getting stronger as Harvey slowly wandered round the room as Lillie, Daniel and Lord Casborn were still talking in the middle of it, then as quick as it had arrived the voices vanished, Harvey shook his head and a cold shiver made his body tremble,

'Brrrr' he said out loud, causing Daniel to turn towards him,

'Are you ok Harv?' he asked 'something spooked you?' he laughed softly,

'I don't know Dan...Felt like someone had walked across my grave or something, I feel all icky now' He moaned as he shook off whatever it was and joined Daniel alongside his father,

'So children..' Lord Casborn said 'this is where I must leave you...this education must be taken, our history needs to be embedded in all of you in order for you to take the next step of your journey, I cannot help you on whatever path it is you choose, You and you alone must make choices, choices that may test you in some way, choices that will test each and every one of you in both a physical and mental way, no matter what happens I will always be proud of you, you have come back to me finally and I would love you to be by my side.'

'I hope we can make you proud then father' said Lillie as she hugged Lord Casborn just that little bit tighter,

'Do yourselves proud children, but please no matter how long it takes take in every piece of information you can as the final test you will all have to carry out will show us all that you truly belong here' Lord Casborn hugged his children again and went to walk off but before he did he stopped and turned towards Harvey,

'Now Harvey...I understand that this must be slightly hard for you but as you are Daniel's true friend I do look upon you as family, I sense a strength in you that I haven't felt in a very long time, just remember to channel it wisely and as I said before take great pride in the opportunity that has been laid out before you' Lord Casborn placed his hand on Harvey's shoulder and stared deep into his soul, his words echoing around inside Harvey's head as he stared right back.

Then Lord Casborn suddenly pulled his head back fast, shaking his head slightly as if dazed,

'Are you ok father?' asked Daniel

'Y..yes..I'm..I'm fine..' he replied 'I just felt odd for a few seconds, there's nothing to worry about, now come on children we must get you started in class, just wait outside please, I just need a quick word with Garin' and off the children went, Garin had seen Casborn looking shaken and walked over to him, a worried look appearing on his face,

'What is it? Are you ok' He asked as Casborn turned away slightly,

'I can't be sure Garin' he replied 'I saw something in that boy...something slightly disturbing, I can't quite put my finger on it though'

'What was it to do with?, did it show anything to you?' replied Garin who could see Casborn visibly shaken now,

'I saw an ending...it involved the children, they were surrounded by an evil of some kind, I couldn't quite see anything else apart from a man..someone I thought I recognised....then it was gone, Garin please watch over the children for me, ALL of them, but be careful of any interference, we cannot afford to lose them, and also please don't relay any of this to my father, if anything develops then I would rather I deal with it head on'

'Yes sir I shall do what it takes, within reason, to keep them safe and heading towards whatever path they may choose'.

And with that they both headed out of the room, Daniel and Harvey were play fighting as Lillie tried to stop them, she grabbed them both in a headlock and pulled them along the corridor behind Garin who seemed slightly edgy now, she let go eventually when they had calmed down, Lord Casborn was following behind, still seemingly taken aback by the events of earlier but he was putting on a smile that was reassuring to the children as the looked back to see if he was still there,

'Father do you think we will be alright, in the classes I mean, we don't know anyone here and it's a bit scary' Daniel asked, sounding slightly worried,

'My children, you shall be fine, you have my word that everyone will take to you just as we have, just enjoy what you are to learn' Casborn smiled back just as they reached the first classroom door which swung open with a CREAK.

Chapter Eighteen
First Day Of Forever

'Ahhh children...do come in' the familiar voice of the King greeted them warmly into the room, as they walked in tentatively they could feel a thousand eyes burning into their souls, all wondering the same thing, who are the new people?, where did they come from?, a thousand questions from a thousand places all wanting the same answer. They looked slightly embarrassed as they continued in when Harvey caught sight of someone he recognised which caused him to tug at Daniel's arm,

'Dan...Look!!' Harvey said as he pointed at the class teacher. In the corner of the room standing just behind the King was a familiar face known to all three of them,

'That's Mrs Marley!!!' exclaimed Daniel 'She was my first teacher when I was small!!', as she stepped forward Daniel knew he had seen her before, a very long time ago, she always had a sort of soft spot for him and seemed rather protective, he remembered her giving him small pieces of advice about how to stay safe and always watch out for those closest to him, which now seemed to make sense seeing where they had ended up now.

'This is Lady Willo children..' said the King as she stepped forward and smiled at them,

'Hello children, first of all I'd like to welcome you to my class, we are known as 'The Dawnfall', there are two other classes like ours which you will learn about in time, as I understand it this will be your class Daniel..' said Lady Willo pointing to an empty table right in the middle of the class,

'I thought we were all going to be put in the same class together' said Harvey as he started to feel a bit uneasy just like he did at Longmeads at the thought of not being with his friend, the King offered his reasons for doing this to the children,

'We must separate you so you aren't influenced in any decisions you make by each other, this ensures that any progress you make towards the final test is born of your mind alone'

'Oh great, bottom of the class again I bet!!' moaned Harvey as he looked even more upset by this,

'Don't be so hard on yourself young Harvey' smiled the King 'you may just surprise yourself here, this schooling is more of a...guideline shall we say, into what we would like you to become'

'Oh that helps!!' said Harvey 'it's still school though, I couldn't stand it then and I'm sure I won't feel any different about it now',

The King knew that Harvey would be the hardest to get through to so made sure he had something good to aim for and appealed to his more excitable side,

'My dear boy, I can see that you are uneasy about what you are about to go through but let me explain that this schooling is beneficial to your future here with us, you will learn so much about yourself, you will learn thing that will keep you safe from harm, you will learn how to defend yourself and how your mind can manipulate the world around you, if you're strong enough I mean, all in all it's a schooling that may just save your life one day'

'Ohhhh right, if you put it like that then...where do we start??' a smile had spread across his face at the thought of something exciting happening to him for once,

'But remember it's not all easy going Harvey, the path ahead is filled with pitfalls as well as highs, and the learning you will be doing will require a lot of concentration' the King hoped to see Harvey's demeanour change, which it did, meaning he was fully focused on what was going to be happening to him here.

'Right children, Daniel you are to stay here with Lady Willo as you know, Lillie and Harvey you are to follow me please'.

Off they went out of the classroom leaving Daniel standing there with everyone just looking at him, he felt so uneasy as he made his way to his table, he pulled the seat out which creaked and screeched across the wooden floor as he did it, hoping no one had noticed it he sat down as if nothing had happened, he turned to his right and smiled at the girl sitting next to him who just stared back blankly, her eyes burning deep into the side of his face,

'Hello…' He said 'I'm Daniel…I'm new here', the girl just kept staring back at him, mouth wide open, without even moving throwing him a look that seemed to suggest she had never seen anyone like him before,

'Oh ok…' Daniel said and turned back towards the front of the class to be met with the face of Lady Willo staring back at him with a look that said 'are we ready to start', Daniel smiled nervously at Lady Willo as he shuffled in his seat and adjusted his robes before looking straight ahead waiting for the class to begin.

'This way Lillie…this is where your class is' the King said as they reached the most colourful door she had ever seen, beautiful carvings filled every inch of it, carvings that seemed to depict a happy environment within, a scenery which showed all of the town laughing and dancing to some sort of festival.

Lillie was enchanted by its beauty and couldn't wait to meet the people behind the door who had created something so beautiful,

'The door opened and a beam of beautiful sunlight filled the corridor as the teacher in the room filled the doorway bathed in a glorious glow,

'This is Mr Flora..' said the King, stretching out his hand to introduce Lillies new teacher,

'Ahhh Lillie…that is a most beautiful name' replied her teacher 'Lillie, like the flower, and my name is linked to flowers, It's like you were meant to be put in my class, how wonderful' he beamed, Lillie smiled back knowing she felt instantly comfortable in her surroundings, Mr Flora could see that Lillie knew she belonged in his class and had the biggest smile spreading across her face as she turned to face her new classmates who seemed just a happy to see her as she was to be there, a few of them waved in her direction causing her to smile back,

'Welcome to your classroom then Lillie' said Mr Flora, 'we are known as 'The Wallbloom', a nod to the flowers that grow up our castle walls, I feel that you will fit right in Lillie. I have kept a table clear in the centre of the classroom for you so you can mingle with the rest of the class, feel free to chat to your new class friend's and get to know them well, we try to encourage social interaction so no one feels out of place',

'Oh thank you sir' Lillie beamed as she walked over to her seat with everyone in the class wanting to say hello to her, the King pulled Mr Flora to one side and said,

'I hope that this child will be allowed the room to grow Mr Flora, I don't want a repeat of what happened last time!!'

'My King..' replied Mr Flora 'no one could have predicted what would have happened with the child, you know I have an excellent record with the children, what happened that day was not of my doing'

'Just see that nothing happens to her, she's a very special individual' the King replied raising a finger as he spoke,

'Yes my King, I will not fail you this time' Mr Flora said as he bowed his head toward the King,

'Good good Mr Flora' replied the King 'she must have no outside influences, I need to see where she belongs', and with that the King turned on his heels and walked out the door shepherding Harvey away from the class,

'Now my dear boy just your class left and then I can finish my own teachings'

'What do you teach if I may ask sir?' asked Harvey as he noticed that they had been walking for a long time now,

'Ahh my boy it is a specialised teaching for certain individuals, but only a select few get to partake in this, it's more for...castle protection purposes…but it takes many years to be allowed into my chambers for that' the King said as he walked down the longest corridor Harvey had ever seen, they walked past a collection of doors, each with a class behind them, Harvey was getting excited at the thought of what his new classmates were going to be like seeing as both Lillie and Daniels classes seemed like good classes to be in,

'So King…' asked Harvey as they neared the end of the corridor 'what's my class like then?, I can't wait to meet them!!'

'Patience Harvey. We are almost there, this class has been carefully selected by the board as best suited for you apparent ability, I expect you to thrive in here' smiled the King as they reached the final door in the longest and darkest part of the castle, he knocked on the door…and nothing, no one came to the door, the King sighed as he knew the class were inside, he could hear noises sounding like the children 'shushing' each other.

The King knocked slower and harder this time, the sound of footsteps could be heard coming towards the door, it creaked open enough for a pair of eyes to become visible to both of them.

'K..King Casborn…Errrm hello…I wasn't expecting to see you today' said the small rounded face with a pair of rather oversized glasses on looked out from behind the battered and beaten door,

'Ahhh hello Mr Scoot' smiled the King 'if you would be so kind as to open the door and let us in, I have your new pupil here..And he's excited to be joining your class', Mr Scoot turned his attention towards Harvey who was standing there sporting a huge smile on his face,

'This is the child?' asked Mr Scoot as he looked Harvey up and down, his eyes bulging as he looked over the top of his glasses,

'Why yes, he is a new addition to our ever expanding family Mr Scoot, so I expect you to show him the same courtesy as you did to the rest of the class when they joined you' the King's tone changed to a more authoritative tone this time which didn't go unnoticed by Mr Scoot who slowly pulled the door open which creaked and groaned as he tugged at it. The door got

221

stuck halfway which caused a room full of sniggering to start up from behind him, Mr Scoot sighed and closed his eyes as he grew increasingly annoyed with every passing second, he looked down to see someone had put a wedge behind the door, stopping it from opening fully,

'Who put that there? Answer me or else there will be consequences for the whole class' came the high pitched response from Mr Scoot who was now turning a dark red colour as he turned towards his room full of children,

'New kid done it…'came the smart response from somewhere deep in the room, Harvey was now shaking slightly at the thought of stepping into the room, Mr Scoot reacted in his normal way towards whoever had come out with the comment by stamping his foot on the ground and wagging his finger strongly,

'DON'T ACT ALL SMART WITH ME' He shouted back 'and I don't want you to start on the new child in the class ok!!' just as he finished a rolled up ball of paper came hurtling through the air and hit Mr Scoot slap bang on the side of the head causing his glasses to fall off and hit the floor,

'RIGHT WHO THREW THAT!!!' he screeched and disappeared inside the room leaving the King and Harvey standing there looking rather bemused, the King turned to Harvey and smiled awkwardly just as Harvey was about to take a peek inside the classroom to see where the teacher had gone, he heard something slamming inside and a voice laughing as it said once again,

'New kid done it…' followed by complete silence.

As footsteps could be heard walking back towards the open door Harvey prepared himself for whatever it was coming his way but he was met by the sight of Mr Scoot again, looking a little disheveled as he adjusted himself,

'Sorry about that sir' he said as he turned his attention back to Harvey, 'just a bit of unruliness that has been sorted for now..'

'Not a good impression for this boy's first day is it Mr Scoot' remarked the King as he stood there very patiently,

'I can only apologise sir...but it's been one of those mornings for them, something seems to have rattled them but I don't know what it is' Mr Scoot replied as he lowered his head in a slightly shameful way,

'Just make sure you get them all inline for the parade please, I don't want any more shame brought upon this class, seeing just how far behind everyone is' the King said as he then looked towards Harvey, he put his hand behind Harvey's back and looked at him straight in the eyes for a few seconds, 'and Mr Scoot...make sure you look after young Harvey here, I have already told you all about him so I expect total cooperation and absolutely NO interference from anyone, DO YOU UNDERSTAND!!'

'Y...yes my King...I understand completely, I will do my best as always...but you know what the children are like sir, a handful at the best of times, and with the new boy joining they might just get slightly worse!!' replied Mr Scoot nervously,

'Then it's your job to keep them inline, seeing as they are your responsibility...you do remember what happened to Mr Tanner don't you Arthur?' the King leant in slightly and used his first name which Mr Scoot knew normally meant trouble for him,

'I...I do sir...and I appreciate how lucky I am to have this position. I...I will do my best I give you my word..' he replied looking rather worried now,

'YOUR word is...worthless' the King replied 'just follow the books and no harm will befall you', and with that the King turned away from Mr Scoot, winked at Harvey as he went to walk away which made him feel a bit less worried about joining the class.

As Harvey was ushered into his new class he felt slightly odd, his head was starting to feel all fuzzy, like he wasn't in control, followed by a voice, one he had heard so many times already,

'For us to succeed you must be strong...give us more' the ghostly voice said before slowly fading away, Harvey shook his head as if trying to shake off whatever it was he was feeling just as he walked past the door to be greeted by row after row of young children, all sitting there quiet...for now, not one of them smiled at Harvey as he inched his way towards his seat

223

which had been placed in the back corner of the room in what looked like the darkest scariest corner ever seen, he was talking to himself as he went 'just keep going...don't look at anyone', all the confidence he felt earlier had suddenly drained from his body and he shuddered as he walked towards his table, pairs of eyes just staring at him, as if looking deep into his soul and beyond.

As he reached his seat in the corner and went to sit down he caught a glimpse of something just close to the door he came in through, a hazy hooded figure stood there for a second then vanished, Harvey just stared at the space where it had been as if he had sort of recognised whatever it was,

'Did I just...I've seen that before I think' he said quietly to himself but loud enough for the boy sitting next to him to be able to hear him talking,

'What did you say Ordie??' the snarling voice snapped back at him out of the semi darkness he was sitting in,

'Ordie??' replied Harvey looking puzzled 'what's one of them? And who are you?', the boy leaned further towards Harvey, sniffed the air around him as if sensing something and still snarling said,

'It's a name for people like you...those who have nothing inside them'

'Oh right that clears it up...thanks for that!!' Harvey said feeling even more confused than ever as he took his seat, just as he did another pupil walked over to him, this time a girl stood there, she leant forwards so her hands were on his desk her face was slightly covered by a mop of long jet black hair, she moved her face closer to his as she stared deeper into his eyes before speaking,

'I see evil in your soul….swirling round like the wind….a cloudy future you have...be afraid of the dark for it will consume you forever'.

Harvey sat back in his chair seemingly too afraid to move,

'Wh...what the heck is going on here!!' his voice trembling as he spoke 'I didn't ask to be in here..just leave me alone!!' he closed his eyes tight hoping they would all go away but when he opened them he was met with

224

the same pairs of eyes staring back at him until one boy at the front of the class got up and stomped to the back to where Harvey was sat,

'Leave him alone Otto!!' came the strong sounding voice 'and you sit back down too Hayla!!, leave him alone right now or I'll turn you both into Leadheads' said the boy as he stared at the other two children with his hand outstretched and a small crackle of lightning seeping from each finger,

'Oooo I'm so scared Pontus!!' replied Otto as he casually laughed at the threat aimed at him 'why not put a spell on your new best friend and make him not look like he's about to cry', all the while Harvey was just sitting there frozen stiff trying not to make eye contact with anyone.

The two children eventually turned away but not before Hayla left Harvey with a message,

'Inside your soul lives something evil, something strong enough to make a difference, when the time comes you must fight...I'm watching you. Always'.

'Don't listen to her' said Pontus 'she's been drinking crazy juice again', Harvey stared at Pontus now who was smiling back at him,

'Th..Thank you for that' he nervously replied, still not sure what to say or do,

'I'm Pontus by the way, class guardian and, as I'm sure you will find out soon enough, Class champion 2 years running, welcome to 'MuddyBog' the class everyone wants to avoid when they arrive here'

'I...I'm Harvey and I have no clue what's going on!' he replied nervously, not knowing whether to smile or just sit there and look at his desk, 'I kind of get the impression I'm not liked that much'

Pontus leaned on Harvey's desk and smiled, it was a smile that seemed to put Harvey at ease a bit,

'Naah, don't worry about any of that' said Pontus 'they are like that with every new kid who joins the class, they like to let them know who's in charge but they know not to mess with me if I get involved' 'Oh why is that?' asked Harvey quizzically

'Well....' replied Pontus 'bit of a long story really but shorter version you only need to hear about is that we had a new kid in here quite a long time back, think his name was Archie. Or something, he was really odd...didn't speak to anyone, didn't do any work and just sat there looking down at his desk, just seemed not right to us. So one day he all of a sudden stood up while Mr Scoot was in the middle of his lesson, jumped up onto his desk and started freaking out quite badly', Harvey was taking in every word as he leant forward to be able to listen better,

'And what happened then?' he asked, his mouth now wide open,

'He was screaming about the voices in his head taking over, and how he didn't want this inside him, then his eyes turned a sort of purple looking colour and it all stopped, stood there on top of his desk with Mr Scoot shouting at him to get down at once, but he was having none of it and let out the most ear piercing scream followed by sort of electricity shooting out of his fingers towards Mr Scoot, that's where I stepped in' Pontus smiled smugly as he stood up straight, arms on his hips like a superhero,

'So what did you do?' Harvey was mesmerized by the whole story now,

'I done what anybody else would of done in that situation..' started Pontus, but Otto as usual was listening in and decided to try and finish his story for him,

'He tripped up on his chair while trying to run away from the class and fell backwards against the desk causing the kid to fall off and knock himself out cold...'

'Shut up Otto!!!' shouted Pontus 'that's rubbish and you know it, the REAL story ends like this, I conjured up my own brand of a freezing spell which, may I add is one I thought up myself during class and developed it to perfection, and stopped him in his tracks. Mr Scoot was far too scared to help so I had to step in, that's why he's such a scaredy Buffle now' Pontus puffed his chest out and stood there as if waiting for applause but Harvey was just staring in awe,

'Oh is that it?' asked Harvey 'wow that is a great story, so where is the boy now?'

226

'No one really knows what happened to him' Pontus said 'but rumour has it that he is somewhere in this castle, locked away deep below ground, still trying to get free from his cell', Otto scoffed at what Pontus was saying,

'Oh and who told you that load of old plonk?' came the reply,

'It's true!!' remarked Pontus 'the last person to go find him never returned, It was the old teacher from 'ElmWood' Mr.....Astrum, yes that's him, they say all that all that was found of him when they went looking was his cloak, glasses and his notebook of spells sitting outside Archie's room, very sad situation, he was a nice teacher too!'

'Oh do shut up Pontus. That story gets better and longer every time you tell it!!' laughed Otto, and with that Pontus picked up his school book and hit Otto round the with it with enough force to make him fall off his seat.

'You'll pay for that Polder' said Otto angrily as he lifted himself up off the chair and raised his hands in a sort of attack stance, a low humming could be heard coming from Otto's direction,

'Don't do it Otto' shouted Pontus as he summoned electricity to his fingertips 'I don't want to have to hurt you again!!' this caused the whole class to turn round now,

'MAGI-FIGHT, MAGI-FIGHT' they chanted together,

Just as they were about to get going Mr Scoot screamed at the top of his voice,

'STOP THIS RIGHT NOW YOU TWO!!, there will be no trouble here today ok, if you have any problems go sort them out in the arena, but not in my class!!, DO I MAKE MYSELF CLEAR?',

'Whatever sir..' muttered Otto 'I'll get you one day Polder, just you wait', Pontus just smiled and winked at Harvey who had now slunk down below desk height and was visibly scared,

'Back to your seat too Pontus if you please, I must get this lesson finished before time runs out, and with that he made his way back to his seat, whistling as he went and leaving Harvey totally scared and even more confused as to what had just happened. He sat upright in his seat and looked around at everyone else who were all now looking towards the front of the room as Mr Scoot carried on with his lesson.

'I'd watch yourself too Ordie…' Otto piped up 'don't get sucked in by anything he says, there's a reason we are all in this classroom and it's not because we are the best at everything, we are the kids no one wanted to teach, we are the kids who they can't control and we are the kids who will do just about ANYTHING to survive, you just remember that ok?'

'R..righto..' muttered Harvey as he closed his eyes tight hoping for this all to go away. As Harvey sat there shaken by what had just happened right in front of him he started thinking about what Otto and Pontus had said to him, 'how am I going to get through this?' he thought 'no one likes me', but just then a voice entered his head and made him sit upright,

'You will succeed boy....become the best....take them all down…' then, as they always done the voice vanished and Harvey's head was silent once again. Just the normal shouting could be heard coming from outside, the Arena was buzzing once more.

Chapter Nineteen
First Days Nerves

As the first day in their new school surroundings continued there seemed to be a buzz of excitement around the corridors and in most of the classrooms as the children got to know their new classmates, laughter could be heard echoing around Lillies new class, loud clapping from behind Daniel's class door and from behind Harvey's classroom door....just the usual sound of Mr Scoot shouting at his class and them not bothering to listen, just a normal day for them in fact.

But back in Lillies class everything seemed to be better than she was expecting, everyone was interacting with her as she was allowed time to get to know her new classmates, they were swapping stories about the school and their families and how they had always wanted to be in the class they had been out in as it was the same one either their mother or father had been in many years before,

'So Lillie, tell us about your family and where you grew up then, we don't really know that much about you other than you turned up suddenly at the castle' said one girl who was sitting next to Lillie,

'Excellent question Daisy' smiled Mr Flora as he had overheard her question 'Would you like to tell us all about your family Lillie?, there's a space right at the front of the class for you, I mean you don't have to do it if you're unsure, no pressure at all', Lillie thought about it for a few seconds, knowing where they had actually come from might make her sound like she was making it up so she decided to bend the truth a little but keep it as close to her real life as she could,

'Errr, ok Mr Flora' she said as she rose to her feet and was given a round of applause by her new friend's as she made her way past each desk which made her slightly embarrassed,

'Well...errr' she started 'The thing is…

'It's ok, don't be embarrassed, we have all been where you are' smiled Mr Flora as he put his hand on her shoulder, Lillie let out a deep breath, which gave her a few seconds of thinking time,

'You see. As you all know I'm not from here, sorry, WE aren't from here. I mean my brother Daniel, his friend Harvey and myself. We came from a place far away from here, on a journey that seems to have taken us a lifetime…' each child in her class was listening intently at their desk, all leaning forwards trying to take in every word Lillie was saying,

'...we didn't want to leave our town but we didn't really have a choice, we just sort of appeared here' she said as she could feel a thousand eyes staring at her,

'So what's the town called you are from Lillie?' asked Mr Flora, wanting to know as much detail as he could get from her which would help her integration into the class,

'I..errr..it's quite a small town quite a way from here' she replied, looking for inspiration from anywhere in the room when she spotted a huge map of Vaymia on the wall to her left, right next to where she was standing, she quickly noticed a small looking town on the other side of the world from where Erwin was, 'It's called...errr...Netherbrook...just here' she pointed directly to the town on the map. Mr Flora suddenly perked up a bit when he heard the name of the town,

'Oh that's interesting' he said ' I have friends around that part of the world Lillie, maybe about four or five towns away from there', panic seemed to set in across Lillies face as he said that,

'Oh...really, that's nice s..sir' she bumbled out a reply, now worrying she might be found out,

'Unfortunately, since the start of the wars I haven't heard anything from them or that area in fact, I believe evil forces have flattened the towns by now' replied Mr Flora seemingly lost in thought, 'Ahh..Yes where were we' he muttered 'do go on please my girl', Lillie seemed to breathe a sigh of relief at his reply,

'Well as I was saying we lived with our mother in the town...and we had a pet do...' she stopped herself as she knew they wouldn't have heard of a dog before and didn't want to have to explain herself again, so once again she scoured the wall looking for inspiration,

'A Dobbler....' she exclaimed, and with that everyone in the class gasped as they heard her say that name,

'A Dobbler Lillie??...' remarked Mr Flora 'are you sure it was one of those' a puzzled look spread across his face which didn't go unnoticed by Lillie,

'Y..yes sir, it definitely was a Dobbler' she replied nervously noticing the mood changing in the room with the children whispering to each other, then she caught sight of what a Dobbler actually looked like as there were pictures across the far wall showing this huge scaly two headed beast attacking what looked like a huge castle somewhere, it's steely ivory eyes sit buried within the creature's bony, hard skull, which gives the creature a rather intimidating looking appearance.

Several enormous horns sit atop its head, just above its thick, dog-like ears. A row of small horns runs down the sides of each of its jaw lines.

Its two noses are flat and have two tiny, slitted nostrils on each head, there are horns running around its chin too. Rows of sharp teeth poke out from the side of its mouth showing the terror hiding inside if anyone were to be unlucky enough to get taken by this huge beast.

A short neck runs down from both its heads and into a huge body. The top is covered in wide scales and a row of smaller scales run down its spine.

Its underbelly is covered in narrow scales and is coloured slightly darker than the rest of its body. Six muscular limbs carry its body and allow the creature to stand up straight as well as walk on all its limbs. Each limb has 6 digits, each of which has razor sharp claws digging into whatever it decides to stand on.

Freakish wings growing from its shoulders and end at the middle of its back. The wings are almost angel-like in their appearance, one of the heads is shooting fire like nothing she had seen before while the other head was breathing ice from its mouth, and part of the beast was invisible.

'So this is the 'pet' you kept then Lillie?' asked Mr Flora as he walked up the drawings which adorned the walls like wallpaper and pointed at one of the pictures 'This destroyer of cities and towns, this unimaginable evil, this….just horrible, horrible creature was a pet of yours?',

'Uh-huh..yep' she replied, her voice quivering slightly as she desperately though of something to come back with, 'well it was a lot smaller when we had him around!!'.

Some of the children sniggered at her answer but she knew she had to keep going with it,

'My brother and I found him out in our woods near where we lived' she started 'we were playing in them one day when we came across Edgar, that's what we called him, he was injured quite badly so we decided to help him. We nursed him back to health over the next few weeks, he was no bigger than us at the time so we took him home and our mother helped up to look after him', once again the children fell silent as Lillies mind ventured off into a different world

'Please do go on Lillie' said Mr Flora 'This sounds fascinating', Lillie didn't know if he was being sarcastic or just enjoying the story,

'Well as I was saying sir when Edgar was almost better mum realised that he was growing very fast and there would come a time when he couldn't stay with us otherwise we would be crushed as he was getting so much bigger now!!' she put in a little snigger to try and make it more light hearted,

'One day when we were outside with him mum made us say our goodbyes, he was almost as tall as our house now so we knew it was the right time to let him go' she lowered her head, pretending to be upset about her 'pet' having to leave, 'Edgar seemed to know it too, he lowered his heads to me and I held his huge head gently and left a kiss on his scaly mouth, then done the same to Edgar two, he whimpered softly as if to say goodbye…',

'Then what happened Lillie?' one child shouted excitedly, wanting to hear the rest of the story,

'Well...as Daniel leaned in to say goodbye Edgars heads came together and Daniel was caught between them, they were only being friendly towards him but Daniel was now struggling to breathe, they moved their heads apart and Daniel flopped to the ground gasping for air, then as Edgar turned to go his body turned sort of....invisible and then he was gone, we never saw him again' Lillies story seemed to have them all mesmerized now, Mr Flora just seemed to sit there as if trying to process her story,

'Wow Lillie…' replied a child at the back 'I bet you miss Edgar don't you!',

'Yes and no I'd say' she replied 'if these drawings are anything to go by then I'm glad he went away!!',

'Ok Lillie go and take your seat again please...and thank you for that amazing 'story' of yours' said Mr Flora 'Now we can get back on with the first days lesson, please open your books at page three children 'The Fourteen Bells Of Peace'..' Mr Floras voice trailed off as Lillie sat at her desk hoping that she had got away with her story, she sat there not really concentrating on anything as her mind wandered off again, small memories kept filling her head of her real past and the life they had come away from, 'Mum' she said in her head as blurry images filled her mind like a tap being turned on, but for some reason she was struggling to remember her old life now, one image began to become clearer in her head as she sat there daydreaming, then just as the image cleared she heard a lot of shouting coming from outside in the Arena which broke her concentration. 'GET HIM….TAKE HIM DOWN…' came the shouts, the whole class rose to look out of the windows to see what was happening, including Mr Flora.

Just along the corridor stood Daniel's new class, a picture hung on the wall of the teacher, Lady Willo, a very happy looking teacher who always looked for the best in everything, her picture radiated with love and kindness, she was the sort of teacher who everyone wanted to be taught by, inside the class Lady Willo was telling the story of 'The Fourteen Bells of Peace' and how they are still guarded to this very day after hundreds of years,

'So children as you now know The Fourteen Bells of Peace are invaluable to the safety and security of our land and their location can never be known for fear of them falling into the wrong hands' she shut her teaching book gently 'Now any questions?',

Not one child raised their hand as most of them had been told their own version about the Bells and their importance by their own parents, Daniel looked round slowly then he raised his hand ever so slowly,

'Errr Miss Willo…' he asked

'It's Lady Willo, Daniel and yes do you have a question?' she replied with a smile,

'Well…you see, I don't really know too much about the Bells apart from I know that if they all fall then it will mean a lot of trouble for us..' Daniel said as the children in the class started whispering to each other, something that Lady Willo had noticed,

'Quieten down children please, it's only right that we answer this for Daniel' she said calmly 'It's really a myth that 'if the Bells fall' ,as you put it, then it will lead to an evil being unleashed over the land, a mere fictional tale passed down through many generations to keep children away from harm,'

'I..I didn't ask about any of that Lady Willo, I was only told it would mean that the land would be unprotected for a while' Daniel's eyes shut slightly as if he had picked up on something totally different,

'Oh..err, yes that's what I meant Daniel, you see there have been many stories passed down over the years about how we will become workers for evil. But I assure you there is nothing to fear' Lady Willo spoke, trying to confuse Daniel with another tale,

'So there's no truth in what you are saying then?, we are all safe here?' Daniel replied hoping to catch her out,

'I swear to the King that no harm will ever fall upon this land or you children' said Lady Willo as she smiled back in Daniel's direction,

'Right. I sort of get it...but if that's true then what is the purpose of that big arena thing outside and why are people training. Or whatever it is they are doing in there? There seems to be a lot of noise coming from it' Daniel said as he pointed out of the window to the huge structure that engulfed the whole courtyard and left most of the classes around it in darkness,

'Oh yes...you've seen that have you?' her face turning slightly red now as she was getting slightly flustered,

'Well you can't exactly miss it can you' Daniel replied smartly ' I mean it's huge and it always seems to be full of people and stuff' as he said that a large army of armour wearing soldiers marched past the window in perfect unison and around the side of the arena towards the front gate, ready for whatever challenge lay ahead.

'Oh you're talking about that arena Daniel' replied Lady Willo 'well that's nothing more than our outdoor activity area, it's somewhere we go rather frequently after lessons are completed, it's normally used for physical exercise and general training but it's being used for something completely different at the minute'

'So it's a place for training soldiers then...I mean you did kind of just tell us Miss' Daniel said as he could see Lady Willo getting more and more flustered,

'Yes...I mean no....it is used for many things Daniel, including the three yearly competition we stage here' Lady Willo said hoping to throw Daniel off its real purpose,

'Oh what's that then?' he asked when, Finn, the boy sitting next to him spoke out loud,

'It's a competition to find the most complete warrior to join The Circle, we call it 'The Tri-Yearly-Night-Games'...'

'Ooooooo' the class called out in unison as Daniel laughed out loud

'The TYNG....haha, oh that so reminds me of home!!' he sniggered as the word took on another meaning for him,

235

'This competition is no laughing matter' replied Lady Willo 'it represents a chance for people from all over the world to participate in these games and hopefully for a lucky few to be able to join the 'Kings Circle' which is his army of most complete and trustworthy soldiers',

'And do we get the chance to try out for the circle thing?' Daniel asked inquisitively, which caused a few of the children to laugh quietly amongst themselves,

'Oh no…' Lady Willo said 'this is only open to entrants from across Vaymia who have completed their own pathway through their town or village where they live and have been put forward in the hope of winning a place here'

'Oh right..' replied Daniel 'so there's no chance of any of us getting in there to do that at all?, or has anyone from here actually managed to get into the Circle?'

'Well there has been one from here...quite a few years back, but it took him quite a few years to finally realise his dream of fighting alongside the King' Lady Willo smiled as she thought about the person who had won their rightful place 'Garin of Arrowbrook. Ahhh he was such a strong competitor...no person could match him for strength or heart but then without any notice he just...vanished, only to appear a little while ago with no recollection of where he had been'

'Garin??' exclaimed Daniel 'Oh he never said anything about that!!', Lady Willo shot Daniel a confused look across the room,

'Oh so you know of Garin do you Daniel?' she replied back,

'Well yes...he was my d...' Daniel looked round to see everyone now staring at him '...doctor?....yes he was my doctor back when I was a small boy, he was always looking after me and my family, but I didn't know his secret until now, he kept it hidden well' smiled Daniel as he knew of his REAL secret but knew the class didn't,

'Well I didn't know he was so medically trained, but I guess everyone has something to hide don't they children' smiled Lady Willo 'Anyway enough of that...so as I was saying...with the night games almost upon us we shall, as we always have done, go and support the competitors at some point' a loud cheer went up when Lady Willo announced that 'but as I have said many times before you must NOT distract any of them while they are competing, we don't want a repeat of last year when Hammond of Baggothill was distracted by a pupil causing him to be brutally taken out of the competition....oh it still gives me nightmares!!' she shuddered at the thought of it 'but the class were warned just like you have been so I expect total cooperation please'

'YES LADY WILLO' the class replied as she looked round the room smiling at the children,

'What did happen to that man then Miss?' asked Daniel 'it couldn't have been that bad surely'

'Daniel..' she replied 'it was horrific in every way, he was one of the favourites to join The Circle but as it proved that when in the Arena total concentration is required at all times, I don't wish to dwell on it any longer'

'I'll tell you later' smiled Tobias, a small boy with a rather disheveled look about him who was sitting to the other side of Daniel 'its gruesome trust me' he smiled, Daniel's face grinned as wide as it could as he couldn't wait for the story,

'Oh great, can't wait!' he said before his attention was caught by the sound of shouting outside,

'GET HIM....TAKE HIM DOWN...' were the raised voices coming from inside the Arena walls,

'It sounds like it's coming from in the Arena!' someone said excitedly

'Is he here?, he's my absolute favourite' said another voice closer to the window,

'Settle down children!!' Lady Willo said loudly 'I'm sure we will get to see them all in action soon'

'See who?' Daniel replied looking slightly confused as to what they were all talking about, Tobias turned to Daniel and said quietly,

'Don't you know Daniel?, Tahmidius of Banglashera is here this year!!', Daniel was now completely lost,

'Who?, sorry Tobias I haven't a clue what you're going on about' he replied,

'Oh yes I forgot you were new, Tahmidius is sort of a celebrity around the world, most of his family have been successful in joining 'The Circle' so he has been following in their footsteps and trying to join them,

'Oh right' replied Daniel still looking totally lost 'so what's so special about him then?'

'Well..' replied Tobias 'this isn't the first time he has been here, in fact he's been coming here for about twelve years or so, every Tri-year he has managed to earn his place here but fell just short in the final test, I think it's been dirty tricks stopping him but that's my opinion anyway, He's everyone's favourite now and we all want to see him win it this year'

'But what makes him stand out though? He sounds sort of average to me' Daniel replied still totally not understanding about any of this, Tobias looked shocked that Daniel could come out with something like that and angrily answered back,

'He is the best competitor ever!!!, his skills are legendary around these parts, his strength and speed are better than any other competitors here, he can do things we can only imagine and his magic is...well, just out of this world, we can only dream of being as good as he is!!'

'Well he didn't actually win it yet so I hope you all get what you want' Daniel replied

'Also this year there's talk of him taking on a child from the school to mentor, he has taken time off from his home life to stay here for a while and teach a child his ways, from what I hear it's the winner of the Inter-Class Cup that gets the place' Tobias said proudly

'The what?' replied Daniel 'this place gets even more confusing!'

'The Inter-Class Cup!!, you haven't heard of that either?' Tobias said now looking at Daniel as if he was from another planet or something, 'Nope..sounds great though' replied Daniel sarcastically,

'The Inter-Class Cup is basically a series of challenges set during the class year and at the end of it the child with the most points gets to go into

238

the Arena to face the final challenges against the two other highest scoring classes, then the winner of that becomes Inter-Class champion' Tobias said enthusiastically as he enjoyed the competition every year,

'To be honest I'm not the sportiest of people so I guess it won't be me' laughed Daniel as he could think of nothing worse than physical activity,

'Oh no Daniel I assure you it's more than just that...' said Tobias happily 'the physical part of it is called 'The Proving Test' and that is the last event, everything before that is made up of a series of class challenges and general yearly tasks set by the head of each department, oh they are such great fun!!', Daniel slunk back onto his seat thinking to himself 'Oh great, school work and sport, I so can't wait for that'.

So as the children's first day wound down slowly Daniel had a feeling of Deja vu, him sitting there in a class he didn't want to be in surrounded by people he thought would never be his friend's, his real friend not even in the same class as him, it was feeling like being back at Longmeads all over again but the one difference was that in this world he had found his family and more importantly his father, he was learning about things he never knew were possible and was looking at a brand new future which was unknown to them all apart from a select few who knew something wasn't right but had no way of knowing for sure. Daniel's mind started wandering again while he was sitting there in class as Lady Willo carried on with the lesson, images of his possible future swirled round in his head, things he had never seen before involving all his new family, then his mind focused on and image speedily approaching him, he could see a woman in the distance, her hair blowing in the wind covering her face, as the image moved closer to Daniel he thought he recognised the woman, someone who he had seen somewhere in his past, someone familiar.......but then his attention was taken by a loud knocking on the door of the classroom, Lady Willo stood up and strode over to answer the door, as she pulled it open she beamed happily at whoever was there, all the children started whispering excitedly amongst each other,

'He's here!!!' one girl shouted loudly as she had seen who was there,

'Oh wow!!, I need to tell mum!!' shouted another as Lady Willo escorted in the person at the door.

All the children screamed with delight as they saw the figure of a man at the front of the class standing there chest puffed out and hands on hips, his armour glistening in the afternoon suns and his long flowing hair hanging behind him, he sported a cape emblazoned with a crest not seen before, it showed the two suns of Vaymia shining down onto a sword held by a silhouetted figure which looked uncannily like the man standing in front of them.

'Who's the big guy?' asked Daniel, not a clue with anything that was going on here now,

'You don't know??' Tobias replied looking very surprised by his answer 'It's Tahmidius!!! He's my hero'

'Oh right' said Daniel, not really bothered by his presence 'wonder why he's here Tobias?'. Then Tahmidius spoke…

Chapter Twenty
The Challenge Awaits….

'Good afternoon children, as most of you know I'm Tahmidius from the small town of Banglashera' he started to speak as every pair of eyes stared at him, most of them awestruck by him actually being there 'And my main reason today is as you may or may not know that I have offered to take on a sort of….apprentice after the Games have been completed, so I am visiting every class inside the school to just say hello and mainly good luck. Now as I understand the school is holding the Inter-Class Cup again this year but I wanted to help in any way I could seeing as I have been here many times before, so I spoke with the teachers and offered one pupil the chance to be mentored by myself. Purely out of class time I mean. It's a chance for one of you to learn new skills and spells that you may not have been able to make before and maybe just maybe help you to be considered worthy enough to join the next Tri-Yearly-Night-Games', excitedly the children clapped and whooped with delight at the thought of being mentored by their hero, something most of them could only dream of until now.

'Settle down children…' Lady Willo said, raising her voice just enough to be heard over the excited chatter of her class

'now, I expect you all to start putting in the hard work from this point onwards as you're journey towards Class Champion begins….now' as the bell rang, signalling the start of the Inter-Class Cup, all the children sat upright in their seats as they were now earning 'Class Points' on every aspect of their school work, ranging from appearance all the way up to projects and challenges set by the teachers. Daniel looked less than impressed by all of this which didn't go unnoticed by Tahmidius who saw him sitting there looking very disinterested,

'You there boy' he said pointing in Daniel's direction,

'Me??' Daniel replied looking around the class to see if it was actually him he was addressing,

'Yes you…'Tahmidius replied 'did you not hear what I was offering?'

'I heard it all right' Daniel said as he let out a yawn 'but to be totally honest I'm not that bothered, first of all I don't have any clue as to who you are and second of all I'm probably going to fail most of this anyway, so this cup thing seems a bit pointless',

'POINTLESS!!!' Tahmidius shouted, totally taken aback by what Daniel was saying 'I can assure you one thing boy, there are people around this world who would give anything to be offered the chance of a lifetime',

'Which is??' Daniel smirked as he could see Tahmidius slowly getting angrier by the second,

'The opportunity to have ME as their mentor, the opportunity for ME to pass on most of my extensive knowledge, and the opportunity for YOU to be surrounded by greatness!' Tahmidius replied as he puffed out his chest in a way that screamed 'I am the best'.

'Oh now you put it like that…' Daniel fired back quickly 'Then I am truly sorry for not knowing about you sir, master, your lordship…or whatever we are supposed to call you, I must be from another planet to not have heard of you!'. Tahmidius was unsure about what Daniel was saying, whether it was sarcastic or he truly was sorry,

'Very well boy…I forgive your naivety' Tahmidius smiled a very odd smile at Daniel 'as I was saying..errrr, oh yes that's it….so good luck to each and every one of you. And remember my motto 'Don't be lucky, be strong and plucky'. No one remembers second place so make every point count, and who knows at the end of your term it could be you standing beside me looking towards greatness!!'.

The whole class clapped as loud as they could as Tahmidius smiled then took a huge step back before bowing to the whole class, then the whooping started again,

'Class...once again settle down' Lady Willo clapped her hands to grab their attention 'And thank you once again Tahmidius, it's an honour to have you come into our class with such excellent news like that, I truly hope the winning pupil comes from our group of young students'

'The pleasure is all mine' he replied as the door was opened for him, 'Oh and children...don't forget that I shall be training in the Arena every day if you want to come and see what I am all about, and what it takes to be a champion' looking directly in Daniel's direction which made Daniel snigger slightly at seeing Tahmidius trying to stare angrily at him, then in one swift movement he flicked his cloak around himself and sped off out of the classroom door which banged shut behind him.

'What...was....that??' Daniel said to Tobias, still sniggering to himself, Tobias felt slightly offended by Daniel's lack of respect for one of his heroes,

'That was a bit rude Daniel' he said 'I mean that soldier is someone I have looked up to since I was young, I have heard stories about his bravery and skill that would put most people to shame!'

'All I saw was a bloke in a cape doing his best to look important but failing massively' Daniel replied 'I mean, seriously, are we meant to believe something good will come from whatever pointless training he gives one of us?, He's more interested in getting his profile up considering he hasn't actually won anything yet'

'Well I believe in him and I believe with a lot of hard work this term I will be the one to be trained by him!' Tobias stated as he raised a finger in the air like he had made a valid point,

'Well good luck to you, you won't see me trying too hard to win it, and he's just a fraud I reckon!' Daniel said as he crossed his arms and sat back in his seat once again looking bored as Lady Willo continued with the lesson.

A loud cheer could be heard from just down the corridor which stirred Daniel from his daydream,

'Sounds like Mr Fake has gone next door' laughed Daniel causing Tobias to slap him on the arm,

'Look Daniel' sighed Tobias 'I believe in Tahmidius even if you don't sp please let's not argue over this, I'm going to watch him train after class in the Arena, I've never actually seen him in action so this is exciting to me',

'Go enjoy the show then Toby' replied Daniel 'don't let me stop you', 'its Tobias by the way!!...The thing is we can't go into the Arena alone and I don't actually have anyone else to go with...' he turned to face Daniel who sort of knew what he was getting at,

'I think I see where this is heading...' laughed Daniel as he raised his eyebrows and flopped back in his chair again,

'I would very much like to go with you to the Arena Daniel' Tobias beamed at him as he stared right into his eyes 'Oh please say yes Daniel. It would mean the world to me..I've never seen him actually train live...oh please say you will...just this once!!'

'If I say yes will you stop pestering me about it??' said Daniel who was now staring at his desk,

'Yes..yes I promise!!' came the excited reply 'so you'll go then??'

'If it keeps you quiet then yes I'll come along, but only this once ok!!' replied Daniel who now felt his arm being shaken rather violently and turned to see a visibly excited Tobias with the biggest grin on his face.

'Just don't expect me to enjoy it ok!!' said Daniel as he pulled Tobias' hand off his arm which had now turned red through him gripping it tightly and looked up to see him still grinning like a Cheshire cat and showing no signs of stopping,

'Stop it!!' said Daniel 'you're giving me the creeps now...give it a rest!!', Tobias eventually stopped shaking and smiling, looking totally exhausted as he turned to face Lady Willo who was none the wiser about what was going on with these two boys,

'I..I can't help it...he's just my absolute hero!!' an exhausted Tobias replied 'I would love to get his autograph to show my parents!!',

'Alright, alright I get it!!' said Daniel who was slowly regretting saying yes to Tobias, but he could see just how much it meant for him to get even closer to someone who he looked up to more than anything in the world so he changed his attitude towards him and smiled back. As Lady Willo continued with the lesson Daniel started wondering about how his sister was doing in the next class and what she might be up to, 'I bet she's loving all this new work she's getting to do' he thought 'bet she's in charge of the class already!!'. But it seemed Lillie was feeling slightly stuck in the middle on that front, she didn't really feel like she was fitting in at all, no matter how hard she tried she just couldn't get any closer to having a new set of friend's to talk to, she was feeling rather alone but it was only the first day and she was maybe trying TOO hard, she couldn't wait for the end of the day when she got to meet up with her brother just for a bit of companionship really, Harvey on the other hand had now been fully integrated into the classroom thanks to Pontus and his heavy handed tactics and was loving being centre of attention for once without being picked on, his confidence had grown dramatically in the few hours he had been in class, every question thrown at him he had answered correctly and confidently, Mr Scoot was pleasantly surprised by the transformation of Harvey since the beginning of the day,

'Well Well Well Harvey...' Mr Scoot said happily 'It seems that you are simply racing ahead in the point's stake today!!' a glint flickered in Harvey's eyes, a look that had been seen before, something....not quite right,

'Yes...I suppose I am sir' a wicked grin spreading across his face as he stared right through Mr Scoot,

'If you keep this up Harvey then I can see the all-time points record for a single day being smashed, and I'm sure Pontus wouldn't mind that' replied Mr Scoot,

'Why is that then sir?' Harvey's eyes squinted slightly as he answered back,

'Because...' remarked Pontus as he rose from his seat and looked down his nose at the class 'I am the record holder for both 'Most points collected in a day' and ' All-time class points holder', oh that was a great year for me' he smiled as he looked around the class smugly only to be met by scores of rolled up paper balls being thrown at him 'OW...stop it!!!' he shouted as one hit him right in the eye 'sir please make them stop!!' he demanded,

'Yes yes Pontus....ok children please stop pelting the paper at him, we don't want another pupil to lose an eye!!' Mr Scoot said smiling to himself, as Pontus stood there rubbing his eye Harvey tugged at his robes causing him to spin round,

'Don't think your records will stand for long Pontus, there's a new boy in town!!' Harvey cackled like never before causing Pontus to feel slightly worried by his new friend's odd tone,

'Ooookkkk' He muttered to himself before sitting down in his seat with Harvey's eyes burning into him, throwing him a look that even he found very off putting, Hayla had heard everything that was going on and turned towards Pontus,

'A dark soul...' she said 'as dark as the night and as cold as the Sea of Souls!!', Pontus felt a cold shiver running through his body,

'Wh..what?' he replied 'what are you talking about?', Hayla leaned in closer,

'What the eyes can't see, the mind will reveal...your friend is not one of us...be wary of him' then she turned round as if nothing had happened leaving Pontus afraid to look at Harvey.

As the lessons in all the classes drew to a close for the first day a low murmur was filling the halls as all the children grew excited at going to watch Tahmidius and the other soldiers training for the games which were due to start, it also gave Lillie, Daniel and Harvey a chance to meet up after being apart all day but Daniel knew he had to tag along with Tobias to watch his 'hero' in action. So when the school horn blared out signalling the end of the day the classroom doors were flung open followed by scores of children eager to get into the Arena to get a good look at whoever they were rooting for in the Games.

246

Harvey was the last out of his class, Pontus and the others had sped out due to Harvey's weird behaviour, Mr Scoot was just getting his paperwork in order which had been piled up on his desk when he saw that Harvey was about to leave,

'Ahhh Harvey, do you have a second?' he called out, Harvey swung round to face him,

'Why yes sir, what can I do for you?' he replied casually,

'I would just like to say a massive well done on your first day here, it seems like you are well ahead of all the other students in the points stakes including Mr Polder, which I'm sure will only make him try harder' Mr Scoot smiled at Harvey as he could see someone eager to get the most from every lesson 'So how have you found your first day here then?'

'It's been...educational' Harvey replied 'I'm looking forward to learning as much as I can about this place AND the history of the castle, I feel there's so much I need to learn, It can only help my mas...' Harvey stopped suddenly which Mr Scoot picked up on

'Your what?' he replied inquisitively

'Errr...my mask...I'm making a mask for the upcoming cup we are in, purely for the physical element you see as I have seen lots of people wearing them' Harvey had to think quickly on his feet for fear of his dark side being revealed,

'Oh yes..' replied Mr Scoot 'That's a wonderful idea, and it certainly helps towards those final points let me tell you!!' and with that Harvey turned and walked out of the class, his eyes still flickering the purple colour that had taken over his normal eye colour, and off he walked down the corridor towards Lillies classroom where she was standing talking to one of her classmates, as Harvey was still slightly in a trance he didn't notice Lillie standing there,

'Harvey...' she said as he kept walking on 'Oi clumsy, are you ignoring me?' she stepped behind him and slapped his arm hard causing him to come out of the trance,

247

'OWWW that hurt!!...oh sorry Lillie, I totally didn't see you there, how was your day?' He asked as he shook his head to clear it of the fuzziness he was feeling,

'I'll catch up with you later....' said the girl Lillie was talking to as Lillie strode over to Harvey,

'Had a fairly odd day today' she said 'bit of an unusual class, but I think I'll be ok, It's just all new to me' just as she said that Mr Flora poked his head out of the class door and shouted down the hall,

'Oh Lillie, a good solid start today, well done, just remember that every action taken goes towards your final points tally for the cup so remember to make the right choices!!'

'Yes sir...I'll do my best' she smiled back as Mr Flora disappeared into his class and shut the door behind him,

'What's he like then?' asked Harvey,

'Seems alright so far, the people in the class are a bit odd though, I can't quite work them out yet' Lillie said as they continued up the corridor towards Daniel's class 'What's your class like then Harv?, are they as weird as you!!' she said as she let out a laugh,

'Not funny Lillie' Harvey replied 'To be honest I can't really remember much of what went on today, it's all a bit of a blur' as he rubbed his head which to him still seemed hazy,

'So what about this competition thing that's going on throughout the year?, are you that interested in it?, seems like a good opportunity to me' Lillie asked Harvey who had both hands on his head now as if trying to keep his brain still,

'What competition?, I haven't got a clue what you're on about?, as I said I can't really remember much about the day, my head's been spinning all afternoon' he replied as he stopped to lean against the wall,

'Oh really?, you don't know about what's going on even though you've been sat at the desk all day!!!' Lillie seemed confused by what was going on 'did you actually listen to anything in class?' just as she said that a couple of Harvey's classmates walked past him and patted him on the head before saying

'Nice going Harvey!! Looks like Pontus is fuming with your points score so far!! Said one boy,

'Reckon you'll beat his record points score, that will show him!!' laughed the other boy,

'Errrr...thanks I think' replied a confused Harvey as the boy's walked off down the corridor,

'And what were they going on about?, the beating his points score thing I mean!!' Lillie said as Harvey just stood there totally confused by everything 'hold on here one minute Harvey...I'll be back in a sec', and with that Lillie sped off down the long corridor and ended up at the door to Harvey's classroom, Mr Scoot was putting the scores up on the board and right at the top was the name

'H.JONES-1573pts',

'What the....' gasped Lillie as she saw just how far ahead he was from the rest of the class. So she shot off back up the corridor to where Harvey was standing,

'Well...what did you see??' asked Harvey

'It seems to me you are actually a class superstar!!, you are about 600 points ahead of the next student in the class!!' exclaimed Lillie who saw the oddest look stretch across Harvey's face,

'Who's in second place then?' he asked 'and what the heck is going on??'

'It's a student called 'P.POLDER' he's just under a thousand points, so what IS going on??, where did all this brain power come from?' Lillie said grabbing hold of his head and pretending to look through his ears for any signs of life,

'Get off me will you you're hurting me!!' replied Harvey angrily 'and as for the class thingy I haven't a clue, I must be just good a something for a change. I do actually listen sometimes!!', and with that he stormed off down the corridor towards Daniel's class, Lillie just stood there laughing and mocking his voice,

'I do actually listen sometimes….yeah right!!, something seems a bit fishy to me...I'll get to the bottom of it !!' and off she strode down the corridor with Harvey looking nervously over his shoulder as she got closer.

As she neared the door to Daniel's class a huge roar could be heard from inside, Lady Willo had kept the class behind for a few minutes just to let the children know how the daily points were coming along,

'So children..' she started 'It seems that Tobias has taken an early lead this year. Wow very well done to you, and the rest of you….please let's make more of an effort tomorrow, It's looking very close in the middle part of the leaderboard after the first day...and Daniel?'

'Yes miss?' Daniel sighed as he turned to face her

'You seem to not have many points, if you fall too far behind you won't be in with a chance of winning this most wonderful experience that we have been so kindly given by Tahmidius today' she calmly spoke back knowing he was proving hard to get through to,

'Oh whoop-de-doo!!' he said quietly to himself but was loud enough for a few pupils to hear who started sniggering,

'What did you say??' Lady Willo asked,

'I said OK miss I'll give it another crack if it makes you happy' his sarcastic answer hitting a cord with her,

'Daniel...this school prides itself on doing the right thing and always making great decisions with regards to its pupils but it does actually mean you need to be involved and helping everyone out before you help yourself, We only want the best children in these classes which are VERY hard to get into, so for your own sake please start afresh tomorrow ok' Lady Willo could see she had got through to him a little bit and smiled a huge smile in his direction,

'Fine…' he replied 'I'll see what I can do tomorrow, I'm not promising anything though' Daniel let out a sigh and leaned back in his chair, Tobias on the other hand was literally dancing in his seat as he knew it was time for class to end, his hand shot up in the air as high as he could stretch,

'Yes Tobias...I see you are desperate to ask something as usual' Lady Willo said,

'Is it time for class to end now?...you see I'm desperate to get into the Arena to see Tahmidius in action and I don't want to miss a single second!!' came his over excited reply,

'Well class. Seeing as it is finally that time then yes you may all leave the class, those of you who are heading into the Arena to watch the training do remember to sit in our own class seating area, we don't want a repeat of what happened between Eldrin Finch and a few of the older boys from 'Phantom Flyers', that poor boy will never be the same again!' Lady Willo said as she stood by the door, opening it so the children could leave 'Oh and before you go do remember that when the practice is over could you all make your way to the King's Chamber, where you will all be given instructions as to what room you have been designated for the term'.

What followed was almost a stampede as the class rose as one and charged towards the door excitedly at the thought of going to watch their favourite soldier training.

'Blimey..' Harvey said as he was almost knocked over by the sudden wave of children leaving the class,

'Where's Daniel?, have you seen him come out yet?' Lillie asked craning her neck over the onrushing children's heads, just then she spotted him slowly walking towards the door with an excited Tobias tugging at his robes,

'Come on Daniel...we can't be late otherwise the best seats will be gone!!' Tobias said as he pulled Daniel along,

'Yeah yeah I'm coming Toby!!' said Daniel as he saw Lillie and Harvey were waiting for him at the door to his class,

'Alright Dan....who's the new kid?' Harvey said with a hint of jealousy as he saw his friend with someone else,

'Toby...this is Harvey, my friend, and my sister Lillie' Daniel replied sheepishly,

'Actually it's Tobias. And I'm Daniel's class friend...we are off to the Arena to watch Tahmidius training so we can't hang about' Tobias replied slightly snootily,

'Oh right...fair enough…can we come too?, I mean there isn't really anything else for us to do now' Harvey answered back looking slightly put out that Daniel had a new friend,

'Oh ANYONE can go but we can't sit together...you do know the rules don't you?' Tobias replied still tugging at Daniel's robes,

'No not really...' Lillie replied, so Tobias went on to explain about the way you had to sit with your own class otherwise you would get bad things done to you,

'Oh great...thanks for clearing that up. Well Dan I guess we will be seeing you later maybe' laughed Lillie as she started to walk off,

'Oh and don't forget to go to the King's Chamber after the practice session is over' shouted Tobias to Lillie who had set off at a pace now,

Harvey was looking totally dejected now as his best friend was being taken away from him by some…..NEW friend,

'Guess I'll see you afterwards mate' said Harvey as he walked off slowly in the direction of the Arena.

'Bye Harv..' came the sad sounding reply from Daniel as he watched his friend walk away.

'Oh come on Daniel. Let's hurry, we might get right at the front if we are quick!!' said Tobias as he pulled Daniel along towards the huge doors to the Arena. The doors opened and Tobias' eyes lit up with excitement, Daniel on the other hand stood there totally open mouthed at what he was seeing in front of him

Chapter Twenty-One
The Arena

Right before Daniel's eyes stood The Arena, an oval shaped area that stretched as far as the eye could see, surrounded by large seating structures which stretched all the way around the entire area, high walls towered over the games surface suggesting that no one was to be able to leave the arena by climbing up them or going through them, the walls were solid and brick like in their appearance and were as thick as they were tall. The seating area contained hundreds of seats for the school pupils to sit and watch whatever was going on inside and on the wall just below them sat a name plaque which held the name of every class at the school which meant that every person who went there knew their place not just by name but by class colour as each stand was painted in the classes chosen colour, there were twelve seating areas reserved for pupils and countless others for anyone else who came to watch and this year was extra special due to the Tri-Yearly-Night-Games being held here which would mean more people than ever would be coming to watch the games taking place. There was a special seating area high up around the centre of the Arena which was reserved for The King and family plus whichever guests he had requested the company of. As expected it was the plushest looking tower of all the areas and could accommodate hundreds of guests at one time and this year would be filled with the most important people from all across Vaymia attending this Tri-Year.

Daniel was totally awestruck at the sheer size of it and couldn't actually move his feet, Tobias was tugging at his robes,

'Daniel...' he said 'we need to get in quick, all the seats are being taken up and I want a good seat to see him'

'Wh...it...it's huge!!' Daniel said not really listening to Tobias and what he was saying, 'how far does it go back?. I mean from outside it doesn't actually look that big!!'

'Well that's the amazing thing about this place, it's sort of magical, I mean it's been built by the most accomplished wizards across the world' Tobias smiled as he explained the story behind the Arena 'from the outside it looks like a small sort of....err...training arena, but the great thing about it is that it's protected by 'The Light of Erwin', it's a sort of magical dome that protects the people inside while they are here'

'Oh right' said Daniel looking still confused 'and what does this dome thingy do apart from that?'

'Well first of all no magic from the outside world can penetrate it meaning everyone inside is safe, anything brought into the Arena can easily be contained as the King holds all power over it and is the only one who can use magic if he is needed to, oh and its party piece is that from the outside it looks like an empty training area, as I said, but inside its size is magnified a hundred times, meaning it is not seen from above and everyone inside can safely watch whatever is going on' Tobias knew every fact about the Arena as he spent most of his time inside it just taking in its size and magical aura,

'I think I get what you're saying...well as long as we are safe in here then that's fine by me' smiled Daniel who seemed to be a little more at ease with every passing second he stood there,

'Oh the last thing I forgot to tell you is that the Arena floor and up to the height of the walls is protected by another dome, that one is only used when we have the games and also the final of the Inter-Class-Cup, it's to protect everyone who is watching' Tobias said as he and Daniel started on their way to find their seating area,

'Oh why did something happen here or something?' asked Daniel

'Well sort of...you see quite a long time ago. Before I was born there was a story which I had been told about, and it was about a traveler who had managed to get into the Final Games, not one person knew his name and no one knows how he made it that far even to this day but some had suspicions of magi-foul play, his story supposedly checked out according to one soldier who was in charge of the entrants, he battled all the way through the heats but he got into the Finals and before anyone could stop him he managed to destroy the entire Arena and the people inside, totally vaporized by him using some sort of dark magic' Tobias shuddered at being reminded of this, Daniel was seemingly fascinated now,

'So what happened after that?' he asked,

'Well it seems that the King at the time was not quick enough to spot the danger this traveler possessed and couldn't do anything to stop him, the traveler escaped somehow and was never seen again, and that's why we now have a 'dome in a dome', meaning if there's any hint of trouble on the Arena floor then it will be contained to the 'inner dome' and we won't be harmed, the King insists on using it wherever possible to keep us safe, he realised that for him to be the King we need he would have to have total control over every aspect of the Arena, so that's why he insisted on using it for every event'

'Oh right I get you!!' replied Daniel who had a look on his face that screamed 'CONFUSED!!!' 'So where do we need to go now?' he asked,

'Well if you stop asking me so many questions then I'll take us to our area, come on...follow me' Tobias said as he sped off past scores of students and teachers who were all making their way to their own class seats, as they neared the centre of the Arena Daniel spotted Harvey about to descend the set of steps that went high up into the heavens, but as he walked forward he accidentally barged into another pupil,

'Watch it Ordie!!!' the boy said angrily as he rubbed his shoulder 'you'll pay for that I promise you!'

'Whoa, whatever, it was only accidental, I'm sorry if my little tap on the shoulder hurt you!!' Daniel replied sarcastically as he always did when faced with someone who wanted to hurt him,

'You'll be sorry for that, don't you know who I am?' the boy asked as if Daniel should actually know,

'Not a clue, are you Barry the wonder dog??.. Or Simon the chicken farmer!!' Daniel laughed out loud as the boy grew angrier by the second,

'He has no clue!!' the boy laughed as he stepped forwards right into Daniel's face almost pressing his nose up against his 'You will know soon enough I promise you, I'm Cahlid...and I run this school, everyone and I mean EVERYONE answers to me got it??' he snarled as Daniel took a step back waving his hand in front of his nose,

'Could you at least brush your teeth next time, your breath is awful!!' Daniel replied whilst laughing out loud,

'Oh that's it now you're gonna get it' Cahlid said as he lunged forwards towards Daniel as if going to attack him but he stopped mid-air, inches from Daniel,

'That's enough!!!!' shouted Garin who had been following Daniel from a distance 'I will have no violence today!!' Garin had frozen Cahlid in mid-air, he stepped in front of him and released the spell causing him to fall to the floor with a 'THUD', 'You will leave this place and go to your stand right now!!',

'Or what??' Cahlid replied hoping to provoke a reaction from Garin,

'Or...Young Cahlid I shall have to bring down on you the punishment that you so desperately deserve, now get out of my sight and DON'T look back!!' Garin pointed to the stand where they were supposed to be going to, Cahlid dusted himself down and muttered under his breath as he stormed off angrily, Daniel smiled at Garin as they both stood there,

'Thanks for that Buck...sorry Garin but I didn't need any help with that boy' Daniel said as Garin stooped forwards slightly,

'Daniel...please remember that this place is new to both you and I it has changed so much since I was last here, I cannot allow you to get hurt, but that boy is evil beyond belief so please just be careful' replied Garin, knowing that he couldn't afford for Daniel to be hurt in any way 'Now go...find your place and please stay out of trouble',

'Yeah yeah..I'll be ok I promise' he said as he turned and started to walk off then he spotted a familiar figure, 'HARVEY...' he called out 'HARV....it's

256

me' Harvey didn't hear him so Daniel shot off towards the 'MuddyBog' stand, he reached the steps and looked up, he could see Harvey just up ahead,

'Harv...wait up mate, I'm shattered running after you!!' but just as he went to climb the steps two huge school pupils stepped out in front of him, they were decked in the uniform of MuddyBog,

'Where do you think you're going Ordie?' asked one of them as he stood there arms crossed and grinding his teeth,

'Errr it's none of your business weirdie!!' Daniel cheekily replied,

'Weirdie??, I reckon he's making fun of you Don' replied the other 'I think we need to teach him a lesson!!' he cackled as he rammed his fist into his other hand,

'Oh you two bone heads are going to teach me a lesson eh?, Oh excellent but I bet I'm smarter than both of you AND can outrun you', Tobias appeared at the bottom of the steps panting heavily,

'There you are Daniel!!, what are you doing on the steps of 'MuddyBog' ?'

'I'm going after Harvey. My friend!!, and these two numbskulls won't let me past!!' Daniel said as he started to feel slightly angry as Harvey had disappeared out of sight now,

'Don't you remember what we said about not being allowed to go into another classes seats?, it's against the school rules for one thing and you're likely to get thumped if you get caught!!' Tobias tugged at Daniel's robes hoping to get him off the steps quickly before something bad happened,

'But I need to see Harvey...and these two aren't going to stop me!!' Daniel said as he tried to push past the pupils who were blocking his path 'Get off me!!' he shouted as he was hoisted up into the air and then thrown to the dusty ground,

'You've about as much chance as getting up there as you have becoming King!!' laughed Jon the smaller of the two pupils 'Now clear off or you'll be sorry!!'

Daniel picked himself up off the floor with Tobias helping to dust his robes down, 'I'll get in there don't you worry!!', not letting those two clowns stop me',

'You know we can't get in there, it's impossible. You'll just have to see him later on in the King's Chamber, now come on we must go find our seats!!' said Tobias who was practically shaking on the spot as he felt he was missing seeing his hero in action. And with that they both headed off to where their class seating area was, at the base of the steps was a huge wooden shield attached to the side of seating wall, 'DAWNFALL' was written across it in two foot high letters to let everyone who didn't belong up there not to enter this area, at the base of it stood a small rectangular plaque, Daniel moved closer to it and squinted his eyes as the lettering was slightly faded and rather small, it read

'THOSE WHO SEEK TO ENTER HERE MUST FIRST BELONG AND SHOW NO FEAR, FOR WHAT AWAITS ABOVE THIS LAND IS SOMETHING SPECIAL SOMETHING GRAND'

'So what does this mean then?' asked Daniel as he read it over and over again,

'It's just something the King has put on every block, a saying to excite the children as they climb the stairs to the top' Tobias replied as he started the climb up the stairs,

'But what does it mean 'those who must first belong and show no fear'' asked Daniel who was having to step up the pace a bit to keep up with Tobias,

'All it means is that....as I look at it....you must be part of the class named on the plaque and...well I think the second part just means that as we are so high up don't get scared maybe?, I never really looked that deep into what it meant really' Tobias said as they kept climbing what seemed to Daniel like a never ending staircase, they were pushing past the other children who were making their way up also,

258

'Excuse me please…'Tobias said as he squeezed past a couple of slow coaches 'we must get to the top..' he continued as he could now feel the breeze on his face meaning they were almost there.

'Wait for me!!' shouted Daniel as he was puffing heavily 'I'm not as fast as you, you've had more practice at this climbing lark!!' but Tobias was slightly out of sight at the top of the stairs as Daniel eventually caught up with him,

'Why...huuuu...didn't...huuu...you...huuu...wait!!' wheezed Daniel as he collapsed on the floor gasping for breath, Tobias was showing no signs of tiredness as he whooped and clapped as loud as anyone,

'Come on Daniel…' he screeched 'there's room at the front for us!!' and off he went descending the wooden steps in front of him, Daniel was slowly pulling himself up off the dusty floor when he saw Tobias gesturing to him to follow,

'Oh great!!! Look at the state of my clothes!!' he said angrily as he slapped his clothes to get the dust off, causing him to splutter as it got into his mouth, 'PAH..' he groaned as he spat out dust 'that's disgusting!!', Tobias was now standing on the chair shouting up to him,

'DANIEL...THIS WAY..YOU'RE GOING TO MISS IT!!'

'Oh yippee!!' he muttered under his breath 'can't wait to see this rubbish, it's not like I wanted to be here anyway!!' he said as he started the descent down the steps towards where Tobias was now waving at him to hurry up,

'Quickly!!' he said to Daniel 'you're going to miss the address'

'I won't miss this 'dress' at all' Daniel sniggered to himself but loud enough for Tobias to hear,

'What are you talking about?, I'm talking about the Kings address, he gives a speech before every Tri-Year tournament to wish everyone entering good luck and safe viewing' Tobias gripped hold of the wooden rail in front of him excitedly as he took a look over the edge and down onto the Arena floor, 'where is he??' he asked the boy sitting next to him, 'I haven't seen him yet' the boy replied 'but I'm sure we will get to see him soon', Daniel leaned forward so his head was over the rail and was greeted with the sight of the Arena floor looking like a barely visible area from their lofty position,

'I can't see a thing!!' he said to Tobias 'why does it look so far away? Is this an arena for ants?' he laughed out loud,

'What's an 'ant'??' asked Tobias quizzically,

'It's a very small creature from where I used to live, as small as a pebble but as strong as an Ox' Daniel said, doing his best to explain

'Oh right...' replied Tobias 'what's an 'Ox??',

'Another creature from where I was raised, it looks like a cow' Daniel replied in his own descriptive way,

'Ahh ok...what's a 'cow'??' replied Tobias now looking even more confused at things he had never heard of, Daniel then realised that he had no clue what he was talking about,

'Oh a cow...it's a...errr...huge three headed beast, with wings as wide as the moon, sharp horns on each of its heads and teeth as razor sharp as the sharpest axe, it also tastes pretty good too!!' laughed Daniel at seeing the look on Tobias' face,

'Gosh I hope I don't run into one of those!! I'd probably cry or something!!' he replied looking visibly scared at the image he was given,

'Yes they do 'mooove' rather fast for such a big creature' Daniel was in fits of laughter as he knew Tobias had no idea why he was laughing when he felt a whack on his arm,

'Shhh Daniel' Tobias said as he turned Daniel around to where everyone was now looking 'the King has just entered, he's going to make his speech!!', the excited chatter and mutterings were slowly dying away as all around the Arena people were shushing each other as their King was present. The whole Arena fell deathly silent as the King stood at the edge of his box and looked around at every part of the ground with a huge smile spreading on his face, Daniel was the only one still looking around as everyone else had their eyes fixed on where the King was standing. Just the creaking and groaning of the Arena doors could be heard from the other end of the ground. From their lofty position all the spectators could see the participants moving into place in front of the Kings stand, they formed row after row of people until it looked like a small army had entered the Arena, each one laid down whatever it was they were holding and stood totally still, eyes transfixed on the King who stood above them.

It was so silent you could hear a pin drop, just the lightest of breezes whipped across the Arena floor taking with it the loose dust that was sitting on top, then it fell silent again until the King cleared his throat gently, and with a voice so deep and bellowy he began his pre prepared speech as per usual,

'My dearest Vaymians...' he started 'once again I would like to thank you all for your continued support in these darker times...to see so many of you still turning up to support these games has not gone unnoticed by myself and my son, Lord Casborn. Now as it stands we seem to have a lot of new entrants this year, that's three hundred up on the last games, which just goes to show you how important and how well received these games have become' a huge cheer spread around the Arena as the King stopped to take it all in before taking a deep breath and carrying on,

'Now these games, as we all know, are set over seven days of competition and each task is just as tough as the previous one. Now as you are also aware that this Tri-Year once again represents the chance for the winner of the games to become a member of 'The Circle' which would mean a lifetime of dedicated training and protection, and most important of all....learning the magical teachings of 'The Wise' a prize so great that it has attracted people from far and wide, all with one goal in mind, But with this Tri-Year being possibly the most important for a long time I must point out that even though I have done my very best to protect us from harm there will still be evil lurking around every corner, And it just shows that no matter what evil we may be faced with here...we will always be united, this land will never be conquered, THIS LAND SHALL NOT FALL!!!' the King raised his hands high which brought everyone in the Arena to its feet, chanting could be heard in every part of the ground, the noise was totally deafening which caused Daniel to put his hands over his ears to try and shut it out. Finally the King gestured to the Arena to hush, even more shushing was now taking place as row after row fell silent again,

'Now my friend's..' the King said as if he was speaking to every person individually 'these games have shown me that together we can overcome anything, they have given me some much pleasure over many years so it's with extreme happiness and excitement that I now declare the Tri-Yearly-Night-Games open!!' and with that a huge fireworks display filled the Arena sky bringing with it plenty of 'Oohhs and Aahhs' from the children as each one exploded overhead, the most beautiful colours filled the Arena, bathing the entire area in a cool warm glow,

'Wow...' said Daniel 'I've never seen anything quite like this before!!' he stood there open mouthed as each one fizzed around the stands coming close to where they were standing 'Whoa!, that one nearly hit me' he said as a shiny gold firework shot past them, Tobias laughed at seeing Daniel flinch,

'It's ok Daniel, they can't hurt you!!' Tobias putting his hand on Daniel's shoulder to turn him towards where the King was standing,

'Yes they blooming well can hurt you!!' added Daniel just before he noticed the King standing right next to the rail and was orchestrating the fireworks, his hands were moving all over the place as if guiding them,

'See!!' laughed Tobias 'they aren't even real, you see ever since we had a small accident in one of the stands a while back the King decided that all fireworks would be fake'

'What happened then?' asked Daniel

'Well what actually happened was, one of the Kings trusted guards was put in charge of the 'Welcome Display', he was practicing in the Arena one day, luckily when it was empty, and he lit this real firework which shot off towards one of the stands, it wedged itself between the beams and the whole thing set alight, it caused a lot of damage not just to that stand but about three others close by',

'Oh right, bet that was a sight to see!!' laughed Daniel

'Well not really, as it was in the Arena he was practicing the dome was in place and shielded the whole thing from the castle, so no one knew anything about it' Tobias said as he recalled the amount of damage it had caused,

'I bet he got in serious trouble though didn't he?' Daniel knew a thing or two about causing untold amounts of damage, especially around his old school,

'Well the King eventually found out about it but only when the gates were opened ready to host the last Games, the smell of burning wood and fabric filled the air around them, as far as anyone knows the Guard was banished to the 'Valley of the Lost Souls', and was never heard of again' Tobias loved telling a good story to anyone who would listen and Daniel was now his captive audience,

'Sounds like he deserved it though I guess, so what's 'The Valley of the Lost Souls' then?' he asked, Daniel was hearing about so many new places every minute and felt he needed to know about each and every one in detail,

'Well...' started Tobias 'It's a Valley...that holds...the Lost Souls, quite simple to understand I'd say!!' he laughed at Daniel's reaction,

'Oh that's it take the mickey out of the new kid!!, I thought there was more to it than that!!' snarled Daniel,

'It's basically a part of Vaymia where no one dares to go any more, you see the legend has it that anyone who dares step even one single foot inside the Valley will be forever hunted by whatever evil is lurking there, anyone who has ever been there has never come back!!' Tobias always shuddered when thinking about that place but Daniel didn't seem that bothered by the story,

'Oh really!!' he smiled 'hmmm, I might have to see for myself' he said quietly as Tobias was too busy looking out for his hero Tahmidius,

'Oh come on...' he muttered 'I want to see him!!', Lady Willo had been listening behind the boy's for the last part and tapped Tobias on the shoulder,

'It won't be long now, there's just the last minute speeches going on down on the Arena floor by their coaches before they can begin their practice, patience is a virtue Tobias!!' she said calmly,

'You know I hate this part miss, it's too long!!' Tobias said as he huffed and crossed his arms, Daniel didn't really know where to look which Lady Willo noticed,

'Are you ok Daniel?, you seem.....bored?' she asked,

'Nah, I'm ok, just don't know what to expect, all this is new to me so I'm trying to take it all in, it's an amazing place this!!' replied Daniel as he squinted down at the Arena floor, 'So how can anyone see what's going on in this place, I mean everyone is so far away!!'

'Well that the magic of this place Daniel' Lady Willo started 'You will see soon enough just how amazing this whole area is, The King has made it a truly magical and wondrous place where everyone is safe and free from any outside influence',

'Well I didn't think this place was this big at first, I mean from the outside it looks like nothing, but when Tobias showed me just how big it was inside and explained about the Arena works I couldn't help but be shocked, My grandf...I mean the King has made an amazing place!!'

'Your what??' Lady Willo had heard Daniel nearly say something he shouldn't have,

'N...nothing I meant it was a grand place he had built' he tried to backtrack, hoping that it wasn't noticed,

'Oh ok Daniel...anyway it looks like it's time for the free practice to start!!' as the King stood once again to face the crowds he first lowered his hands to the floor, the silence fell again around the Arena, with a crackle he swiftly raised his hands upwards causing all the new visitors to the Arena to suddenly gasp in astonishment.

Chapter Twenty-Two
The Fun of the Games

Daniel stood there slightly open mouthed as he just witnessed something rather special as all of a sudden it seemed as if the whole floor had suddenly risen up to make everything visible to all who were watching, now every person who was involved in the games was what seemed to be within touching distance of the crowds,

'D..did I just see that??' he asked Tobias who knew what had happened and was watching Daniel's face the whole time 'I...I mean. The floor...it just...Huh?',

'Oh Daniel have you never seen that done before?' laughed Tobias as he put his hand on Daniel's shoulder 'Well you did say you couldn't see anything on the Arena floor and this is kind of the Kings special trick, it's the inner 'dome' which is used as sort of a magnifying glass, it makes the whole place seem closer than what it is, we have to sit up high so we don't get caught by any misguided magic or weapons'

'Oooohhhh, I get it now!!, wow that's amazing' said Daniel who seemed to be now slowly falling for this special place 'I don't feel as scared as I did earlier when I was leaning over the side looking down, you can see everything now!!' he laughed as he watched the competitors lined up in front of the Kings stand and one by one them nodding their head towards the King with the other arm across their chest in a respectful salute to the person who had made this all possible, something caught Tobias' eye as he watched every competitor bow the walk off to their respected area for practice,

'Ooh ooh ooh' he excitedly said waving and pointing his finger towards the competitor at the back of the queue 'It's him!!!, I can see him now!!' excitedly he turned towards the nearest person to him and grabbed them by the robes 'Can you see him too!!!, I can't believe we get to see him train' the boy whose clothes he grabbed his arms and said 'Let go Tobias!!, you'll ruin my clothes!!'.

He wasn't the only one to spot who most of them were here to see as a rumbling murmur descended across every stand in the Arena, 'is it really him?' and 'I want to be his friend' were the sort of comments being heard coming from all over the Arena descending down from every stand like a wave of sound which seemed to bounce of the 'dome' and spread them all over the place.

As Tahmidius made his way towards the front of the queue he knew that by being last every pair of eyes would be on him, something which he played on as he waved to every part of the Arena and got back a huge roar of whistles and shouting, He bowed to the King who saw it was him and felt he needed to say something,

'Ahhh Tahmidius…' the King started 'I'm so glad you are back again, as I understand it you were very close to being beaten. Well that was my understanding'

'It wasn't that close I can assure you my King' Tahmidius replied confidently 'the last round of action was a bit of a breeze really, you see the person I was up against wasn't really up for the challenge so he dropped his weapons and fled like a coward' he laughed at recalling this story,

'Well Tahmidius..' the King replied in a way that he knew would get at him 'I have an extensive network of scouts scattered throughout this land and from what they tell me you only came good in the last few rounds so it seems you were very lucky on this occasion, but I do know how much this means to you and I know that you brother's and father would wish you all the luck in these games if they were in the Arena today so for once please drop the act and concentrate on excelling at the Games, I have VERY high hopes for you this year, Don't let me down!!' The King warned Tahmidius with a wagging finger,

'Y..yes sire' he nervously replied back and off he went towards his area of training like a scalded schoolboy, head bowed low and him kicking the dirt on the floor. The King chuckled to himself as he turned to be greeted by Tahmidius' father who had been hidden behind a row of soldiers not wanting his son to see him for fear of him being put off by his presence,

'I hope I wasn't too hard on the boy, Joda, he looked positively scared when I was talking to him' laughed the King as he ascended the steps towards his seat,

'Not at all sire, I honestly didn't think you were hard enough on him' Joda laughed back 'I mean he's a very confident young man but he can come across very arrogant, but now I'm sure he will put in maximum effort and hopefully surprise us all this Tri Year,',

'Oh I do hope you are right' replied the King 'I have been keeping an eye on him at every games we have hosted, maybe it will be his year, who knows though, we have a lot of good competition who have come through from all over the world who would love the chance to join our 'Circle', let's hope he doesn't let you down', the King patted Joda on the shoulder as he went to sit in his seat to watch some of the practice, as he sat down on his cushioned seat he let out a sigh of relief,

'Ahhhh that's better!!, I don't like all this standing around, it doesn't do these old bones any good' the King's servant brought him his favourite drink and sat it down on the table next to him,

'I understand sire' the servant replied 'that is why I've taken the liberty of making your drink but adding in a special pain relief potion that we have been working for some time, I'm sure this will go some way to helping with the pain'

'Oh right thank you Olin...you are one of a kind, I'd be lost without you these days!' smiled the King 'So tell me, what's this made out of?' he carried on as Olin crouched down beside the King

'Well sire' he started 'it's a fairly new concoction we came across recently, I have tested it on myself so I'm very confident in its healing abilities, it's a mixture of a few things that I found out about from my mother which had been passed down through the generations but only now has she passed them onto me, it consists of a plant called 'Blue Bank

Milkweed', a dash of 'Sneezewort', and the final plant which was the hardest to find called 'Pocan Ashflower', which may I add was found only by accident in the Valley of the Lost Souls. These three mixed together give off an aroma like no other...', the King took a mouthful of it and immediately smiled,

'Oh this is good!!, this is really good Olin' he said as he took another gulp of it,

'If anything can help me through what's happening to me lately then this will do just fine, what do you call it?' Olins face changed as he watched the King drink the rest of it in one go,

'It's called 'Ferunem' sire, it means 'Life extended' in Erwininum. I'll make up another batch then sire, it will take me a few hours to make enough to keep you going for a few days but by that time we should be able to make it in bulk and keep it in the stores. Sire...I have one more question though if I may be so bold as to ask' Olin asked with an air of nervousness in his voice,

'Please ask away...but do not allow any person here to listen in, you know how much I don't like my private life spread around' replied the King as he leant across towards Olin,

'Do you think you should maybe....tell Lord Casborn about what's happening to you..I mean I don't know what else I can prepare to help you with the pain you are in, I don't mean to be so harsh sire but I think maybe with the rate at which it's spreading it might be wise to...take it a little easier until the time is right I mean' Olin knew the extent of the Kings pain but as with every member of staff he had been sworn to secrecy,

'Olin...' the King turned his head slightly towards him 'My ailments are of no concern to anyone else at the minute... considering the state of the world around us and the impending battle which has been foretold I cannot afford to let weakness show to our enemies!!, I need to just rest and only use my powers when absolutely necessary, that is why I need you and your team to keep making this medicine, that's all I ask'.

'But sire...' replied an exasperated Olin,

'But nothing!!!!' the King replied sternly 'just do as I ask, nothing more!!'

'Yes sire, you know how I feel about this but as you wish' Olin said as he then sighed and walked off up the steps and disappeared out into the back of the stand. The King had seen one of his many close friends from one of the other districts of Vaymia and gestured him to come over just as the free practice got underway in the Arena.

Down on the Arena floor Tahmidius had finally got over the chat he had had with the King earlier, his trainer was going through his usual warm up routine with him, the usual boring stuff that Tahmidius hated doing,

'Don't forget stretch out your back properly this time please' his trainer said as he remembered what happened the last time he was involved which was seemingly still on his mind,

'Yes yes...If I stretch it any more I will probably pull something!!' he replied back slightly angrily 'Look Brewster....I'm in the best shape I have ever been in ok!!, all this exercising is pointless, I mean just look around you, I'm not really facing that much stiff competition this Tri Year am I?' he laughed as he dug his pole into the ground and surveyed the rest of the competition who looked like they had never actually competed before.

On one side there was this huge man who looked like he might pose a threat, until he picked up his weapon of choice and as he swung it around to get used to it when he accidentally let go of it and it shot across the Arena and slammed into the wall, embedded so far in that they were having trouble pulling it back out, causing the man to turn away and pretend it wasn't him, Tahmidius laughed as he saw another couple of competitors struggling to stand up with their armour on and crashing into each other causing Tahmidius to burst out laughing,

'See what I mean, It's painful to watch' and with that he flicked his pole out of the ground with the outside of his foot and began spinning it around his head like an accomplished warrior, as his pole swished through the air it drew gasps from the stands, followed by thunderous applause and cheering as he connected with the practice dummy that his trainer had brought out onto the Arena floor, he knew he was being watched so decided to put on a bit of a show for them before he really got into his practice,

'Just watch this!!' Tahmidius said to himself smugly as he began his normal show off routine which involved him leaping and rolling around his training area,

'WOW!!..' shouted Tobias as he was hunched over the rail in front of him trying to get a better look at his hero 'he's amazing. I want to be just like him one day' he said as he whipped his hands through the air as if he was in training just like his hero was doing when he swung his arm too far and whacked Daniel on the side of the head,

'OWWWW....' he shouted 'that blooming hurt!!, stop with the arm waving it's really putting me off!!' Daniel rubbed the part of his face that he had just been hit on 'That's going to leave a mark now...be more careful or else I'm going!!'

'S..sorry Daniel' Tobias said 'I'm just too excited now, I mean look...he's amazing!!' as he pointed over to Tahmidius, who was lapping up the adulation from the crowds above, still spinning and jumping around as if possessed by spirits,

'It looks like he's been stung by a Bee to me!!' laughed Daniel as he watched Tahmidius in action,

'What's a 'Bee' then?' asked Tobias as he stopped flinging his arms round,

'Big teeth. Big claws...huge wings' Daniel replied keeping as straight a face as he could,

'Oh sounds positively awful' Tobias replied, with the image of something that didn't even resemble a bee in any way stuck in his head, 'do you get many other odd creatures where you are from then Daniel?' he asked hesitantly as it seemed every creature where Daniel said he was from sounded like it could eat you in one go,

'Oh yes we have loads of them, I sometimes wonder how I stayed alive for so long in such a dangerous place!!' he sniggered to himself as he knew this could run and run for a long time.

'Well I'd love to learn more about these fearful creatures one day, but not yet as I'm watching him in action' Tobias said as he turned away from Daniel and concentrated on watching Tahmidius who was still twisting and flicking his way around the Arena floor, the chants from the stands filled the air, most of them for Tahmidius, as the competitors who had stopped to watch him in action had seemingly got bored and started to carry out their own warm up routines while trying to block out the overwhelming chants for their hero, who was now in the final throes of his routine, Tahmidius leapt up high in the air followed by a few spins then slammed his stick down onto the floor below. As the dust settled on the floor around him a few huge letters could be made out, Tahmidius had managed to scrape the word 'THANK YOU' into the floor, he stood up straight and threw his arms out to the side as the ripples of applause cascaded down towards him like before, he took a bow and smiled until he caught a glimpse of the King looking largely unimpressed with his complete show of arrogance and threw him a look that Tahmidius knew had got him into trouble,

'What is that boy doing now??' questioned the King as he stood up to get a better view, 'I give him a talk that is supposed to give him the kick up the backside he needs and he goes and shows off like that!!', Joda had stepped forward looking rather embarrassed now as his son had seemingly cast doubt over his ability to do well in this year's competition,

'I'm so sorry sire, shall I go and have a word with him?, he may well listen to me, I cannot believe he's showing off again!!' Joda said as he tried to look away from his sons antics muttering 'that boy will be the death of me!!...not impressed Kirk!!!, so not impressed',

'No don't do that Joda...he needs bringing down a peg or two...' a wry smile crept across the Kings face as he stood up from his seat and inhaled deeply, his chest rising and falling with every breath then in one swift movement he flicked his right arm out and as if sliding it sideways he made the ground beneath the competitors shake and rumble, followed by a wall of dust some thirty feet high shoot its way from the centre of the Arena all the way along to where Tahmidius was standing, still taking in the adulation of the crowd, or so he thought, but they were shouting at him to turn round and see what they were seeing. The wall blew ever closer until at the last minute he spun round and was faced with this huge dust cloud which brushed away what he had written on the floor and threw him across the Arena with such force.

'OOOF' Tahmidius winced and moaned as he had landed upside down in a huge pile of straw and hay that was sat around the edges of the Arena 'what just happened??' he said as he slowly clambered off the rather padded landing area, he stood up as straight as he could causing his back to click then noticed a lot of people were laughing at him and the mess he was in,

'TAHMIDIUS....' came a booming voice from in the distance,

'Father, is that you???' he answered back with a slightly scared tone in his voice,

'MUCH WORSE THAN THAT...' the voice once again echoed around the Arena causing total silence to descend, 'I warned you about your attitude and behaviour...and you have totally forgotten every single word I said, so for that I am penalising you...a thousand points are being taken away from your final score at the end of the week for this complete lack of respect' Tahmidius now knew it was the King talking to him and didn't know what to do,

'B...but Sire, I...I didn't mean to...' he replied with his head slightly bowed,

'Are you questioning my decision here?' the King angrily replied to him as he stepped forwards to place his hands on the rail at the front of the stand, more for support than anything else,

'N..no sire, I just think maybe that's a bit harsh...' came the quivering answer back in the King's direction,

'Ok...TWO thousand points!!!, answer me back anymore and it will be a record points deduction...and I assure you that following that amount of points deducted you will not fulfil your dream!!' the Kings steely eyes went straight through Tahmidius like an arrow, he opened his mouth as if to speak again,

'Something to say??....' the King said as he placed his hand up to his ear and cupped it, Tahmidius just huffed and dropped his shoulders before walking off looking very dejected following his latest tongue lashing from the King,

'That boy infuriates me so much!!' said the King as he turned to see his son standing there beside him, he placed his hand on his shoulder and gently squeezed it,

'Who are you talking about father?, It seems there's a lot of commotion coming from the stands, what's happened?' Lord Casborn said as he scoured the stands, as if looking for something,

'The son of Joda...I mean he IS an excellent candidate for 'The Circle' but his arrogance is holding his progression back, he needs to be totally focused on the task ahead, I am hard on him as he's in the top one percent of Vaymians who I feel are ready to make the step up' the King said with an air of doubt surrounding his every word. As Lord Casborn watched Tahmidius very carefully while he had actually started his training properly he could see what the King was talking about with regards to his skill,

'He is good, father...I mean I've never seen or felt that much confidence in one individual before, even his father doesn't possess that much skill, and Joda is the finest soldier in 'The Circle', his magic usage is excellent also' Lord Casborn said as he watched Tahmidius expertly conjure up a levitation spell that lifted his equipment up above his head and move it across towards the Arena wall,

'As I said he's infuriatingly good but he just needs to rein it in a little otherwise he will blow his big chance, I'm expecting him to sail through this Tri-Year' huffed the King 'but it remains to be seen whether he can overcome the points deduction I gave him',

'Do you believe you were wrong to do that father?' asked Lord Casborn 'or do you believe that by doing that will give him the extra focus he needs to come out on top and show you he deserves to be in 'The Circle', I

273

believe this can only help him' he smiled as he gently patted the King on the shoulder 'but for now I must find Garin, he's keeping an eye on the children don't forget, I need to find out how they are getting on' and with that he placed his thumb and two fingers onto his head as if communicating telepathically, he then breathed out as he could feel the presence of Garin somewhere close by,

'Garin...' he said as he searched the stands for him,

'Sir?' came the reply

'Ahh excellent...you are here then, how are the children?' Lord Casborn replied.

Over the far side of the Arena just at the top of the stand where Daniel and Tobias were sat, Garin was standing up against the wooden pillar, his hood lifted up over his face so he couldn't be recognised by anyone,

'From what I can gather they are all in good spirits, no issues so far and it seems as if they are enjoying this experience, especially Lillie' Garin replied as he too had his thumb and two fingers against the side of his head,

'Shall we meet in the King's Chamber for a detailed update?' replied Lord Casborn to him 'I want to know how the children are coping with all this, I shall see you very soon ok?',

'Yes sir...I shall be leaving very shortly, I just need to visit the other boy before I come....there's an odd feeling surrounding him, I just need to check it out then I shall be over' Garin replied as he turned as quick as a flash and shot down the stairs towards where Harvey's stand was situated.

As the day wore on the children in the stands were treated to a spectacle like nothing they had ever seen before, there was of course the competitors practicing for the upcoming games, each displaying their own level of strength and magic to the watching crowds who were cheering for their favourite, plus the King had laid on a little treat to finish off the evening, a small show that had been put together by some of the younger members of the school which explained the history of the Tri-Yearly-Night-Games to anyone who didn't know much about it. As fireworks filled the

Arena, buzzing around like small fireflies as they shot off, a few of the boy's from 'ArrowHead' had seen enough and decided to sneak out,

'Come on boys, let's go down to the hideout..' said one boy who was known as Cahlid, the leader of his small group of friends, 'I'm not staying here to be even more bored than I already am!!' he moaned as they descended the steps towards the exit, but there were a couple of guards standing between them and the Arena exit,

'What do we do now Cahlid?' said another of the boy's as they stood around pretending not to be up to much,

'Hmmm...Just leave it to me, but be ready to run when you get my signal' laughed Cahlid as he walked away from the group,

'What's the signal??' shouted another of the boy's, but Cahlid had already disappeared 'Well that's just great!!' he continued 'how can we run if we don't know what's going on'. Just as he finished his sentence a huge commotion was taking place just over the other side of the Arena walkway, what sounded like a load of shouting quickly turned into a small fight between a couple of the children who were surrounded by a big group of children all trying to get a look at what was going on, then the guards rushed over to where it was all kicking off just as Cahlid came running back towards the exit and pushed at the doors,

'Come on you lot let's get out of here!!' he shouted as the Arena doors swung open just enough for them all to squeeze through as the doors then slammed shut behind them with a BANG.

'What did you do in there?' the smallest boy asked, Pip was his nickname due to his size more than anything, Cahlid laughed as he told them what had gone on.

'Well I saw Drace from 'FieldBloom' talking to Jamar, one of his old friends from 'FuryChasm', and you know how much Elrin from 'RainFall' doesn't like Drace talking to him as there was something bad that happened between them a while back. Well as Drace and Elrin are supposed to be good friend's I accidentally whispered to him that we had seen Drace and Jamar spending rather a lot of time together in the food hall, laughing and joking away just like old times which strangely seemed to anger him a lot, don't know why. So then Drace was confronted by his friend who was shouting all sorts of things in his face which then escalated into the fight, causing those stupid guards to run over to sort it out, meaning we could escape this boring place' as he led the boy's away from the Arena doors and around the side of it 'Now come on let's get out of here I can't stand this place'. As he led the group over to the corner of the darkest part of the castle wall Cahlid moved back a large wooden box and pile of rags which revealed a hole in the side of the castle wall just big enough for them to squeeze through, well almost all of them as the last boy to try and get through managed to get himself wedged in the hole,

'OWWW…' he wailed 'I'm stuck!!, can you help me please, I'm caught on my robes!!' the more he struggled the more he became stuck and the more noise he was making,

'Shhhh..' said Cahlid as he raised his finger to his lips 'Do you want us to get caught??',

'Well I don't fancy staying stuck in here so can you please get me out!!' said the boy as Cahlid told the others to help him out of the hole,

'Grab his arms and drag him out please boy's, I don't want to stay here a minute longer, that new boy has got me wound up too' he snarled as he could hear the roaring from inside the Arena from the gathered crowds 'I can't wait for this place to fall!!' and with that the boy's heaved and tugged at their friend who was still stuck in the hole in the wall until finally they pulled him free with a 'pop' causing them to lose their balance and slide down the hill on the side of the castle straight into the woods below. Cahlid just stood there shaking his head as he watched them disappear through the bushes that lined the start of the woods,

'Idiots…' he sighed heavily 'total idiots, not a single brain cell amongst them', as Cahlid followed a different path down from the side of the castle he seemed deep in thought and was talking out loud as if talking to someone beside him,

'There must be a way to get my own back on this place...there must be something I can do to make people fear me...I will get my revenge, I promise you that. DO YOU HEAR ME!!! I WILL MAKE YOU ALL KNEEL BEFORE ME!!' he shouted up at the castle with a rage burning inside him that he had never felt before. He stood there for a few seconds before laughing to himself, a cackling laugh so evil it would terrify anyone. Then as he reached the start of the woods he couldn't see any of his friend's waiting for him,

'Err guys??' he said quietly 'where are you?, I can't see you anywhere, stop hiding or I'll have you!!', Then a crackling sound came from directly on front of his followed by a breeze that whipped around him like an excited child,

'Wh...who are you??' he stood completely still, frozen to the spot as a figure appeared in front of him floating above the ground, it's hood pulled right over its face,

'Ahhh Cahlid...' the figure spoke in a ghostly tone as he just stood there unable to move 'I've been waiting for you boys...the Master will see you now!!' Skaff had seeked out these children on his master's explicit orders and the next part of his plan was beginning to take shape. Cahlid was in some sort of trance as he disappeared off into the woods following behind the figure, then as if by magic they vanished.

Chapter Twenty-Three
Understanding The Change

Back at the castle Daniel and Tobias were talking about the practice session that had been put on for them earlier, Daniel's attitude seemed to have changed towards the games themselves,

'Wow Toby' he said smiling as they made their way down the flight of wooden stairs towards the bottom 'I must admit that was quite a show, I actually can't wait for the games to begin now!!',

'Please stop calling me Toby, my name is Tobias, and finally I'm glad you can see what I can see, I love these games so much' he smiled as he knew Daniel was now beginning to feel part of this large community all three of them had found themselves in, 'Come on Daniel, we need to get to the King's Chamber remember, I can't wait to find out what room we've been put into this time' Tobias was literally skipping along as excited as he had ever felt because he knew that the room they were going to be allocated would define their future.

'So what do you mean 'room'?' he asked 'I've already got a room here with my sister and Harvey, I don't want another one' replied Daniel who was looking slightly confused by what Tobias was telling him,

'Well Daniel I'm guessing you have been staying in the guest rooms here at the castle, am I right?' Tobias said as they followed the huge crowd of children towards the far end of the castle,

'We've been staying in 'a' room together, but I didn't know it was for guests, I thought that was going to be our room for however long we are here' he replied as more and more excited children pushed their way past the two boys and through the huge door at the end of the corridor which slammed shut behind the last group of children. As Daniel and Tobias were still talking about what was going on Harvey had sneaked up behind Daniel and was readying himself to pounce, he crouched down slightly behind him just as they reached the King's Chamber door and threw his arms out to spook Daniel,

'BOO!!!' Harvey said as he leapt onto his friend causing them to fall through the door and end up in a crumpled heap on the floor of the Kings Chamber,

'Harv...you idiot!!, you scare me half to dea...' Daniel stopped when he noticed that everyone in the room was now staring at the three of them lying face down on the carpet, Tobias was trying to push himself off of the floor but was struggling to move with Harvey landing right on top of him 'Get off me you great lump!!' he shouted as he wriggled free and stood up, dusting himself down as he sighed heavily to himself.

'Ahhhh boy's...' came a familiar voice from the other end of the room, as the room full of children parted and they were met with the sight of King Casborn standing high up on a platform looking down over everyone before him, 'please stand up and join your classes please, we have been waiting for all children to enter so we can begin'

'Begin what?, what's going on here gra....grand...leader' Daniel said as he nearly gave away who the King actually was to him,

'All will be revealed boy's' smiled the King as he turned back towards the rest of the children, cleared his throat and thrust out his hands

'Welcome children...' the King began 'as you all know this new school year has finally started with a great amount of expectation being placed upon quite a number of you, as you may or may not know we have had a record number of new starters to the school this time around which gives us a lot more hope for the future safety of this wonderful place we live in....', the King kept talking about the values they were going to be learning as Daniel kept looking around the room where he spotted his sister standing midway down the rows of children looking slightly confused just as Daniel felt too, she saw him looking at her and smiled to him but Daniel could tell she wasn't her usual confident self for some reason,

'Are you ok?' mouthed Daniel to her but Lillie couldn't make out what he was saying so she lifted her hands up as if to say 'I don't understand' 'are you ok??' Daniel said a little louder causing Tobias to nudge him in the ribs and 'shushing' him at the same time but Daniel was still looking at his sister who had turned away now, her eyes fixed somewhere else as the sound of footsteps clumped across the wooden floor in the direction of Daniel and Tobias,

'Lillie….' he said 'Lillie!!!' he called once again as the footsteps suddenly stopped and a shadow loomed over him like a dark cloud over the land, the King stood there arms folded as Daniel turned back to be met by his grandfather looking down at him,

'You boy…' the King said in his deep bellowy tone which was normally enough to strike fear into the smallest of children but as Daniel knew him he was as calm as ever,

'Oh hello' Daniel replied 'are you ok?,

'What's your name boy??' the King asked, knowing he needed to make people believe they weren't related so there would be no jealousy towards him,

'Eh??...but you…' stuttered Daniel as he stared at the King with the blankest expression on his face,

'I asked you a question boy!!' the King replied 'and I expect an answer!!' his tone changed as he knew all eyes were fixed on him but his grandson couldn't see what was going on,

'Oooo tetchy!!' Daniel laughed out loud as he thought they were playing some kind of game 'my name is Freddie McGumball, third in line to the throne of the Land of Cabbages...Ohhhh that's a good one, must remember that' he laughed as he looked back at the King who was looking less than impressed with his grandsons lack of respect towards him in front of the rest of the school.

'Hilarious..' the King said as he sighed heavily at his grandsons response, 'your REAL name if you please, and no more back chat!!'

'Sorry!!..' Daniel said with an air of annoyance as he was trying to have a little fun 'my name is Daniel Carter...I'm twelve years old...and I can't stand brussel sprouts'

'Daniel you say...Hmmmm I've not seen you here before, are you new to Castle Erwin?' asked the King with a wry little smile spreading across his face as he looked at Daniel,

'Well yes sort of...I guess...I mean...I don't think I've been here before but I'm not sure' replied Daniel as he squirmed awkwardly on the spot with hundreds of eyes staring right at him,

'Ha ha, it's ok, I'm only joking with you, and from now on could you please pay attention as it is from this point on that your future will be decided' the King smiled as he swiftly turned on the spot and walked back towards the front of the room and climbed back up onto the platform he had been standing on, as he took a deep breath the King looked out over hundreds of expectant faces all waiting for his first day speech, as he looked across the children he could see that most of them had a look of excitement while others looked as nervous as they had ever done so he knew his speech needed to appeal to all the children, a huge smile spread across his face as he began to address the children with warmth and compassion, the class teachers dotted around the room as if forming a sort of protective barrier around them,

'Children...' the King began

'as you all know this year is particularly busy with all the new additions to the school, and I know a lot of you have spent some time here before your actual first day but I hope that this year will be one that we can look back on with a collective amount of joy and happiness and us being able to watch you all grow into the most wonderful people that have ever graced this wonderful place, but as always there are forces that lurk beyond the safety of these walls which are trying to upset the balance here, but I assure you that as your first school year passes with us you will have gone some way to being able to spot the danger signs that threaten to upset our way of living and you will be equally adept at defending yourselves with the

281

aid of Professor Deveraux and his class for defence and wizardry…' the King lifted his hand up to the place where Professor Deveraux was sat which upon hearing his name he rose from his seat so the whole room could see who it was the King was talking about, he smiled and bowed his head slightly towards the children but didn't utter a single word allowing the King to continue his speech 'I do hope that you take his class very seriously as I have been particularly active in recruiting only the best teachers to serve at this school this year, and he comes with the most glowing reputation as one of the best defence teachers across the land….I would hate for his time to be wasted by any of you' a murmur spread around the chamber as the King paused for a few seconds to catch his breath, every child was whispering amongst themselves apart from Harvey who was just standing there completely still as if frozen and was staring at the wall at the end of the room as if he could see right through it.

'Settle down please, all of you….Now we all know the reason why we are all here don't we children?' the King began speaking to the room again with a slightly more upbeat tone as he leaned against his platform and smiled,

'ALLOCATION DAY!!!!' the children shouted as they threw their arms in the air whooping wildly at the thought of what was happening next.

Allocation day was the most important day in the children's school calendar as this was the day that the King and his staff would give each class their own dormitory, these were to be their rooms for the rest of their school term but the rooms came with a hidden secret, something that none of the new pupils knew about and which would be revealed to them soon enough,

'So children..' the King raised his hands aloft and smiled again 'I know just how excited you all are about finding out which dormitory will be yours but if you can just contain your excitement for just a few moments more, I just need to speak to the other teachers regarding your placements' so the King stepped down and ushered the teachers to the far end of the room as a quiet murmur filled the room, followed by a rumbling of noise as the

282

children began talking rather loudly amongst themselves now, Daniel just stood there looking rather bemused by what he was hearing,

'So Tobes...' he said as he turned towards his classmate who had been in conversation with the child standing next to him 'I think I get what's going on now...so the room we had been staying in wasn't actually our room?, but to me it seems we will all be staying together in one big room now, kind of like one of those big halls the Army use', Tobias placed a hand on Daniels shoulder and laughed out loud, enough for Lillie to be distracted from her chat with the girl she was standing next to,

'Ohhhh you don't know do you?' laughed Tobias ' It's so much better than that I can assure you Daniel, what the King was saying was that each class is given their own dormitory to stay in, it's so we can all get to know each other better and form bonds or something'

'Sort of like a camp you mean?' replied Daniel,

'Yes....maybe, I guess, a camp...now that does sound great, yes it's done so we can all help each other in any way which is needed, it's a place where we can study and have fun without the pressure of being in class' Tobias had been looking forward to this day for so long now that he was beginning to get extra excited at the thought of finding out which dormitory would be theirs 'I've also heard there is some sort of surprise being left in each dormitory, but that's as much as I know...now Shhhh the Kings on his way back'.

The King stepped back onto his platform and addressed the children once again 'My children...now the time has come, the most exciting day in the history of this castle...now let's get you children allocated...', a huge roar greeted the King's last comment, the children were high fiving each other and talking excitedly about what room they were being given, 'ALRIGHT children...'shouted the King 'let's get started.....step forward the class of ForestEdge' as the class stepped forward the King smiled warmly 'after much deliberation we have decided to offer you the dormitory of....Elder Siren', the class began excitedly shouting in appreciation at the dormitory they had been given 'now if you will follow your teacher Mrs

Higgitt she will escort you to your new dwelling, all your things have already been placed in each room ready for you. Oh and don't forget what we talked about Mrs Higgitt, wait for my signal ok?' the King smiled as the class exited the room out of the side door and off into the echoey corridor

'Yes my King, I shall be standing by' Mrs Higgitt smiled as she left the room after her extremely excited class.

'Now who is next??...Ahhhh yes Rivers Cove. Please step forward, you have been offered the dormitory of....LunarFog' once again loud and excited shouting followed what seemed to be a very popular decision amongst the class as they were ushered out of the door by their teacher Mr Ragnar after being given the same instruction as Mrs Higgitt.

So for the next few minutes the King reeled off name after name of classes and dormitories, slowly the numbers dwindled until he got down to the final few classes, Lillie's, Harvey's and of course Daniel's. A low murmur filled the room as the last few classes stood side by side in the Chamber,

'And now the last few....step forward...MuddyBog' the whole of Harvey's class fell completely silent awaiting their dormitory room, 'now as you may already know you three classes that are left have always been seen as a higher performing class year after year which is why I have allocated you one of the top three dormitories this castle can offer....Titans Trinity!!!' gasps spread amongst the children as they knew this was a massive honour for their entire class to be offered a dormitory as wonderful as this one 'Now Mr Scoot you know what to do, await my signal in the room please, and children do behave!!' as they all ran towards the door it seemed Harvey had been swallowed up by the number of children desperate to get to their new room, something which Daniel had noticed,

'Oh bye then Harv!!!' he said as he watched the class managed to squeeze through the door and off out of sight in a whirlwind of whoops and screams,

'I'm sure you will get to see him soon, this is the most exciting part of the day for us, don't worry' smiled Tobias as he grabbed hold of Daniel by the shoulders 'I'm so excited myself!!!, I can't wait to find out what we have been allocated!!, I'm literally bursting!!'

'Oh whoop-de-doo' laughed Daniel 'I just need a rest I'm shattered!!', the King cleared his throat which was to get the attention of the last couple of classes who were still muttering to themselves,

'Ahhh just the two left now…' smiled the King 'now step forward….WallBloom please' a collective clomping started as the whole class moved forward at once 'now this was a very close thing between you and DawnFall as to who got the last two Dormitories but after much careful thought we have decided that you will be allocated….StarFall',

'Oh my goodness that's the best room isn't it??' asked one pupil from Lillie's class,

'It's just as good as the other one trust me' said another pupil, Mr Flora smiled as he held out his arm for the children to follow,

'Come along children…' he said 'we have a bit of a walk ahead of us so please do try and keep up' he smiled as an excited class exited the

room in an orderly fashion with Lillie not really having a clue as to what was going on now and seemed to be just following the crowd for once, she did catch Daniel's eye as she turned round and waved to him with a worried look spreading across her face which Daniel noticed but was unable to do anything about.

'And then there was one..' Daniel said under his breath as he looked as lost as he had ever felt before, not knowing what was going to happen now but judging by Tobias's reaction he knew it couldn't be a bad thing,

'And finally….DawnFall' the King said as he smiled broadly at the remaining class standing in front of him and the last of the teachers 'now seeing as we have a new pupil who knows nothing of this castle or just how special it is we...as a collective... feel that the only room we could give you all would be one of enormous importance, not only to the school but to the people of this fine land itself, that is why we have allocated you the dormitory of….' as the suspense built up regarding their room Tobias was standing there, eyes closed and clamping his hands together as if praying

285

while muttering to himself over and over again 'shadow blaze...shadow blaze. Shadow blaze' Daniel just looked at him with an expression that shouted 'what's he doing??', Tobias was starting to turn a darker shade of red as he clenched his hands together tighter and tighter,

'Fruitcake..' laughed Daniel as he thought it was funny seeing someone as excited and desperate at the same time.

'Shadow Blaze!!!!' the King finally said as Tobias opened his eyes and let go the biggest smile he could muster,

'YESSSSSSS' he shouted, punching the air as he said it, not really that bothered by anyone else around him but just so excited that he had been allocated the best dormitory this castle had to offer 'I can't believe it Daniel!!!....I've only ever dreamed of this' he said as he looked at Daniel who didn't know where to look as he watched Tobias turn even weirder than he had seen already, 'aren't you excited too??' he said as Daniel just stood there not knowing what was actually going on,

'Yay...' Daniel said meekly as he half-heartedly lifted his arms up with clenched fists 'Shadow Blaze...Is that a good thing??' he asked as he felt numerous pairs of eyes now staring in his direction,

'Why Daniel...it is the most sought after dormitory in the castle' the King had decided that he needed to explain further to his grandson about the room itself 'you see my boy, this room has housed some of the finest warriors ever seen on the battlefield, before they were warriors I mean, this room has helped forge hundreds of friendships and produce countless champions who have all gone on to join our Army so for you select few to be given the chance to room here is one of the biggest honours ever bestowed on such a young class, so I expect you all to knuckle down and work as hard as you have ever done' the King winked in Daniel's direction when he had finished his speech causing Daniel to smile which put him at ease slightly as he stood there alongside the rest of the excited class, 'Lady Willo, would you be so kind as to escort the class to their new dormitory please'

'Yes my King, I shall take them right away' Lady Willo replied as she walked over to the door shepherding the children as she went 'Come on children let's go, it's rather a long walk to your dormitory'

'Oh Lady Willo...would you mind if I had a quick word with this young boy here?, I want to make sure he understands what's going on' said the King as he pulled Daniel back from the crowd,

'Not a problem at all my King, shall I come back for him soon?' asked Lady Willo,

'That won't be necessary, I shall escort him to the dormitory very soon, I only need a few minutes of his time' the King said as he turned and walked Daniel back to the front of the room just as the door slammed shut behind them.

'Sit down my boy' smiled the King as he patted his hand on the seat next to where he had sat down, Daniel sat right next to his grandfather and looked right into his eyes as he stared at his face,

'So what is going on then if you don't mind me asking?' Daniel said, his attention was taken away by the sound of the Kings Chamber door being opened and in stepped his father Lord Casborn and Garin, Daniel's face lit up as he saw his father standing there with a huge smile on his face,

'Daniel...' Lord Casborn smiled as he threw out his arms wide which

when Daniel saw that he ran to him and jumped right into his arms, 'whoa...steady Daniel, you nearly knocked me off my feet, haha' as they stood there embracing each other the King sat back smiling as he watched his family looking happy,

'We are complete...' he muttered under his breath happily, 'now Daniel, as I was saying, the reason I kept you back was for nothing in particular, I just wanted to get your thoughts on the day so far, don't look so worried' the King laughed out loud as he could see Daniel was still looking nervous around him, 'come, come, sit right here with me' as Daniel looked up at his father he received a huge smile back from him,

'It's ok son, I'll be right here' Lord Casborn walked Daniel up to the front of the room again, only the sound of soldiers walking past could be heard from outside the door, Garin kept watch so that they weren't interrupted,

'Sire, the corridors are clear now' he said shutting the door behind him and clicking the lock into place,

'Now Daniel...' the King started 'what are your thoughts on the first day here?, I can understand how daunting this must be for you, oh and your sister also, but I hope we have been able to integrate you in gently to the school and without anyone knowing who you actually are'

'It's been a weird day' said Daniel as he rubbed his head 'I don't really know what the heck is actually going on, it's been crazy since we got here really, feels like my feet haven't touched the ground'

'I can assure you the days will get easier my boy, we just needed to see how you reacted to this day before we decided what steps to take next, but I can see that you seemed to have coped better than we though, wouldn't you agree son?' the King turned his head in Lord Casborns direction,

'I would agree there father, I mean the feedback from Garin has been invaluable, Daniel...we had Garin follow you around but from a safe distance just so we could watch how you interact with the children and teachers, and I must say they have had nothing but good things to say, we always get a class report sent to us at the end of each day just so we can keep tabs on how everyone is coping within the school itself' Lord Casborn smiled at his son and placed a hand on his shoulder as he spoke softly to him,

'Oh ok...I guess' replied Daniel as he stared at the ground looking slightly embarrassed by what was going on,

'Oh no need to look like that my son, you and your sister are coming along fine, but your friend is a bit....odd' laughed Lord Casborn 'I mean one minute he's as dedicated as I have ever seen anyone on their first day then the next minute he's as crazy as a HornBill, I really can't figure him out yet',

'So why else am I here?' asked Daniel as he still seemed to be not getting the real reason for him being kept back 'I don't think your telling me everything'

'Daniel...when the time is right I will reveal all to you, but let me just say that as things stand we have nothing to worry about, your future will be whatever it becomes, but if all goes as I anticipated then the future of this land will be in safe hands and the Bells shall not fall anymore!!' the King said defiantly as he stood up straight and smiled at his grandson who was sitting on the chair still, 'Now as you are aware for things to go as they need to we cannot let anyone know of your connection to our family otherwise that will have a major impact on whatever is going to happen from now on'

'I haven't said anything to anyone yet, and I'm sure Lillie hasn't either....' said Daniel, suddenly his eyes widened slightly as if alarmed

'Oh there was this one woman who guessed who I was, just after we arrived here...', a look of panic spread across the faces of the King, Lord Casborn and Garin at hearing this news,

'Oh and what did this woman look like?' asked Lord Casborn

'I can't really remember much...' Daniel sat there racking his brains for any information he could think of 'Oh...she was wearing this huge red and blue cloak I think'

'Oh...I think I know who that is sire!!' Garin said 'there's only one person who wears such bright colours on her person...Ruby Cloven...the woman with a thousand personalities, I'm sure our secret will be safe if it is her that you spoke to' laughed Garin as he stepped away from the door and down towards the front of the room 'so my King as all seems well so far shall I escort young Daniel to his dormitory?'

'Yes Garin thank you that would be most helpful...' smiled the King 'and Daniel...remember you must not tell a soul, I shall speak with your sister very soon and make sure she is feeling welcomed, but for now you must go and join the rest of your class at Shadow Blaze dormitory, I can assure you that we shall not interfere in anything you do, any decision you make or any act you see fit to carry out, this is your time and your place and I....we need you to develop as you intend to, enjoy your time here my boy and don't allow yourself to be swayed by a wrong decision or something that might endanger you or your sister, ok?'

'No problem. I'll do my best to do the right thing by you all, and father...Lillie and me are so happy we have found you, I just wish mum was here to see this' replied Daniel a little downhearted as he stood up from his seat and headed towards the door with Garin.

'Do not worry about what 'has been' but focus on 'what will be' my child, every situation has a solution and I'm sure you will figure out what is best, but for now go with Garin and take your place in the dormitory with the other children who will be waiting patiently' the King smiled Daniel as he joined him at the door, he knelt down in front of him and placed his arms around his grandson, instantly putting Daniel back at ease,

'I believe you will fulfil your potential and go on to do great things my boy but to achieve that you must be ready to face whatever challenges come your way and not give into the evil that surrounds this place, but....I'm sure you will succeed in whatever it is you do, so go with Garin and...Daniel....' the King said,

'Yes grandfather??' replied Daniel curiously,

'Go become YOU!!' laughed the King as Daniel smiled and set off out of the door with Garin at his side, off they walked to the other side of the castle where Lady Willo and the other members of his class were waiting patiently for him to arrive,

'Ahhh there you are Daniel' Lady Willo said as she smiled broadly at Daniel who went and stood with Tobias just at the entrance to the dormitory door, 'this is the bit I enjoy the most' she smiled as she clapped her hands together in excitement, she clapped her hands and the dormitory doors flung open wide, all the children gasped as they were greeted with the sight of the Shadow Blaze dormitory right in front of them,

'Step inside, children..' she said as her smile grew even wider.

Chapter Twenty-Four
Let's Get You All Settled

As the children stepped inside their dormitory they were met with the sight of a slightly darkened room, dimly lit lanterns filled the corners of the room, a huge stained glass window sat proud at the end of the room overlooking the Hills of the Howling Wind and the Lake of the Frozen, the wind howled against the window as they all stood there waiting nervously for Lady Willo to enter the room,

'Doesn't look like much to me' said Daniel to Tobias 'bit of a let-down I'd say!!'

'Shh Daniel…' replied Tobias 'I want to believe in this place, don't ruin it for me!!'

'I was only saying!!!' Daniel replied

'Well please keep your comments to yourself, I have waited my whole life to be given this dormitory, I don't care how awful you may think it looks because to me this is the most magical room in this whole castle, can't you just feel it's aura??' Tobias said with a huge smile as he rubbed his hands up the wooden door frames trying to take everything in,

'The only thing I'm feeling is cold!!, surely this can't be the right room??' just as Daniel said that Lady Willo made her way into the room after a lengthy discussion with Garin who was now walking off down the corridor,

'I'm sorry for the delay children but Garin and I just needed a little chat about an important school matter' Lady Willo said as she stepped a few paces further into the room and stood in front of a large table which was placed in the centre of the room

'oh I wish someone would of cleaned this place a little beforehand, it's so…..dusty!!' she said wiping her hand over the table, picking up a dusty layer as she did so,

'Errrm excuse me' said Daniel as he raise his hand high in the air

'Yes Daniel, please speak' Lady Willo replied,

'Is this the actual room we are staying in as I think it looks nasty and dirty, feel I might catch something horrible if I stay in here too long' Daniel replied as he pulled a disgusted face towards the teacher.

'Well Daniel, first of all yes this is the dormitory you and your class will be staying in for the entire term, Ahhh my favourite place in the castle' Lady Willo said as she wandered around the table slowly, taking in the feel of this mighty room 'and secondly, welcome to the dormitory of Shadow Blaze!!!' as she clicked her fingers something magical happened. The dark room that they were in was suddenly transformed in front of their eyes, a shimmering light filled every inch of their dormitory, colours filled the room swooping around like a bird on the wind, brightening up every wall and glistening in the light. The children stood there mouths wide open as the room kept changing beneath their feet, Lady Willo was flicking her hands around, casting a spell on the room,

'WOW!!!' the class shouted out at once, Tobias was on the verge of falling over due to the excitement and had to hold on to Daniel as they stood there still open mouthed,

'Oh it's better than I imagined!!' Tobias screeched excitedly

'We aren't done yet' smiled Lady Willo as with the flick of her hand the walls in the dormitory creaked and groaned and all of a sudden started to move sideways, making the room they were in as big as any room they had ever seen, new rooms were appearing before their very eyes, huge comfy seats filled every corner of the room and a table as big as the King's sat at the far end of the room with huge chairs lining each side of it with plates and cups and cutlery laid out in complete symmetry across it. The last part of the room to be changed was a corner of the room which had been filled with a huge wooden door with the Shadow Blaze crest right in the middle of it,

'That looks creepy!!' one of the children at the back of the group said,

'Bet that's the best bedroom in this dorm' said another smartly, but none of them were anywhere near close to what was actually behind the door, something which Lady Willo was quick to point out.

'Children..' she started as the final pieces of the room revealed more and more space 'as you can all see now that this room is yours for the rest of the school term, only this class can enter here and no one else, many of you who know this room once housed some of the most fearsome soldiers that protect us, even to this day may I add, so I want you treat this dormitory with the utmost respect and care ok!!'

'YES LADY WILLO' came the collective reply as the whole class were still in awe at the beauty of the room they were standing in compared to how it looked earlier,

'Errr Miss…' said Daniel with a raised hand causing everyone to turn round to look at him as he did so, something which made him feel slightly uncomfortable 'what just happened?'

'What do you mean Daniel?' came the reply from Lady Willo

'Well one minute we are standing in one of the most grottiest rooms I've seen, apart from my bedroom, then the next thing I know we have been transported or something to this place!!' Daniel was totally confused by this and made his brain spin,

'Oh Daniel' laughed Lady Willo 'we haven't gone anywhere at all, this is the same room, with a few upgrades...shall we say, call it the Kings personal touch' as Lady Willo stood there arms outstretched looking pleased with what had been created before the children's eyes,

'Nope...still totally lost' Daniel replied as he shrugged his shoulders heavily,

'Daniel...this room is sort of an extension of the Arena' Lady Willo felt that her explanation would clear this all up for him 'you see this room is exactly the same size, it hasn't altered in size or shape on the outside but inside it sits a protective dome, just like the one which is protecting the Arena, so we can make this room as large or as small as we want to and make it into any shape too, whatever suits your requirements',

'Oh right, I think I get it...well sort of...maybe just a little bit...my brain hurts' said Daniel holding his hands on his head as if he was feeling woozy,

'It really is that simple Daniel, we just use the Dome to make the most of the space we have so it gives you the best chance of being totally relaxed in your own space, free from the pressures of school lessons and the ability to form close friendships with your fellow students which will help you in the future I'm sure' smiled Lady Willo as she felt just by looking at Daniel that he was now more up to speed with what was going on,

'So this place won't get any bigger than this?' he asked again as a groan filled the air as a few of the children were now getting slightly annoyed with Daniel's lack of understanding,

'Leave Daniel alone!!' barked Tobias, sticking up for his friend 'it's not his fault he doesn't know anything about this place, I mean he might not be the cleverest one here but....' he didn't get to finish what he was saying as Daniel whipped his head round rather quickly,

'Oi!!!!....thanks for that TOBY' came Daniel's stinging reply 'blooming cheek!!'

'Oh I'm sorry Daniel I didn't mean it in that way...' came the apologetic reply 'and please call me Tobias...not Toby, I can't stand that name!!',

'Don't call me thick then!!' Daniel replied angrily at his lack of knowledge being questioned 'and Miss...What's that in the corner there??' he asked pointing to the large wooden door that was now fully unmasked and shining like a beacon for all to see,

'Ah ha!!' said Lady Willo 'I was hoping that you would see that, that room is a fairly new addition to this school, it has taken many years for the leading wizards to perfect the programme used behind this door, we needed to make sure it was safe before we let you children loose in there',

'So what is actually in there then??' said Daniel 'Is there a huge dragon or something' he laughed out loud at the thought,

'Well there may be some sort of creatures lurking in there but it's not what you think Daniel, but the truth is children that is what we call the 'Acceleration Chamber', it's a room designed to allow you to express

294

yourself to the maximum without the stresses of actual physical contact' Lady Willo explained, but the children still looked totally lost,

'Eh??, Miss...Still not getting it' replied Daniel, who's face had a look of complete confusion now,

'Ok children. I understand that this does sound confusing but in time you will be able to see what we are trying to achieve here, but this room will allow you to perfect any skills or such at an accelerated rate, meaning anything you have learnt in the wizardry lesson you can practice here without getting hurt, one minute out here equals one hour in the chamber, so time speeds up for you allowing you to put maximum effort in and making your transition into a soldier, or whatever it is you want to become, a lot less daunting', Lady Willo felt the children were a bit more clued up on it now so explained to them that the room would be shared equally amongst them all so no one is seen to have it more than anyone else, 'In time you will come to respect the Chamber and it will come to respect you and your choices, but do remember that we monitor this room every day so please behave and show us that we can trust you all to do the right thing, ok'

'YES LADY WILLO' the class said in unison,

'Right children..' she said again ' I shall now be leaving you to become better acquainted with each other, but the Chamber stays locked until required so no trying to sneak a look or else there will be serious consequences'

'No problem' Tobias smiled 'I shall keep an eye out for you and let you know if anyone tries to get into it' as he saluted towards Lady Willo a sniggering started amongst the children, Daniel included,

'Yes, very good Tobias' Lady Willo replied gesturing to him to lower his hand 'thank you, but there is no need for you to do that, as I said earlier all rooms are monitored by the Elders so be warned that you ARE being watched'

'Lady Willo..' shouted one of the boy's in the small group that had gathered by the table,

'Yes Samuel what is it?' she replied

'Well...so this room is only able to be used by us?...I..I mean what if someone from another dormitory comes in here and mucks about' Samuel replied nervously as he stood there looking awkward,

'Well, these rooms are designed for you and you alone, if, per say, someone other than this class did manage to get into here then the room would instantly revert back to the state it was when we came in' Lady Willo said as each pupil seemed very interested in how the room worked,

'Sort of like a security thing Miss' said Daniel as his eyes lit up 'so what happens to the people left inside?, do we get vaporized or something?' Daniel laughed out loud at what he had just said causing more laughter to follow from the rest of the class,

'Oh very good Daniel, but no such luck there, what happens is the person who isn't meant to be in there is met with the room only, any of your class that is in here when this happens will stay in the adapted room and won't be seen by anyone else' Lady Willo smiled at her class once again,

'Ohhhhhh sort of a parallel universe type thing, oh I like the sound of that' smiled Daniel broadly, 'so what about if we need to leave the room and the person is still inside?, what happens then?'

'Well absolutely nothing, it will be as if you are in two separate rooms so you can come and go as you please without fear of anyone interrupting you or your studies, does that answer your questions sufficiently children?' Lady Willo said as she started to walk towards the window at the end of the room,

'Absolutely spot on Lady Willo' beamed Tobias as he stood there proudly, Daniel stood there behind him mimicking what he was doing which caused the rest of the class to laugh at Tobias,

'Calm down children!!, and Tobias thank you for your excellent manners as usual, I think you may find a few more points added to your total before the day is out!' Lady Willo said as she started walking towards the door. As she reached the door she turned round to watch as the children were still looking in awe of the room they were in, a few of them had wandered off to

296

have a look around while the rest just seemed to stand close to the central table,

'Go explore my children' said Lady Willo softly, she opened the door and smiled at the thought of knowing just what they had achieved with this room, she knew that the future would be one filled with everything good as long as the group of children carried on this path.

The door slammed shut behind them and the children were left to get acquainted properly, some of them had been friends for a very long time but others were as new as Daniel felt even though he had Tobias hanging off him plus Harvey and Lillie were somewhere close by,

'This room is spectacular!!' said Daniel as he ran his fingers across the huge wooden table top 'I could do with a drink though, I'm so thirsty...' no sooner had he finished what he was saying when all of a sudden the glasses on the table filled up on their own with water,

'D...did you just see that??' said Daniel pointing at the now filled cups 'they filled themselves I'm sure of it!!', Tobias turned towards Daniel and questioned what he had just seen,

'Errr Daniel, I'm sure they were like that when we came in here' he replied,

'Well watch this then...' as Daniel picked up one of the glasses and drank the contents in one go, placing the empty glass back on the table after he had finished 'Ahhh that's better...' he said 'now refill this glass please' the glass started to fill up again causing a small crowd to gather to watch what was happening,

'Oh wow!!' said a voice in the crowd,

'We've got a magic room guys!!' shouted another as gasps filled the air, every child in the room feeling even more excited at this latest new thing they had discovered,

'See Tobias...told you I wasn't seeing things, now who's the clever one eh!!' Daniel laughed as he playfully pushed Tobias on the arm,

'Oh I love this room even more now!!!' Tobias squealed with delight and clapped his hands together excitedly 'let's see what else it can do!!' rubbing his hands together as he surveyed the room for any other signs of magic,

'Oooo oooo oooo, I've got just the thing to ask....' as a twinkle appeared in the corner of his eye 'I'm so hungry now, who else is??'

'WE ALL ARE!!!' came the collective cry as all of a sudden the table filled with the most delightful feast, from end to end it was covered in every type of meat going, weird shaped fruits filled the surface of the table, drinks popped up from nowhere, napkins flying overhead before landing in front of the plates folded up in all sorts of odd shapes, the most glorious colours leapt up off the table like a rainbow streaking across the sky, all the children gasped as the food kept appearing from nowhere until finally the table had been filled, not a space was left on the table, the smell of the feast filled the nostrils of the children followed by a collective rumbling from thirty stomachs,

'Oh...my...gosh!!' Tobias said as his jaw dropped down almost to the floor as his eyes bulged at the sight before him, as his eyes scoured the table of food he saw something out of the corner of his eye so flicked his head round to see Daniel had already sat down and was stuffing his face with all kinds of meat and fruits,

'Mmpphh...Gooood' he mumbled as he crunched down on something as delicious as the last piece of food he had just eaten. Everyone just stared right at him as he kept on eating his way through a huge plate of food,

'What??...' Daniel said as he looked up to see his classmates just looking at him, totally taken in by the huge mound of food he was attempting to shove in his mouth 'come on guys tuck in...' he laughed as all of a sudden the whole class dragged their chairs out and laughed out loud as they also started to fill their plates with the feast laid out before them. Lady Willo poked her head back in the door and smiled as this was what she had wanted to see from her class, a unity amongst them all, them all getting along which would help them in the future, she stood there for a few seconds more just long enough for her to hear someone shout across the table in Daniel's direction,

'A massive thank you to Daniel I'd say for getting us all to sit together and getting us to speak to people we haven't spoken to before, something that I personally struggled with in the past, I hope that we can all become great friend's now, so Daniel you truly belong with us now in DawnFall' the voice came from Riley Ray, the smallest boy in the class and by far the shyest child,

'Thank you Daniel' came numerous voices from around the table

'Looking forward to what lies ahead with you' said another child sat at the far end of the table,

Lady Willo quietly shut the door behind her and felt a warm glow spread over her body 'Ahhh Daniel...' she said 'it looks like this class is ready now...all thanks to you, that calls for extra points!!' as she walked off down the corridor softly singing to herself knowing that her class was coming together nicely.

As Tobias and Daniel sat there starting to talk like old friends and interacting with the rest of the class it seemed Harvey was just as popular in his dormitory, he seemed to be ordering everyone around as if he was in charge, the class of MuddyBog had also figured out how to get food and had been given their pep talk by Mr Scoot so they felt excited about what lay ahead for them.

'Pontus I'd like a drink...' ordered Harvey to his closest ally, who whipped his head round quickly at being told to get Harvey a drink

'Get it yourself Harvey....I'm not your slave!!!' Pontus replied angrily,

'You will all be my slaves...one day!!' he muttered under his breath softly,

'What did you say Harvey??' replied Pontus as he heard him quietly speak, Harvey shook his head, looked up at Pontus with a pair of confused eyes and replied,

'Eh??, I didn't say anything, I'm as confused as everyone else seems to be' Harvey pointed around the room at the other children who looked just as stumped by the beauty of this new room they had been left in, 'so anyway….what's that door for over there??' he continued as he then pointed to the door to the Acceleration Chamber which was adorned with the Titan Trinity badge of honour,

'Did you not hear what Mr Scoot said about it earlier Harvey?, which planet are you on!!' laughed Otto as he sniggered, causing a few of the others to join in,

'I didn't hear a thing' replied Harvey 'Must of been your stupid face putting me off Otto!!'. Pontus laughed out loud as Otto stood there looking angry, he stood up and pushed his chair back with his legs causing everyone to gasp, Otto then raised his hands up as he muttered something under his breath causing crackles of light to fill his hands 'I've had just about enough of you Ordie...time I taught you a lesson!!!' and with that he whipped his hands forward and shot the crackles of light at Harvey causing him to stagger backwards slightly but not actually doing him any harm,

'Wha...what's going on!!!' said Otto 'he should be fried by now...why aren't my powers working!!' angrily he slammed his hands against his legs which stopped the light from shooting out of his hands, Pontus noticed a withered looking parchment had appeared on the table in front of him, he picked it up and read it out loud for all to hear,

'**The room you occupy is free from harm,
There shall be no use of harmful powers,
Anyone attempting to use such evil will be
properly dealt with by the laws of the
School,
This room is a non-harmful training room
which has been designed to allow you to
practice your own personal skill set without
incident,
This room is your haven, be respectful to this
room,**

YOU WILL BE WATCHED CLOSELY AT ALL TIMES.

E.Casborn

'Oh Otto, it looks like your powers are as useless as you are' laughed Pontus as he handed over the parchment for him to read,

'B...but that is so unfair!!!' he replied angrily before turning towards Harvey who seemed to be frozen in terror and was shaking uncontrollably 'your time will come Ordie...mark my words' and with that he slammed the paper down on the table and stormed off through one of the side doors, slamming it shut behind him. A loud crash could be heard from behind the door followed by an angry yell, the door flung back open and Otto appeared looking annoyed,

'It's a blooming cupboard...' he said as his face reddened with embarrassment which caused a lot of laughter to fill the room as he marched towards another door 'shut up you lot...or you'll be sorry' he continued ranting as he opened another door and walked through it, it closed behind him again and silence for a second until a door on the other side opened and he appeared again, now looking totally confused,

'What is going on here!!!' he whined as he could see he was back in exactly the same room as where he started 'this place is crazy!!, I need a sit down, my head hurts now!' Otto marched over to the seating at the end of the room and slumped down in a huge armchair, head in hands and muttering to himself as he sat there stewing. Harvey just stood there completely shocked and scared not knowing what to do, his eyes fixed on nowhere in particular as Pontus noticed him looking terrified, 'Harvey...' he said 'Harvey...are you in there?' as he moved his hand up and down in front of Harvey's eyes which didn't flicker, then Pontus realised he needed to do something to snap him out of his trance so he slapped him hard round the face causing Harvey to scream out,

'YEOWCH that hurt!!!...what are you doing??' he asked as he stood there rubbing his cheek gingerly,

'Sorry Harvey. But you were in some sort of weird trance for a minute' replied Pontus as he stood there sniggering softly,

'Oh I remember now.....why didn't I get blown away by King Idiot over there?' Harvey said as Otto poked his head out from behind the seat with an angry stare,

'I heard that Jones!!!' said Otto 'You'll get yours don't worry!!',

'Oh give it a rest you imbecile!!' said Pontus as he huffed out loud 'always idle threats from you, they are getting very tiresome now!!'

'Oh don't worry 'Perfect Pontus', you're not safe either mark my words!!' Otto said as he turned back around in the armchair laughing to himself,

'Don't worry about him Harvey, he's just a bully, anyway you can't get hurt in this room. It seems like there is a sort of protection spell in place. Read this' Pontus handed Harvey the parchment paper to read.

'Oh ok so I kind of get it I guess, if what I'm reading is right then we can't get hurt if we stay in this room, meaning we get to practice whatever we need to without actually getting hurt!!!, Ohhhh I like the sound of that' smiled Harvey 'so that means I can do this...' He kicked his leg out catching Pontus right on the shin, he didn't flinch at all but just stood there smiling at Harvey, 'well what about this too..' and Harvey swung his hand out and cracked Pontus right on the side of the cheek, still no movement,

'Didn't feel a thing Harvey' Pontus laughed as Harvey kept aiming slaps and kicks in his direction like a martial arts expert but still no flicker of pain showed on Pontus' face,

'Oh this is going to be fun' laughed Harvey as they two boy's cracked up into a fit of giggles which then started everyone else off into what resembled a scene from the wild west with children conjuring all sorts of spells on each other without fear of them being hurt, flailing arms catching whoever was in the way but not actually doing any damage, the sound of laughter filled the room as every child was now involved.

Suddenly a familiar voice appeared from somewhere above them,

'WOULD ALL CHILDREN PLEASE NOW SETTLE DOWN, I UNDERSTAND HOW MUCH FUN THIS CAN BE BUT IT IS TIME FOR YOU ALL TO REST BEFORE TOMORROW'S ACTIVITIES'

The loud unmistakable voice of Lady Willo filled the room as the children stopped in their tracks to listen to what she was saying,

'NOW EACH ONE OF YOU HAS BEEN DESIGNATED A ROOM WITH ONE OF YOUR CLASSMATES, SO PLEASE NOW FIND YOUR OWN ROOM WHERE YOU WILL FIND ALL YOUR BELONGINGS INSIDE'.

As the children set off to find their room they could see their name appear as if by magic right beside the door itself in big bold letters, Harvey had been paired up with Pontus which he seemed pleased about,

'Oh I'm so glad I'm with you, couldn't stand it if I was with Otto!!' said Harvey as they opened the door to their room and stepped inside looking rather pleased,

'I can't wait to see what tomorrow brings' smiled Pontus as he closed the door behind them with a 'CLICK'.

As the castle settled down for the night the last of the torches dimmed but rustling could be heard from the darkest corner

'Come...follow me boys...it's time to make our mark!!' as Cahlid appeared out of the darkness with his gang of friend's all looking like trouble was about to be thrust upon the whole castle, His wicked laugh filled the cold night air as they made their way across the courtyard and sneaked in through the side door of the school ready to unleash evil on a massive scale.

Chapter Twenty-Five
A New Dawn Approaches

As the children awoke for their first day in their new dormitory there seemed to be an air of excitement buzzing around the castle, the sound of children laughing and hollering filled every room no matter which dormitory you walked past, something that the teachers came to notice on their early morning walkabout,

'It's awfully noisy today isn't it!!' laughed Lady Willo as she and Mr Flora walked along the corridors of the castle checking in on every dormitory as they went,

'I totally agree Lady Willo, I have a good feeling about this day, I can't quite put my finger on it but I have a feeling something magical is just around the corner!!' Mr Flora laughed as they turned onto the last corridor to be met by the sight of Pip floating out through the door of the RiversCove dormitory shouting as he was being spun around in mid-air,

'Please stop Cahlid..' came his whimpering voice 'I'm feeling sick!!!, pleaseeeee stop it!!'.

A bellowing laugh echoed around the hall as Lady Willo and Mr Flora made their way towards the open room door as Cahlid walked out waving his hands as if directing the way Pip span,

'Mr Undren….' Mr Flora shouted out as he stood there arms crossed and looking angry,

'Ahhhh Mr Flora….' replied Cahlid sarcastically 'so nice to see you again, how are you?' he laughed out loud but it was a laugh that didn't seem like Cahlid's normal one,

'Just what do you think you are doing to that poor boy?' Mr Flora retorted as he gestured to lower him to the floor,

'Well Mr Flora....Oh and hello to you also Lady Willo' Cahlid replied as he winked at her 'I was just teaching this silly young boy a lesson...you see he has been very disrespectful to me and I cannot tolerate insolence in any form, I'm hoping he sees this as a very valuable lesson as not to disrespect me anymore....Isn't that right. Boy!!' Pip was still spinning round like a top, his face was starting to go as green as the grass too,

'Y...yes Cahlid...I'm sorry...I'm really sorry, I didn't mean it, It was just a joke!!' Pip was close to tears now and feeling like his breakfast was on its way up,

'DOWN...NOW!!!!' Lady Willo demanded as she stared straight into the darkened eyes of Cahlid who smirked before dropping his hands to his side causing Pip to fall straight onto the cold floor with a THUD,

'OWWWW my nose!!!, that really hurt' Pip cried out as he got up feeling very wobbly and unsteady on his feet 'I think I'm going to be sick!!' Pip said as he pushed his way past the teachers and scampered off down the corridor, weaving all over the place as he ran, bumping and banging into the walls on his way to the bathroom,

'I hope you are proud of yourself Cahlid!!!' Mr Flora said as he stood there hands on hips looking very angry,

'Oh I can assure you...Sir...I am VERY proud!!!' Cahlid laughed out loud without even the slightest hint of regret 'That boy deserved everything he got...and he won't be the last to feel my wrath!!'

'I suggest you get back into your dormitory Cahlid' said Mr Flora

'Oh I don't know...Sir...I may just go for a little wander around this....place' Cahlid replied with a sinister tone in his voice,

'I've had enough of this...awful behaviour Cahlid, you are hereby removed from the Inter-Class Cup effective immediately....' Lady Willo said as Cahlids name disappeared off the class leader board which sat in the King's Chamber, the King looked up and smirked before burying his head back into the papers he had been reading,

'Oh pipe down!!!! Cahlid shouted back 'do you really think I care about that stupid cup and this awful place...I have better things to do' and with that he raised his hands up above his head and clapped them three times before disappearing into thin air leaving the teachers looking very bemused and at a loss to explain what had happened to Cahlid, they both stepped into the dormitory and closed the door behind them.

As each dormitory bell sounded more and more of the children rose from their beds and got ready for a new day and the first proper day of school, excitement and nervousness filled the air as the children reflected back on the events of yesterday, each scoreboard sat proudly above the door of their individual Acceleration Chamber giving the children something to talk about during the coming term and making their bond stronger.

The class of WallBloom had been awake for a while and were scattered around the room talking amongst themselves, some were sitting at the table eating breakfast, others were sitting in the seating area laughing and joking, Lillie on the other hand was just lying in her bed quiet and still and just staring at the wall on the other side of the room, her eyes seemed vacant and lost, it seemed as if she was struggling with the change she was going through,

'Mum...' she mouthed softly as a single tear fell down her cheek and onto her pillow, just as she wiped it away the door burst open and in stepped a girl, her body casting a shadow in the room as she entered,

'Hello new girl I'm Freya...Freya Delora, are you getting up soon?', everyone wants to say hello' the Girl smiled as she stepped forward into the light sporting a huge smile on her face 'are you ok?' she asked 'it looks like you've been crying',

'No...I...I'm ok, just feeling a little odd' Lillie replied looking puffy faced, she sat up and swung her legs off the bed before allowing a smile to stretch across her face 'I'm Lillie...Carter, this is all new to me and I feel so far away from home that I'm struggling a little', Freya sat herself down on the bed next to Lillie and placed her arm around her gently before reassuring her,

'It's ok Lillie Carter…' smiled Freya 'as yesterday passed by so quickly we didn't really get a chance to chat properly, oh I'm so glad we have been given StarFall as our dormitory!!' she giggled as her excitement grew,

'Why is that…is this a good place?? Asked Lillie inquisitively,

'Oh this is the dormitory my parents were given when they were pupils at the school, this is where they first met…and this is where they fell in love, mum used to tell me the stories about her time here when she found out I had been accepted to the school' Freya smiled as she thought about all the wonderful things she had been told of about this school and the dormitory her mum and dad had been given, but a tinge of sadness spread across her face when she thought of her dad,

'And I bet your dad was pleased wasn't he!!' Lillie smiled as she felt slightly easier until Freya responded gently and with a sadness that made her eyes tear slightly,

'My father isn't here anymore…'she said 'he was taken from us in the Great War some years back so he never got to know I would be following in their footsteps'. Lillie sat completely still as she could see Freya was upset and didn't really know how to approach her,

'I..I'm so sorry to hear that…' she replied 'I don't really know what else to say…I..I mean I'm sort of in the same boat on that',

'You mean you've lost YOUR father also?' Freya replied

'Oh no, not my father…but I can't really remember my mother for some reason, it's as if she….' Lillie paused for a few seconds racking her brain for any information on her mother,

'Do carry on… 'She what' Lillie?' Freya replied anxiously

'As if she doesn't exist!!!' Lillie sat bolt upright staring at the wall in front of her hoping for some kind of explanation 'I need to go and see my brother…' said Lillie as she jumped up off the bed and hurriedly got into her school robes, Freya grabbed her arm gently and squeezed it,

'Please come and have something to eat first Lillie…everyone has been waiting to see you again, away from the classroom' she smiled softly at

Lillie as she stood up next to her 'come on...please', Lillie smiled warmly at Freya who was now standing in the doorway holding the door open,

'Oh ok, but I do need to find my brother after that' Lillie replied as she walked through the door arm in arm with her new friend.

Sat around the table were all her new classmates who were all sitting there smiling at her while putting food onto their plates ready for the morning feast. At the end of the table was an empty seat which was being held out for her to sit down,

'Please sit here' smiled Freya as she walked her to it 'I've had some food put on your plate already, I hope that's ok',

'Thank you very much Freya...I don't know what to say, I think this place needs to grow on me more, I still feel like I don't belong' Lillie said feeling slightly embarrassed at the generosity of her new friend's,

'You don't have to say anything if you don't want to Lillie. We have a whole term to find out about each other' she smiled back 'now please eat. And can I officially welcome you to StarFall', this caused a lot of clapping and whooping to fill the room followed by a lot of laughter which was putting Lillie at ease and making her totally forget what she was supposed to do after.

Mrs Higgitt, who was the teacher of Forest Edge, had opened the door slightly to listen in on the class and was pleasantly surprised with how the children in the dormitory were getting along causing her to smile just as Mr Fessler walked past,

'Sounds like another class happily getting along Erik' she said as the door creaked behind her as she closed it,

'It seems as if this isn't the only class like that' Mr Fessler said with a grin 'I've had word that almost all the classes have been this positive, I've not heard news like that for quite a few years I can tell you',

'The King will be pleased I'm sure, we may even have a record number of new recruits by the end of it all!!' Mrs Higgitt said as they walked off down the corridor laughing to themselves,

'Let the games begin!!' said Mr Fessler rather loudly and with a slight snort as he spoke 'I cannot wait to see what's going to happen!!', They both disappeared around the corner at the far end of the corridor and out of sight, laughter still echoing around the halls as they went by.

Outside the castle walls in a part of the grounds that wasn't patrolled stood Cahlid completely still on the edge of a huge drop which fell away towards the woods below, he seemed to be talking to himself at first until a familiar figure came out of nowhere and stood right behind him,

'Ahhh my boy...' Skaff said as he placed a hand on Cahlids shoulder and got him to turn round to face this hooded figure 'let me look into your mind for a moment..' as Skaff place Cahlids head in the palm of his hand and seemingly transferred whatever information he could from the boy, 'My..You have been busy...disruption and rage...I like it very much...and so will the Master!!!', Cahlid was completely under his spell as Skaff carried on removing what he could,

'W..What is the next step?' asked Cahlid,

'Ahhhh you will know soon enough...boy, now you must return and await the signal...' Skaff said as he released Cahlid from the spell,

'The signal??' he replied 'the signal for what?'

'To end all!!!' Skaff said as he disappeared from sight like a ghost in the shadows 'now go....boy....be our eyes, be our ears!!' Skaffs whispery voice filled Cahlids head with all sorts of instructions causing him to turn and go back towards the castle with a grin on his face, a grin that just screamed of evil.

'Yes!!!...' he said 'it's time to take it all back!!' said Cahlid with the most evil laugh as he squeezed back through the hole in the wall and into the grounds of the castle only to run into the castle security team who were patrolling the grounds as normal.

'Excuse me young sir but shouldn't you be in your dormitory?' said the guard as Cahlid looked on vacantly,

'I'm talking to you...' he continued

'Don't think he's on this planet Gorlan!!' laughed the second guard as Cahlid still stood there not showing any sign of life,

'Come on young un, you need to get back to your dormitory now, it's too early for you to be out' said Gorlan, the first guard. All of a sudden Cahlid turned towards the guards, his eyes turned a dark purple colour as he raised his hands and chanted out loud, crackles of light appearing at his fingertips as his chanting increased,

'ACK A SEETA, MALA BAROOM!!!' Cahlids eyes turned completely black as the guards stood there totally stunned, unable to move,

'Wh...What's going on??' said the second guard,

'I can't move...' Gorlan said, those proved to be their last words as Cahlid slammed his hands together, emitting a light as bright as anything ever seen, the two guards turned in to a pile of dust in front of him, unable to scream as they vanished, Cahlid laughed out loud as everything around him settled, the wind blowing around the castle walls whipping up the dust which was once the guards and carrying it off into the distance,

'Oh that was so easy...' he laughed as he surveyed the rest of the castle for anyone else who may have seen what had just happened but it seems they were alone 'Nowww....Cahlid..' the voice in his head ringing about, knowing what had happened would come out soon 'do not let anyone find out...we need you to stay 'hidden' from the rest of them' the voice disappeared like a gentle breeze blowing through him.

Cahlid then clapped his hands above his head again and the beam of light swirled around him all the way down to the floor, he vanished into thin air only re-appearing outside his dormitory door.

He shook his head and awoke from his trance like state,

'Where the heck am I and why am I here??' he questioned as his eyebrows lowered in a way that had him feeling totally confused,

'And what's all this dust on me??' he said brushing it all off his clothes causing him to sneeze out loudly which alerted his classmates inside as the door flung open and a group of faces appeared in the doorway,

'What are you lot looking at??' he grimaced at them 'You never seen me before or something?,

'N...no Cahlid...it's just...' Pip said nervously over,

'Just what Pip?, go on spit it out!!' his angry tone causing a few of them to step back into the room,

'J..just after what happened earlier with me and you in the corridor, you kind of freaked everyone out!!' Pip stood there head bowed waiting for another tongue lashing or one of his floating spells to be cast again,

'I haven't got a clue what you are on about Pip!!!, are you feeling sick or something as you look a bit green in the cheeks!!' laughed Cahlid

'Well the spinning round didn't help, and why did you do that to me?' Pip replied again but noticing Cahlid was trying to figure out what he was talking about 'you do remember don't you??',

'Errr I'd remember doing something like that Pip trust me, even if I did do that you probably deserved it!!' he laughed as Pip retreated into the room a few steps further,

'Why did you disappear like that though?, I mean one minute you were here and the next.....gone, vanished, the teachers didn't know what to say but I've never seen fear on their faces like that before!!' said Pip as he edged closer to the door again,

'But I'm right here, I can't recall that!!' said a totally confused Cahlid now 'I remember us in the classroom trying to sneak a look in that Chamber thing but I am completely lost now...are you sure you haven't got a fever or something??',

'It's true Cahlid...' said Rubeus Clarke, the class know-it-all 'I saw it with my very own eyes....all that whirling and screaming from Pip had us worried, I have never seen magic like that on one so...young before, it's as if you were possessed or something' he raised his nose upwards and sniffed loudly in a 'I'm totally right' kind of way,

'So why can't I remember any of this??' he replied shaking his head,

'As I said maybe there are dark forces at work here, those who prey on the weak minded and foolish to carry out their dirty work!!' Rubeus said without any sign of a smirk or giggle, speaking his mind was one of his many annoying habits,

'WEAK MINDED??, FOOLISH??, I would stop right there Clarke!! Before I get you back!!' Cahlid pushed his way past them all causing the children to end up in a heap on the floor 'now come here so I can clonk you one!!' Cahlid chased him around the room angrily as Rubeus fled as fast as he could,

'I was merely being honest...please do stop!!' he shouted out as Cahlid caught up with him and pressed him up against the wall fist pulled back as if to thump him when all of a sudden he was frozen still,

'Wh..what's this?, who's doing that??' Cahlid tried to move but to no avail,

'PUT HIM DOWN..' boomed a voice which seemed to be coming out of every wall and crevice in the dormitory 'THERE SHALL BE NO VIOLENCE IN THESE DORMITORIES....YOU SHALL BE REMOVED'. Before Rubeus very eyes Cahlid slowly disappeared from right in front of him in a ball of light as if being transported away,

'Well that was a turn up for the books guys..' said Rubeus as he re-adjusted his clothes and dusted himself down 'I really thought he was going to hurt me..' everyone was staring at Rubeus now as he looked around the room for an exit, 'I errr...I need to get ready for class...so if you please I'd let to get past and go to my room now', as the class parted enough for him to get through he shot off very quickly into his room and slammed the door shut, just as a note appeared on the table in front of the children, Pip picked it up and read it out to them

TIMETABLE FOR TODAY

8.30am-10.30am Recap of first day in class with Form Tutor
10.30am-12.30am Protective spell teaching (Professor Deveraux)
12.30pm-13.30pm Lunch Break

13.30pm-15.30pm Inter-Class Cup update in the Arena
15.30pm-17.30pm History Teachings
17.30pm-21.00pm Dormitory Review followed by access to
Acceleration Chamber
21.00pm-22.00pm Reflection time
22.00pm-07.00am All students must retire to bed

**ANY STUDENT FOUND NOT IN THE CORRECT AREA WILL BE
SENT TO THE MAIN OFFICE FOR EXPLANATION.**

The note had ended up in every dormitory but each class had a slightly different timetable due to the number of children at the castle,

Daniel was slightly more relaxed today knowing what they had coming and the fact he had seemingly found a new group of friend's to hang around with,

'So what can I expect today Tobias, seeing as you are a fountain of knowledge about this place' laughed Daniel as he poked him in the ribs gently causing his friend to splutter his breakfast over the table,

'Oh thank you very much Daniel!!, that wasn't very clever!!' he replied as he wiped his chin which had been plastered with whatever it was he had been eating, 'it's all over my robes too!, well done!!',

'Oh sorry Mr Serious. I was only asking you a question, jeez don't get too upset' Daniel sniggered as he picked up a tissue and whipped it out in front of Tobias, 'would you like mummy to wipe your chinny winny for you?' as he belly laughed like he hadn't done for a long time at the face Tobias was now pulling,

'Oh yes that's it...' he replied 'laugh at the messy one, oh that's hilarious!!' he snatched the tissue out of Daniel's hand and wiped himself down before scrunching it up and throwing it over his shoulder, it hit the wall and dropped to the floor, Daniel just stared at Tobias with a puzzled look, 'I bet that went in the bin didn't it!!' he laughed before fist pumping in triumph,

'Errr I think you were a bit out Tobes!!' laughed Daniel 'the bin is over there in front of you, well done on hitting that spot on the wall though' Daniel sarcastically applauded Tobias who didn't know which way to look,

'I swear the bin was behind me!!, you must of moved it!!' Tobias huffed as he sat there when all of a sudden a note appeared in front of him which caused him to pick it up and read it

Absolutely no littering in the class or anywhere else on the castle grounds. Deduction of one hundred points per misdemeanour.

T.Gracewell -Deduction of one hundred points
B.Bearbrook-Deduction of one hundred points
S.Evandine -Deduction of one hundred points

'Oh no look at that!!' exclaimed Tobias as he handed Daniel the note,

'Oh that's bad Tobias!!' laughed Daniel 'you've gone from Mr Goodie Two Shoes to class litterbug in one throw of a tissue, I hope they severely punish you, Throw him in the dungeons!!' laughed Daniel out loud as a crowd gathered around him to look at the note too causing Tobias to shrink in his seat out of pure embarrassment,

'Oh be quiet Daniel. Now look what you've done, everyone will know now!!' he replied as Daniel sat there wagging a finger at him,

'Any way do you want me to tell you what's going on then or are you going to make fun of me all day?' said Tobias trying to turn Daniel's attention back to what he had originally asked,

'Oooo that's a tough one..' he laughed 'I suppose you best enlighten me with your school knowledge, so go on fill your boots!!' Daniel said as he got ready for a Tobias story,

'I don't understand Daniel. My feet are already in my boots so you could say they are filled already' Tobias replied looking oddly confused by what Daniel had said,

'It's just a saying where I come from. It means carry on and talk!!' Daniel slapped his hand to his face in despair,

'Oh ok...well in that case I shall proceed...' Tobias said as he went on to tell Daniel everything about the second day of school and probably more than he needed to know, he sat there like a nodding dog as Tobias waffled on in great detail about each class and teacher that

they would have and how he was looking to go down to the Arena floor and being able to actually touch the hallowed ground, Daniel just sat there looking like he was about to nod off to sleep with every word Tobias was feeding him until finally he stopped and the door sprung open with Lady Willo standing there smiling at the class,

'Now come on children..' she started 'it's time to get ready for class, you have fifteen minutes, I expect you all to be on time today, we have a lot to cover' swiftly shutting the door behind her as she finished,

'Can't wait, this is going to be a boring day!!' muttered Daniel as a clap of thunder rumbled across the skies above the castle...

Chapter Twenty-Six

Countdown….

As the children exited their dormitories Daniel finally caught sight of Harvey just up ahead of him, he could spot him anywhere with his floppy hair and odd laugh filling the air,

'Harvey…' he shouted dementedly waving his arms as Harvey turned around 'HARV….wait up please mate' as he jogged down the corridor towards him,

'Ahh hi Dan...Wow it seems like ages since I saw you last!!' smiled Harvey as he walked towards his friend, hi-fiving as they got closer,

'Oh my gosh mate this place is crazy!!, I feel so connected to this place for some reason!!' Harvey smiled as he felt ready to burst,

'It's alright I suppose Harv...but I still have a nagging feeling something isn't quite right. I can't put my finger on it…' replied Daniel as he stood there with Harvey,

'So what do you reckon to this cup thingy we are doing?' Harvey replied excitedly 'somehow I'm at the top after the first day and I have no clue how that happened!!!...Isn't that mad' he laughed as he rested a hand on Daniel's shoulder,

'To be honest Harv I haven't really been that interested in what's going on in class, I've been sort of...distracted, I keep getting these images of an old house surrounded by trees, and a garden with a woman in it, for some reason I can't remember anything about who or what it is' Daniel's shoulders slumped as he stood there talking away about how he was feeling and why couldn't he remember his past,

'Nope...not a clue on that front Dan…' Harvey replied seemingly clueless on his friend's visions 'but I must say I had an odd dream last night...it was so weird that it woke me up!!',

'Oh right' replied Daniel as the thoughts he had seemed to disappear from his mind 'tell me then Harv...but let's walk to class together', and off they walked down the long corridor towards their own classrooms with Harvey extremely animated as usual,

'Well. I was in these woods, you weren't anywhere to be seen, when I started hearing this voice telling me to follow the sound, which me being me, I did and it led me to this weird looking castle which I've never seen anything like it before, it was as tall as it was long. The walls outside were covered in bones and stuff, the voice was calling me from what sounded like the castle...' Harvey's eyes widened as he told of his dream, Daniel was totally taken in so far and demanded more,

'So then what happened??' he asked

'Well the next thing I know this huge drawbridge slammed down in front of me and the voice called for me to enter, it was the most evil sounding voice I'd ever heard, worse than my mu......' Harvey paused for a few seconds racking his brain for the answer,

'Your what Harv??' Daniel had picked up on something he was trying to remember but he looked blankly back at him,

'Oh I've forgotten what I was going to say...' Harvey said as he shrugged his shoulders,

'Ahh well...but as I was saying as I got into the castle I was drawn towards this huge door covered in more skulls, the voice kept telling me to come into the room so I pushed the doors with all of my might until it creaked it's way open where I was greeted with the sight of this ghostly looking figure floating above the floor just staring down at me, I couldn't move at all and just stood on the spot, oh but the weirdest bit was it called out my name...',

'What was it saying, I bet it was 'You Stupid Ordie' haha ' laughed Otto as he barged past Harvey and Daniel upon hearing what Harvey was saying,

'Oh get lost Otto!!!, your such an idiot' Harvey snarled as Otto made his way down the corridor laughing along with his friend's while Daniel and Harvey stood there looking angry,

'Don't worry about him Harv, he'll get what's coming to him!!' vowed Daniel

'So anyway you were saying…'

'Errr…oh yes so as I was saying this figure called out to me, it stretched out this weird bony hand towards me calling out 'Harveyyyyy' and 'you are our eyes', weird or what!!' he said as Daniel listened intently to him,

'Wonder what it means??' replied Daniel 'but I wouldn't rule anything out in this place!!' he laughed just as he felt a slap on the back of his neck forcing him to slump forwards,

'OWWW what was that??' he said as he turned round to see Lillie standing there doubled over in fits of laughter,

'Haha, oh that was so easy Dan!!!' she kept on laughing as Daniel slowly stood up 'Did that hurt much?' she asked in between sniggering,

'You know it did, what was the point of it!!' Daniel angrily replied

'Oh shut up Dan…It's been ages since I gave you a little slap, Ahhh how I've missed that, and I see your still hanging around with rat boy there!' Lillie said pointing at Harvey who whipped his head round swiftly ready to bite back at her remark,

'Who are you calling 'rat boy'?' Harvey snapped back

'Well…you, slush for brains!!' laughed Lillie as she could see Harvey getting redder in the face,

'Leave it out sis…we are all feeling a bit strange today I'd say' Daniel said 'anyway, what's been happening with you?, have barely seen you since the start of all this'

'To be honest Dan…I can't get to grips with all of…whatever is happening, I'm struggling to remember stuff for some reason and my dream last night was so weird that it woke me up!!' Lillie said scratching her head,

'Oh you as well' Harvey piped up 'the dream I had was super odd, I was just telling Daniel about it, you see I was in these woods when....'

'And no one cares...' Lillie sniggered,

'But you see I was sure I'd seen....' Harvey spluttered as he tried to carry on with his dream,

'You're STILL talking. And STILL nobody cares!!..' Lillie glared at Harvey,

'Oh so sorry jeez, all you had to do was ask nicely, I do have feelings you know!!' Harvey replied with a shaky voice as if he was getting slightly upset,

'The only feeling you'll have is a fat lip if you keep on waffling. Just button it for now there's a good.....rat boy!!' Lillie laughed out loud as Harvey huffed and started to walk off mumbling to himself,

'Oh well done sis!!' Daniel said back to his sister 'you've probably upset him even more now!!'

'I'm sure he will get over it Dan....' she replied back but Daniel felt he had to go after him,

'Look I'm going to catch up with him and check he's ok, that wasn't called for at all so please apologise to him when you see him again' Daniel angrily pointed at his sister before running off down the halls after Harvey,

'Yeah yeah whatever...' laughed Lillie as she slowly walked off towards her class alone, just as she got to the end of the corridor a note appeared in her hand, slowly she unfolded it and it read,

L.Carter-Deduction Two Hundred Points for causing harm to others
Deduction One Hundred Points for provocation of a fellow student

Lillie scrunched up the paper and threw it on the floor with a carefree attitude when another note appeared,

L.Carter-Deduction One Hundred Points for littering of the school grounds

PLEASE REMEMBER STUDENTS ARE UNDER OBSERVATION AT ALL TIMES!!!

'Oh that's just great!' she remarked as she stormed off towards her class still clutching the new note in her hand 'this is so unfair!!, I don't want another day like yesterday!' Lillie mumbled as she stormed off only to be met at her classroom door by her teacher Mr Flora,

'Ahhh there you are Lillie, I've been waiting for you, is all ok? You seem a little down this morning' Mr Flora said as he could see the state Lillie was in as she approached the classroom door,

'I..err, It's nothing Mr Flora, it's just very overwhelming here for me, it feels like I'm losing my mind a little and I can't explain why' Lillie replied with her head slightly bowed as if embarrassed,

'Ahhh yes…' said Mr Flora ' I think I might know what is up with you' he smiled at Lillie kindly 'but I assure you it's nothing to worry about'

'What do you mean?' She asked back 'now I'm totally confused'

'It's what we call 'The Re-Birth' Lillie' Mr Flora said 'what I mean by that is when someone is born away from this planet they live their life as normal, they have thoughts, memories, a whole lifetime of images...but when they arrive in this world a transformation takes place within themselves and they slowly over time become 'attached' to this wonderful place we call home'

'Attached???, I'm totally lost now!!' Lillie struggling to understand what was going on was causing her to feel slightly sick as she leant against the wall,

'What I mean by 'attached' is more of a telepathic connection, a way of becoming at one with the whole planet and the people who live here, it's our way of detecting any….shall we say...non-world occupants. The longer you are present here the more you become part of our culture' Mr Flora said hoping that Lillie was following him as he explained about what was happening to her,

'Errrr, still struggling a bit here sir' Lillie said scratching her head

'The connection you have here suppresses any former memories or an attachment with other people you may have had from wherever you came from, it's sort of a way of you being fully integrated into our culture and allows us to assess your future, it gives you a sort of clean slate...shall we say a re-birth' Mr Flora explained further which seemed to help Lillie understand it slightly better,

'Ahhh ok...so anything I done in the past is erased from my memory, but what about my brother??' Lillie asked,

'Ahhh those feelings and thoughts are kept separate from what happens to you, so any family who are with you here will not be erased' Mr Flora said 'but anyway Lillie let's go into class and start a new day afresh and I need a positive mind and positive attitude, it's going to get a lot more strange I promise you' he laughed as he shepherded Lillie into the class and shut the door behind her.

Harvey's class was brimming with excitement as Mr Scoot started his morning speech outlining the events of the day before and the amazing impact Harvey had had already,

'So Class...' Mr Scoot started 'as you can see by the early leader board it seems we have a bit of a shock developing here....Harvey Jones would you please stand up for me', as Harvey rose from his seat Otto started making kissing noises behind him,

'Oooo teacher's new favourite toy...' Otto said out loud as a few of his classmates sniggered 'Go on Ordie...give him a big hug for us!!'

'Settle down class..' Mr Scoot said to the children, who had raised their volume levels slightly above the sound of an airplane taking off, Harvey turned round and scowled at Otto who was almost bent over his desk chuckling, what Otto hadn't noticed was that Harvey hat completely turned round and was leaning on his desk, he looked up to be met with a pair of eyes piercing into his very soul, purple in colour and with a swirling mist filling every corner, Otto seemed drawn into them and was caught in the hypnotic gaze unable to break contact when a voice filled his head, the sort of ghostly voice Harvey had been hearing,

'Harm will not befall him...reset your anger...' then with a whoosh the voice faded and Otto flickered his eyes, unable to remember what had just happened to him as he looked up and Harvey was now facing the other way smiling as the class were applauding him for his first days efforts,

'So well done Harvey and I do hope you carry on with this path' smiled Mr Scoot as he returned to his chair and sat down before opening a book sat on his desk 'Well class if we get through this part of the class then we will have a bit of free time before Professor Deveraux and his protection spell class so let's get started...' Mr Scoot stood up again and placed himself on the front of his desk as he addressed the class and began his day off talking about how the first day had gone, most of the class were listening as he kept on talking but Otto was just sitting there in complete silence not able to focus on anything whereas Harvey was really getting into the swing of being popular at school for once, every question he answered was met with a steady stream of added points to his class total making him pull even further away from the rest of the class which made him excited inside.

Lillie's class were running through the same daily routine as Harvey's class, Mr Flora was running through the state of the class leader board as Lillie sat there not really coping that well with her new surroundings, she was unusually quiet which wasn't like her, she kept getting fleeting images of where she had come from and the life she used to have but they lasted only a few seconds before disappearing from her mind,

'What's wrong with me??' she quizzed herself while sitting in her seat 'my memories...I can still see them!!', a girl sitting right next to Lillie heard her talking to herself and leaned across to speak,

'I'm sorry for interrupting but I couldn't help but overhear what you were saying...' the girl smiled as Lillie turned to face her,

'S..sorry what??' she replied looking slightly puzzled,

'I'm Tia Gracewell....and I think I know what you are on about. You see I'm rather new to this place too and it took me a long time to feel like I belonged until one day I just.....gave in to it' she smiled warmly at Lillie,

'Gave in to what?, I'm so confused still' Lillie replied slightly exasperated,

'This world. You have to just relax and be taken in by it, then you will feel truly free I promise you' Tia said as she placed a hand warmly on Lillies which made her suddenly sit up, a warm feeling filled her whole body as she let out a smile,

'I keep getting memories from somewhere I used to know though...Mr Flora said they would go but still I see things I think I used to get up to...and my mothe.....' Lillie paused for a few seconds as her mind worked overtime trying to think of the last images she was having as her eyes screwed up tightly and a tear sat in the corner of her eye ready to fall like a leaf on an autumn tree,

'Are you ok Lillie?' asked Tia softly 'what were you going to say?'

'I...errr...I can't remember...' Lillie replied again as she turned her face towards her desk 'I've forgotten again, can't have been that important' she said scratching her head again,

'It's ok, I totally understand how strange this must feel, it took me a long time to figure out what was happening but now I feel free' smiled Tia as she looked at Lillie trying to get her to relax 'I'll help you with all this if you would like me to', Lillie turned towards her and smiled

'Oh ok...but I think I need to try and figure this out for myself, thank you anyway' Lillie smiled awkwardly at Tia as she looked towards the front of the class again to where Mr Flora was standing there still talking away,

'Is everything ok at the back you girls?' asked Mr Flora 'there seems to be a lot of talking going on, anything you would like to share with the class??', Lillie shook her head as she readied herself to reply,

'No Mr Flora, it was my fault' Tia butted in 'I was asking Lillie a question, I didn't mean to interrupt you sir and I am sorry'

'Thank you for owning up, good manners and true honesty is always rewarded' smiled Mr Flora, the scoreboard flickered as Tia's name flashed up moving her up the board to sixth place,

'One hundred points awarded to you Tia, well done and as I said yesterday you are always being watched' Mr Flora clapped his hands once then walked to his chair, 'right children, as we have already discussed today the events of yesterday and seeing as we have a bit of free time before the start of your next class you may want to brush up on the history of the school or anything else just as productive...but remember everything you do and every decision you make reflects in your scores' Mr Flora smiled at the children warmly,

'So are we allowed to draw and stuff sir?' asked a young boy who was sitting in the corner,

'Why yes Lupo, you are most welcome to draw about anything that is relevant to the school, if it is something that appeals to the schools image then it may well be hung up on the wall of the classroom for all to see' Mr Flora smiled warmly at him as Lillie and Tia started talking quietly amongst themselves, Lillie seemed slightly more at ease with how her day was going to go now seeing as she had a new friend to help her through all of this change she was having, Daniel's class however were still listening to the ramblings of their teacher Lady Willo who was now talking at great length about their first day and the events leading up to now,

'So class…' said Lady Willo 'it would seem that you are all progressing rather well so far and the scoreboard certainly reflects that...well almost all of us are progressing' a small grin appeared on her face as she threw a quick glance at Daniel who noticed it and screwed his face up,

'As if I'm that bothered by this stupid cup thing anyway' Daniel snarled softly 'I'm probably too far behind you lot anyway'

'On the contrary Daniel' replied Tobias 'as we have been constantly told by everyone here that everything we do and decision we make is seen and points are given for good behaviour or honesty, you will be surprised I promise you',

'Fair enough Toby...I'll see what I can do, I'm not a suck up though so don't expect me to be all nicey nicey to everyone' Daniel replied as he faced the front of the class again with Lady Willo still talking away to the class who were now that bored that the children near the back of the class were copying her every movement, sniggering was travelling around the class as it seemed it was mainly from the far corner of the room, Tobias slapped Daniel on the arm quite hard this time,

'It's Tobias.... T.O.B.I.A.S. not Toby!!, I really don't like that name so once again please stop calling me that!!' he sniffed as Daniel sat there looking shocked,

'Oooo sorryyyyyyy...' Daniel replied as he rubbed his arm gingerly 'I was only messing around, just don't hit me anymore!!' Daniel warned Tobias who could see Daniel was getting a bit annoyed so he backed off and stared straight at the front of the class again.

'So children. As you are now aware from your new class timetables..' started Lady Willo '..your next lesson will be with Professor Deveraux in his 'Protection Spell' class, and please do pay complete attention to what he will be teaching you as there may come a time when you might need to use it!!' warned Lady Willo as the class fell silent all of a sudden until a small voice piped up at the back

'Will we get to...you know...do fighting and stuff in his class??' the boy asked,

'Oh why doesn't that surprise me that it's you asking that Hector!!' laughed the teacher 'and unfortunately it's not that sort of class for you first years', a collective 'AWWWWW' rang around the classroom as it seemed their hopes had been dashed,

'But do remember class that your first year performances will be taken into consideration at the end of term to see if any of you would benefit from a bit of extra tutelage and the possibility of stepping up into the upper class with Professor Deveraux!!' Lady Willo could see that she had their full attention now, 'so remember class full attention at ALL times!!!'

As the bell rang for the end of their first class of the day a buzz of excitement had filled the halls as the new pupils were looking forward to their next class, there were two teachers who carried out this class due to the amount of pupils, first of all Professor Ignus who had been at the school since he was a first year pupil and also the main 'Head of Spells' Professor Deveraux a seemingly quiet but focused teacher who would go out of his way to make sure every pupil was capable of using his spells, not one person had a bad word to say about either of them which made his classes the most sought after class in the school year.

The classes had to run in two of the largest halls at the school due to the amount of people wanting to attend, the rooms sat at the far end of the castle in two very large and round towers with seating stretching all the way round the small stage which sat in the middle of the room so every pupil could see what was going on.

As the children all made their way towards their next class the two friend's bumped into each other in the corridor close to where the class was being held, with Lillie lagging slightly behind,

'Oh hi Dan' smiled Harvey as they walked on,

'Harv!!!' smiled Daniel as he threw an arm around him 'not seen you for a while, you looking forward to whatever is happening next mate?'

'To be honest I haven't really got a clue what's going on at the moment' Harvey replied 'all I know is that we are going to a class for protection or something!',

'Well from what I can work out we are going to learn how to protect ourselves' said Daniel as he saw Harvey's eyes light up,

'What you mean like fighting with swords and stuff?, just like back ho....oh...it's gone' Harvey seemed to be having a slight recollection of his past,

'What has Harv?, what were you going to say?' replied Daniel,

'Oh nothing...it's totally gone from my mind...can't even remember what I was talking about' he laughed when all of a sudden he felt a slap on the back of his head,

'Hey boy's...' a familiar voice filled their ears as they turned round, Lillie stood there smiling at the pair of them,

'Oh hi sis...how are you?, how's the classes going?' asked Daniel

'Meh...don't know what to make of all this really, but I've heard this next class is one to not miss!!, a few of the kids in the class have been telling me all about it so I may as well give it a go I suppose' she smiled,

'I can't wait now!!' Daniel said excitedly 'Toby said this lesson is made for me...can't think why he said that really, it doesn't sound like my kind of thing, all this magic stuff I mean!!'

'Oh I'm not so sure Dan' replied Harvey 'you do remember that invisible spell thing you done for us don't you, maybe this will help you use it properly!!',

'Hmmm, maybe Harv...I'll ask the teacher when we get into class to see what he thinks, so which hall are you in you two?' asked Daniel as they approached the split in the corridor, one way led to Valcam East Hall and the other led to Trendare West Hall,

'Oh I'm in Trendare today' said Lillie 'seems like we all are' she smiled as she looked at their timetable sheets,

'So come on let's go guys' smiled Daniel as they opened the hall doors wide and stepped inside slowly.

Chapter Twenty-Seven
Lesson Learnt….

As the children stood there in the hall doorway they were met with a glorious sight inside. The walls of the round hall were decked in the coat of arms of Erwin itself, also pictures of the former Kings sat proudly behind every area of seating as if watching over the pupils as the sat there ready for the lesson to start,

'Wow….this place is huge!!' said Harvey as he stared up at the never ending staircase that wrapped itself around the walls of the hall disappearing up out of sight, 'I wonder what's at the top of those stairs!!' he said pointed up at the ceiling which showed the staircase disappear up to a large wooden floor right at the top of the hall.

'I…..don't really care Harvey' laughed Lillie 'now come on let's go find our seats' as she dragged her brother and Harvey off at a speed which left them dragging their feet on the floor as they climbed the stairs to reach a row of unoccupied seats at the back of the hall,

'Move along dimwit!!' said Lillie as she pushed Harvey along as he was attempting to sit down right near the edge of the seats,

'I'm moving, I'm moving!!, no need to be so rough Lillie' Harvey replied angrily 'I just want to sit near the end so we can get out quicker!!',

'As if that's going to happen plank!!' laughed Lillie as she drew his attention to the hordes of children who had now filled the hall and were chattering loudly amongst themselves, all as excited as each other at what was about to happen for them, not a spare seat could be seen inside the hall as they awaited the start of the next lesson.

'All eyes were now focusing on the small square stage that sat in the centre of the hall as a hush descended the room in anticipation for what was going to happen,

'It's a bit quiet in here now!!' said Daniel as he clapped his hands together causing an echo to reverberate around the hall, the children around him turned around and glared at him,

'Oooo sorry guys!!' he said sniggering as he let out a small 'whoop' which echoed once again of every wall and every window in the hall causing virtually the whole class to turn around and stare at him now,

'Sorry…I couldn't resist' Daniel laughed out loud as Lillie tried to put a hand over his mouth to stop him carrying on,

'SILENCE!!!' boomed a voice which seemingly came out of every part of the wall causing the whole hall to descend into a quiet hum,

'Who is that??' asked Harvey as he strained his neck over the children in front of him, trying to look for any sign of who was shouting out. Just as his eyes met the stage a figure appeared on it, a tall man wearing a long dark robe with gold stitching forming the crest of the castle stitched into the back of it, his eyes were as clear as a marble and his beard hung down onto his chest but was neatly trimmed, in his hand he held a small bottle with writing on the label which was smudged and smeared so you couldn't make out what it said,

'My name….' the man addressed the whole hall as he turned around slowly '…is Professor Deveraux and I am the teacher for this class, it is my job to provide you with the basic protection skills that might just allow you to come to no harm if…god forbid…anything evil should befall you',

'Blimey…he's a bit full on isn't he' whispered Harvey to Daniel as he sniggered to himself, Professor Deveraux stopped mid-sentence while he was still addressing the class and popped the lid off the bottle tipping a small amount of the liquid into his hand, no sooner had the first drop hit his hand he disappeared in a puff of smoke from where he had been standing before reappearing right in front of Harvey causing him to jump back in his chair with a 'WHOA',

'You scared the living daylights out of me sir, my heart is thumping here, I nearly had an accident!!' Harvey said looking extremely rattled,

329

'What is your name boy?' asked the Professor staring intently at Harvey now,

'Wh..who me??' he replied looking rather confused and pointing a finger at his own chest,

'Not you, the boy sitting behind you...' Professor Deveraux said sighing heavily causing Harvey to turn and be met with the sight of a brick wall staring him in the face,

'But there's....' he stammered slightly before turning back as the Professor folded his arms '...ohhhh I get it, you were being sarcastic'

'Of course I meant you boy..I want to know who it is who is talking during my class...I don't think you realise just how important this class might be for everyone who enters those doors' Professor Deveraux stood up and bellowed loud enough for everyone to hear he wouldn't be standing for any interruptions or bad behaviour,

'I...I'm sorry....my name is Harvey...Harvey Jones, I'm new to this school' he said confidently as the Professor towered over him trying to figure him out, staring deep into his eyes as Harvey looked right at him

'Hmmm, interesting..' the Professor said as he raised a hand to his beard and began to stroke it gently,

'Wh..what do you mean by that?' asked Harvey 'where are you looking?',

'I haven't seen eyes that distant for a long......' his attention was broken by the sound of the hall door creaking open as his class assistant Kaley entered the room carrying a box,

'Sorry to interrupt you Professor but here is the equipment you requested earlier, I had a bit of trouble tracking down a few bits but I'm sure it's all there now' she said as she laid the box carefully on the stage in the centre of the room,

'Ahhhh Hawkins...I am most grateful, I trust you brought the Manix Catcher along also?' replied the Professor as his head was turned to the side with Harvey still looking scared in his seat, not daring to move,

'Yes sir, I have fully prepared it for you this time so we can't have any more...accidents' she smiled awkwardly as she stood there rubbing her arm with one hand,

'Good good, now thank you and run along please, Oh and Kaley...please prepare the equipment for my next class if you please, I have a good feeling about today' the Professor smiled at her as she creaked the door open again and slipped out, shutting it with a gentle thud,

'So anyway...where were we?' asked the Professor 'Ahhh yes I remember...you had offered to be my first classroom assistant of the day' smiled Professor Deveraux as made Harvey stand up from his seat,

'Huh??' Harvey was now looking confused as the Professor placed a hand on his shoulder and clicked his fingers, both of them vanished in a spiral of colour before reappearing on the stage, Harvey standing there wide eyed and looking petrified, his arms stuck to his side as Professor Deveraux clapped his hands together ready to address the class,

'Well good morning once again class..' the Professor started 'I'm sorry for the slight disruption to the beginning of the lesson but as you can now see that I would require your FULL attention from this point on, do I make myself clear?',

'YES SIR' the class shouted out in one voice,

'Excellent, so shall we begin?' the Professor said as he turned back to Harvey who was still standing there looking scared

'YAAAHHHHHH' he shouted out, panting heavily as he tried to catch his breath 'WHAT...JUST...HAPPENED???' he asked as he stood there shaking now,

'That...Mr Jones... was a small taster of what this class can help you with the ability to remove yourself from one place when threatened and allow yourself to appear safe from harm' Professor Deveraux smiled as he looked around the class and saw every child hanging from every word he was saying now, 'So as you can see I have a willing volunteer here to help me with the first part of the lesson...Protection', Harvey snapped out of his trance long enough to see the Professor walking around the edges of the stage slowly addressing everyone in the class, his head felt a bit groggy as he tried to shake off the effects of the spell,

'Now children...' the Professor started getting himself into a position likened to a defensive stance '...I will use this boy here to show you the right way to implement the shield spell or 'Repelis' as we like to call it, now what this spell does is allows the user to extend a semi invisible shield around anyone lucky enough to be close to them at the time allowing total protection from any harm coming their way, but with practice this shield will be able to extend over a wider area that what you will be capable of casting right now' as the Professor readied himself to cast the spell a voice shouted out from high up in the seats,

'So how long does the shield last for when you cast it?, I mean is it a quick use spell or what?' said the small boy who now had hundreds of pairs of eyes staring right at him causing him to shrink into his seat slightly,

'In answer to your slightly interrupting question young boy the spell you cast depends on how experienced you are at holding the cast, some might only be able to hold it for a few seconds, whereas some may be able to hold it for a lot longer which helps with how far it will cast' sighed the Professor as he calmly set himself again,

'Now boy...' he said as he turned back to look Harvey straight in the eyes 'in that box on the floor is something I need you to pick out and use for me',

'Oooo...kkk??' replied Harvey as he lifted the lid on the box to reveal a huge rock sitting in the middle which he duly picked up out of it, 'is this it??' he asked as he turned back towards the Professor,

'Yes boy that is correct...now what I want you to do is throw it with all your might towards me ok!!' the Professor said confidently as Harvey stared at him blankly,

'Are you sure sir??, I mean I don't fancy hurting you, I am actually a good shot you see!!' replied Harvey as he looked down at the rock, feeling the weight of it in his hand 'It's really heavy too!!',

'I promise you that nothing bad will happen, you have my word, now throw it at me boy as hard as you can!!' the Professor began muttering to himself as Harvey wound his arm up and unleashed the stone from his hand which zipped through the air towards the Professor, heading right for his face until he shouted 'REPELIS', the rock seemed to stop in mid-air inches from the Professors face before falling to the ground making a clattering sound on the wooden stage. The children whooped and clapped all around the hall at what they had just witnessed, even Harvey stood there mesmerised,

'H...how did you do that??, that was amazing!!' he spluttered as the Professor just stood up with a slight smirk on his face and addressed the class,

'Now children..you will all get the chance to practice this spell along with many other protection spells which will take place throughout the year, in each of your rooms an individual book will sit, and with every class you attend with myself then the spell we perform that day will appear in it so you can practice of your own accord, but it will only appear at the end of the class. So what I have just shown you is the most basic of protection spells which I expect you all to master at some point and this boy...Henry wasn't it....will now demonstrate his casting ability for us to see' the Professor looked right at Harvey who had whipped his head round so fast he nearly lost his balance on the stage,

'Errr...Ha..Harvey sir, its Harvey and I don't think I can do what you just done...I mean. I'm not magical or anything!!' he protested as he raised his hands up towards his chest but the Professor reassured him softly as he stood there,

'Do not worry boy, I have seen something in you, you will be fine' as he felt a hand on his shoulder Harvey listened as the Professor whispered the words of the spell for him to cast 'just relax your mind. Feel it flowing through you like a river, let it control you're senses'.

Harvey shut his eyes and breathed slowly and puffed out his cheeks as he spoke the words in his head over and over again as the Professor stepped back towards the edge of the stage again,

'That's it boy...free your mind, feel the energy building inside you...' Professor Deveraux bent down and picked up a smaller rock that was sat in the corner of the box on the stage as he looked at Harvey who was muttering the words of the spell to himself still,

'now....ROCK!!!!' the Professor shouted as he threw the smaller rock in Harvey's direction, Harvey screeched out loud like a banshee as his eyes stayed shut tight,

'YAAHHHHH....' he shouted, too scared to open his eyes as he expected to feel some sort of pain from the rock hitting him but he felt nothing so he popped open one eye carefully,

'Huh??...' he said as he saw the rock floating there right in front of his eyes as if under his spell,

'Wh..what just happened' Harvey asked 'did I just do that??'

'Why yes Henry...that was all you, I told you I could feel something inside you, no pupil has ever been able to conjure a spell of that strength so quickly before...I am mightily impressed',

'Th..thank you sir. But my name is still Harvey!!' as he let go of his concentration and let out a huge huff,

'Yes yes..a minor detail boy, so children as you can see it can be performed by anyone willing enough to let it take over their body and soul' Harvey stood there wiping his brow of the sweat that had formed on it as the Professor turned around to address the class and secretly showed them the bigger rock in his hands 'Just one more try...' Professor Deveraux said wickedly as he spun around on the spot and shouted once again giving Harvey little time to cast the spell,

'ROCK!!!' the Professor put everything into the throw as Harvey cowered in front of him but somehow he had managed to cast the spell again, his eyes were squinting this time as he managed to see the huge rock shooting off past the face of Professor Deveraux and stop with a bang against the far wall and land on the floor below.

'Hmm...Interesting...very interesting' he said as he stroked his beard gingerly 'it seems you are stronger than you think boy'

'Wh..what do you mean?' asked Harvey as he stood there open mouthed as he noticed the rock had shot across the room and was slowly spinning on the spot at the base of the chairs, which then caused him to fall to his knees as if completely drained of energy now.

'It seems you casting area is larger than I thought it would be!!, you seem to be able to protect over a very large area for someone so new!!' the Professor said with what sounded like a slight worried tone in his voice, the Professor turned his back away from Harvey and picked up what looked like a large wooden walking stick by the side of the stage which he duly banged on the wooden area. The door swung open and Kaley appeared,

'Ahh Kaley...' the Professor said 'can you please approach the stage for me if you please, I need an errand running'

'Yes Professor, what do I need to do?' she asked as she stood in front of the Professor who leant forward and whispered into her ear quietly.

Harvey was still trying to get his energy back as he sat there breathing heavily to himself when he could overhear a few words of what Professor Deveraux was saying to Kaley, words like 'speak to the King' and 'something not right with...' but that was it, he slowly got back to his feet and coughed, Kaley hurriedly made her way out of the door and could be heard running off down the stone corridor.

'Is there something wrong sir?' asked Harvey as he dusted himself down,

'No no my boy everything is fine' replied the Professor with a nervous smile aimed at Harvey 'now let's get you back to your seat so I can carry on with the lesson, thank you for your help today, you were...a complete surprise', the Professor clicked his fingers causing Harvey to disappear once again in a puff of smoke and reappear back at his seat,

'STOP DOING THAT!!!' Harvey shouted out as he flopped back in his seat with a sweat on and his ears ringing constantly.

So as the Professor carried on with his lesson and keeping one eye in Harvey's direction he allowed every pupil to step down onto the stage and attempt the spell he was trying to teach them, some were more confident than others while others still needed more coaching, the Professor then split them into twos due to the huge number he was faced with which seemed to go better as the children began to relax and cast some excellent protection spells of their own, Daniel though was still looking on in semi amazement at Harvey's ability to cast his spell,

'I still can't believe what you done Harv...that was amazing!!' he said as Harvey sat in his chair still feeling the effects of his reappearance,

'I..I don't know what happened Dan..It was like I wasn't in control or something!!' Harvey replied with a confused sounding tone,

'No...what I mean is you can't even make a sandwich properly, so for you to somehow do whatever it was you just done was mad!!' laughed Daniel as he slapped Harvey gently on the arm, Lillie just sat there looking stunned too,

'Wow Harvey, I must say for the first time ever I am speechless...In a good way I mean' said Lillie who was able to recognise something that might just help them stay safe here in Erwin.

So as the lesson continued Daniel and Lillie got to practice the spell under the watchful eye of Professor Deveraux who had been filled in on the importance of Daniel's presence here at the castle, he was one of the Kings most trusted teachers and his most reliable ally from 'The Circle' as his task was to protect the last of 'The Bells of Peace', he was the watcher of 'The Overgaard' and controller of the Book of the Silent so he was one of the most respected members ever seen at the castle, so when he noticed something in the eyes of Harvey he knew that there was something not right and he was duty bound to pass on his findings to the King as the safety of Erwin was the single most important thing to him.

'REPELIS' shouted Daniel as he raised his arms up just as Lillie threw a small stick at him which duly hovered in mid-air in front of his face before falling to the ground, he smiled at Lillie as he stood there arms aloft feeling rather pleased with himself,

'See told you I could do it sis!!' he said as he blew a raspberry at his sister who had the hump because she wanted the stick to hit him on the nose,

'Lucky more than anything Dan!!' she replied angrily 'but don't worry you won't stop the next lot!' and with that Lillie launched a whole handful of sticks in Daniel's direction but he was wise to it and had already cast the spell, each stick pinging off in different directions just as Professor Deveraux walked past,

'Ahhh, very good there...Daniel isn't it?' he smiled

'Yes sir, Daniel Carter' he smiled back 'and this is my sister Lillie' as he finished what he was saying he was hit on the side of the face by one of the sticks Lillie had been holding,

'Oh haha that's too funny' she laughed doubled over, tears running down her cheek as watched Daniel rubbing his cheek gingerly,

'Owww!!!!, that really hurt you idiot!!, now look what you've done, bet that's left a mark!!' Daniel cried out as he rubbed his cheek harder,

'Now Lillie that wasn't very nice was it' the Professor replied, cutting her a look that stopped her in her tracks 'I would appreciate an apology for your brother please!!',

'Oh that's so unfair!!, he started it sir!!' Lillie replied trying to shift the blame onto her brother,

'Well I only saw what you just done so if you please!!' the Professor asked again 'I won't ask again...the next time you will be ejected from my lesson and will be dealt with accordingly',

'Humph' she sighed 'all right all right!!!, jeez I'm sorry for having a bit of fun!! Daniel I'M sorry for whacking you in the face and all that...' Lillie shrugged her shoulders,

'There that wasn't so bad was it' replied the Professor 'now Daniel I would like you to pick up the sticks by your feet and it is now your sisters turn to cast the spell'

'You ready sis?' quizzed Daniel as he readied himself to throw the first one in his sisters direction,

'Yeah yeah, easy peasy!!' Lillie replied confidently,

'Don't forget to free...' stared Daniel before his sister interrupted him,

'Free my mind...yep, simple!!' as she readied herself on the spot, just as Daniel threw the stick towards her Lillie shouted out 'REPELIS' as instructed but the stick showed no sign of stopping as it arched its way towards her and past where the shield should of been before slapping her right on the side of the head as she turned away squealing,

'WAAAHH' she shouted as she felt a wave of pain across her face

'Wh...What happened??' she asked nervously 'I done what you said to do!!',

Daniel sniggered to himself as Professor Deveraux stepped forwards and stood in front of her,

'The problem is my girl...' he started 'you don't respect the use of the spell!!',

'Eh??, I haven't a clue what you're going on about sir!!' said Lillie who was looking completely confused now,

'What I mean is you didn't have any faith in the spell actually working, you dismissed the words used to cast it as just words and not having any magical effect!!' the Professor said as he pointed a finger at her head 'you see up here...in this head of yours...is the key to unlocking any spell you desire to use, you just need to believe the words will work and believe in what I am trying to get across to you!' the Professor sounded exasperated as he turned round and smiled at Daniel before going to walk off where he saw Harvey just staring right through him which unnerved him slightly but couldn't show any signs of him being worried,

'Right children...' he started 'I think that we have covered enough in this lesson today and I hope that each and every one of you can take

338

something away from here and move forward with confidence, so as instructed the Chamber door will be unlocked in each of your dormitories so you will be able to practice what you have learnt here today but as you should know there is a list of who can enter and at what time, so I thank you for your time and remember to use any spell wisely and safely as it may save your life one day!!' the Professor finished before disappearing in a puff of smoke from the stage causing every child in the hall to stand there amazed by what they had just seen.

'That...was....amazing Harv!!' screeched Daniel as he clapped his hands together in excitement 'Oh I hope my names down for the Chamber today!!, did you see me?' he asked Harvey who was still transfixed on something in the distance

'Harvey...' said Daniel as he waved a hand in front of his face

'Harvey...are you in there??....Harv...' Harvey managed to come round when Daniel slapped him across the cheek,

'Wh....oh yep, I'm ready to go Dan' Harvey replied as he stood up as if about to leave,

'Your acting all weird again Harv!!' replied Daniel 'you feeling ok??'

'Ermmmm I think so, I must be hungry, my stomach is hurting and my head feels odd' he replied looking slightly off colour 'come on guys let's go and get lunch I could eat all day!!' said Harvey as he raced off down the steps and through the hall door with Daniel and Lillie in tow,

'Wait for us mate I don't know where we have to go!!!' shouted Daniel as they raced off after Harvey down the corridors.

Chapter Twenty-Eight
Time to Relax...For Now

As the children reached the canteen area of the castle they were met by Garin along the way who was always close by but not enough for them to see him, he sneaked up behind Harvey and grabbed him around the waist,

'BOO!!!' he shouted causing Harvey to almost jump out of his skin,

'YAAAHH!!!' he screeched back 'will you stop doing that 'dog', I'm already nervous enough as it is!!',

Garin laughed out loud as Harvey stood there arms crossed with a face like thunder,

'Oh Harvey...I am so sorry but it was too good an opportunity to pass up, how are you all feeling after Professor Deveraux's class?, it is one of the most popular classes we have here at this school children' said Garin,

'It's the strangest thing I've ever done in my life!!' said Daniel 'but it was the most amazing experience also, I never knew I could do that!!' he smiled as Garin placed an arm around Daniel's shoulder softly, 'Well Daniel I was watching very closely and I must say you have a bit of a gift it seems, I'm sure your fath...err I mean your family will be so proud of your efforts' he said as Daniel noticed Garin give him a little wink just so no one else would cotton on as to what Daniel's actual relationship was to anyone here in Castle Erwin,

'Oh...err yes I'm sure they will be happy, It was crazy in there, I felt I could do anything I set my mind to, I'm so looking forward to using the Chamber to see what it's all about' smiled Daniel as he clapped his hands with excitement, Lillie on the other hand wasn't so joyful and wasn't really bothered about talking to anyone,

'And what is the matter with you Lillie?? You have been very quiet today' said Garin as he knew what Lillie was going to say,

'Oh as if you didn't know!!, I'm really trying to fit in here but it's too hard!!, I never asked to come here, but I can't actually remember how we ended up here, I've tried my hardest in the spell class we just had but I couldn't even do that properly' Lillie moaned as Garin listened,

'Look Lillie..' said Garin with a reassuring tone in his voice as the two boy's listened in '...not everyone who comes here to Erwin can do everything that is asked of them, we all have to start somewhere you see, I'm sure that after a while you will forget we had this conversation when you are pulling off spells left, right and centre!!',

'I can't see me doing that Garin..' Lillie replied 'I mean I feel like a complete failure, I couldn't even conjure up the most basic of spells and ended up being hit in the face with the things Daniel threw at me!!', Daniel put his hand over his mouth and sniggered to himself just as Harvey turned round to see him struggling to contain it which in turn started him off too, that then turned into fits of laughter and both the boy's ended up hunched over struggling to breath as they were laughing so hard,

'Oh that's it take the mickey out of me!!' Lillie angrily said as she went to take a swipe at her brother but Garin stopped her,

'Lillie, contain yourself please, there is no need to be upset. Do not worry about these two boys, I'm sure they will come unstuck somewhere along the way then it will be you who is laughing at them, if you don't first fail then how can you succeed' Garin said as he pulled her to one side and tried his best to reassure her,

'Remember that I have watched you both grow up and seen what you can both actually do and I wouldn't say this if I didn't believe good things were just around the corner, I promise you that your strength will lie in another area, something that offers so much more to so many, so please don't beat yourself up over this ok?' Garin smiled warmly at Lillie

'Sigh...I'll do my best, that's all I seem to be saying lately though and it's really getting me down' Lillie seemingly getting upset so Garin pulled her in close for a hug,

'Lillie....you will be fine I promise you, I will always be there for you and Daniel just like I have been since you were little, I promise you nothing will ever keep me away from you, I'm always around if you need advice or just a bit of space from whatever is upsetting you, ok' Garin pulled her away slowly and wiped away the tears that were rolling down her cheek, Daniel and Harvey were just standing there looking at the state Lillie was in as they had never seen her like that before,

'She DOES have feelings!!' laughed Harvey 'the ice queen has melted!!' as he slapped Daniel on the back unable to control his laughter any more 'I think I'm going to wet myself!!!'

'Shut up you idiot!!!!' shouted Lillie who was still upset 'see what I have to deal with!!'

'Boy's, I want you both to go inside the canteen please, leave Lillie alone, you are not helping!!!' Garin said raising his voice slightly,

'But Garin....' Daniel replied

'GO NOW....BOTH OF YOU!!!' Garin shouted back which startled the boys causing them to step back towards the door to the canteen,

'Jeez, keep your hair on!!!' Harvey replied as he opened the door 'come on Dan let's go before we get moaned at again!!', Daniel backed up slowly still staring at Lillie and Garin who were both looking in his direction,

'Shut the door behind you' Garin said as Daniel then turned on his heels and skulked off through the door after Harvey.

'Now they have gone Lillie, so I want you to remember everything I said to you right here in this moment ok?, I mean every word I say, I am always here, you children are my world and have been since I first came into your lives' Lillie grabbed hold of Garin again and hugged him as tight as she could,

'Thank you Garin...with you around I know things will get better for me I can feel it' she smiled as Garin held her tight,

'Now go Lillie...Go join your brother, it's time you became that person I know is in there!!' Garin smiled as he let Lillie go so, she walked towards the door to the canteen feeling better than she had done in a long time and turned back to see Garin smiling away at her,

'Remember...I'm always here!!!' he said as Lillie slipped inside the canteen door to find her brother.

As she walked in she was met by a wall of the most delightful smells which danced through her nostrils like a ballerina, she inhaled heavily as she walked down through the enormous hall past row after row of benches, some already filled up with children who were tucking into their favourite food like they hadn't eaten for a week while others were busy chatting about the past few days at the castle, she smiled for the first time in a long time as the words of Garin filled her head and made her feel extremely positive about life here at Castle Erwin, as she looked around the Canteen area at all the laughing faces and happy children her mind seemed to wander to a place she thought she recognised, images of her and Daniel having fun out in a huge grassy garden filled with what looked like toys scattered across the green land, there then appeared a woman at the door to a house which she thought she recognised, the woman's face was covered in darkness but she could feel the warmth and love radiating from her as she watched them playing happily together, then....she was gone and Lillie was back in the Canteen with Tia standing right in front of her grinning like a Cheshire cat,

'Oh there you are Lillie!!!' she squealed with excitement as Tia grabbed her by the arms 'I've been looking everywhere for you, I ended up in Valcam for the lesson so I missed you, so how was it??'

'Oh...errr, yeah it was ok I guess' she replied, still feeling a bit fuzzy in the head 'I...errr...I found it quite overwhelming at first',

'But did you get to try the spell Lillie?? The protection one I mean?' asked Tia as Lillie's cheeks turned a slightly red colour,

'Errr yes I tried it but...' she stood there awkwardly not noticing she was standing in front of Harvey and Daniel,

'But the spell didn't work and she got smashed in the face by the sticks, oh it was so funny!!!' Harvey laughed as he banged his fist on the table,

'Give it a rest Harvey!!' said Daniel angrily on seeing Lillie was getting slightly upset again,

'Oooo sorryyyyyyy!!....' Harvey said sarcastically as Daniel turned towards him and slapped him on the back of the head hard 'I was only messing around, it's not like she's never been horrible to me is it!!'

'Just leave it Harv OK!!!' Daniel was feeling overprotective of his sister who he could see was struggling to contain her emotions again, 'come on Lils, let's go get some food,' he said 'I've saved you a seat next to me if you want it', Lillie smiled broadly as he led her by the arm down towards the front of the canteen where they were met with an array of the most weird and wonderful looking foods they had seen, Daniel had spotted the spiky fruit they had found in the woods when they were looking for food,

'Look sis, remember these??' he laughed as he picked one of them up and threw it at the table top, where it's spikes fell off to reveal the fruit inside, 'oooo this tastes like strawberries!!' said Daniel as he filled his mouth with the delicious fruit inside, Lillie had grabbed a plate and was carefully putting things onto it but not actually knowing what it was that she was taking,

'It all looks so good sis!!' Daniel smiled as he nudged his sister's arm softly,

'Yeah but what is it we are actually eating? It all looks....strange' replied Lillie,

'Who cares Lillie!!, just imagine it's one of those.....oh I've forgotten....Ahhh well you get the idea!!' smiled Daniel as he piled food onto his plate before going to sit down next to Harvey. Lillie turned round and sighed out loud as she scoured her eyes around the canteen area just wishing she could fit in more when she spotted Garin standing there right at the back of the hall, smiling to her, she smiled back knowing he was close by before making her way to where Daniel and Harvey were sitting,

'Is it ok if I sit down boys??' she asked politely, Harvey almost spluttered out his food in amazement,

'Are you feeling alright Lillie??, I mean you never asked us nicely for anything before!!' Harvey said as he coughed out the last few bits of food stuck in his throat,

'To be honest I don't really know how I'm feeling right now but I'm trying to become more than I am now' she replied as Lillie felt spirits lift slightly 'Look, I haven't been the best person to be around but I'm willing to have a go at all this and change my attitude if you will both help me'

'Of course we will sis…'smiled Daniel as he stood up and put his arms around his sister 'we need to stick together no matter what happens!!', Harvey moved his head away slightly as he curled up his mouth,

'Don't think I'm giving her a hug Dan!!' said Harvey 'I'm not getting all lovey-dovey with her!!', as he turned his head around he felt a slap on the back of his head as Daniel gave him a playful wallop, 'oh that's it start on me again!!' he said rubbing the back of his head,

'Shut up Harv!!' laughed Daniel as he sat down on his chair with Lillie sitting beside him holding his hand tight 'look sis, I know it's going to be tough, for us two as well, but I promise we will get through this and you'll see the good at the end of this ok?'

'I hope so Daniel' replied Lillie 'suddenly I do feel more positive!!', Garin was watching from his place by the door when he lifted his hand up to his ear, someone was talking to him which made him have one last look over at the children before he exited the canteen and disappeared from sight, Lillie turned round looking for him but could see he wasn't there anymore so with a small smile she turned back around and began tucking into her food as Harvey stood up sharpish,

'I'm off for seconds!!' he barked as he picked up his plate,

'Seconds Harv?? That's the fourth plate you've had since we sat down!!' laughed Daniel as he watched Harvey waddle off down to the front of the room to pile more food onto his plate as Daniel turned back to face Lillie again,

'So sis…'Daniel said '..I know this place is kinda weird but it's really growing on me now...I mean look at us, we have found our father after thinking the worst had happened, we have a family here and things are feeling...well pretty perfect to me I'd say'

'I do wish I could agree with you there Dan but I have just the weirdest feeling running through me...' said Lillie as she scratched he head,

'What sort of feeling??' asked Daniel

'A feeling like something bad is going to happen, I've been feeling like this for a while now, it's like I'm not supposed to forget it or something, like I'm needed to protect something....' Lillie's sentence trailed of as she seemed deep in thought now with Daniel looking more and more confused,

'Protect what?' he asked 'now I'm lost sis!!' as he turned back just as Harvey sat down in his seat with the biggest pile of food Daniel had ever seen,

'Got enough food there Harv?' he laughed as Harvey started to tuck into it 'think you missed a bit!!' pointing at some sort of animal leg that was sat on Daniel's plate on its own,

'Oh cheers Dan' he smiled as he whipped out a hand and scooped it up, placing it on top of his pile,

'I have no words!!' laughed Daniel as he turned back to face his sister who was staring at her small plate of food,

'Sorry sis...what were you saying??' he asked

'Oh...errr, I can't remember. Whatever it was couldn't of been that important Daniel' she said as she tucked into her food

'Mmm, it's not actually that bad' said Lillie as she took another bite

'Ahhh ok, well whatever it was I'm sure will come back to you at some point' Daniel replied as he smiled warmly at her,

'Hey guys...' said Harvey with a mouthful of food 'have you heard about what's going on after lunch??' he asked

'Not a sausage Harv...but I bet you're about to tell us aren't you' laughed Daniel 'come on sis let's get ready for Harvey's story time...' he continued as he swung around to face him,

'No need to be like that Dan..I'm only passing on what I've heard!!' Harvey replied slightly angry,

'No no please do go on Harv...this should be good!!' Daniel said as he gestured for him to start,

'Well...' he said 'while you two were sitting there getting all brotherly and sisterly I overheard those two boy's over there speaking about the Arena' Harvey pointed at two excited boys who were making their way past them towards the door, they could be heard saying 'can't wait for this cup to get going properly!!' while the other boy said 'come on let's go now so we get good places to watch from',

'it turns out that we all have to go to the Arena for some sort of update on the next part of the Cup' Harvey continued 'I overheard one of them saying the King and members of 'The Circle' were going to be there to address us all or something as this year's competition is supposed to be the biggest and best ever as it runs alongside the Tri-Yearly-Night-Games' Harvey continued as Daniel sat there pretending to yawn as Lillie let out a little laugh,

'Oh come on Harv...' laughed Daniel 'you sounded like a good little robot then, trying to sell us this competition thing, look I know how exciting this might be getting to most of the kids here, Toby especially, but do you think I'm totally bothered by this?',

'Well I'd rather have something to look forward to than just sort of give up Dan!!' Harvey replied angrily 'and any way I'm doing rather well so far so I want to see what's at the end of it',

'Whoa!!!!!, calm down Harv, I didn't realise you were mad on this, jeez I'll stop if it's getting you this wound up!!' Daniel replied sharply as he turned towards Lillie and puffed out his cheeks as she sniggered in between bites of food,

'Oh that's it laugh at me!!!' Harvey retorted as he crossed his arms before turning his back on the pair of them 'well forget you then!!!, I'm off to the Arena with the other kids, don't follow me please, and don't stand anywhere near me when or if you decide to come out!!' and with that Harvey stood up, slammed his chair backwards and stormed off out of the canteen door closely followed by Cahlid and his small group of friends who were deep in conversation as they left.

'Thank heavens he's gone Dan!!!' laughed Lillie as her shoulders dropped in relief

'I know sis!!' Daniel replied 'what was all that about??, I thought he was going to cry or something'

'I reckon we will find him blubbing like a baby when we go out after lunch!!' said Lillie as for the first time in ages she seemed calmer,

'So anyway sis...what were you and Garin talking about earlier when you were outside I mean' asked Daniel as he tapped his fork on the table gently,

'Oh not much really Dan..You know just stuff' Lillie replied sheepishly as to not tell him too much,

'Stuff???, no actually I don't what you mean, was it about us??, Look I know how you have been feeling and I'm sorry I haven't been there for you but it's been crazy for me too' Daniel said getting slightly exasperated

'I don't want to go into too much detail Dan but let's just say that I feel a lot better with things here now, Garin told me a few things that sat nicely with me and made me look at all this with a positive attitude, we are so lucky he's around for us Dan' smiled Lillie as she sat back thinking about what had been said outside earlier,

'Well if you're sure that's all it is sis then I'm glad you feel better, I hated seeing you looking sad and that' Daniel smiled lovingly at his sister as they sat there talking like they hadn't done for a very long time, the air filling with laughter and joy not just from them but from the whole canteen area itself, excitement was building all around them as every child had a story to tell about what the Arena was like for them, then the end bell rang and a voice boomed out

'CHILDREN OF ERWIN.....THE END OF LUNCH IS UPON US, SO I ASK YOU TO TIDY AWAY YOUR DISHES AND LINE UP IN FRONT OF THE SIDE CANTEEN DOORS, FROM HERE YOU WILL BE ESCORTED

BY THE TEACHERS TO THE ARENA FLOOR, FROM HERE YOU WILL LINE UP IN YOUR CLASSES WHERE THE KING WILL ADDRESS THE SCHOOL IN PERSON ALONG WITH MANY OTHER HIGH RANKING MEMBERS OF THE CIRCLE...

SO AS ALWAYS BE RESPECTFUL...BE KEEN...AND ABOVE ALL ELSE BE YOURSELVES!!...THAT IS ALL'

As the voice died down a low murmur rang around the canteen as everyone started talking about what had just been said, scores of children shrieked as their excitement levels grew with the impending date in the Arena where they would learn about the next step in the Inter Class Cup and what would be happening during the rest of the term.

So as the children lined up at the side doors to the canteen Lillie had grabbed hold of Daniel by the arm, she seemed to be feeling slightly uneasy as the doors to the yard opened and fresh air filled the stuffy room they were just in,

'Daniel...' Lillie said as she tugged at his robes 'Dan....something doesn't feel right!!'

'What are you talking about sis??' he replied

'I...I can't put my finger on it..but I'm getting the weirdest feeling something bad is going to happen...can we not go to this meeting thing??' Lillie was visibly upset now, her whole body beginning to shake with fear,

'Look Lils...I'm sure it's going to be fine, let's just go to this and then go back to the Dormitory afterwards and you can relax and forget about whatever it is you're feeling ok?' Daniel said as he placed a hand on her shoulder trying to reassure her that everything was going to be ok but Lillie wasn't feeling reassured, everywhere she looked felt wrong for some reason but she couldn't quite put her finger on it,

'Please Dan...It's like I have some sort of new sense..I can feel evil in every part of the Castle and it keeps calling to me!!!' Lillie tried to pull Daniel backwards out of the line but he was having none of it,

'Lillie please. While I'm here nothing will happen to us, especially with the King around...do you think he will let anything harm us...his family??, you're worrying too much!!' replied Daniel still hoping Lillie would see sense,

'I get that he will want us safe but this feeling is stronger than anything I've felt so far and I'm just really worried!!, we might be safe but what about the other children who aren't related to him??, maybe this was what Garin was talking about after all!!' Lillie said all of a sudden as if something clicked in her head,

'Garin??' asked Daniel ' what do you mean?, what did he say then?' replied Daniel

'Well that talk we had outside was him trying to reassure me that I didn't have to worry about what had gone on in the last class, he said that my strength might lie in another area and I'd know when I felt it...oh I get it now!!!' she smiled broadly at her brother,

'Maybe Garin was just trying to be nice....as he could see you were upset sis' Daniel said as the line got closer to the rear entrance of the Arena which was being protected by two of the Castles finest guards as this was an important meeting,

'Look Dan...Please let's just give this a miss!! I'm begging you again, I don't know what's going to happen if we go in there and I'm scared!!' said Lillie as she couldn't free herself from Daniel's grip on her arm,

'I promise it will be ok....It's my turn to look after you sis, we are family and need to stick together, we need to go to this meeting thingy as it's supposed to be mega important. According to Tobias' Daniel said as he led Lillie closer and closer to the doors as scores of children filed past the two guards who stood there as still as statues, some of the children trying to get the guards to break concentration by blowing raspberries at them and poking their legs as they walked past but nothing fazed them,

'Daniel....please, I need to keep u safe and I don't think this place is very safe, we can apologise to everyone later when this is all over...I beg you to follow me..' said Lillie just as Lord Casborn appeared as if from nowhere,

'Is everything ok here children??' he asked

'No problems on my part but Lillie is acting a bit strange' Daniel replied, Lord Casborn turned to Lillie and smiled warmly,

'What is the matter then?, you do seem a little strange, I can feel it'

'I can't figure it out...sir' she said 'but I feel like something bad is going to happen but I don't know what it is and don't know how to stop this, I just wanted to leave but Daniel wouldn't let me',

'Lillie I assure you that you are in the safest of Arenas in this land, nothing from the outside can cause harm to those inside. We are protected at all times by higher powers' Lord Casborn said,

'Yes. But...' she said trying to explain,

'No buts my dear girl...' Casborn replied 'come with me and I shall take you to the front, you are safe with me, now please trust me' he smiled as the children walked inside and the door shut behind them.

Chapter Twenty-Nine
As The Dust Settles….

As the children were led to the far end of the Arena the excitement level grew even more as they were split back into their classes, each row of children excitedly talking about the impending announcement and what was going to happen next,

'I'm so excited!!!' shouted Tobias as he spotted Daniel and ran over to him, jumping on his back and knocking him forwards slightly,

'Owww watch what you're doing Toby!!!, that blooming hurt!!!' shouted Daniel as he staggered forwards with the whole weight of Tobias on his back,

'It's Tobias...how many times do I have to tell you Daniel!!, and any way I'm too excited to care about you calling me that!!, I can't wait to hear what is going to happen next' he shrieked with excitement as the volume grew to almost deafening levels all around them,

'Think my eardrums are going to burst!!!' shouted Daniel as he dropped Tobias on the floor and covered his ears, then just as he felt slight relief from the shouting a huge roar filled the Arena as the children began clapping and shouting,

'Here they come!!!!' said one voice,

'Oh wow...they look so huge' said another voice, Tobias was jumping around behind Daniel as he was struggling to see who it was that had arrived,

'Daniel…' he said 'can I get on your shoulders please, I can't see what's going on'

'As long as you don't hurt me!!, otherwise I'll drop you on the floor like a stone!!' Daniel warned Tobias as he crouched down and he got onto

Daniel's shoulders, 'jeez you're heavier than I thought' laughed Daniel as puffed his cheeks out to lift him up,

'Oh wow….they are all here!!!' clapped Tobias excitedly as his moving caused Daniel to sway from side to side,

'Stay still Tobias...I'm going to drop you otherwise!!' he said as he steadied his feet, Daniel managed to catch a glimpse of a group of smartly attired men standing up on the platform ahead of them, their armour glistening in the morning suns and capes bustling in the breeze that whipped around the Arena floor and danced around the feet of the children,

'Who are they??' asked Daniel as he was being blinded by the sun bouncing of the groups stunningly polished armour,

'Really Daniel??.. You really don't have a clue who they are, where have you been hiding all this time!!' laughed Tobias as he clapped his hands with excitement,

'I've been in a cave all this time!!!' said Daniel 'but before that I have no idea!!' said Daniel as he squinted his eyes to get a better look,

'That group up there are the most feared soldiers in all the land. They are 'The Circle', oh I so wish I would be the one to join them!!, I have waited my whole life to be even this close to them!!' Tobias said as he stared deep into the eyes of one of the soldiers who caught him staring and smiled and waved back at him,

'D….did he just wave at me??' asked Tobias 'oh wow...my life is finally complete!!' as he slumped down into Daniel's shoulders this caused him to slide backwards off of Daniel causing him to lose his balance,

'Whoa!!!!' Tobias said as him and Daniel ended up lying on their backs in the dirt,

'Oh well done you numpty!!!' said Daniel 'now look what you've done to my robes!!, they are dirty!!', as he dusted himself down another cheer filled the Arena as more and more voices shouted out in excitement,

'There he is!!!' one shouted

'It's all three of them!!!, wow all in one place!!' said another,

Daniel lifted his head up and put his hand to his eyes to see what the fuss was all about and was greeted by the sight of his father, Lord Casborn and the King walking up the platform towards the front closely followed by Garin who was doing his best to stay sort of in the background, as the King stepped forwards he was helped slightly by Lord Casborn who knew his father wasn't looking or feeling at his best today, the King leant against the small altar that had been placed at the front of the platform so as not to draw too much attention to his ailing condition, he smiled a huge smile as he looked out over the Arena floor to be met with hundreds of happy smiling faces looking back at him in eager anticipation, the King composed himself and raised himself up onto his arms as Lord Casborn and Garin looked on nervously, the King inhaled deeply before addressing the gathered crowds, a hush descended across the Arena floor as the King began to speak,

'My children....' he started 'firstly welcome to the Arena's main staging ground, a place so secret and so well guarded that no one apart from you all know this area exists. Now as you all know there is a double competition going on this year, firstly the schools Inter Class Cup, which as I'm told is progressing nicely so far with a few surprises coming through, and secondly we once again are hosting the Tri-Yearly-Night-Games, and as many of you have seen that all the competitors are training hard to be the one who comes out on top and joins 'The Circle', now I must ask you to please respect the competitors and their privacy this year as we cannot afford a repeat of what happened at the last tournament which resulted in the loss of the school pet, Clovis, after some un named boys decided to mess with someone's wand and set it to explode!!'

'Ohhh that sounds bad!!!' Tobias said as he held his chest with one hand,

'Sounds blooming funny if you ask me' laughed Daniel as he thought of some animal type pet being blown to smithereens, he could hear Harvey's cackle too as the King said what had happened causing them to turn to face each other and snigger,

'Shhhh' said Pontus to Harvey as he nudged him in the back 'I'm trying to listen'

'Ooooo sorry!!' replied Harvey as he chuckled to himself still 'just found the thought of that thing exploding hilarious'

'Well considering that when it happened the King was in close vicinity of it as he was watching the competitors, he wasn't best pleased I can tell you!!' replied Pontus 'now please be a bit quieter, the King is still talking!!'.

As the King continued his speech not a voice could be heard, it seemed he had an amazing connection with all the children this year especially, something just felt good and more like family than it had ever done before,

'Now children, as we progress through this wonderful activity filled first school year you will come across many challenges that will test you, but they are all aimed at showing us how you will react in certain situations which gives us a good idea of which path you will follow later in the school year.' the King paused briefly so he could get his breath back before addressing the children once again,

'now I have it on good faith that some of the children are having a stand out few days so far and are looking very strong but there are a few boys and girls who shall we say.....require extra help. Now I do not want any of you to take this schooling for granted as it is a huge opportunity for each and every one of you children to fulfil your potential here, that is why we hold the Inter Class Cup every year to assess how our students are doing as they look to reach the top and stand out amongst the whole school', the King paused for a few seconds as the children whooped and clapped in appreciation of the King's speech so far,

'So as the year progresses on children I will be keeping a close eye on events throughout the term, just so I can see it's all going the way it needs to so I would appreciate maximum effort and a positive attitude towards each and every man, woman and child who visits the Castle as well as the people who are staying here', more clapping followed towards the King as Lord Casborn stepped forwards and whispered something in his ear before taking a step back to his original position,

'Ahhh yes, one other order of business is as you well know by now that the Tri-Yearly-Night-Games is also being held here and it is with great pleasure that I once again welcome the competitors to our Castle once again...'

'WOOOOO' a voice screeched from the side of the Arena as every head turned to see who it was that had shouted out, hundreds of pairs of eyes trained themselves on the culprit and it happened to be Tahmidius standing there with his arm aloft looking over confident as he always did, the King turned round with a slight smirk when he noticed Joda's face had turned an angry shade of red as he threw his son a look that would take down an marauding Howler in full flow,

'Wh..why are you all looking at me??' asked Tahmidius nervously,

'Son... just practice the art of silence for once!!!' Joda replied angrily,

'I'm so sorry for my son's....outburst my King...' he said a she turned back to the front looking rather embarrassed,

'It is ok Joda' smiled the King 'I'm sure he will be put in his place soon enough!!',

'So as we reach the near end of this almost perfect day I would personally like to show my appreciation........' the King continued to speak on as all of a sudden a few children started to slip away from their class and move around the platform slowly, taking care not to be seen by anyone as they slowly moved into a sort of circular position around the base,

Then Cahlid stepped forwards out of the shadow of the crowd with his hood up totally covering his face, he moved people out of the way to get right into the Kings eye line and as the King was delivering his end of day speech Cahlid and his group all clapped their hands in unison which caused the King to suddenly stop in the middle of his speech and stepped forwards to the edge of his platform,

'What is the meaning of this???' the King shouted down to the person who had interrupted him not knowing who it actually was that was standing right in front of him 'guards....deal with this please!!!' the King ordered as the guards from the 'Outer Circle' stepped forwards but as they got near

Cahlid and his group all raised their hands up with Cahlid shouting out in a voice so unworldly that it scared some of the children,

'You shall not interfere. You shall not harm us...we are the few. We are the dark' he said as a pulse reverberated from within the group causing the guards to suddenly stop dead in their tracks, frozen and unable to free themselves from their invisible prison.

'Whoever you are I demand you release my guards and be ready to explain yourself fully, Do you know who you are dealing with?' angrily the King slammed his cane down on the platform floor causing it to boom out across the Arena floor as gasps could be heard coming from the crowds of children gathered all around the group. An eerie silence fell around the Arena as no one dared mutter a word, Cahlid and his group stood there absolutely motionless, hoods still raised.

Once again the voice filled the Arena, from every corner it could be heard making its way towards the gathered crowd

'We are the darkness you fear....the pain that holds you still...we are the storm that keeps you hidden...',

Lord Casborn stepped forward, staying close to his father and whispered something in his ear which was met with a nod, whereas Garin had disappeared from the platform and was making his way quietly down towards the Arena floor as the voice grew louder around them, the King was getting visibly angry now as he took in a deep breath and exhaled then he had decided that enough was enough,

'ENOUGH....' the King shouted as the chanting suddenly stopped but a huge gust of wind filled the Arena, blowing dust all around them as they stood still. The children were covering their faces, unable to see anything and not sure what to do so they stood there huddled together tightly packed and frightened now, 'you are to stop this immediately....do not think for one minute I don't know who you are and what you think you will achieve but I assure you this will not work...SKAFF!!!!!',

The King had been informed that Skaff was behind this as it bore many traits of his such as the mind control and the eerie voice.

Cahlid stepped forward a few steps and, hood still raised and the voice came from his mouth but wasn't his own,

'Ahhhhh....yessss, why....hello there...King!!!!' said Skaffs voice with a cackle 'howwww nice to talk to you againnn...' he continued

'And what is it that you are trying to achieve here...do you think intimidating us will get you what you need??' asked the King, the next voice came from another member of the group but still with Skaffs voice,

'Achieve???, we haven't set out to achieve anythingggg...' the voice protested 'we. As a collective are merely trying to reclaim what is so rightfully ours, and in order to do this we shall do it by whatever means are necessaryyyy' Skaffs voice echoed around the Arena like a leaf caught in the wind as the King held tightly onto Lord Casborn,

'And pray tell what is it that you are claiming is rightfully yours??' laughed the King as the voice rang out again from another direction,

'Ahhhh now that would be tellingggg..' the voice said with an air of laughter about it '...but you see in order for me to find out what I needed to know I had to enlist the help of a number of weak minded individuals to help me achieve this!!' laugh the voice of Skaff as the group lowered their hoods to reveal that Cahlid and his friend's had been brainwashed and were completely under Skaffs control.

A huge gasp filled the Arena as each hood fell, followed by a loud muttering from each group as they recognised the children involved,

The King felt a cold shiver run through him as he stood there looking into the vacant eyes of a group of children who were from the Castle, their eyes glowing purple as they stood completely still,

'What have you done??' the King said with his voice quivering in fear 'I demand you release these children at once Skaff or so help me...',

'I have no intention of releasing my...playthingssss' laughed Skaff as his voice grew louder 'I have many plans for these childrennnn....they are a means to an endddd',

Lord Casborn stepped forward to where his father was and felt he needed to address Skaff,

'Skaff....' he started 'I can tell you now that whatever it is that you are after will not be handed over to you...you forget who I am...who we are and what we stand for...there is no way you will ever get anything from us and I will protect everyone with my last breath to make sure that doesn't happen!!' Lord Casborn said angrily with real intent in his voice as Cahlid and his group still stood in a circle around the platform without a flicker of life felt in their souls,

'Your last breath?...Casbornnnnn...' Skaffs voice said with an interesting tone 'Ahhh that is an interesting thought and I'm sure the Master will be the first to watch that happen...when it does happen I meannnn', the King had heard Skaff talk about 'his Master' which caused him to speak out again,

'Ahhh it all becomes clear now, I should've known that you never work alone Skaff...' the King said 'I mean you are too weak a character to do this alone!!', this caused Skaff to laugh,

'Your attempts to anger me are pointless. Kingggg' said the voice of Skaff which was once again coming from one of the group of boys under his control 'you see I have been around for centuriessss...watching...waiting....learningggg, the Armies that protect 'The Bells' have grown few, I have been around to witness their demise...and you stand there warning me to leave but now is our time...our fight...and you shall all fall. This world as you know it will be no more!!!!' warned Skaff as the children who were under his spell all looked up at the King with the purple glowing eyes that had drained their souls,

'This is your final warning Skaff, if you do not release the children then I shall be forced to take serious action, we shall hunt you...and we shall find you' Lord Casborn said as he stepped forward towards the platform edge 'I will not rest until you have been found and I will personally deal with you....so if you do not stop then so it begins!!',

'Oh I've had enough of these threats...Casborn, you have been a real pain for the Master. And you will fall!!!!' Skaff threatened them all now as the plan that Aret Del and Skaff had planned was falling into place nicely so

359

far, and with that Cahlid raised his arm and muttered something under his breath. A bolt of light shot out from his finger and slammed into the chest of the King causing him to fall backwards onto the stage floor,

'FATHER!!!!!' shouted Lord Casborn as he leapt over to him and scooped his head up, his face looking scared at what he might see but the King was conscious and not seemingly too badly hurt

'I...I'm ok son, whatever that was only meant to scare me' replied the King, but little did he know Skaff had hidden something in that spell that he wouldn't be able to detect, something that would have grave consequences for the King.

An evil cackle now filled the Arena as Skaffs voice flew around it like a wild bird caught on the wind before an eerie silence fell across the ground,

'Oh King!!' laughed Skaffs voice 'that was just a taster of the power we now possess, the Master shall be pleased with the progress and even more pleased when the children carry out the final act that will bring this Castle crashing down before your very eyes and we will be free to finish what was started so long ago, this place will be no more....',

Lord Casborn jumped up to his feet and readied himself for whatever was coming next with a look in his eyes that meant business until he caught sight of Daniel and Lillie looking utterly scared which caused his heart to drop,

'Chi..children...' he said to himself with a trembling voice until he noticed Garin was edging ever closer to them 'now you shall feel MY pow....' before he could finish his sentence Cahlid and the group of boys raised their hands above their chest and shouted out in one voice

'IGNITUNO....IGNITUNO'.

A flash of light filled the Arena blinding everyone who looked at it, then followed the sound of wood breaking as the stands around them creaked and cracked as the whole place began to fall from within, stone began splitting and exploding as the light grew stronger, the walls which covered the edge of the Arena exploded and showered the whole place with stones, the children were screaming as they held onto each other totally gripped with a fear of their lives, the whole Arena became a whirlwind of dust, stone and wood as every inch of it was ripped from its holdings and flung around the floor with Cahlid and his group still chanting the same thing over and over again, panic set in amongst everyone who was close to the group until with a thunderous clap the light vanished and the wind stopped howling, in that moment Cahlid and his group had disappeared in a puff of smoke, each child in the group clicking their fingers as they disappeared from the Arena floor and Skaffs voice had faded.

As the Arena was still filled with dust making it hard for anyone to see the children were wondering why they hadn't been harmed, a small collection of them were groaning as it seemed they had caught the brunt of the debris flying around.

'Wh...what just happened???' asked one child as he lifted himself off of the floor,

'Owwww my arm….my leg...I think it's broken' screamed another child, it seemed that most of the members of the Circle had managed to put in place the protection spell around them.

Lillies class were all lying on the floor in a huddle when Freya rubbed her eyes roughly and was met by the sight of Lillie standing in front of them having been able to cast the protection spell she had struggled to do, she had saved her group from harm which surprised everyone.

Harvey seemingly knew what was going to happen and had already cast his protection spell before the Arena imploded around him and was now dusting himself down but across at Daniel's class only a handful of the children could be seen out in the open, looking dazed and confused as they got to their feet,

'Cough cough...' went Daniel as held his arms across his stomach, the cough causing him pain as he tried to move but realised his legs were trapped under something,

'Wh..what's going on??' he said in some pain 'I can't move my legs!!!!, HELPPPPP...' but no-one came, an eerie silence filled his ears as he lay there on the floor of the Arena trying to focus his eyes upwards but the dust surrounding them was too thick for him to make out anything, a collection of children groaning could be heard all around him as he fought to free himself from whatever it was that was stopping him from getting to his feet, his body ached and his throat stung from the mixture of dust that was swirling around and his ears were ringing constantly, then through the dust and mist a figure strode towards him, Daniel rubbed his eyes as he lay there trying to make out who it was, then feeling a little dazed he reached out his arms to try and move again and the image of Bucksy appeared in front of him,

'Bucks???....wh...how??' said Daniel as he felt his body go limp, he had a feeling of him being pulled from where he lay as his eyes began to close he looked at the image of Bucksy dragging him clear to a place where he felt he was safe, He licked Daniel's face and softly barked just as he heard Lillie shouting his name, then Bucksy's image faded as Lillie raced into his eye line just as Daniel's eyes closed and it all went dark.

As Daniel lay there on the ground images flashed through his head from a life he couldn't remember anymore, laughter filled his dream as Bucksy chased him around a field before catching him and pushing him over, licking his face as they lay there with Bucksy barking with excitement, the next image he saw was of a house he thought he recognised, he followed Bucksy in through the open door past room after room with pictures placed all around showing Daniel, Lillie and Bucksy all looking happy. As he reached a door which led into the kitchen he had a feeling of he knew this place really well, he pushed the door open and walked inside, Bucksy was sitting beside a figure wagging his tail as the figure had their back turned to him, the person bent down to pat Bucksy on the head,

'Good boy..' said the voice of a woman 'you brought him back', Daniel stood there looking confused as he felt he knew who the woman was who was talking to him, she then turned round but as she did Daniel awoke from his dream and was greeted by the sight of Lillie and Harvey standing over him looking worried,

'Dan...Are you ok??' asked Lillie as she held him close,

'Thought we'd lost you mate' laughed Harvey as he leant in close to his face,

'Back up please Harv...your breath is nasty!!' replied Daniel as he was helped to his feet by his sister,

'Yep he's ok I'd say' Lillie sniggered as she pulled him in tight for a hug,

'What happened??, I can't remember much apart from a feeling of something holding me back from something evil that was trying to get me' Daniel said as he rubbed his face and eyes gingerly,

'Something very bad Dan' replied Harvey as he shuddered at the thought of what had just happened 'something pure evil...no one saw this coming!!!',

Daniel and Harvey were still talking when all of a sudden Lillie shouted out in what seemed like terror as she saw something that filled her with a sense of dread,

'Daniel, Harvey come here quickly!!!!!' she said with tears streaming down her face, as the boy's reached her Daniel saw what she was looking at and dropped to his knees in a state of shock as staring back at him was something he recognised, sticking out of the rubble and wood which used to be the stands around them was the arm of someone he knew, he recognised the small tattoo on his hand with the initials D and L underneath,

'Garin!!!!!' he shouted with tears filling his eyes.

THE END

37503143R00214

Printed in Poland
by Amazon Fulfillment
Poland Sp. z o.o., Wrocław